CRIMSON SHADOW: NOIR

NATHAN SQUIERS

Published by
Tiger Dynasty Publishing, LLC

ISBN: 978-1-940634-00-5

DEDICATION

To all my friends and family who kept me alive and writing to see Xander's origins to the end so that I could find my start.

To all my colleagues and supporters who make every day a gem.

And to anybody out there who, like Xander, needs a reason of their own.

Chelsea,
Great talking
to you at
Ryu-Kun 2014.
Hope you enjoy!

Stay gnarly!

Nathan
Squiers
(LDE)

PRAISE FOR

CRIMSON SHADOW:
NOIR

"Very well written and perfectly paced the author has given us a great read and a skillfully developed character in Xander. I will say that this type of story about supernatural powers and the struggle for personal control and self-discipline has been done many times before but this is one of the few times where I actually bought it."
~*Christoph Fischer (Top Amazon Reviewer)*

"I'd recommend this book to any lover of horror or anyone riding the vampire wave. This is an exciting, new and fresh novel that everyone should check out. It's a little on the dark side, but it brings back the true darkness of the vampire myth."
~*Joseph J. Langan (Author)*

"Xander Stryker, is a tormented soul with a lot of baggage and you cant help but be pulled into this story and feeling all of what Xander goes through. It's an extremely touching, awesome, and remarkable story about a boy/man full of power, magic, surprises, love, hate, sadness, laughter and two awesome, kick ass guns named Yin and Yang. A MUST read!! This book will leaving you wanting more of Xander Stryker and his adventures."
~*Jenny Bynum (Black Words-White Page)*

ACKNOWLEDGEMENTS

Major thanks and love to my fellow Tiger Dynasty Publishing colleagues for making this book shine brighter than it ever has before; between my wonderful editor and business partner, Kristina Gehring, and my astounding fiancé/partner/formatting queen, Megan J. Parker, and our incredibly diligent and talented assistant, Danael McGuire, I honestly feel that the awesomeness of this project has long-since stopped being mine to claim.

To all of Tiger Dynasty's supporters and followers, I extend an immense and heartfelt thanks. We are still young, but our progress at this stage has made me confident that we'll be growing into something as beautiful and powerful as our namesake.

A very special shoutout goes to the anti-suicide/self-harm movement, To Write Love On Her Arms. As it was with previous publications of "Crimson Shadow: Noir", a portion of this book's proceeds will be donated to help support young people who are suffering from anxiety and depression. The growing suicide issue with our youth needs the efforts of groups like this, and we owe it to future generations to show them that they *do* matter and that killing yourself is *never* the answer.

I'd also like to thank all of my readers with The Legion (I will never stoop so low to call such a phenomenal group of followers "fans"; you all rock hardcore) for your continued enthusiasm. You make it all worthwhile!

Many thanks & much love,
Nathan Squiers
(The Literary Dark Emperor)

"Sometimes the most profound of awakenings come wrapped in the quietest of moments."
-Stephen Crane (1871-1900)

CHAPTER ONE
RITUALS

ANOTHER NIGHT.

Another chance to finally die.

Pulling the cigarette from his mouth, Xander set it into the old glass ashtray on the nightstand to his right and let out a deep, smoky breath. To his left, lying in wait on the floor, was the wooden box bearing the Yin-Yang symbol on the lid. As he let the taste of smoke and regret linger a moment longer, he allowed his fingertips to brush the polished surface

1

and dared another exhale, hoping it would be one of his last.

For the moment, however, he let himself remember.

After all, it was the only time of day he allowed the memories to come.

Reaching away from his cigarette—not daring to move his other hand from the box—he reached up to his bare chest and lightly ran his fingers across the pendant.

His mother's pendant...

It had looked so much better—so much more appropriate—around her neck.

But she wasn't around to wear it anymore.

Not since Kyle...

She wouldn't want you to keep doing this to yourself, you know. Trepis' voice was soft, almost unnoticeable inside his head. His involvement with Xander's ritual varied from night to night, but one thing was clear: he was never in favor. Xander didn't blame him. Under any other sort of circumstances he probably wouldn't be either. The painful truth of the matter, though, was that things were bad enough five years earlier to warrant the attempt, and they certainly hadn't gotten any better. *I certainly don't want to see you doing this to yourself.*

Xander shook his head, "Then close your eyes."

They're your *eyes too, smartass!* Trepis' scorned voice was a tickle in Xander's mind.

"Don't worry, then," Xander said, sliding the lid off the wooden box. "I'll close them for both of us."

Oh, aren't we cryptic.

Xander ignored his lifelong friend's sarcasm and, giving only a brief, sidelong glance, drew the solid black, eight-chambered revolver from the satin-lined interior, leaving its ivory twin untouched.

Yin and Yang, his late-grandfather's custom-made

pieces, were, other than the pendant, his only treasures. Ever since he'd first come across the guns and the remaining round in Yin's chamber he'd performed the ritual:

One bullet.

Eight chambers.

Once a night.

For almost five years his solitary, suicidal game had gone on and not once in all that time had Yin's hammer ever found purchase on anything but an empty chamber.

That dull click haunted him each night in his dreams.

Please! Trepis said, pulling Xander from his thoughts. *Can you stop doing this to yourself?*

Xander shook his head, "Tonight might be the night, Trep."

You say that every night! And every night proves to not be 'the' night. Doesn't that mean something to you?

"Yea," Xander smirked, "that I'm not trying hard enough."

That's not funny.

Xander weighed Yin in his hand and let it hang loosely in his grip, "Sure it is." He thought for a moment and frowned, "What do you think it means?"

There was a soft tickle over Xander's ear as Trepis scoffed. *It means that fate or destiny or whatever-you-think it is DOES NOT want you dead!*

"You know that's not what I believe," Xander said, scowling.

Then what do you believe, Xander? Huh? You sure don't believe strongly enough in dying, or you would've just done it by now! The fact that this has become your only potential way out and that it's not working has got to mean something.

Xander bit his lip, focusing on Yin's barrel. "It means it

wasn't my time."

That's right!

Xander nodded, "But tonight could be it."

Dammit, Xander, no! That's not—

Before Trepis could get another word in Xander popped the cylinder open and checked—though he was certain that it was there—to make sure the round occupied one of the chambers. Spotting his would-be prize, he spun the wheel and slapped it back into place. With Trepis' words still rattling in his head he jammed the barrel into his mouth and thumbed back the hammer, feeling the resonation rattle against his teeth like it did every night. With his right hand still tightly wrapped around his mother's pendant he clenched his eyes shut and pulled the trigger.

A flash of red and black tore across the vast darkness behind his eyelids like a bloody bolt of lightning.

A rustling around him like a whirlwind; across the room, some papers on his desk shifted and fell to the floor.

A dull, empty click.

As the energies settled around him Xander relaxed his muscles, his left arm sagging and drawing the revolver out of his mouth. Before the gun hit the floor he stayed his hand, glaring at the piece.

Trepis stayed quiet then as Xander let out a heavy sigh—one of many till the next night would arrive—and set Yin back inside the box with Yang and slid it under the bed. Certain that the twins were hidden from his grandmother for another day he picked up the ashtray and clenched the cigarette between his lips as he set about getting ready for bed.

He'd been condemned to another day.

CHAPTER TWO
DILEMMA

"SON OF A FUCKING BITCH!"

The Beretta pitched in Marcus' grip; the echoes of the gunshots resounding off the walls of the mansion's underground shooting range. Several-hundred yards away, a paper target disintegrated under the assault until the ammunition clip had been emptied. Sighing, he ejected the spent clip and set the weapon down on the counter in front of him. The fourth round had done just as much to settle his nerves as the first three: nothing.

"Marcus!" Depok's voice roared and the others' nervous glances moved from Marcus to their leader long enough to bow their heads.

He hadn't even realized how much attention his furious shouts and merciless firing had attracted from the other clan warriors. Turning towards the head of the Odin Clan, he bowed his head. Positive that he was in for a lecture he braced himself only to be surprised to see that Depok was smiling as he approached.

Depok, despite his many years, had the appearance of a well-kept middle-aged man. His grayed hair was pulled back in a tight ponytail that was bound with strips of leather. His golden eyes—now mirroring his bright smile—took Marcus in for a long moment before finally blinking.

When he was close enough he laid a hand on Marcus' shoulder. "You're troubled."

It wasn't a question and neither of them treated it as one.

For a short while Marcus stayed quiet, toying with the idea of lying; of maybe going so far as to tell his leader that nothing was wrong. This thought was short lived, however. Lying, of any sort, was incredibly difficult when Depok was involved.

Letting out a heavy sigh, he nodded, opting for the truth:

"It's the Stryker situation," he said, finding the issue easier to address than it should have been. Upon hearing the name, several of the nearby shooters quickly packed their gear and moved away. Marcus couldn't blame them. "I still don't understand why we're waiting!"

Depok took a calculated breath, "Believe me when I say that I'm just as eager as you to bring him in; everybody is. But there is a right way and a wrong way to go about it."

"Oh come on! If Joseph was still alive—"

"*If* he was still alive he would be just as obligated to follow the oath as the rest of us!" Depok's voice rang with rage both in and outside Marcus' skull.

Marcus, embarrassed by his brashness, lowered his head, "I understand"—he lied—"I'm sorry. I'm just… impatient."

Depok smiled, "I know. But it will be dealt with when and *if* the situation calls for it. Like it or not we are bound by our promise."

Marcus lowered his gaze to the floor, "I understand."

Depok stared at him, his face painted with his own irritation, before he gave a slight nod and turned away. "Have some patience," he called out as he left, "Our late comrade's son is not the only one who's at risk from all of this."

Marcus stood, watching the clan's leader leave. Despite the elder's soothing speech, his tension was unrelenting and, though he hated to admit it, he was bored with shooting.

Now he wanted to hit something.

Stepping out, he took the stairs to the upper levels of the mansion and headed towards the gym.

"Depok read you the riot act," Sophie's voice chimed ahead of him.

Marcus rolled his eyes as he passed her, "Were you watching in or are you in my head again?"

His friend stepped away from the wall and fell into a matching pace beside him. "You really should know better than to bring it up," she said, ignoring his question. "The entire clan is already boiling over about it. Still, I think it's bothering him the most."

Marcus rolled his eyes, "Joseph's kid is going to get himself killed and we're just sitting on our hands and hoping that we don't get shit on them."

"Charming," Sophie sneered, "You really should calm down. After all, there's nothing we can do."

"Bull-fucking-shit! The only things holding us back are a few limp-dick laws and a crazy old bitch!"

"We're being 'held back'—as you put it—by a promise!" Sophie said.

"A promise that never should have been made," Marcus grumbled, stepping into the gym.

Sophie sighed, standing in the doorway a moment before following him in and beginning to stretch. "It's really not up to us at this point."

Marcus scoffed and drove his fist into a triple-reinforced sandbag that hung from the ceiling. As the supporting chains creaked he turned towards Sophie. "Can't we just *talk* to him? Would it really be so bad if we gave him the choice?"

Sophie stopped stretching and looked at him, "We're not allowed to approach him at all! If she sensed us anywhere near Xander—"

"Yea yea. It'd be a shit-fit. I know." He thought a moment longer and smiled, "But what if she *didn't* sense us?"

Sophie leaned forward, a blond eyebrow rising, "You got something in mind?"

"I might," Marcus smirked, "And I think it's something that even Depok can agree to."

CHAPTER THREE
MO(U)RNING

THE SUN'S OPTIMISTIC RAYS PIERCED

through the window and into Xander's face, creating a blinding, neon kaleidoscope inside his eyelids and forcing him into consciousness. Like every morning, dragging himself out of sleep's embrace was nothing short of torturous. He tried to struggle against nature's attempts at rousing him and groaned as he rolled over to hide himself from the brightness...

Only to have the alarm clock go off in his face.

Anguished, he sighed and reached up to silence the alarm's howl. Life had won yet another round against his efforts, and he finally succumbed to its demands and sat up, bracing himself for what was to come.

He had a life to live.

No matter how much he resented it.

Groaning, he forced himself to his feet and grabbed his cigarettes. His lighter—a cheap, black BIC he'd stolen from the teacher's lounge—was almost out of fluid and took four strikes on the flint to birth a flame. He scowled and took in the first drag, promising himself he'd buy a Zippo after school.

It didn't take long to get down to the filter, which he crumpled between his fingers before hiding it at the bottom of a trash bin by his desk. Confident that the evidence was well-hidden, he went back to his bedside table and stashed the ash-filled tray beneath a stack of papers in a drawer and retrieved the aerosol can therein. After a healthy spray of air freshener to hide his "dirty habit", he put it back.

His grandmother's labored snores echoed through the hall as he padded by her bedroom door. Swallowing away the growing lump of sympathy in his throat, he quickened his pace until he reached the bathroom and shut the door behind him.

The overhead florescent lights flickered for a moment and, overcome by the brightness, Xander blinked several times. Finally, he turned towards the old Clawfoot tub and leaned in to turn the faucet. The shower sputtered to life and let loose a freezing stream of water onto the back of his neck, making him cry out.

Trepis' laugh echoed in his mind.

"…it's not funny," Xander grumbled, shaking the dampness from his hair.

I thought it was hilarious.

"Shut up," Xander adjusted the water.

The tattered tee and loose-fitting boxers that served as his pajamas were peeled away and cast aside before he pulled off his mother's necklace with meticulous care and delicately set it down on the counter by the sink, being careful not to tangle or kink the chain. The ruby eye—inlayed in the center of a diamond-shaped, sterling silver pendant—caught the light and shone with intense brilliance. He gazed at it, transfixed, and felt the memories begin to bleed through his mental barrier.

He looked down at the scars that decorated his forearms and chewed the corner of his lip. There had been nights, several years before, when he'd felt that Yin's refusal had been unjust. On those nights he'd turned to a razor for relief. With the nail of his index finger, he followed the length of one of the pale marks—a mock-repetition of the motion that had birthed it.

His grandma had found him the last time he'd cut; unconscious and nearly dead, a puddle of blood spreading across the tile. After a trip to the hospital and a long time in the psychiatric ward, Xander decided to leave his fate in Yin's barrel.

Casting away the thoughts, he stepped into the shower and drew the cheap, red shower curtain. The water, now hotter than he'd anticipated, scorched his skin and he suppressed a shudder as he made a final adjustment to the temperature and dipped his head into the flow and held it there. The current soaked into his hair, draping it across his face. After several slow, calculated exhales, he reached for the shampoo bottle.

Bathing was, unfortunately, only beneficial to the surface. It was a shame that there was no way to wash away the stains that lingered within him; the imperfections that everyone else seemed to notice but he, himself, could not discern. It *was* a shame, but drenched in warmth and encased in a crimson cocoon he felt serene. It was one of his few—if not his only—moments of peace in the day.

Like all good things in his life, however, it was short-lived.

The rush of cold air to his wet skin was yet another rude awakening and he heaved a sigh as he dragged himself out of the tub.

You could always skip school today. Trepis said.

"And—what?—take twice the beating from Christian tomorrow?" Xander shook his head. He reached for a towel and draped it over his head and began to dry his hair, "Besides, Grandma would know something was up if I did."

So go somewhere else. Try and have a relaxing day for once. We could go see a movie!

Xander frowned and paused, knowing he *should* have liked the idea of doing something entertaining. Had he really grown so distant from everything? What kind of a life could he live if he couldn't even find enjoyment in anything?

"There's nothing I want to see," he said.

There was a sensation in his mind that he recognized as Trepis sighing. *Come on, Xander.*

"Step off it already, Trep! I don't want to go to a fucking movie!"

You're no fun. Trepis whined.

Xander nodded to himself and finished drying off. "I know."

Wrapping the towel around his waist, he stepped in front of the mirror and wiped the steam from the glass. His reflection, partially hidden under a curtain of black hair, glared at him. His jaw shifted and tightened and his hazel-green eyes narrowed.

"I hate you."

Trepis stayed quiet.

Xander appreciated it.

He exhaled through his nose, taking one last glance at himself before carefully scooping up his mother's necklace and going back to his room.

The process of finding what clothes to wear was a simple one. Having long ago abandoned any sense of style and adhering to a tight budget, Xander had found the second-hand shops to be a valuable resource. The only true rule he followed was one of hygiene—after all, he was already bullied enough without adding body odor to the mix. He fetched a pair of jeans from the dresser drawer and sniffed it to be sure before tossing it on the bed. Opening another drawer, he snatched a balled-up shirt from the top of a dark pile, giving it the same attention as the pants.

He was happy, for the time being, that he was still at least a few days from having to visit the laundromat. The dirty looks he got while there were made all the worse by the need to stay until the process of washing his clothes was finished. He sighed, wondering if his grandma would ever get the washer fixed, and shoved his foot through the first pant leg and, as he hopped into the second, his mind drifted to a bumper sticker mantra that he'd come to know all-too-well:

Same shit, different day. Trepis echoed his thoughts.

He nodded, pushing his arms through the shirt and pulling it on. "You bet your ass."

I might—Trepis chuckled, a soft tickling sensation—*if I had an ass.*

Rolling his eyes, he pulled the shirt on and stuffed his

cigarettes into his pocket. Finally dressed, he draped his mother's pendant around his neck and ran his thumb slowly across its surface. For a long moment he couldn't bring himself to do anything other than rhythmically caress the ruby and let himself remember.

Best to not let your mind wander. Trepis warned.

Xander frowned but nodded, pulling himself to the present and letting the necklace go. "Right. Thanks."

Anytime.

Like every morning, Xander was careful not to wake his grandma as he headed downstairs and into the kitchen. With the sound of her snores left behind, he was able to relax and grabbed a discolored coffee mug from the cabinet over the sink and filled it at the tap. As he maneuvered through the kitchen he opened the window and he turned one of the stove's burners to "High". When this was done, he continued on to another cabinet and pulled a tea bag from a box of English Breakfast.

With everything ready, he took a deep breath and held the mug in his left hand and closed his eyes. Silence engulfed the room as he stood motionless, focusing his energies. Tightening his grip, Xander felt the familiar tingling sensation as it crept from his shoulder, down his arm, and into his hand. Outside, a neighbor's dog barked at a passing car and a lawn sprinkler hissed. Xander focused harder, his hand starting to shake. Though the passing car was long gone, the dog continued to bark. Nearby, the dishes from the previous night's dinner—still sitting in the sink where he'd left them—started to shake and rattle, and as he continued to focus his energies the chair closest to him shifted and started to drag across the floor. After another moment a tiny bubble formed at the base of the mug and floated to the surface. Encouraged by this, Xander continued to focus—his hand shaking from the exertion and threatening to spill the contents of the mug—and ignored the blistering pain growing in his palm. Finally, a small group of bubbles ascended to the water's surface, followed soon after by another, then another. Steam began to rise and Xander clenched his eyes harder and tightened his grip, worried that the mug might break under the pressure. Still ignoring the pain, he coaxed the growing number of bubbles to continue coming until it finally erupted into a full boil.

Smirking at his personal victory, Xander relaxed both his mind and his grip and put the cup down on the counter, dropping in the tea bag. He looked at his hand, still shaking and bright-red, and ran it under the cold tap for a moment.

Don't you think the microwave would be easier? Trepis teased.

Xander smirked, turning off the faucet. "Where's the fun in that?"

There was an odd sensation as Trepis scoffed. *The arts are tainting you.*

Xander thought for a moment as he watched the hot water darken. "They always do."

The knowledge of magic, like Trepis, had been with him his entire life. He wasn't sure for how long he'd had the power, or even how he'd learned to control it—though the control part had recently become something of an issue—but he knew that it felt right. Nevertheless, he had the power and, though he couldn't bring himself to use it against others, it sure made a great cup of tea.

With his breakfast brewing, he opened the refrigerator and grabbed a carton of milk, pouring a splash into the mug along with a spoonful of sugar. When he was finished, he took his first sip; letting the warmth and flavor linger in his mouth before gulping it down.

The burner, Trepis reminded him.

Xander glanced over at the stove, seeing that the metal coil was, indeed, bright orange and waiting. The sight triggered a tremble at his core—an old scar at his back beginning to itch—before he buried the memory and pushed himself to approach the stove. "Thanks," he grumbled as he reached into his pocket and retrieved the pack of cigarettes and pulled one of the cylinders free with his teeth. Still clenching down on the filter, he bowed down and touched the tip to the burner and inhaled.

You are an odd one. Trepis said.

Xander shook his head. "You say that every morning."

And it's never any less true.

He chuckled at this before taking the cigarette from his mouth and chugging the rest of his breakfast. A few more deep drags later and the cig had been reduced to nothing but its filter. This he crumpled and dowsed with water before wrapping it in a paper towel and tossing it into the garbage. Finally, certain that his grandma wouldn't suspect anything, he closed and locked the window and started for the door.

Coat, Trepis reminded him.

Xander rolled his eyes and started to turn back before stopping, a sly grin creeping across his face.

That feeling of freedom was calling to him once more.

Focusing his energies again, he stretched his hand out in the direction of his coat—still hanging on the rack at the other side of the kitchen. Directed all of his attention on the garment, he watched through squinted eyes as it began to shake. Finally, the force of its tremors became too great and it freed itself from the rack and…

Fell to the floor.

"Dammit!" Xander crossed the kitchen and picked it up.

There was a slight chitter in the back of his mind that signified his friend's laughter. *The Force is weak with this one!*

"Shut up!"

Trepis sighed, *The arts have tainted you, my friend.*

Xander frowned, "They always do."

CHAPTER FOUR
STRANGE DAYS

XANDER WATCHED WITH ALMOST NO surprise as the bus skipped his stop once again. The driver had become selective about stopping at his house ever since he'd gotten in trouble for "starting an incident" on the ride to school. Nobody had cared too much that the incident in question had left him with a torn lip and a ripped shirt that later got him sent to the principal's office for "inappropriate attire".

With the diesel exhaust still burning in his nostrils and the bus growing smaller with distance he watched as a few of his peers ran to the back window to taunt him. Turning away from the beginning of the day's tortures, he sighed and walked back towards his house.

Did you honestly think that the driver would stop?

Xander frowned, "He could have."

But did you think he would?

Xander stared off for a moment; *had* he expected the driver to stop? Or was he waiting for something else? He looked around slowly; perhaps it wasn't the bus he was out there for.

I just wonder why you do this to yourse—

"Wait…" Xander could feel something; a tickle in his mind.

Turning around, he was surprised to find a young boy— no older than eight or nine—standing just behind him. He shook his head, confused. Xander stared a moment longer, captivated. The boy seemed out of place, standing, unmoving, in a well-tailored blue suit and freshly combed blond hair.

Suddenly, as though a switch had been flipped, the child blinked and life emerged behind his blue eyes. Xander frowned and took a step away. The boy smiled then, reaching out his hand.

"You will come with me now?" he asked in a small voice that seemed to echo in Xander's ears.

Xander shuddered and took another step away.

The boy saw this and tilted his head, staring for a long moment before turning away.

No more words were spoken.

No purposes expressed.

Xander frowned. "Creepy little shit."

What was that all about? Trepis asked.

"Fuck if I know. Not like it's anything new," Xander

said. Though he hated the attention, he'd gotten used to people—especially children—acting weird around him.

He seemed different.

"You mean because he wasn't afraid of me?"

No! It was his mind!

Xander frowned, "What about it?"

There was nothing there!

Xander rolled his eyes, "Then he was retarded! Will you forget about it?"

No! You don't understand! Trepis urged. *There was* nothing *there at all!*

Xander had long-since given up trying to figure out how Trepis could look into peoples' heads and had come to accept it. "What's that supposed to mean?"

I don't know. Trepis answered with a sigh—an airy sensation inside Xander's head.

He shook his head in disbelief, "Why would you not be able to see inside his mind? He couldn't have been powerful enough to put up a shield!"

That's what confuses me.

The old Volvo hacked to life; coughing up a black cloud of smoke that smelled like burning oil and rust. The once red paint was chipped and faded and was now the shade of dried blood. Grandma shifted into gear and cringed at the sudden screech of metal against metal as the transmission stuck.

"Damn clutch!" she cursed.

Xander chuckled. She might have been older than the sun, but she was still full of life; still vibrant despite losing a husband, a son, and a daughter in law and inheriting a miserable, traumatized grandson.

His smile melted away and he turned to look out the window, wondering which one of them would have to suffer the loss of the other. Could he handle another loss? Would the pain of her death be the last twist of the knife, or would Yin finally take pity on him and take his life before she met her own end? She'd already suffered so much, having lost her husband so many years back. And then there was her son—Xander's father—who had been killed in a mugging months before Xander had been born.

And then there was her daughter-in-law…

The car whined and belched out another cloud of black smoke that was carried away by a soft October wind. The sound and smell were enough to pull him out of his thoughts and he sighed as he saw that they had arrived at the school.

Old hinges squealed as the door was forced open and Xander cringed as several passersby looked his way. His grandma, seeing his reluctance, gave him a reassuring smile.

"Try to have a good day, sweetie," she called behind him.

Xander stumbled and turned to face her, forcing a weak smile in return. "Thanks, Grandma. I'm going to walk home this afternoon, so you don't need to worry about picking me up."

She nodded and an awkward silence followed as they waited to see if the other would say anything else. Finally, Xander pushed the door shut and watched as the car pulled away.

Another day in Hell, eh? Trepis said.

"This isn't Hell," Xander grumbled as he started towards the entrance, "The Devil's not that wicked."

CHAPTER FIVE
FRIENDS: OLD AND NEW

IT HAD BEEN A WHILE SINCE XANDER

had had a *real* friend.

Trepis, of course, had always been there—since as far back as he could remember, in fact—but the ever-constant voice in his head could never replace the company of another human being. Unfortunately, his last—and, for all intents and purposes, his *only*—real friendship had long since passed along with his childhood.

Estella...

Even then, in the comforting embrace of innocence and

youth, Xander had a bully problem and had already learned that his safest option was to stay quiet and do nothing to attract unwanted attention. It was for this reason that the day the new girl stepped through the door, her shoulder-length black hair tied back with a red ribbon for her first day and a pair of bright and exuberant blue eyes that searched around the colorful room, he did not look up or speak. Even when the teacher instructed the class to greet their "new friend", young Xander knew better than to let his voice be heard. He knew better than to get involved. There was not a doubt in his mind that this newcomer would be like all the others: cruel and uncaring. Instead he sat, hunched over a piece of yellow construction paper, and busied himself with a set of crayons.

It was only after the new girl had pulled out the seat next to him and settled down that he had bothered to look up. Unlike the others she didn't seem shy or nervous around him; nor did she sneer at the sight of him or insult him like everyone else! Instead she smiled—the first he'd ever seen directed at him from a classmate—and began to draw as well.

That day, on the playground during recess, Xander had retreated to the shade of a tree next to the fence that penned them in. Comfortable in his peaceful solitude, he'd pulled the apple that his mother had given to him out of his Ninja Turtles lunch box and began to eat. The tree was one of the few places that nobody else had played around; the others preferring the jungle gym that occupied the center of the playground. This worked to Xander's advantage, allowing him to both avoid those who would make him eat dirt and talk in secret to Trepis.

He'd been halfway through his treat that day when the first of the screams started. Peeking around the trunk, he saw that the source of the wailing was the new girl who, sitting in the center of the sandbox, continued to cry out as she wiped frantically at her face. Standing over her and holding a fresh handful of sand and cackling was one of the boys that regularly bullied Xander. At that point, just as the boy tossed his second helping of sand in the girl's face, the ribbon had come undone and fallen into the sandbox. Other kids circled around to watch, some beginning to laugh. Unsure of what to do but desperately wanting to help, Xander had left the security of his tree and hurried towards them.

Another handful of sand was thrown, this one filling the girl's open mouth and causing her to cough and gag. Reaching the sandbox, Xander had tried to pull the boy away, screaming at him to stop. Seeing who was dragging on him, the bully had yelled a bad word and pushed him away.

All of this had occurred in the span of several seconds, and by the time their teacher had gotten to the scene to break up the situation the two were coated in a fresh layer of sand. With the bully being dragged inside for his punishment, the two had brushed themselves off and retreated to the safety of Xander's tree.

That day saw the beginning of their friendship; a friendship that both were certain would last forever...

But, like everything in Xander's life, that too had gone sour.

Stepping through the double doors and into the bustling high-school hallway, Xander spotted his old friend at her locker; her now-short hair hiding most of her face from the side. He stared for a moment, thinking of the friendship they'd once shared and, like every time he spotted her, regretting the loss. Finally collecting all her things, she slammed the locker closed, the impact jarring Xander back to the moment, and walked down the hall towards her first class.

Xander... Trepis' voice rang with pity.

Xander knew he was in for a lecture if he didn't act fast: "Don't!"

But she—

"I don't care!" Xander lied to himself and his friend as he turned a bend in the hall and stopped abruptly, side-stepping to avoid a group of gossiping girls.

There was a slight rattle inside his head—Trepis was obviously annoyed—and he rubbed at his temple with his thumb as he stepped through the door to his first class and scurried to the rear corner of the room. Letting his bag slip from his shoulder, he stuffed it under his desk before taking his seat, avoiding any sort of eye contact with his classmates as he did.

For some reason he couldn't shake the bubbling thoughts of the little boy from earlier or the ever-growing and unsettling sensation that he'd felt since that morning. The entire situation made his head spin; a deep exhaustion beginning to overtake him. He yawned just as the final bell rang and, crossing his arms on his desk, set his head down to try and ease the dizziness.

Trepis was and always had been a mystery; a mystery that had been with Xander his entire life. The self-named voice—which had served as Xander's longest lasting and truest friendship—had existed since as far back as he could remember.

For a short while the idea was toyed with that the voice was nothing more than a result of some mental illness, and the two of them discussed this possibility in depth. But something in that didn't seem right. Though there was no evidence to support the claim, Xander knew the truth:

He wasn't crazy; Trepis *was* real!

Though his mom had always insisted that he take the bus home from school, Xander knew it was safer for him if he just walked. He didn't mind it, though. It wasn't too far and the path was a straight shot from school; though it did call for the occasional cut through some backyards and the climbing of a few fences. More than anything, though, the walk was an opportunity to chat with Trepis.

His only regret was that his house was in the opposite direction of Estella's and he couldn't walk home with her. A couple of times she'd asked if she could walk with him and go to his house, and though the idea seemed exciting at first he knew that what was waiting for him at home was not something he wanted Estella to experience. At first she was persistent with the request and it seemed that he might run out of excuses, but she soon became discouraged and never asked again.

So each day, rain or shine, he walked home alone and talked with the voice inside his head.

Until the day came that Trepis proved himself to be so much more.

That spring day had brought with it a warm and inviting afternoon. The last of lingering snow had melted, leaving behind damp grass and well-fed weeds that poked up through cracks in the sidewalk. The beauty of the day and the pleasant exchange with Trepis had young Xander almost forgetting about the potential torture he was heading home to.

He had become aware of the sudden threat much too late for his own good, recognizing the sound of wheels on pavement and beads on bicycle spokes. At first he had refused to turn around, hoping that they'd leave him alone, but whoever it was refused to pass. Eventually it became too much to bear and he peeked over his shoulder to get a look at who was following him.

There were five of them: two that he recognized from class and three older boys he'd never seen before. They circled him; two blocking him on their bikes while a third swayed back and forth on the other side in a pair of inline skates. The two he recognized—both holding skateboards at their sides—took their places, boxing him in.

The older boys chuckled while the others waited for them to make the first move. Finally, bored with waiting, one of the kids behind Xander shoved him forward and into one of the older kids, who smirked and pushed him again. With nobody on the other side to stop his fall he hit the pavement, his hands—spread out in front of him to stop the fall— catching the corners.

Xander had learned earlier not to encourage bullies by crying out, and as the pain flooded his body he gritted his teeth to keep himself from making a sound. His eyes burned as tears began to surface and he quickly clenched his lids against them.

"He went down so easy!" One of the older boys teased.

Another laughed. "I'm not surprised."

The entire group cracked up and the boy on the inline skates rolled forward. Xander had begun to lift himself from the ground and began to dislodge the small rocks from his palms. As he rose, one of the boys jabbed him in the ribs with his skateboard. Xander cringed and a pained hiss forced itself past his clenched teeth.

Why? He'd wondered to himself. *Why do they hate me?*

Let me help! Trepis called out.

Xander frowned.

Help?

What help could a voice offer?

It made no sense!

A foot came down on his back and caused him to finally cry out as he once again fell to the ground. As the attacker ground their toe into the base of his spine a red-hot anger grew deep within him. He wanted these boys to feel the agony they and everyone like them had put him through.

Trepis answered the call.

It had begun with the strange sensation that he was falling; an intense nausea sweeping over him. Then he watched as his body acted without his orders, and he knew that this was the help that his friend had offered. Trepis, in full control of the body, pushed out against the older boy. Letting out a baffled grunt, the boy stumbled as the seemingly weak nine-year old swung out with his left arm, knocking his standing leg out from under him. With nothing to support himself with, the boy fell forward.

Xander watched from the back of his own mind as the boy's face met with the sidewalk and let out a wet gasp as he tried to suck in a breath. Slowly, he pulled himself up and spit out a mouthful of blood and let out a sharp sob before running off, cupping his mouth with his hands and leaving his bike behind.

Trepis, no longer pinned down, pulled the body to its feet and turned towards one of the younger boys, who gripped his skateboard and swung at him. Trepis ducked under the attack and grabbed onto the boy's shirt, and yanked. The bully's eyes went wide with surprise as their victim, a boy who had never fought back before, threw him into the other older kid—still perched on his bicycle—and knocked them both down. The younger boy cried out as he struggled to get up, only to discover he had gotten caught in the bike's chain. The bike's owner, trying to get out from under the metal frame, cried out as the other's weight came down on him. Those who remained standing gawked at what had transpired before taking a cautious step back, giving Trepis the opportunity to sprint away.

A quarter-of-a-mile later, leaning against the garage of his neighbor's house, Xander was given control of his body.

"How... how did you do that?" he'd stammered.

I'm not sure. Trepis answered after a long pause. *I just knew I had to do something.*

With the rush of adrenaline still flooding his system and too many questions that he knew weren't about to be soon answered, Xander pushed himself to walk to his porch, hoping that it would be an uneventful evening.

Only to be greeted by an all-too-familiar sound.

No matter how many times he'd heard it, he could never get used to the sound of his mother crying. As her sobs resonated past the front door Xander, desperate to see what was wrong but hesitant to unveil the truth, held his hand on the knob for a long moment. Finally, after a deep breath, he stepped inside.

His mother was sprawled on the hall floor, inching back in terror from Kyle. Xander stared, his young body frozen in place and shaking against his will as he watched his stepfather inhale deeply. He stood over the terrified woman a moment longer before his shoulders tightened and he turned around with a smirk towards Xander.

In a nightmarish flash, Kyle threw open the coat closet and stuffed Xander's mom inside, slamming the door in her face and wedging it shut with a broom handle.

"NO!" she'd wailed, pounding furiously against the door, "LEAVE HIM ALONE, YOU BASTARD!"

Confident that his time with Xander would be uninterrupted, Kyle curled his lip upward in a sadistic grin and took a step closer to Xander, who, despite Trepis' encouragement, was unable to move. With another satisfied inhale, Kyle pulled off his belt and doubled over the strip of leather.

"Have a good day at school, son?"

"I'M NOT YOUR GOD DAMN SON!" Xander shrieked, bracing himself for the familiar agony of Kyle's belt. His eyes flew open as he shot upright. Sweeping some strands of hair from his sweat-soaked brow, his panicked heart finally settled in his chest as he saw that he was not at the mercy of his stepfather.

Instead, his entire first period class stared at him.

Somebody up front snickered as others turned to whisper to their neighbors. Feeling his face redden, Xander did his best to ignore his peers and took a deep breath.

"Stryker!"

Xander cringed and watched as Mister Nimbe navigated his way from the chalkboard towards him. In a lot of ways seeing the portly teacher calmed him. Letting out a slow breath, he reassured himself of the truth:

Kyle was dead.

"… enough, Stryker!"

Hearing his name, Xander snapped out of his thoughts and looked up at Mister Nimbe.

"Huh?"

The teacher's jaw shifted before he slapped a heavy palm down on the desktop. Xander stared at him, continuing to ignore his peers as they gossiped and laughed.

He didn't want this kind of attention.

"Don't play games with me, you little punk!" Mister Nimbe's voice seeped through clenched yellow teeth, "The next time you decide to act up in my class, it's your funeral!"

A girl sitting nearby cackled, "That'll be the day!"

There was another bout of laughter.

Xander forced himself not to look away from Mister Nimbe, who seemed to bask in the approval of his class. Unable to handle another moment of the humiliation, he snatched his backpack by the strap and pulled it with him as he stood from his desk and hurried for the door. Behind him he heard Mister Nimbe yell after him, but he was already too far out the door to hear it or care.

"Fucking assholes," Xander spat. The burning in his cheeks had spread and now his entire body felt hot with his growing rage.

You need to calm down, Trepis said.

Xander shook his head at the advice. He let out a growl and threw a balled fist into a nearby locker; a jolt of magical energy following through. Withdrawing his hand he saw that he had nearly torn the metal off its hinges. He smirked at the results and started walking again.

Trepis sighed, *Was that really necessary?*

"Is any of this *really* necessary?" he retorted.

Trepis, after an airy sigh, went silent.

Xander nodded to himself, satisfied that the voice in his head was finally done criticizing him and continued down the hall. Gripping the pack of cigarettes in his pocket, he turned down the East Wing, dragging the fingers of his left hand across the rows of lockers as he walked.

Going to see Stan?

"You know it," Xander said as he turned another corner and stopped just before the cafeteria, pushing open the door labeled "TEACHER'S LOUNGE" without hesitation.

An old coffee machine to his right gurgled and belched its greeting as a fresh batch of sludge dripped into a carbon-stained pot. Nearby, a wild-haired woman who Xander recognized as one of the English teachers sat with a crossword puzzle while an over-caffeinated math teacher grunted something about a failing sports team. Reaching blindly for his coffee, he knocked the mug, spilling the contents onto his crotch and swearing as a cloud of steam rose from his pants.

As expected, neither noticed Xander as he walked in.

Unable to wait any longer, he retrieved a cigarette and began working to light it. The worn-out lighter sparked uselessly.

"Damn it!" Xander said, scowling at the lighter before tossing it into the trash.

"Need a light?" Stan's voice emerged from the corner of the lounge.

Xander smiled, "Would you?"

"Hey!" the coffee-stained teacher frowned at Xander, "You're not supposed to be in—"

The man's eyes went dull, followed soon after by the woman's, before both stood and walked out the door, closing it behind them as they did.

Once they were alone, Xander turned towards his friend and smirked, "You're going to have to teach me how to do that."

Stan's dirty-blonde hair shifted as he shook his head. "Xander, Xander, Xander... it's not even second period," he scolded as he held out his hand.

Xander watched as the cigarette sparked and magically ignited and he was rewarded with a rush of flavor. He smiled and took a long drag before taking it between his fingers and sitting beside his friend.

"Had the dream again."

Stan nodded, his blue-green eyes going solemn, and leaned his head back.

Xander thought for a moment that he might offer Stan a cigarette as a joke, but thought better of it. Stan always said that the things were a poison and putting those substances in your system was like allowing your own personal Trojan horse into your body time and time again.

Scowling, Stan turned his head towards him, "What are you going to do with your life, Xander? I see the potential, but..." he sighed then, shaking his head.

Xander didn't take his eyes from the floor, "Maybe Yin will take me tonight. Then I won't have to worry about where I'm going, right?"

Stan rolled his eyes. "I doubt you're going to find your escape tonight. Or tomorrow, or even the day after that," he chuckled. "I mean, if I seriously thought you were in any danger I'd have had you put away long ago."

"So why haven't you?" Xander allowed his eyes to shift in Stan's direction.

Stan shrugged, "It's that whole potential thing I was talking about. You're not worth much to the world in a padded cell."

Xander scoffed, "Wouldn't say I'm worth much to the world *at all*."

"Or maybe you just don't see that potential yet," Stan curled his lip.

Xander frowned, "Then can you tell me what's going to happen?"

Stan shook his head, "I've told you before: the future can't be seen. It hasn't been written yet."

"But you must know something!" Xander did what he could to hide his aggravation, but his lingering rage and growing confusion became too much and the wall groaned against the magical energy and cracked under the pressure.

Stan sighed, "I *know* that I'm tired of mending this damn wall!"

Xander nodded, "Sorry."

He had lost count of all the times his friend had used his magic to fix what he had broken with his own. This time wasn't any different.

Stan focused on the wall; his eyes narrowing with the same intensity they'd shown when lighting Xander's cigarette. After a silent moment, the pieces of cracked plywood shifted and cracked as they bonded together and the drywall reformed, leaving the wall looking good as new. When it was done, he went back to staring at the ceiling. "How's Trepis?"

"He's... still Trepis."

Stan tilted his head and gave him a skeptical look, "Trep?"

Doing fine, Trepis answered in Xander's head, *Kid's just being a brat.*

Both Stan and Trepis laughed.

Xander frowned.

"Oh, stop being so sensitive!" Stan gave him a few hard pats on the back; his energy stinging like lightning under his skin before it spread like a sweet drug through his system.

"You can't take everything so seriously!"

Xander smiled against the bizarre sensation and leaned into the couch. "Yea, right," he didn't bother trying to mask the sarcasm in his voice.

Stan, ignoring Xander's attitude, stared back up at the ceiling, "So what do you want for your birthday?"

Xander sighed and took another long drag, not stopping until he'd burned up the cig to the filter and blowing the smoke out slow, "I want freedom, Stan."

CHAPTER SIX
THAT WHICH BIRTHS RAGE

THE SCHOOL DAY ENDED WITH THE
piercing call of the bell and the sound of hurried footsteps
and slamming locker doors.

Most of the students scurried for the buses that had
lined up outside, their diesel engines rumbling as they waited
for their loyal cargo to board. Others started off across the
parking lot towards the street on bicycles or skateboards
while a select few, envied by many, strutted proudly to their
own cars.

The entire process, in Xander's mind, was another excuse for the world to shove, pull and trip him several more times before leaving. It wasn't until he'd gotten past the parking lot—where student drivers honked and yelled obscenities—and crossed into the football field that things began to calm down.

Once on the gridiron, he let out a sigh of relief.

"God! They're like animals!"

Trepis sighed, *I don't think that's fair to the animals, Xander.*

"Tell me about it," Xander scoffed.

With nothing left to say he started towards the far end of the field. Past that and beyond the fence were the neighboring woods which formed a triangular patch that divided the school, the rest of town and the beginning of the residential area. Most of the time, when walking home, Xander needed only to bank right past that fence and walk a few miles to get home. Today, however, he would head towards the left so that he could go into town and get the new lighter he'd promised himself.

As he crossed the thirty yard line, he mapped it all out in his mind: after about a mile-or-so he'd come to the library, and across the street from that was the shop run by the all-too-trusting older family who never checked for ID. It was there that Xander had gone for nearly three years to supply him with cigarettes and, when the occasion called for it, a beer or two.

He was nearly to the fence when he heard the familiar laughter growing in volume behind him and his shoulders sagged.

"Stryker!" Christian's voice sent a nervous shudder down his spine.

Don't turn around!

"Hey! I'm talking to you, freak-show!"

Ignore him.

The voices got closer and Xander did what he could to discreetly pick up the pace towards the fence. He made it several more steps before, with the rising chorus of laughter, something hit him in the back of the head. The world went fuzzy as he went down, twisting in the process and landing hard on his shoulder.

As his eyes uncrossed and his vision cleared he watched the ball that had hit him roll a short distance away. Studying its shape, he wondered why footballs had to be pointed, and, furthermore, if one of those pointed ends had just broken his skull. Dizzy and disoriented, he rolled onto his back and stared up at the portion of sky that wasn't hidden behind his bangs.

Get up, Xander! Get the hell up NOW!

It was too late, though; the laughter was over him and out of the corner of his vision he could see Christian and his friends looking down at him. Running wasn't an option. He knew just as well as they did that they would catch him.

Give me control! Trepis called out, *Let me take care of this!*

Xander shook his aching head, "What's the point?"

Christian laughed, "I think he's finally lost it!" There was a brief moment where he and his friends laughed before: "Get him up!"

The other two, a pair of gorillas that Xander recognized from past beatings, grabbed him and hoisted him to his feet—holding his arms on either side so he couldn't struggle. Picking up the football, Christian tossed it playfully in the air.

"So are you thinking about joining the team, then?" he asked with a malicious grin, jabbing the ball into Xander's ribs in between each word.

Xander frowned and looked away, refusing to meet his tormentor's gaze.

Christian scowled and swung with a right hook that tore Xander from the gorillas' hold and threw him back to the ground. He curled up, trying to protect his sides, only to have Christian drive his foot into his stomach. Xander doubled over, throwing up on the grass...

...and Christian's Nikes.

"You fucking freak!" Christian spat in disgust as he grabbed at Xander and gripped the chain of his necklace.

As Christian pulled, the metal strained and finally snapped, dropping the pendant into the grass. For a moment Xander could do little more than stare at it as Christian took in the shock in his eyes over the jewelry. Growing gleeful at having found a new technique to torment Xander, he raised his foot and prepared to stomp down on it.

Xander, seeing this, felt the familiar, burning rage erupt within him. Ignoring the lingering pain, he jumped to his feet and he swung, catching his tormenter of several years in the left temple. Christian let out a pained and surprised grunt as he toppled over.

Just then, one of the gorillas caught him from behind and tackled him. With a roar of fury, he twisted around, throwing his foot into his attacker's throat and forcing him back. Seeing an opportunity, Xander snatched up his mother's pendant and the broken chain before hopping the fence and sprinting into the forest.

CHAPTER SEVEN
NIGHTMARE

STAN HAD BEEN RIGHT ABOUT YIN.

He was always right about those types of things. Xander sighed and wondered in silent anguish how he could know the fate of his nightly ritual but not know what the future held.

His new Zippo, however, worked like a charm, giving quick life to his cigarette, which he held tightly between his lips as he went to work on mending the broken chain. When he was confident that it would hold, he slipped on his mother's pendant and set it on the nightstand. The ruby caught the light from the last burning candle, which he concentrated on and, after some effort, magically snuffed.

Lying back, he focused on the glowing red tip of the cigarette in his mouth. Trepis talked, though most of the conversation was one-sided, and Xander closed his eyes and let his mind wander to strange worlds where he felt welcomed and meaningful.

A world where...

His grandma coughed suddenly from her room.

Xander blinked, noticing that the ash of his cigarette had grown too long and was about to collapse. Carefully, he took the dwindled cigarette from between his lips and put it out in his ashtray.

What had he been thinking of?

He closed his eyes again, hoping to revisit the serenity he'd had a moment earlier...

It's dark, and a sliver of light emerges like a gash.

Light bleeds into Xander's shelter and the screams follow. He wants to get out—needs to get out—and digs and pushes against a mountain of coats to get free.

The claustrophobic darkness closes in until it's too much to bear and he throws himself forward in one last effort. An opening emerges and he slips free—feeling born again. As he turns towards the womb he'd just emerged from he's greeted by a screaming, bloodied corpse with a writhing creature inside its depths.

Before the monster can free itself, there's a flash and the blinding light wraps around the body as it morphs into a towering figure. It stands over Xander, looming and making him feel scared and weak. Somewhere in the blinding light, a woman screams and Xander looks around frantically.

"Mom!"

He sees her necklace; sees her ghostly silhouette coming into focus—struggling to fit itself with its jewelry—and reaching out to him in desperation. Sound dulls and time slows and Xander hears the metallic snap *as the necklace is torn from its rightful owner's neck.*

It echoes…

The sound ripples the scene and the image distorts before it explodes and he finds himself watching five monsters crawl over a shrieking angel. Blood and feathers fly from the mass as it's torn apart and a horrified Xander stumbles back as the gore pools on the floor and spreads like a hungry stain. The screams echo and warp into a swarm of angry bees that sting at him inside and out.

He cries out and runs—hating himself for his cowardice—to the coat closet and slams the door shut against the monsters and the stinging screams.

It's dark—so very, very dark—and a sliver of light emerges like a…

"NO! NO! NOT AGAIN!"

Xander pounds on the wall and the world shatters like a mirror. He is trapped as the shards swirl around him, leaving fragments of the horror in their path. The images of the monsters appear in the fragments, which grow spider legs and rise until they tower over him. He closes his eyes and when he opens them again he's lying with his mother as she reads him a story.

As the melodic words of Dr. Seuss flow he looks up towards their source and cowers as her face begins to melt away and exposes an orb of maggots and flies that buzz at him and try to crawl up his nose and into his mouth.

As he fights the nauseating invasion, Kyle emerges, breaking through like a summoned demon, and stands in front of him. Kyle's approach continues, and as he does he begins to grow into a monstrous creature.

Xander drops to his knees in tears.

The Kyle-monster's laughter echoes as its face stretches until the mouth's edges wrap halfway around its head, its teeth gapped and allowing dark horrors to spill out.

And still he grows; stretching into the darkness like a demonic balloon. His mother—the corpse—continues to read, unaware of her fate, and the growing monstrosity plunges its sharpened hand into her left breast again and again. Silence spreads and sucks everything into it.

Xander twists and plummets into the nothingness and sees salvation in the shape of a closet door.

It's dark, and a sliver of light emerges like a gash...

The calm, quiet night shattered as Xander shot up in bed, screaming in rage and agony. The sweat-soaked sheets clung to his cold, clammy skin and he thrashed to get free from them, falling out of bed. The walls strained, groaning, as he released wave upon wave of energy that finally shattered through the windows.

Still screaming, the magical energy collected and hurled his bookcase across the room where it smashed into the wall, littering the floor with horror and fantasy novels. He stood and staggered backwards and bumped into his desk, bruising his hip. Heaving, he turned to steady himself on the surface only to have it crack in half down the middle. His rage poured forth and his energy picked up and whipped texts and pages in a furious tornado around the room.

He couldn't control it.

He couldn't stop it.

Behind him, his grandmother opened the door and calmly approached him through the magical whirlwind, finally taking his left hand in her right. Xander felt the touch like a soothing chill that relaxed him. He felt his eyes flutter as tears formed and he looked into his grandmother's face. She released his hand, looking back at him, boring into his eyes as if there was an answer to the madness hidden within them.

Xander collapsed on the floor and whimpered, the images of his dream slowly fading from his mind. He was distantly aware that Trepis was talking to him, but he couldn't decipher the words.

With his vision fading, he uttered the only thing left bubbling in his mind:

"Mom…"

CHAPTER EIGHT
STRENGTH VS. GRACE

OCTOBER'S SPELL HAD TOUCHED THE
trees, taking the dull greens and turning them to vibrant
yellows, browns, and reds. It was Saturday and Xander's
grandmother sat on the front porch in her whicker rocker
sipping iced tea.

She could feel Xander's tension inside the house as he
woke up, clearly still on edge from his nightmare. It had taken
a lot of energy to calm his rage and she was both proud of his
heritage and terrified by his potential. All the same, she felt
sorry for him and all he had gone through. She had seen the
cuts and bruises that were left from the school kids that
picked on him and was constantly reminded of the bullying

problems that his father had suffered so many, many years ago. She often wondered if telling Xander about his father would help him in some way, but had decided long ago that she wanted him to live a simple life.

Inside, Xander's waking mind tried to grasp the strange dreams he'd had the night before; dreams of losing control and tearing his room apart with his magic. He nervously scanned his bedroom for any signs of the destructive forces he'd unleashed, only to find everything exactly as it should have been. Then, after a long moment, she sensed his acceptance that it had all been a dream.

She sighed and returned to herself and took another sip of her tea.

Yes, she felt sorry for her grandson and everything he had gone through, but she was more concerned about what was coming. There was no doubt in her mind that her son's comrades were looking for him. But, despite their deceptions, she also knew of the others that were coming for him.

She sighed; the time was coming, and though this upset her, she had to admit that she wouldn't have been able to protect him from their world forever. Nevertheless, she'd made up her mind to care for him as long as she could.

She smiled.

At least he had someone watching over him.

"Joseph..."

"You say something, Grandma?" Xander stepped out the front door onto the porch.

She looked up at her grandson as he plopped down in the neighboring chair. He was wearing a massacred pair of blue jeans that exposed more leg than denim and a shirt that was cut up at the shoulders, leaving jagged tears where the sleeves should have been.

"No, dear. I'm afraid there was nobody to say anything to."

Xander hunched forward in the chair and looked at the floorboards of the deck, "Well, you got somebody now."

"I suppose I do," she couldn't help but smile. Through all the pain that had occurred in his life—despite all the hatred towards humanity that burned within him—he was never unkind to her.

"Are you thirsty?" she asked, motioning towards a second glass that was waiting for him beside her own.

He studied it for a moment before casting aside his confusions and went about pouring himself a drink.

She breathed in deeply and looked at the sky, "Do you know why I like tigers, Xander?" she asked. "It's their character. There is so much power; such raw energy and strength. But"—she paused and allowed a warm smile to tug at her age-weathered features—"they symbolize grace and intelligence."

Xander frowned and looked at her, "Tigers?"

She nodded, "Yes. Don't you like them?"

Xander laughed nervously and sipped his iced tea. "Actually, they're my favorite animal. I just never told you that."

His grandmother nodded, "You told me once. You just don't remember." She smiled and sipped her tea, "So... how did you sleep?"

Xander tensed at the question and opened his mouth to answer as a car across the street began to pull from the driveway and stopped abruptly, brakes squealing, as a rusted pickup truck honked its horn and sped by. The loud noise—coupled with the tension he was already feeling—ignited his rage.

His mind was so tormented:

Calm down!... fuckers!... "li'l faggot"... hate them!... "hope you rot and die you fuc—"... Xander!... "Devil-spawn"... stop it!... Trepis?... Bleed!... burning!... "HOLD HER BOYS... GET HER"... MY FUCKING SKIN'S ON FIRE!!... "XAANDDDER"... I hate them all!... leave this putrid place and go far away... HATE THEM!... Please... I HATE THEM!... Why?... I FUCKING HATE THEM!

"... so much power, but so much grace," his grandma spoke softly, her right hand patting his left.

Xander's mind was suddenly calm; the burning in his skin had disappeared.

But what...?

"Grace is what makes power worth having, Xander," she nodded to herself, "Grace. Always remember that, Xander, and always remember that I love you"

He frowned for a moment, taken back by the randomness of his grandmother's words. After a moment, though, he smiled and looked up at her.

"I love you too," he answered sincerely.

CHAPTER NINE
SOMETHING'S WRONG...

SUNDAY MORNING.

Again Yin's hammer had fallen on an empty chamber.

It was nearly eight-thirty in the morning when Xander's grandma knocked on the door and told him—sounding unnaturally eager—that she had to run some errands. He considered asking if she wanted company, but before he had the chance to make the offer he heard her soft footsteps as she scurried down the hall and went down the stairs.

Xander frowned at this.

That was certainly odd. Trepis said.

"Yea," he bit his lip, "Wonder what was so important…"

Still confused and more than a little hurt by his grandmother's behavior, he plodded down the stairs and went to the kitchen, making a bee-line to the liquor cabinet. Without even bothering to browse the selection, he grabbed the first bottle his fingers fell upon before returning to his room. The stolen liquor—a nearly-full bottle of vodka—was placed on the nightstand to allow Xander to light up a cigarette. He pulled in a long breath and blew the smoke out slow as he snatched his prize and began to chug its contents.

His drink was cut short, however.

Somebody was outside.

He could sense them.

"Who the hell…?" he muttered to himself as he set down the bottle. Hurrying to the window, he glanced out and saw the little boy from the other day gazing up at him from the backyard. "What the fuck?" he turned and rushed for the stairs.

What is it? Trepis asked.

Xander frowned, "Are you kidding me? It's that damn kid again!"

Trepis laughed, *Another visit from the fan club?*

"Shut up!"

Xander was downstairs, through the hall and out the back door in an instant. The little boy—still dressed in the same suit as before—remained motionless, his body rigid and his eyes lifeless as he stared back at Xander.

Creepy.

"Shut. Up," Xander repeated, hoping not to scare away the kid before he had a chance to talk to him. Taking a slow step towards him, he tried to calm his voice: "Who are you?"

The boy didn't answer; he didn't even move!

Xander flinched. He suddenly had a headache.

A bad one.

He felt a burning tingle in his arms and legs as his

impatience grew into anger.

His fists clenched on their own, "Who the hell are you?" he stomped towards the child, hoping to scare an answer out of him.

Seeing Xander approaching, the little boy's eyes sparked to life and he held out his hand, suddenly looking desperate, "You will come with me now!"

Xander scowled, growing more and more exhausted—more and more *enraged*—with the whole situation. "Wh-what?" he stammered, having difficulty masking the nervousness in his voice. "Why the hell should I go anywhere with you?"

The boy continued to reach out towards him, flexing his fingers in desperation, "You are in danger and must come with me!"

Xander stepped back, feeling more and more uncomfortable with the situation, "J-just get lost! You hear me, you little shit? Go back home to your—"

"We can protect you!" the boy interrupted.

"Who the hell is 'we'?"

"We are—"

Xander shook his head, "You know what? I don't even care! Just get out of here! Leave me alone!"

The boy cocked his head, a look of confusion adding to the desperation, "But you are in *danger*!"

"*You're* the one who's in danger!" Xander stomped towards the boy again, hoping to scare him off this time.

The child stood his ground and smiled expectantly as Xander approached, his hand still outstretched, "You will come with me now?"

"NO!" Xander was beyond furious. The burning rage had overwhelmed his entire body, which shook uncontrollably.

The boy's eyes showed no sign of alarm as he calmly turned and walked away, "It won't be long now, Stryker."

Xander stood and stared after the boy, his breath coming out jagged and his fists still clenched as he watched him leave. All around him, the grass was whipped about by the energy that flowed from him. As the rage seeped deeper Xander dropped to his knees—dizzy, tired and suddenly panicked.

There was no sound of the back gate's squeaky latch or the crunch of gravel underfoot, but when he looked up to glare at the retreating child, he saw that he was alone.

It took five cigarettes and the rest of the vodka before Xander was able to calm down; though neither helped to shake the feeling that something wasn't right. He was glad that what had remained of the booze had not been enough to get him wasted—he didn't want to get drunk.

Not now, at least.

Not when he was so close to losing control already.

As the alcohol took its course he decided that what he really needed was something to eat. Letting out a heavy sigh and, in the process, issuing forth a cloud of smoke he got up and went to the kitchen again.

Raiding through the contents of the fridge, he came across a disposable baking pan that still held nearly half a meatloaf. Paying little mind to the process, he carved a thick slice and threw it on a plate next to a large puddle of spicy A-1 sauce. Satisfied that the hunk of food was enough, he went into the living room and plopped down on the sofa—respecting the sanctity of the worn out recliner that was his grandmother's—and turned on the TV, landing on CNN:

"... *victim: 27 year old Rachel Bayen, was brutally murdered in an alley on Church Street. A possible suspect...*"

Xander rolled his eyes and switched the channel to MTV and sat back, trying to shake off the edgy, panicky sensation that still itched in the back of his mind.

Though he couldn't quite place it, he knew that something wasn't right.

The phone rang and he resentfully got up to answer it. "Hello?"

A muffled voice grumbled something incoherent before coming in clear: "Yes! Hello, may I please speak with Xander Stricker?"

Great! A damn telemarketer... Xander thought, his muscles tightening in aggravation as he sighed, "You are speaking to Xander *Stryker*."

The voice went silent for a moment. Then: "Son, I have some—"

"I'm not your goddam son!" Xander growled into the receiver, his skin starting to feel hot again.

Xander, don't... Trepis pleaded.

"Er... yes, of course. But I..." a voice in the background cut off the speaker.

Xander felt his teeth clenching and was sure that at any moment they'd shatter under their own pressure.

Xander, calm down!

He ignored Trepis, "Whoever the hell this is: get your shit figured out and give me a call when your head is out of your ass!" With that he killed the call with the push of a button.

Groaning in pain, Xander stumbled, the cordless phone slipping from his grip as he threw out both hands to catch himself on the table. His body was on fire; roasting under his own skin! The sensation only grew more intense, crawling up his torso until his entire body was swallowed in the fire.

You have to relax! Trepis' words echoed in his mind, *Don't do this to yourself!*

Desperate for a relief from the burning, he yanked off his shirt and threw the garment across the room where it horse-shoed around a lamp and pulled it over, shattering the bulb. The sound, amplified by his rage, rang in his head and he clapped his hands over his ears to try and keep out the noise.

Where was his grandma?

Why wasn't she back yet?

Xander, you have to relax!

The burning continued, wrapping more and more around him and threatening to cook him from the inside-out. As the room filled with his magical energy the furniture began to shake and drag across the floor. The TV—still blaring music videos—shook for a moment before something inside of it popped and the screen went black. Eyes widening, he turned at the sound of a strained creaking and saw a spider web pattern of cracks forming on the window.

"No! No! NO!" he rushed towards the breaking glass, focusing his mind on stopping the process.

He was too late.

The window exploded as he reached for it. Jagged pieces of glass rained down and, startled, he yanked back and snagged his forearm on one of the shards. As blood poured from his shredded arm onto the wood floor, Xander—finally soothed by a cool breeze that ran into the living room—collapsed to the floor in a fit of tears and choking sobs. He curled his head down and hugged his knees to his bare chest, not caring that his face and hair now lay on his bloodied right arm.

"Grandma…"

Xander! You're arm—

"Something's wrong!" he cried out with a sob, "Something is *very* wrong!"

CHAPTER TEN
RUDE AWAKENINGS

XANDER, YOU AWAKE? TREPIS' VOICE urged him from the depths of unconsciousness.

Xander groaned, his eyes opening only slightly and giving him a bright, blinding view of a whitewashed ceiling. He wondered how long he'd been out. As his senses returned to him he became aware of a full-body ache that started from the back of his head to the tip of his toes, an incredibly bad case of cotton mouth, the sounds of medical equipment, and the horrendous smells of the hospital:

Sickness.

Blood.

Death.

Ammonia.

Jesus, man, you gave me a scare! Trepis went on: *I thought I was going to be trapped in the mind of a vegetable!*

"Glad to know… you still care," Xander quipped as best he could.

"Doctor! He's waking up," a woman's voice chimed, followed by the melodic clicking of approaching footsteps. Then: "Xander? Can you hear me?"

Xander blinked against the dark shape looming over him and scowled, "H-how'd I get here?"

"Same as most: an ambulance."

There was suddenly another light—brighter and more focused than the ones overhead. It darted back and forth for a moment, pausing briefly over each of his eyes before disappearing.

Flinching, Xander tried to pull away, "S-stop it! What am I doing here?"

"Xander, how long have you been suicidal?"

"W-what?" Xander's eyes widened at the question, "What are you talking about?" He felt a pair of hands lift his right arm and he growled, yanking it away and yelping from the pain as his IV was yanked.

"We received a call from your neighbors, Xander. They said they watched you punch through your window and cut yourself with the glass. Do you remember this?"

Xander frowned, blinking his eyes, "No! I mean,"—he shook his head—"that's not the way it happened!"

"Then would you care to explain how it happened?" the

woman's voice was skeptical; already unbelieving.

"Missy?" a man's voice sounded from a short distance away, "They want to know if they can see him."

"Already?" the woman's voice was irritated, "Dammit! He's barely awake!" Xander heard her sigh and his arm was released. "See them in, I suppose. Impatient bastards!"

Xander frowned, careful to rest his right arm on the hospital bed before raising his left hand and wiping some of the grogginess from his vision. As the sound of heavy footsteps resonated from the left, he turned his head to face the newcomers.

"Xander? Xander Stryker?" a man's voice called out.

Xander frowned and blinked, "Who the hell are you?" As his sight cleared, the overwhelming white faded and gave way to others shades and, eventually, shapes. Closest to him and coming closer was an older man with gray hair and a bushy mustache. Behind him, a taller-yet-younger black man followed. Both wore dark-blue police uniforms. Seeing this, Xander tensed and tried to sit up, only to be rewarded with a wave of dizziness. "Wh-what do you want?"

The older police officer frowned at his reaction, "It's alright, Xander, you're not in any trouble."

"Then what's going on?" Xander demanded still feeling unnerved from waking up in the hospital.

"I'm officer Shady," the older man introduced himself, his mustache dancing with the movement of his lips, "we spoke briefly on the phone."

Xander sighed and tried to control his breathing as he felt his rage begin to boil up. "I see," he frowned and reached over with his left hand to pull the IV out of his right arm, "Finally got your head out of your ass, I see."

The other cop glared and moved to step around Shady,

"Hey! That's enough! That's no way to—"

"Tom, stop! He's been through a lot!" Shady put out an arm, holding him back. The other officer—Tom, as it appeared to be—stepped back, still looking angry but keeping it to himself. "I-I'm pretty sure that's supposed to stay in."

Xander finished extracting the IV and flexed his arm several times, ignoring the spot of blood that seeped out behind the needle. Below it, wrapped around his forearm, was a length of bandage that traveled from his wrist to just below his elbow.

"I hate hospitals," Xander mumbled.

"I still don't think—"

"What did you come here to tell me?" Xander asked, looking back at Shady as he started to sit up again, "Must be important for you to have come all the way out here."

Tom stepped forward again, reaching out, "You're not trying to *leave*, are you?"

Xander frowned and shot a glare at him as he stood from the bed on shaky legs, "I can't stay here," he said, trying to keep the shakiness out of his voice. He'd spent too much time in hospitals in the past, and he was in no mood to be kept in this one any longer.

Tom shook his head, "There's not really much of a choice in the—"

"Tom," Shady interrupted his partner again, "let me and the kid talk," Tom grumbled and turned away, leaving the room with more attitude than necessary. Shady waited till he was out of the room and looked back at Xander, "Happy?"

Xander scoffed and shook his head, "Hardly."

Shady's mustache teetered back and forth like a see-saw before he cleared his throat, "I've shown you a lot of patience so far, I'd appreciate a little in return! Now, are you ready to hear what I was trying to tell you before?"

Xander frowned, looking up into the officer's eyes. He felt suddenly uneasy and his head hurt like hell, "What is it?"

Shady nodded, glad to finally be getting somewhere, "It's your grandma. She—"

"Stop!" Xander bit the corner of his lip. He had felt his grandmother's death hours ago. While it had taken a great deal of effort to finally admit the truth, it was no longer a mystery what had set him off earlier. All that aside, he didn't feel like hearing it out loud, "I already know."

Shady frowned at this, "You know?"

"Overheard one of the nurses," Xander shifted his eyes away and hoped the cop wouldn't catch him in his lie.

Shady put a hand on his shoulder, "I'm sorry, son."

"I'm not..." Xander stopped himself and pulled away from the officer's touch, "I'm fine!"

Shady, unsure of what else to say, stood silently.

Xander sighed, keeping his eyes glued to the floor, "How did it happen?"

"I don't think I should—"

"HOW DID SHE DIE?" Xander said through gritted teeth, glaring up at the cop.

Shady took a step back before remembering his place and adjusted his footing, "We think it was an attempted mugging."

"You *think*?" Xander gave him a look.

Shady nodded, "No witnesses have surfaced so we have to go based solely on—"

"Who did it?" Xander fought to speak around the lump forming in his throat.

"Just some punk kids," Shady frowned then and looked away, "Nothing's concrete yet, but we don't think it was

planned that way. They were probably after her purse or
something like that, but like I said—"

There was a loud pop then and the window to the right
of the bed shattered, raining broken glass all over the floor.
Before Xander could tell what had happened, Shady fell to
the ground with a smoking hole the size of a golf ball on the
right side of his head.

Shortly after, the door burst open and Tom ran in, gun
drawn. Seeing his partner dead on the floor, he whimpered
and dropped to his knees.

RUN! Trepis bellowed in his head.

Xander, seeing no reason not to listen, sprinted across
the room and out the open door. As he turned down the hall,
he could hear Tom's voice stammering as he called for
backup. With the sound of the cop's cries fading behind him,
Xander took another turn only to be greeted by another
empty corridor.

Where was everybody?

The evenly spaced lights that lined the hall hummed and
shone down with a sickly sterile glow that made the barren
stretch seem longer. Xander shivered nervously as a cold
sensation swept over him.

Hurrying around a corner, he skidded to a stop in front
of a smiling, tattooed woman with fiery hair. Something in
her grin sent another shiver up Xander's spine and his head
throbbed harder. He took a step back, staggering in the
process and nearly falling. The woman echoed his retreat with
a fluid advance, her high heels sounding in the empty hall.
Slack jawed and terrified, he watched as she lifted off of the
ground. She hovered for a moment, a menacing chuckle
escaping her well painted lips before she shot towards him.

Shit! Go back!

Xander spun on his heels and dashed back down the hall the way he'd come. He turned his head back and saw that his pursuer—toes dragging across the tile floor—was close behind. Startled by the sight, his feet caught and he toppled over. As he struggled to get up, the bulbs lining the hallway burst and rained glass down on either side of him. With the woman's haunting laughter closing in, Xander pulled himself to his feet and started back for the room. Eager to be back in the company of the armed officer he sprinted with everything he had. As the lights lining the hall continued to explode, forcing him to run through the broken glass, his shoes skidded and scraped on the shards, threatening to send him toppling once again.

Once inside the room he slammed the door behind him and jammed a nearby chair under the knob to keep it closed. Not wanting to present himself as a target, Xander dropped down onto his belly and joined Tom, who had overturned the hospital bed in an attempt to shield himself from the shooter's sights. He felt helpless as he ducked his head deeper behind the cover of the stained mattress and steel frame.

The gun! Trepis called out.

"Since when are you so goddam aware?" Xander growled, ignoring the officer's confused look.

Uncertain of what his friend meant, he scanned the room until he spotted Shady's body, still sprawled in the middle of the room, and the firearm still secured in the holster at its side. Frowning, he crept towards the corpse, his hand outstretched in an attempt to retrieve the weapon. With only several inches separating him from the pistol, the door began to shake momentarily against the chair before being ripped from the wall entirely.

Xander turned his head—arm still outstretched for the

gun—and saw the redhead floating at the entrance. Wasting no time, he unlatched the clasp that secured the weapon and turned to aim it at the woman, who narrowed her eyes at the sight of the gun. At that moment, an invisible grip snared the pistol, yanking it from Xander's grip and disassembling it in front of him.

Tom, releasing the grip on his radio, shot up to his feet and drew his own gun, holding it steady with both hands, "Hands where I can see 'em, lady!"

The redhead lifted an eyebrow, still floating in midair.

Xander's eyes went wide, "Are you fucking serious?"

The woman smiled wickedly, locking her scary eyes on Xander, "What's the matter, Stryker? Don't you still want to die?"

Xander scowled, "WHAT THE FUCK DO YOU WANT?" his anger flared up and the bed shook and dragged across the floor several inches.

Tom jumped at the sound of the shifting bed but avoided looking behind him as he tightened his grip on the gun, "I said show me your hands, bitch!"

The woman grinned, looking innocently at the cop for the first time and holding her hands up. She moved back and glanced down the hall, smiling and allowing a hulking pale man with greased-back black hair to enter. Seeing Xander, the newcomer gave a toothy smile.

A loud roar came from outside and Xander—not taking his eyes off the newcomer—crouched down, afraid that the shooter had started up again. It wasn't until the shadow was cast from the passing police helicopter that he relaxed. Tom stood rigid, made all the more confident from the arrival of the requested backup, and tightened his grip on his pistol. Uncertain, he shifted his aim back-and-forth between the floating woman and the man.

Unafraid of the cop or the weapon he wielded, the woman slowly settled down to the ground, a soft giggle ringing out, "Tiro?" she cooed.

The man stiffened and turned with a glare towards Tom, a long step bringing him dangerously close. Seeing the approaching threat, Tom squeezed the trigger.

The man grimaced and twitched as a flower of gore blossomed on his left shoulder. Tom shivered nervously as the man looked back up at him, smirking, before he suddenly vanished. Xander blinked in astonishment and when his eyes opened again the man stood inches in front of him. Tom's body shook slightly and dropped, his head now resembling a crushed fruit.

The pale man growled in Xander's face and grabbed him by the throat, lifting until the tips of his shoes scraped against the floor. He smiled and his lips twitched slightly as a pair of fangs began to extend, "To drink from the son of Stryker,"— he began to lean his face closer—"what a privilege."

Xander's eyes opened in fear as he saw the man's face grow nearer and he screamed, throwing out a wave of energy in a panic. The impact struck him square in the chest, knocking him back and forcing him to drop Xander in order to regain his footing. Free of the iron grip, Xander was caught off guard by a bestial growl that crawled up the strange man's throat and burst from his mouth along with the stink of death. The odor lingered in Xander's throat and he gagged as he was grabbed and flung across the room.

"Just kill him, you moron!" The woman yelled; the contents of the room quaking as she did.

The man frowned and lumbered towards him once again. Seeing no other option, Xander hopped to his feet and, head still reeling, jumped through the window frame. The fire escape outside shook slightly as he steadied himself on it and the cool air stung his bare, heaving chest. From there he could see he was several floors up from the busy street and, confirming that the man was still coming at him, began to descend the ladder.

The roar of the police helicopter caught his attention as he gripped a rung and stared at the reinforcements Tom had called for as they closed-in on the building across the street and hovered over a crouched figure on the rooftop. A booming voice shot out like a cannon:

"POLICE! PUT YOUR HANDS IN THE AIR AND STEP AWAY FROM THE WEAPON!"

The figure, perched at the peak of the office building, stood up straight. Xander squinted against the mid-afternoon sun, watching as the gunner extended his arm towards the helicopter. Though he couldn't be sure from the distance, Xander was sure that the man was giving the helicopter and the police inside it the finger before securing his weapon and jumping down from his post.

The helicopter, unable to keep track of the fleeing assailant, shot forward and began to hook around for a better angle. Frowning at the scene, Xander watched as the gunner stopped briefly, looking out in his direction, and shivered under the cold stare.

"Get him, you idiot!" the woman's voice boomed above Xander's head.

"Are you insane?" the man scoffed at her, "We need to get out of here NOW!"

The roar of the approaching helicopter grew louder as the police brought it around and Xander dared a glance back towards the opposite rooftop.

Seeing the cops coming his way, the gunner adjusted the rifle on his back before taking off at a full, swift sprint across the rooftop. Xander's eyes went wide, palms growing sweaty against the fire escape as the man who had been trying to kill him kicked up a cloud of dust in his wake as he headed for the edge. Just as Xander was sure that he had nowhere else to go the gunner shuddered and dropped forward, adding his hands to the effort, and began running like a wild animal on all fours.

"There's no way," Xander muttered under his breath, "He's not going to…"

As he ran out of rooftop, the gunner hurled himself over the edge of the building and allowed himself to drop like an Olympic diver. He lingered in midair for several seconds longer before reaching out and grabbing onto a window-washing scaffold and swinging through one of the windows. The startled cries and shouts of the office's inhabitants could be heard from across the street and, before disappearing completely into the dim interior of the building, Xander watched for an uncomfortable moment as the man turned and looked back at him with an animal sneer.

The helicopter slowed then and Xander growled in frustration as it hovered in the air.

Above him, there was a loud crash from the room he had just escaped from followed by an even louder bellow from the man:

"Fucking mutt!" he roared. There was another crash, "Some great shot he turned out to be!"

Xander frowned, deciding it was in his best interest to get as far away from the scene as possible.

The cab ride home was an unpleasant one; reeking of stale farts that the driver replaced with new ones without the slightest sign of embarrassment. Xander, ignoring the gross driver as best he could, checked behind them several times for anything that could be following. When he was certain there was no immediate threat, he faced forward and tried to relax; catching sight of a hanging section of fat that hung from the driver's neck that rippled with each imperfection in the road and stifled a dry heave.

Finally, the cab pulled up at the address that Xander had specified and he opened the door and stepped out.

"Th' fare's twen'ee-eight fort'five," the cabby grumbled.

"I haven't got it," Xander muttered.

"Sonababitch!" the cabby yelled as he threw open the door and hoisted himself out, his gut snagging the steering wheel and giving birth to a new wave of obscenities, "Im'a kill ya', ya' robbing b'stard!"

"Disgusting!" Xander muttered as he started across the lawn.

No argument here. Trepis chimed in.

The address he'd given the driver was several blocks away from his own home. He had known from the start that he didn't have the money to pay the fare but felt that he needed a safer way to get home than walking. Running around the back of the house, he hopped the fence and cut through several bushes that separated the one house from another. From there, he crossed through the yard on the opposite side and slowed to a walk, leaving the cursing cabby several houses back.

He was a block away when he first saw the smoke.

As he got closer, his fears were confirmed: the roof of his house collapsing in a violent greeting of his return. Standing in front of the smoldering wreckage were three figures, all wearing black sweatshirts and long, black pants. Two of the three had black baseball caps on while the third wore a black bowler. Xander watched, horrified, from a distance as the last of his life burned to the ground, wondering why nobody else had seemed to notice or bothered to call the fire department.

It's time. The small boy's voice echoed in his head. It was the first time he'd ever heard a voice besides Trepis' and he wondered if he was finally going insane.

Having seen enough of his burning home, he turned his attention to the three, who had noticed his arrival and were now approaching. The closest—a younger-looking man—cracked his knuckles. As he neared, Xander noticed a pinkish stain on his chin and a shudder forced its way up his spine. The other cap-wearer was a dark-skinned woman with a tattoo of a snake that breached her collar and ended on her cheek. The figure in the bowler was a man whose black hair hung from under the hat in front of his left eye.

Too much…

It was all too much for him.

Too much pain. Too much suffering. Too much anguish and guilt and doubt.

Too much to hold back.

Too much to keep it all locked in…

As an unbearable itch—carrying with it an infernal heat—crept over Xander's body, the young man in front of him crouched down like an angry cat then and launched himself several stories into the air. Squinting, Xander fought

68

to keep his eyes focused on the unnatural spectacle as it was lost in the sun; after all that had happened, he once again began to question his sanity and begged reality to return the stranger's feet back to the ground where they belonged. Still gawking into the sky, he was caught off guard by a powerful force and thrown down the length of the street, skipping like a stone over the concrete surface several times before finally rolling to a stop against the curb.

Too much…

It was too—

His eyes rolled in his skull as he wrestled to get his bearings; the world spinning beneath him and keeping him off balance. Getting his left foot centered beneath him, he adjusted his right and tried to stand, only to feel the ground roll under him and drop him all over again.

Behind him there was a soft *thud*, and Xander gave up on the effort to stand up in the hopes of coaxing his blurred vision to focus.

Distortion…

A kaleidoscope of fractured light and rolling shadows…

Xander groaned and blinked, watching as the previously airborne young man stepped towards him.

The familiar sensation of a foot being driven into his ribs; harder and more sudden than he'd expected. As a dry heave ripped the oxygen from his lungs, Xander found himself once again crashing to the unforgiving street.

… too much.

Head still reeling, Xander fought to fill his empty lungs as he was lifted from the ground in an iron grip and shaken before being thrown…

Xander could feel the impending heat growing as he hurdled towards the inferno that was consuming his home.

Consuming his life!

The brittle remains of the house proved too frail to stop Xander as he careened through the sidewall—an avalanche of ash and memories crashing down around him—and slammed into a flaming support beam. No longer able to support the burden of its purpose, the structure crumbled with a fiery hiss and he found himself trapped beneath the mass. Pinned under the scalding pressure and seeing every stolen moment of happiness he'd ever had go up in smoke, he began to succumb.

"JUST FUCKING LET ME DIE!" he roared at the flames.

Dammit, Xander! Fight!

Xander blinked, feeling his tears evaporate before they could fall. "Mom…"

Nothing can be done about that! Now get up! Get the fuck up!

"Grandma…"

Stop it! Sadness fixes nothing! Anger motivates change! USE YOUR ANGER AND FIGHT! FIGHT, GOD DAMN YOU!

The sudden wave of intense heat overwhelmed everything else, and Xander did nothing to stop it from consuming him. Though he could feel the burning remains of the beam holding him down—could smell the burning denim and flesh that had begun to feed it—he knew this new fire had nothing to do with his surroundings. Crying against everything that had befallen him, he pushed up and shook off the offending piece of wood and pulled himself to his feet. He saw his mother, her sweet smile and her slightly curled strawberry-blonde hair. Her green eyes, long since closed, burned in his mind. He saw his Grandmother, with all her wisdom and calmness.

Gone.

All gone.

He closed his eyes and let the visions of those he loved burn in his mind.

And then he imagined Kyle…

Use his anger? Up until then all his magical rages had been done by instinct—chaotic events that had turned themselves on.

But what if he could control it?

Though his eyes remained closed he could sense the strangers as they approached; the young man taking up the lead again. Inside his mind, Xander could practically see the extended snarl stretching the jaws of each of his attackers; could feel their determination and hatred roll off of them in waves.

Hatred?

What could they know about hatred?

"He's still alive!" Xander felt a swell of disgust roll from the snake-woman—could practically *see* her thin lips curl in a sneer from the other side of the collapsed wall—and he felt another wave of energy rocketing towards him.

Frantic to hold his ground, Xander threw his arms out in an attempt to hold himself up. The swell of energy he'd come to recognize as his own kicked up, then, and the ash and debris around him scattered in a momentary gust as his attackers' wave collided with the house. As the dividing barricade burst towards him, the gust shifted and pushed back; the burning chunks of wood and furniture parting around Xander and splaying out in either direction. Growling against the whipping hair in his eyes, Xander fought to maintain his footing as his shoe dragged across the ashes of his home until the force finally died down around him.

The three stopped in mid-stride as the dense cloud between them settled.

Xander felt a swell of excitement at the sight of their confusion.

They had power; there was no doubt about that.

But he did, too.

And now they saw it.

"He got lucky," the snake-woman growled; her words nearly inaudible to Xander, "Kill him!"

The three started toward him again, and the swell of their emotions once again grew; the force becoming so strong that their bodies seemed to radiate with it.

But it was too much.

Xander was too angry to be afraid.

Too eager to see them suffer for *everything* that had happened.

Do it! Trepis urged him.

"It… it can't be," the snake-woman's eyes widened then, her purposeful advance ceasing as she stared at Xander in disbelief. The analytic gaze melted to one of concern, and the woman took a step back, followed soon after by another, "S-Stryker?"

The other two, unaware of their companion's retreat, continued to stride forward.

Trepis' voice echoed in Xander's head: *DO IT!*

"Oh no…" the woman held out her hand, "Get back!"

But the warning came too late. The excruciating heat in Xander's body churned about in him like a boiling whirlpool; a new purpose driving it to spread. As he concentrated on the sensation, he felt the gust pick up and swirl around him, growing in intensity. When the force became too much for him to contain—too much for him to hold back any longer—

he shut his eyes and unleashed it on them.

There was a series of snapping and crunching sounds accompanied by panicked screams. Driven by this, he increased the intensity of his attack. Even when the screams were silenced, he continued to let the energy whip around him; let it rip and tear until there was nothing left to feed the destructive force.

Until there was no energy left in him, and, feeling drained, he stumbled and collapsed into the dying embers.

When he finally looked up, the little boy was standing over him, his hand outstretched. As he watched through blurred vision, a man and a woman appeared behind the boy, who faded away and disappeared.

You will come with us now?

As the effort to keep himself conscious became too much, Xander finally offered a weak nod.

CHAPTER ELEVEN
THE ODIN CLAN

IMMEDIATELY AFTER AGREEING TO GO

with them, the woman had reached down and touched her right hand on the back of his neck and a calm fog engulfed him. As the rest of the world faded away, Trepis' voice became Xander's only focus.

"T-Trep?" he tested his voice, unsure if he was still able to speak, "Where... where am I?"

Somewhere safe.

"How do you know?"

Trepis was slow to answer, *This just seems... familiar.*

The car came to a slow stop and idled as a pair of strong hands helped him out of the backseat. Once out and on his feet, he was gently led inside. The building, he remembered, used to be a factory; one that had long-since gone out of business and now only served as a hangout for his peers to get drunk. The interior was decayed from years of abandonment; mildew and other offensive smells invaded his nostrils as he was led through, pulling him from his daze long enough to gag. Two voices sounded behind him, though he could not make out the words.

"What's happening?" Xander slurred.

Just relax.

"Why are you so calm? How did you know about the people at the hospital? How—"

I don't know! I just did! Now shut up and relax!

Though nobody had pressed a call button, an old elevator groaned and emerged from the basement. Old and unused doors squeaked loudly as the man forced them open and stood aside for them, shaking a stubborn cobweb from his palm. The woman, still holding the back of his neck, helped him over the gap and into the lift as the doors were closed behind them.

They began to descend, and the structure shook with the strain of use and their combined weight. Xander, too lost in his mental haze, could not muster the worry of the old contraption's weaknesses and instead continued with his conversation.

"Are we going to die?"

No.

"Are you sure?"

Very much so.

"How?"

I told you: I don't know.

The elevator reached the lower level, which proved itself to be in even worse condition than the one above it. The hand that rested on his neck moved away and Xander felt suddenly aware, the concern and fear flooding back. The voices, before foggy and incoherent, now came in clearly:

"Are you hurt?" the man's voice cut through the fading haze.

Xander blinked, confused by the sudden wave of awareness.

"Stryker!" The voice was harsher; more demanding, "Are you hurt?"

Frowning, he turned towards the voice and was surprised to see that the speaker, though not large, possessed an intimidating quality in the way he stood. His hair was thick and dark brown, and his eyes seemed almost *too* green.

The man continued to stare him down, waiting on an answer, and Xander finally shook his head, "No. I'm... I'm fine."

The woman stepped around him and came into view. She had blonde hair and blue eyes that seemed to glow with an almost electric force. Her teeth, when she smiled at him, shone like immaculate pearls.

After all the foul-breathed, scary-looking monsters that had been after him, the two were a breath of fresh air.

"Where am I?" Xander demanded, the last of the haze gone from his mind.

Xander! I already told you—

Xander shook his head to interrupt his friend and focused his eyes on the two in front of him.

The man looked at him for a moment, and then shifted his gaze over to the woman, who stepped to the side of the room and bent back as if she were about to sit down. Xander watched, bewildered, as she let gravity take her and she began to fall back before suddenly stopping in midair; reclining comfortably on *nothing*. Xander stepped back, terrified that he had been taken to a secluded place by the same freaks that had tried to kill him. As he retreated, the woman looked calmly at him and brushed a strand of hair from the corner of her face.

"We're not freaks, and you *are* safe," she said with a reassuring smile, "You should listen to"—she smirked— "Trepis for once."

Xander narrowed his eyes at her, "How did you—"

She giggled, "We'll explain it all to you in time."

Xander shook his head, already fed-up with mind games, "I didn't ask if I was safe! I asked where—"

"I know what you asked, sweetheart, but just because you asked that question first doesn't mean that *that* was what you wanted answered. As to where you are"—she glanced around at their surroundings—"you're in a dump." She scowled, turning to her companion, "We *really* couldn't find a better safe house?"

Xander felt around his jeans for his pack of cigs and pulled it out. He struck the flint on his Zippo and lit the end before finally nodding in agreement. "*This* is supposed to be a safe house?" he scoffed, "You know we nearly died on that elevator, right?"

She laughed and Xander reared back in surprise. Though there was nothing special in the sound—nothing abnormal or disturbing—he was taken aback by the strange echo of laughter *inside* his head. Suddenly feeling unsure once again, he took two steps back and bumped into the man, who had somehow moved from the other side of the room.

"I know it's a trip at first. Believe me: I'm not even used to it! But it's nothing to be afraid of," he assured him.

Xander frowned back at the man and took a nervous drag off his cigarette, "I've been chased and attacked all day by people like you—people who could do the *same* things that you're doing! Why should I trust you?"

The man opened his mouth to speak, but stopped and looked at the woman, who still floated in a seated position.

"You should trust us because, after everything that's happened to you, you are finally where you've always belonged."

Though deep down inside he felt it was true, Xander felt angered by this. "What sort of answer is that? What the hell do you know about me?"

The woman leaned forward, "I know that you have known nothing but pain for most of your life. I know that you hate humanity and yourself as well. I know that every night you take a black revolver you call 'Yin' from a velvet-lined case and hope that the one bullet within it will take your life." She pouted her lips sadly at this, looking discomforted before continuing, "And I know that your mother—"

"STOP!" Xander screamed, jabbing a shaky finger in her direction, "Don't say another goddam word!"

The walls of the basement shook and rained down chunks of itself on the three of them. As it did, the woman shook in midair and dropped to the ground, a look of shock on her face. The man, looking a bit concerned, cautiously stepped away.

Without the use of her hands or feet, the woman lifted herself up, floating for a moment before her feet touched down to the dirty floor and she dusted herself off, "I'm... I'm sorry."

The man put his hands back on Xander's shoulder, and, though he didn't squeeze or make a move to hurt him, there was an undeniable strength behind the grip that he knew could present itself at any moment. Knowing better to press his luck he sighed and forced himself to relax. Resentfully, he nodded to the woman in an acceptance of her apology.

She smiled slightly and went on: "I also know things about you that you don't know about yourself."

He couldn't help but wonder what she meant by this and, despite the anger that still welled within him, calmed his voice, "What sort of things?"

"I—*we*—know about your father and the great things he accomplished for us during his life." She smiled proudly, "I knew him well and was personally trained by him. Actually, he trained many of us."

"And who is 'us'?" Xander asked, taking a hard, unsteady drag from his cigarette.

There was pride in the voice of the man behind Xander as he answered the question: "The Odin Clan."

Xander sighed. Like everything else that day, the answer only brought up more questions.

Several hours passed while Xander's escorts, who introduced themselves as Marcus and Sophia, waited for the sun to go down. Sophia, who expressed a preference towards 'Sophie', stayed silent during the wait. She stood close to Xander the whole time, keeping her hand rested on his right arm. Though there was a strange tickle from her touch, he didn't complain.

"As I'm sure you've noticed by now there's *a lot* of

baddies creeping around just aching to turn you into a stain!" Marcus kept his voice down, "Most of them are amateurs at best, but there's plenty gunning for you who could have easily tracked us."

Head still reeling from the events of that day, Xander scowled at the explanation, "But *why* would they—"

"We'll explain everything to you later," Sophie offered as she gave his arm a gentle squeeze, "For now you're just going to have to trust us."

"Trust you? Do you know what I've been through today; how many *freaks* just like you have tried to kill me since I got up this morning?" Xander scoffed, making a point of looking around their surroundings, "Just look where you've taken me! Why the fuck should I trust you?"

Marcus' eyes flashed with anger as they narrowed to furious slits and bore into him, "Because if I wanted to kill your punk-ass you wouldn't have even seen me coming before you were dead!" He began to curl back his lip but stopped when Sophie cleared her throat. Scowling, he looked away, "And trust me, kid, you haven't seen a 'freak' yet!"

Sophie sighed, "We're not happy about being down here either, sweetie, but we couldn't risk leading anything dangerous back to our home."

Soon after the sun went down Marcus took out a cell phone and punched a number on the speed dial, "We're good."

Moments later Sophie stared towards the wall, her eyes darting back and forth for a moment before she nodded to Marcus, who returned the nod. Both motioned for Xander to follow and they headed out of the back and up a flight of stairs. Once in the car—which seemed to be the same make and model if not the same car as before—Xander faced the two and demanded to know what was going on.

It took a while to answer the question, consuming most of the long car ride. It wasn't a hard question to answer, or at least Marcus and Sophie didn't seem to think so, but they had to repeat themselves several times.

"So you're all vampires?" Xander asked again with another scoff. It was the fifth time that he'd questioned the explanation, but they seemed to continue to play the game and refused to simply break off into giggles and confess that the entire thing had been a joke.

The car came to a stop and Marcus motioned for Xander to get out. He sighed and lifted himself from the back of the car and began to follow them up the path towards a large mansion. The structure was huge and, as far as Xander was concerned, awe inspiring.

It hardly looked like the headquarters for a cult...

They're telling the truth. Trepis said.

Xander rolled his eyes, "How would you know?"

Xander, you have always known there was something more to this world, why would you stop believing now?

There was a long silence as Xander grudgingly accepted this. "Know-it-all," he muttered.

Sophie giggled and Xander glanced at her. He wasn't used to anybody but Stan being able to hear Trepis and it wasn't something he was easily coming to grips with. He shook his head in defeat and followed his two escorts towards the building.

A woman, dressed in an elegant black gown, stepped through the door. She paused on her way down the stairs and looked over to the three, lingering on Xander. A deep, red smile spread across her face then that exposed a pair of fangs.

"Is that...?" her voice was saturated in excitement.

Marcus nodded, his serious face giving way to something more.

She started towards them, her hands clasped together, "Stryker! I can't believe—"

"Not yet," Sophie held out a hand to stop the advancing woman. "He's not ready."

The woman stopped and stepped back, looking nervously at the two and then sympathetically at Xander before nodding, "My apologies."

With that she vanished from the room.

Xander stepped back into his escorts, unnerved, and hugged his arms around his chest. The fingers of his left hand grazed his right arm and he realized that he felt no pain. Looking down in astonishment at his forearm, he began to unwrap the bandage and saw only the jagged black patterns of his stitches.

The skin that had been torn and shredded was fully healed!

His mind raced before he looked over at Sophie, recalling her constant contact with his arm back at the old factory and the strange itch he'd felt.

He looked towards the mansion once more, taking in more sights before finally accepting the truth:

"So, you're all vampires…"

CHAPTER TWELVE
VAMPIRE CRASH COURSE

GRIMACING, XANDER PULLED ON A strand of thread that was still networked in his fully-healed arm. After being shown to his room—a massive, empty space with dark-purple wallpaper and thick, matching curtains—he'd gone straight to work on them; carefully pulling them out one-by-one.

Go to sleep. Trepis ordered.

Xander frowned, resisting the urge to yank the strand in an effort to free it, "I'm trying."

Trepis sighed, *No you're not.*

Sighing, he gave up and rolled over in bed, juggling everything he'd been introduced to that day.

He thought back to the morning several days before—had it only been that long?—and recalled Trepis telling him that the arts had tainted him. Although it was true that most who trained in the art of magic were somehow stained by the effects, he was beginning to realize that what had had the biggest impact on him was ignoring the depths of the supernatural world.

He once again kicked himself for being so ignorant.

After being shown around the building, Marcus and Sophie had taken him to a private room on the lower level. Marcus had been quick to straddle a chair and rest his chin and arms on the back and checking his watch while Sophie, ignoring his anxious behavior, allowed herself to fall back and once again "recline" in midair.

"So you recognize the existence of our kind," she began.

Xander knew that it wasn't a question and didn't bother to answer, not audibly anyhow.

"So what do you want explained first?" Marcus asked.

Having so many questions but not knowing where to begin, Xander stared off for a moment in an attempt to collect his thoughts. Trepis, seeming to understand some of the situation already, had remained silent.

After a long silence, Xander thought of his first question: "My father…"

Marcus smiled and nodded, "Your father was one of the most powerful aurics—"

"I thought you said he was a vampire," Xander had frowned at the word.

A heavy and impatient sigh came from Marcus then and he looked to Sophie with a pleading look.

"He was, sweetheart," she'd said, "but you have to understand that 'vampire' is simply a word—a *species*. There's not just *one* type."

Xander recalled feeling agitated at how easy she'd made it sound as he drew another strand of thread from his arm.

"Calm down, Xander," Sophie had said in response to his thoughts, "It really isn't that complex. The term 'vampire' is really just a generic label." She smirked, "I prefer to call us 'life-feeders'. To put it simply, there are those that feed on psychic energy: aurics—those like myself—and those who rely on blood to survive; sangsuigas," she gestured to Marcus then, who, at that moment, had pulled something from his teeth, exposing for a brief moment a pair of fangs. Sophie shook her head at the display and continued, "Anyway, like all creatures, aurics and sangsuigas—or 'sangs' as they've come to be called—have abilities to make hunting and feeding easier. Sangsuigas, for example, have strength and speed while aurics rely on an energy field called an 'aura'—"

"I'm sure you've heard the term before," Marcus had cut in, glancing again at his watch.

Sophie, sighing at the interruption, shot him a glare, "It's with this energy field"—she spoke slowly and deliberately, daring Marcus to interrupt—"that we are able to feed.

"Energy can also be taken through physical contact, usually through the writing hand of the auric user. The same goes for giving energy, just with the opposite hand."

"*Giving* energy?" Xander asked, not bothering to hide the skepticism in his voice, "Doesn't that sort of defeat the purpose of being a vampire?"

Sophie had laughed at that before motioning to his stitched-up arm, "You'd be surprised how often it comes in handy."

Rubbing at his healed arm and the useless stitches therein, Xander had nodded his understanding.

"Those are only the basic feeding abilities, however. Advanced control of one's aura allows aurics to manipulate what's around them," she made a note of this by floating slightly higher, though Xander hadn't needed any more proof by that point. "Your fits of rage have had similar effects, but because you were not aware of your aura you were throwing it around blindly. You see, though your father was an auric your abilities are—for some strange reason—limited, and, unfortunately, what you *do* have has not been nurtured," Sophie had said with a frown. "You just haven't been taught the essential skills."

Marcus scoffed then, "Like control."

Sophie glared at him again, "Aside from a subconscious control of your aura and a natural drive towards magic, you *are* human," she shook her head, "and your mother and grandmother had decided, after your father's death, that you would be safer if you lived your life as one."

A lump had begun to form in Xander's throat; one that had lingered and still plagued him, "My mother…"

Sophie nodded, "Yes. Though many were upset with his decision to do so, your father was honest with her from the start."

Looking down, Xander fought back the wave of emotions that had started to flood his mind.

Sophie nodded, "After your mother—"

Xander had thrown a hard look at her before she could finish.

She stopped herself and thought out her words: "Well… afterwards, your grandma took you in. She thought that as you grew older your abilities might mature as well and she wanted to be there to help you if things ever got out of hand."

Marcus scoffed at that, "She even attacked Depok when he tried to change her mind." He shook his head, "Though she *was* more than two-hundred years older than him!"

Though Xander wasn't sure what a "Depok" was, there had been more pressing matters: "I'm finding it hard to believe that my grandmother was a vampire and I never knew about it!" he'd said as he pulled out a cigarette, noticing there were only two left in the pack.

"Is it really so hard to accept?" Sophie asked, "How many times had she calmed your rage with nothing more than a touch?"

Xander had been taken aback by that, "So every time she touched me…"

"She was calming your rage and absorbing your excess powers," Sophie nodded.

He thought for a moment, suddenly remembering what Marcus had just said: more than two-hundred years?

"So are vampires really immortal?" he'd asked.

Marcus' laugh had been loud and sudden, startling both Xander and Sophie, who nearly fell.

"Nothing's immortal, numb-nuts," he'd answered, still laughing, "We just don't age like humans."

"So how old are you?" Xander asked.

"Turning eighty-six in a few months," Marcus had boasted.

The corner of Sophie's lip had curled upward, "A lady never tells."

Though her answer hadn't satisfied his curiosity, there was still more pressing questions on his mind: "So why am I here now if my mom and grandma both wanted me to live a normal life?"

"They wanted to protect you," Sophie explained, "They didn't want to see you be a part of the world that had killed your father."

"But we figured the shit would hit the fan sooner or later," Marcus had added. "I mean, we aren't the only ones who know that Joseph Stryker had a kid. It was only a matter of time till somebody would try to find you and kill you. When we found out that others were out looking for you, we decided to beat 'em to it."

"But why now?" Xander had asked.

Sophie finally let her feet touch down to the ground, "Your powers are maturing," she explained, taking a few steps towards him, "But you don't know how to control them properly. When your powers started…" she stopped.

"You were broadcasting auric signals that painted a target squarely on your ass," Marcus had finished for her, "And when your grandma 'saw'"—he had made a point of air quoting the word—"the trouble that was coming your way she went out to try and stop them herself."

Xander's eyes had widened and welled with tears, "My grandma died because of…"

Sophie had frowned but gave a slight nod.

Xander had frowned, fighting the urge to cry. His entire week had been one long string of bizarre happenings that had culminated in the ultimate tragedy, and it was his fault!

All his fault…

All because he was too busy getting worked up over some snot-nosed kid!

Who was he? What was his role in all of this?

"You're thinking about my Billy," Sophie had smiled.

He frowned and cursed at her in his mind, watching her

flinch as he did. Despite the invasion on his mind he nodded, "Who is he?"

Sophie's smile wavered but remained plastered on her face. "I made him," she answered, her voice flooded with pride.

Xander, confused, stared at her, "You made him?"

She'd nodded, "It was Marcus' idea. We needed to reach you without coming too close, so I fabricated him as a means of trying to reach you."

"So you were in my head each time I saw that kid?" Xander spoke through clenched teeth.

Sophie squirmed under his glare and nodded once.

"Why not just come and get me yourselves?" he'd demanded.

"Your grandma would have sensed one of us from a mile away, and if she looked in your head and saw a clan member she'd have known we were trying to reach you!" Marcus answered, coming to the still-nervous Sophie's aide, "That, and any other mythos that was out for your blood could have tracked us to get to you."

Xander frowned, "Mythos?"

Marcus nodded, "That's the cute term for creatures that humans would consider mythological."

Xander looked down, feeling the lump grow in his throat, "So I'm the target of a bunch of... mythos?" he asked, suddenly remembering the cigarette between his fingers and taking a deep drag.

Both had nodded.

"How many?"

"Enough," Marcus replied with an icy stare, "There's no shortage of creatures across the globe that hold some kind of grudge against your father; a lot of them feel that killing his offspring is the next best thing."

There had been a long, uncomfortable silence.

"So what made him so special?" Xander finally asked, "Why would so many want me dead because of him?"

"Your father had plans," Sophie had said, "Plans that would've changed the world; not just ours, but the humans', as well."

Marcus nodded, "He believed that the way things were going would lead to chaos for all mythos; that our way of things would lead to a decay of the entire world."

"In the end"—Sophie had let out a deep sigh—"it all comes down to a bunch of narrow-minded mythos who didn't want anything to change."

Marcus shook his head, "Most are content with the way things are: believing that the laws we have are enough."

Xander had looked in Marcus' direction, "Laws?"

Smirking, Marcus gave a nod, "Yup. We have all sorts of laws. Most of them are passed to keep mythos from doing anything stupid that might give the humans reason to suspect our existence."

"So who makes the laws?" Xander asked.

Sophie smiled, "Clans have a big hand in the process of *creating* laws, but the end decision of what passes is made by The Council."

Xander looked between them for a moment, unable to stomach the idea of laws for creatures that, several hours earlier, he'd thought were only works of fiction.

Neither seemed to notice his skepticism, and Marcus continued the explanation: "Clans—certified ones, at least— act as branches to The Council. Many of us are warriors who make sure that the laws are obeyed. Before your father, clans were nothing more than families. At that time The Council struggled to uphold its order. It was your father who thought of forming a clan that supported them. It's taken a while, but now most of the clans that are in power work as enforcers."

Xander shook his head, too exhausted with the whole ordeal to go on any further with the discussion. Seeing that he wasn't ready for any more information that night, Sophie had then walked him to his room as Marcus hurried off.

Xander sighed, continuing to cycle the events in his mind until his head ached and the last of the stitches had been pulled from his arm.

Go to sleep. Trepis repeated.

Xander nodded and closed his eyes, still replaying the events.

CHAPTER THIRTEEN
TAG/A BLOOD BATHED LOVER

IT HAD BEEN A LONG TIME SINCE

Marcus had last seen Brad, and he sighed, working against a wave of nostalgia, as he picked the lock of his old friend's apartment. When finished, he put his tools away and snuck in, stepping into the main hall. Before moving any further he checked his gun and adjusted his combat knife that rested uncomfortably against his ribs. Finally, he set down the bowling bag by the door and moved down the hall.

When they were children they would often play tag in

the park; darting around the playground's obstacles for hours, laughing and screaming as their game grew more and more hectic. Often their mothers would be forced to separate the two in fear that their rambunctious antics would get one or both of them hurt. Later on, as the years passed, the two played high school football and, eventually, joined the army together in hopes of putting their athletic talents to good use.

The army...

Marcus let out a quiet breath.

Their commanding officer had been a madman named Robertson. Most were put off by him and shivered under his cold stare as he had them run surprise drills in the middle of the night. During the day, Robertson was a softie, but more than four times a week he would wake the troops; suddenly exhibiting a ruthless energy in his training methods. His oddities set aside, Marcus and Brad felt motivated by the man and even came to know him as a close and trusted friend.

Looking back on it, Marcus realized that Robertson's trust in them had run deeper than he'd ever thought possible.

One night, sitting over a round of shots, he'd confessed to the two that he was a vampire—a "blood-drinking monster" as he'd put it. When they refused to believe him he dragged them outside of the bar and drew back his upper lip to expose his fangs.

Brad, he remembered as he crept through the darkened apartment, had thrown up his shots and fainted at the sight.

Later, when both were conscious once again, Robertson had explained that he didn't want to see their natural-born talents go to waste. He told them that, though it would piss a lot of other vampires off, he could change them. With the promise of becoming superhuman soldiers, Marcus, ever the enthusiast, was quick to agree and pushed Brad to do the same. Though it took a few hours and several more shots, the young soldier had finally agreed.

Marcus frowned as his probing eyes fell on a massive entertainment center with a big screen HD TV with surround sound. The sight interrupted his memories and he stared for a short moment, shaking his head.

So much for being a starving artist. He thought, *Can't believe how much the son-of-a-bitch has changed!*

Though he'd tried to keep in touch with Brad as best he could, they eventually realized that the two of them had become too different to maintain the same relationship they'd once enjoyed. He had grown fond of being a soldier and the duties that came with it while Brad, on the other hand, hadn't done well with the military scene. After a few months he'd disappeared; eventually hooking up with an artsy French vamp.

That was the last time Marcus had heard from—or of—his old friend…

Until the reports started piling up.

Brad's head was wanted for crimes against the mythos community. According to the many files, he'd been grave-robbing from burial grounds.

Teeth.

Bones.

Organs.

It seemed that there was nothing that he wasn't willing to make off with.

But that was just one act of treason in a list of many; a list that Marcus hadn't bothered to memorize all of. He did know, however, that Brad's biggest crime had been advertising the existence of their kind to the human world.

That alone called for a death penalty, and Marcus figured

it was the least he could do to ensure that his old friend died a quick and clean death.

He clenched his teeth as a floorboard squeaked and he stopped several yards from the door of his target's bedroom. The light was still on in the hall, and he knew that if he got too close his shadow would show from under the door and give him away. He stood back and listened, preparing for the right moment to strike.

"I love you."

"I love you too."

Erika beamed as she wrapped her arms around Brad, something that never ceased to get her stolen blood pumping. The darkness' hold on the room was relinquished momentarily as her lover lit a match and brought the dancing flame to the two cigarettes already held between his perfect lips. He was motionless—a still-life statue of the perfect man illuminated by a single flame as it flickered and threatened to die and steal the image away.

The cigarettes took the flame and Brad shook the burning match to death, leaving only the twin embers hanging from his lips as evidence. Erika inhaled then, taking in the combined scents of fire and tobacco and, of course, Brad as she accepted one of the offered cigarettes. The first drag after love making—like the first drop of blood after a long fast—always tasted best.

Careful not to touch the tip to Brad's chest, she once again lay her head down against it and thought of her history of past romances—if they could actually be called that. It had never been like this, though. She giggled at her fortune and, though the darkness would've stolen the sight from a human's vision, she saw Brad glance down at her and smile longingly. She closed her eyes and pondered how she had come to be lying on a god's chest; rising and falling with each of his breaths.

She had fucked and been fucked her entire life. Others around her had preached, time and time again, that the term was vulgar and offensive but she knew the truth:

Fucking was fucking, no matter what title it is given.

"A lay by any other name," she would say to them with a laugh.

That all changed after she met Brad.

Their first meeting, strangely enough, had been in a gay bar. She had been going there for some time because the music was kick-ass, the drinks were strong and cheap, and she was never hit on.

Brad had been there with a nervous friend who had just come out after nearly fifty years. All Brad had to do was keep an eye out and make sure that his friend's adventure didn't turn sour. Brad had obliged—eager for a chance to just be out of his apartment.

Erika had known from his wardrobe—a pair of plain jeans and a faded jacket—and the non-neon drink on the counter that he was straight, and she had known from his scent that he was a vampire.

And he was cute to boot!

He'd kept his bright amber eyes locked squarely on his mug in an attempt to not send any unwanted messages, though his untamed mass of light-brown hair seemed to work against him in that effort.

Finding a cute, straight man in a gay bar was a good night; finding a cute, straight *vampire* in a gay bar…

Erika had decided then and there that she wanted him and hurried to the ladies' room to put on some lipstick and push up her tits to be sure to get the right kind of attention. She had inspected herself with all the scrutiny of a woman determined; her raven-black hair hanging in silky waves around her face and hugging her neck. Once she was satisfied, a green eye winked at her in the mirror and she'd approached her target.

"If I told you I wasn't a man would you hold it against me?" she had asked, leaning over the bar so her assets lay visible on the counter.

Brad, noticing the offering, wet his lips before smiling the kind of smile that made for a damp night, "Actually, that's the only way I'd hold it against you."

That night, after several hours of deep conversation, Erika had made love for the first time.

Damn if those preaching bastards hadn't been right about everything!

Brad, it turned out, lived a good life selling photographs and paintings. The market for the dark and bizarre had certainly grown a great deal, and all of Brad's pieces— depicting the nightmarish beauty of their kind—sated the ever-constant hunger for that flavor. Her favorite piece, "A Blood-Bathed Lover", showed Erika lying in a bathtub filled with blood and had been tweaked so that all but the blood was black and white. She liked to look at the image of herself bathed in crimson, skin whiter than a china doll's, and found the overall effect both stunning and tasteful. Despite numerous offers from eager buyers, however, Brad had refused to sell it.

Finishing his cigarette, Brad crushed the filter in a ceramic ashtray he'd sculpted into the shape of a screaming, fanged mouth. She watched his movements with silent awe before handing him her own diminished cig to see the same fate.

With the glowing embers gone, the only light came from the golden frame of the hall light shining through the edges of the closed door and the digital clock across the room that told her that it was almost quarter-till-three in the morning. With a soft sigh, Erika shut her eyes and focused on the sound of Brad's heartbeat.

Brad's voice.

Confirmation of target.

The woman, whoever she was, was an innocent, and Marcus wasn't so bloodthirsty that he'd exterminate her for fucking a traitor.

No one night stand was worth the death penalty.

With the gun gripped in his right hand, he checked his watch:

Oh-three and forty-three hours.

No better time, I suppose.

He took a deep breath and jumped into overdrive. As the world slowed down around him, he cleared the rest of the hall in an instant and pulled back his leg, kicking the door.

As the impact cratered the wood, sending cracks weaving across its surface and tearing it off the hinges, the door flew outward in a blur then slowed to a crawl in midair. The two vampires, lying in the bed in front of him, had barely begun to turn their startled gazes towards him, their movements slowed down in contrast to his superhuman speed.

Marcus' eyes took in the whole scene in an instant: Brad sitting up slightly with the woman's head resting on his chest. He frowned. He needed Brad's whole head to bring back as evidence of the kill and a clean shot to his heart was impossible without putting a bullet through the girl's skull. Seeing no other options, he lined up his shot before dropping out of overdrive and pulling the trigger four times.

Erika's eyes flew open at the sound of the chaos that had erupted in the room. The door lay in splinters on the floor as a strange vampire appeared in the doorway, eclipsed the light from the hall like a demonic vision, a smoking gun gripped in his hand.

"M-Marcus?" Brad's voice was a struggled gurgle and Erika turned to face him and gasped. There was a sickening sound of tortured and labored breath as Brad tried to inhale despite multiple bullet holes on the right side of his chest. Wheezing, he stared, wide-eyed, at his attacker as he holstered his gun and approached.

Hearing his name hurt like hell and Marcus had to tighten his jaw to keep his composure. He put his gun away and hurried towards the bed as he grabbed the knife's handle. When he was close enough, he gripped Brad by the hair and pulled it tight enough to expose his neck for a clean cut.

The knife sported a long, curved blade that he expertly stabbed into his target's throat. He swung his arm wide, getting from just below Brad's chin to the back of his neck.

The ensuing blood spray caught him across the chest and was accompanied by a wet sound as the head, with a sharp tug, popped free.

The girl whimpered as Brad's body collapsed into the blood-soaked sheets and Marcus looked at her. The shock in her eyes was visible, and he wondered, for a moment, if she could see the pain in his own. He thought, briefly, that their relationship might have been more than a fleeting one, but didn't entertain the thought long. It only made the pain sting that much more.

With no soothing or reassuring words to offer the girl, he turned away and walked out the door with Brad's head.

Erika looked at Brad's body.

Brad's perfect body.

She sat over him and cried, thinking of the eternity they'd spoken of having together and weighed it against the mere decade they'd been given. Though his killer was long gone, she still held the bloody comforter over her naked body. Finally, she lifted Brad's lifeless hand that only several hours before had caressed her with warmth and love and pressed her lips to it.

"Immortal love for eternal spirits," she choked out.

With nothing left to do, she got dressed and took "A Blood-Bathed Lover" from above the bed and bit her lip as the image filled her vision.

She no longer felt beautiful. She no longer felt anything but a driving and ever-growing hate.

For a moment she thought of killing herself; of finally seeing the sunrise and watching it travel over the sky while it took her piece-by-piece. While she welcomed the idea of an entire day of scalding torture over the seconds of hell she'd been given, she couldn't bring herself to join Brad just yet. Her life was now a weapon, and she had revenge to plan.

Marcus took the first shot of many, laying his hand down on the now-filled bowling bag sitting on the counter beside him. He knew that he'd have to call for a cleanup crew to take care of the body, but for the time being he wanted one last drink with his friend.

CHAPTER FOURTEEN
THE WISDOM OF DEPOK

XANDER'S EYES SHOT OPEN AND HE
bolted to an upright position. "Who's there?" he demanded,
turning to face a darkened corner of the room.

Xander... there's nobody—

"No, Trep! There's somebody in here!"

"Quite right," a voice with a faint accent called out from
the corner. As he watched, a pair of gold eyes emerged,
shimmering as an outline formed around them, followed
shortly after by a pale, middle-aged face. "I'm impressed. Not

everyone can sense an auric that easily," the stranger's lips curled, "Especially when that auric is me."

Xander frowned, "And who the hell are you?"

The stranger ignored his question and moved—his steps almost fluid—towards the door. "Come," he called over his shoulder.

Xander had *always* hated being told what to do, as well as ignored and startled; this stranger had done all three in less than a minute, and he didn't even know who he was!

He knew that he should be feeling the same hot rage he had known his entire life, but, for some reason, he didn't. It was as if someone had flipped a switch in his head. With his curiosity peaked, he got out of bed and followed.

"I was hoping to have a chance to talk to you when you first arrived. Unfortunately, I had some matters to attend to and was delayed. By the time I was free to meet with you I was informed that you'd already gone to asleep," he chuckled as he glanced over his shoulder at Xander. "I didn't mean to wake you, but I honestly couldn't resist a visit." There was more than a touch of pride in his voice as he continued, "Your sensing me at such an early stage in your maturation is an astounding display, really." He looked back down the hall, and a grayish-white ponytail fell over his shoulder and swung across his shoulder.

"You have any idea how creepy all of that sounds?" Xander glared after the old man.

Xander! Don't! Trepis' voice was more desperate than usual.

The stranger paused for a moment, "Creepy, eh?" He gave a slow nod, "I suppose I can see how it could appear that way. As it is, however, you were asleep for nearly seventeen hours! I figured you had to wake up some—"

Xander stopped abruptly, "Seventeen hours?"

The stranger nodded, not slowing his pace and forcing Xander to continue, "Quite a long nap, eh Stryker?" He laughed and began to descend a stairway decorated with fine art.

"You never told me who you are."

"I'm aware."

Xander looked down, wondering what was going on. In the course of less than a week his entire life had been twisted, torn, dirtied, burned and collapsed. The only other time he'd felt this lost was…

He shook his head and continued to follow the stranger, who was quick and constant in his stride. He paused to look at a painting of two naked men surrounded by wolves in a dense forest setting. The title, inscribed on the bottom of the piece, read "Midnight Hunt: Venir and Ujop's Odyssey". Looking back towards the stranger, Xander found that he was no longer in sight and hurried down the stairs, eager to be back in the presence of the eerie man and no longer alone in the dimly lit stairwell with its creepy décor.

Is that panic that I'm sensing from the son of the great Joseph Stryker? The stranger's voice echoed in his head, startling him.

Something clicked in his head and Xander suddenly felt the rage rising up. His muscles tightened and he heaved in a breath of air to try and cool the fire that was traveling through his body, "SHOW YOURSELF, OLD MAN. I'M GETTING TIRED OF THESE GAMES!"

Suddenly the darkness was gone, and the man was standing there in front of him as if he'd been there all along.

"I like games, Stryker. After all my years, I find it's one of the few things that never grow tiring," he snapped his fingers then and Xander's rage shut off again. The stranger, looking proud of himself, turned and continued downward, "And you'd better watch that temper, son."

"I'm not your…" Xander stopped himself. For some odd reason, the burning resentment that he'd always felt towards being called "son" was gone. Normally, whenever he heard it he saw Kyle in his head repeating the same line to him, but this time he actually felt eased by it.

The stranger nodded. "You're right, you *aren't* my son, but I'd like to be able to think of you as my nephew," he smiled.

Xander couldn't help but smile in return.

A long silence followed as the two continued their long, spiraled descent. Each step was met with more darkness and mystery and though he knew that fear should not have been far behind Xander felt strangely confident and secure with the man guiding him.

"Where are we going?" he asked, breaking the long silence.

"To the library."

He narrowed his eyes and frowned, "Yes, of course! The library! It's so obvious!"

"Yes, it's really quite beautiful. I go there as often as I can."

Xander sneered after him, "You know what sarcasm is, old man?"

There was no response.

"You still haven't told me who you are."

"Or is it that you still haven't heard it?" the stranger chuckled.

Xander sighed, "Psychic shit set aside, can you tell me your name?"

"I must say I'm disappointed," the old man stopped and

sighed. "My name is Depok."

There was a strange sense of energy in the name. Though Xander tried not to show that he felt some sort of inadequacy at the sensation, as it ran up his spine in cold waves he couldn't hold back a shiver.

At the same time, however, there was something in the name that felt familiar…

Finally the stairs ended, leading into a marble-floored hall that stretched in either direction. In front of them, a large set of wooden doors towered. While Xander had never been one for admiration of any kind, even he had to admit that the intricate details that had been carved into the doors' surfaces were something to behold.

"Nice, eh?" Depok asked.

Xander tore his gaze from the doors and nodded, "Yea, I guess." He felt the stress of the recent events tug at his lungs, "Mind if I have a smoke?"

Depok frowned, "I do, but I also know it won't stop you."

Xander nodded, already reaching into his pocket. He grabbed the pack and dug inside it with his fingertips, finding only one left. Going in for his lighter he stopped and sighed at the realization that he'd left his Zippo back in the room. With the driving urge growing worse he stared at the cigarette still clasped between his lips. Depok sighed and a thin wisp of smoke rose from the tip. Staring in amazement, Xander was suddenly met with a rush of soothing flavor.

Xander nodded his appreciation and took a long drag, "Nice trick."

"Thank you," Depok bowed his head.

"But I've seen it before," Xander smirked.

Depok returned the smirk with one of his own, "I know.

I thought I might bring some familiarity to the situation."

Xander looked away and took the cigarette out of his mouth. Holding it delicately between his thumb and index finger, he scratched an itch on his left arm above a year-old scar.

Depok looked down at it with a frown and turned away, "Did you do anything like that before your mother died?" he asked as the doors groaned and began to open.

Xander looked down at his forearm—ignoring the new magic trick—and traced along the pale length with his pinky, "I…"—he sighed and looked up and away from the scars, "I didn't need to." He shuddered and returned the cigarette to his lips.

Depok nodded with a frown as the doors squealed to a halt. Before heading inside he paused to look over his shoulder, "Kyle?"

Xander looked down and closed his eyes. He took in another relieving inhale on the cigarette and let it out, "Kyle…"

"We'll discuss that later," Depok said.

Xander returned his gaze towards him, getting agitated, "I'd rather not." He took one last drag and threw what was left to the floor and stomped it out.

Depok's voice turned serious: "That doesn't change the fact that it *needs* to be discussed. And I'll thank you not to make a mess on my floor!" At that the ashes and remnants of filter and tobacco swirled in midair and burned away into nothing. When this was finished, the scorch marks that had been left behind on the floor began to recess and were pulled away, leaving it spotless.

Xander had no way to argue after that display; all he could do was scowl and follow Depok into the library, only to stop halfway and gawk. The room—occupied with rows of old, hardwood desks and expensive-looking office chairs— was vast, taking up more space than the town's public library. The shelves, all of which were so packed with books that the wood around them had begun to warp, were easily a hundred feet tall and stretched across the enormous walls and towered in breath-taking rows.

Depok put a hand on Xander's shoulder and directed him towards the largest of the desks; littered with open books and papers. Taking a seat, he motioned to the chair on the other side, which Xander, after a brief pause, sat down in.

Depok pushed some of the clutter out of the way, making a clearing in the center and pausing to look at a page that was open in a large, old book. After smiling at his reading he looked at Xander and tapped his finger on the table.

Xander shifted uncomfortably. His entire life he'd been seen as a freak, and he'd grown quite used to the attention that came with that title. Lately, however, he was getting quite a lot of attention of a foreign nature, and he couldn't help but feel unnerved by it.

Depok stared, his eyes burning into him. Though this bothered him all he could do was try to maintain eye contact and not fold in on himself like his body wanted to.

It's okay. You can trust him. Trepis spoke up.

Xander scowled, "How the hell could you know—"

"He knows because a part of him remembers me," Depok answered.

"Huh?" Xander looked at him, "H-how could he remember you?"

Depok looked down at the desk and tapped his fingers a few more times on its surface, "That's a subject that I don't think you're ready to deal with yet."

"Then what am I ready to deal with?" Xander demanded.

Despite the hostility in Xander's voice Depok smiled, "That's up to you."

Xander growled and looked away and began scanning the room, avoiding direct contact with Depok.

Depok cocked his head, "I fully understand that all of this is quite a lot to take on all at once. But it will—"

"Stop digging in my mind! I don't give two shits if you are the biggest clown in this whole circus, but I will not be treated like one of your old, dusty books!" Xander's muscles were tensed and shook with the familiar rage. Though he was terrified of what Depok could do to him, he couldn't help but finally vent, "If you want to talk to me then you turn off that annoying little habit first!"

Depok stared back at him, looking stunned, though not surprised, and Xander wondered if anybody had ever talked to him like that before. He also wondered, considering how powerful he appeared to be, if he had just vented himself into an early grave.

Depok, after a long moment, grinned and nodded, "Consider it turned off." Xander exhaled, the fear of death lifted, and leaned back in his seat, "Now, most of the basic facts I'll leave to Marcus to supply you with." Depok was quick to change the subject, "He will be your, well—for the sake of simplicity—let's call it a 'mentor'."

"Don't you people—or whatever you are—ever call something what it is?" Xander asked, feeling that things were once again being overcomplicated.

Depok laughed and shrugged, "You'll find that much of what humans remain ignorant of tends to be difficult to label.

Probably one of the reasons most myths and religions are so misdirected."

Xander shook his head, "I used to believe that all religion *was* was a misdirection."

Depok smirked, "Not quite right, though I'm glad to hear that you have your own views on the subject. If nothing else, however, you should remember that one must avoid ignorance in their pursuit for knowledge. Though I suppose we'll talk about that on another occasion. It really is such a complicated subject that—"

"If it's all the same," Xander interrupted, his interest in a meaningful conversation reaching its peak, "I'd like to talk about it now. After all this vampire stuff that's been thrown at me lately, I don't see any reason to hold back on other things that I've thought of as fiction."

Depok chuckled, "Just like your father," he shook his head and motioned to the rest of the room, "He actually helped build this library." His smile widened, "Probably read almost every book on these shelves, too. Anyway… your skepticisms are quickly beginning to prove justified, aren't they?" He stood up from his chair with another chuckle and paced as he spoke. "You've been raised in a society where creatures like us and others are myth," he ran his fingertips across a row of books behind him, "I find it's healthy for a mind to exercise skepticism; the greatest minds often do." He frowned and started to pace again, "But I digress…"

"But now that I find that these"—Xander paused for a moment, trying to remember the term Sophie and Marcus had used—"'mythos', right?" Depok nodded, pleased that he was catching on. "Now that I know they exist, I can't help but wonder what else is real?" Xander looked up nervously, "Is every so-called 'bullshit' myth actually real?"

Depok raised an eyebrow, "Such as?"

Xander shrugged. "Uh… like ghosts and angels and demons. Are those real too?"

Depok smiled and sat back down, "That is an excellent question, and, ironically, an easy one to answer: all three are actually one in the same. The term 'ghost' implies that the remains of the deceased have some consciousness, which is impossible. You see, after death, biological energies—whether you want to call them a 'soul' or an 'aura' or what-have-you—leave the body, but the mind—its awareness and, therefore, its consciousness—is left behind. Without this, there is no real consciousness to drive it, only need." Depok paused and smirked as Xander's eyes started to glaze over, "Anyway, these energies move on to…" he paused again to think, "… well, to another place."

"My mind's starting to go to another place," Xander smirked.

Depok raised an eyebrow, "Would you like to change the subject?"

Xander frowned and shook his head.

Depok nodded and took a deep breath before continuing, "Now, occasionally these energies have been known to come back to our world, and it's when this happens that people have their encounters with ghosts or angels or demons. Though there is no real distinction between them, only the severity of the anomaly and whether the witnesses are affected in a positive or negative way."

Xander nodded slowly when he was sure that Depok had finished.

Depok's smirk returned and Xander narrowed his eyes at him, beginning to wonder if he secretly enjoyed making people's heads spin, "Unfortunately," Depok went on, "the universe doesn't get much more complicated than the laws of nature and energy. You know full well the incongruities between *real* magic and what people like to see in movies and on stage. The truth is humans seem to enjoy confusing themselves by making everything seem too complex."

Xander grinned, "I don't think humans are the only ones who like to make things 'too complex'."

Depok laughed harder at this, "Indeed. But things do get somewhat more complex when you go digging beyond our realm."

Xander bit his lip and leaned forward, "Beyond our *realm*?"

"Mmhm," Depok nodded, "Most of the time, when someone prays or even attempts to call forth a being—angelic *or* demonic—all they're really doing is digging deeper into themselves; giving themselves the courage they need to ask for that raise or to finally talk to somebody they've had their eye on. In other, far rarer situations, they end up inadvertently casting spells."

"Normal people casting spells?" Xander shook his head, "But how can somebody who's never practiced the arts do anything with them—mistake or not?"

Depok gave a casual shrug, "Most of the time they can't, but what you have to realize is that the only difference between those who do practice the arts and those who do it by accident is the knowledge of what they're doing. While the magic cast by normal people is rarely very potent, there *are* times—again, very rare times—that someone might put enough energy into a prayer to see actual results. It's still all very basic, though, nothing as powerful as what stronger users can do.

"So people pray, and usually it does nothing. While they

expect their pleas to reach Heaven or Hell they never realize that those places are in their mind. Though I'll tell you now that this is a *very* complex universe, one thing that I *am* certain of is that there is only *one* 'other side', and it is there that the magical energies—souls or auras or what-have-you—go to become a part of a greater force."

Xander nodded, intrigued, "So what do you call this greater force?"

Depok shook his head, "Nobody's really named it yet because not enough people believe in it to give it a name."

"Then why do you believe in it?"

"Because I've seen it for myself." He paused and shook his head, "Well, you don't exactly 'see' it, but I've at least *experienced* it… anyway! Though its origins are a mystery, what I and a few others who have been lucky enough to find out is that it is one single entity made up of the aforementioned energies. Now, this being—or *beings*, however you want to imagine it—has been known to visit a select few who go about calling to it the right way."

"So," Xander looked at Depok for a moment, "this creature—built up of all these other creatures—just shows up to *anybody* if the right words are uttered?"

"Not exactly," Depok shook his head, "First off, it's not a 'creature', nor is it built of anything that's alive. It's…" He paused for a moment, "It's like a wall of consciousness made of bricks, and these bricks are always being added on— feeding into it. Only instead of bricks, it's built of biological energies."

Xander nodded, though he didn't fully understand.

"Furthermore," Depok's runaway train of an explanation charged on, "it doesn't show up in its entirety. Instead, when an invocation is strong enough to reach it, it sends out smaller portions to answer the call. Usually, they're sent over to collect a particularly 'tasty' looking energy that refuses to cross over, or even to try and kill something that it wants too much to wait for. However, if someone can get through to it and entice it enough to respond, deals can be made, knowledge can be gained, and power can be wrought."

Xander narrowed his eyes, "How *do* you know all of this?"

Depok beamed and Xander realized that this had been the point he'd been leading to all along, "Because I know somebody who succeeded in invoking it and who gained a great deal of power; somebody who learned the magical arts from me and your father. Somebody, I might add, that you know personally."

Xander looked at him with astonishment. He knew who was powerful enough to invoke such a powerful entity; the only person he knew who could dig into the cosmos and entice a being by will-power alone.

"Stan!"

CHAPTER FIFTEEN
REUNION

I ALWAYS KNEW THERE WAS
something *about him*, Trepis said.

"Figures that he's tied into all this," Xander grumbled as he took another drag off of one of his new cigarettes.

On his way back from the library he'd met a sympathetic sang who had given him a nearly full pack. He'd explained that after being turned he had no longer felt the addiction but smoked them anyway out of habit. Xander hadn't cared about the details but was appreciative nonetheless.

Sort of makes sense, though; in a strange, twisted kinda way, I mean, Trepis continued.

Xander snorted, "This entire fucking week has been a series of 'strange twists'!" He sighed before bringing the cigarette to his lips and taking one last drag.

You sound upset about that.

Xander paused. *Was* he upset about it? After all that had happened, did he really feel any regret that he was where he was? He shook his head, afraid to ponder the question any longer, "You know me, Trep; I always have to have something to bitch about." He exhaled the smoke and put out the spent cigarette.

Feeling that, for the moment, he'd satisfied his nicotine craving, he lay back in bed. It was his third day in the Odin Clan's mansion. After the talk with Depok the night before, he had gone back to his room and collapsed back into his bed only to fall asleep all day.

So are we going lie here all day then? Trepis asked, a note of irritation riding on his voice.

Xander sighed, "And where would you have me go?"

Trepis lingered on the question for a moment and there was a tickle over Xander's left ear that he'd come to associate as a shrug from his friend, *I don't know. This is just boring!*

Sighing, Xander hoisted himself up with a groan and sat on the corner of the bed, "Is there something you know that you're not telling me?"

I wish I knew.

Xander growled, "What the hell does that mean?"

There was another tickle.

"Since when are you at a loss for words?"

I can't explain it! There's a familiarity here, but it's hard to remember—like I've seen it in a dream or something. Trepis explained.

Xander shook his head, "Since when do you dream?"

I've been a part of yours since before you were born, smartass.

Xander sighed; Trepis had him there. Looking at the door that led to the hall and into the strangeness of the vampire clan, he smiled.

"Would you like to take control for a while?"

You would do that?

Xander grinned at the astonishment in Trepis' voice. He was usually uncomfortable being a passenger in his own body and Trepis, knowing this, had given up expecting it. He shrugged, "Not like I know where anything is around here. This place is apparently more foreign to me than it is to you. Who knows what we'll find if you're behind the wheel."

No sooner had the words been spoken than his body began to shake. By some bizarre miracle, the body was able to remain upright as it quaked. There was a sharp pull and Xander felt himself separate from the rest of him. A sensation, as if his mind was being crumpled up like a sheet of paper, followed soon after. When at last the mental whirl-pool died down, he was resting in the back of his own mind "seeing" through the eyes of Trepis as he took control.

How's it feel to be back on the outside? Xander called out.

The body's jaw stretched for a moment before Trepis spoke through it, "Feels good." He tested the joints' flexibility, "Forgot how stiff everything felt."

Xander understood. Where he was, there was no feeling of restriction. It felt like he was simply a ball of floating liquid with no confinements whatsoever. He could see why a sudden change from this into a world of solids and gravity would be jarring.

So are we going to lie here all day then? He mocked.

Trepis shook the head slightly and walked towards the door, fumbling briefly with the handle before finally turning it and stepping into the hall.

Xander watched as Trepis explored the mansion, seeming to already know where everything was. Every now and again, there would be a momentary fog of confusion, then Trepis would steer the body back until it was on a recognizable path once again.

Coming across a stairwell with a nearby elevator shaft, Trepis stabbed the thumb into the call button. As the polished doors slid open, Trepis hurried to step over the gap and nearly fell over before righting himself against the far wall of the elevator cab.

God dammit! Xander cried out as he felt the body stumble.

Some vampires walking nearby watched in silent confusion as Stryker's son—the big-deal talk of the whole clan—laughed at himself for such a blunder and carefully pressed his index finger against the button for the first floor. As the doors shut and the elevator lurched downward, Trepis wavered and fell back, catching himself along a chrome rail.

Real slick, Xander laughed, *I wonder what they think of the son of the great Joseph Stryker now.*

"It's not as easy as you've made it look!" Trepis said in his defense, "And besides, you're a lot taller than you were the last time I did this."

Xander would have rolled his eyes if he'd had control of them, *Good thing you didn't take the stairs. You'd have broken my neck!*

The elevator slowed to a stop and the doors slid open. Trepis made a note of being more graceful as he exited and looked around. After some hesitation, he navigated down a long hall and kept walking straight until a single step down turned the floor from luxurious carpeting to lightly stained wood. At the end of the "new" hall was a Japanese-style sliding door made of light wood and paper, which, after a brief pause, Trepis pulled open and stepped through.

The aromatic smell of tea wafted through the opening and swirled out into the hall. As Trepis looked around the room, Xander could see that the floor, walls and even the ceiling were lined with bamboo. Along each wall, evenly spaced and perfectly symmetrical scrolls hung; each baring a Japanese symbol written in red ink, which contrasted sharply against the light yellow hue of the rest of the room.

At last, his exploring eyes came to rest on a little bald oriental boy who sat near the far wall with a cup of tea. Though he didn't look older than twelve or thirteen, he had a posture that seemed far more matured. As Xander watched from the back of his own mind, Trepis began to move towards him.

Though the boy hadn't seemed to notice their entrance, he looked unsurprised when he lifted his head and saw them coming. "Welcome back, Stryker-san," his voice was soft-but-strong.

Xander watched, his confusion growing, as Trepis bowed formally to the little boy and sat down across from him, "Hello, Sensei."

Xander would have frowned had he the face to do so, *Who is this?*

He is called 'Sensei'. Trepis answered back, communicating in private—something that Xander had never figured out how to accomplish.

Yea, I heard that part. But how do you know who he is? Xander asked.

Trepis paused, looking down for a moment. Then he sighed, *I don't know.*

The little boy—Sensei—took a sip of his tea and smiled, "You've taken the boy where he needed to be, now let me speak with him."

Another strong, sudden pull took Xander by surprise then. He felt as if he was being dragged by his chest into a brick wall that gradually began to swallow him piece-by-piece. As he was consumed, his senses came back to him, allowing reality to fall back into place until he was once again in control.

"That must be quite a trip, I imagine," the boy said with a grin.

Xander blinked away the dizziness, "That's one way of putting it." He reached into his pocket and pulled out the pack of cigs and his lighter.

Sensei frowned at the sight, "You will not smoke in here."

Shaking his head, Xander pulled a cigarette out of the pack and put it between his lips, "Kid, if you'd gone through what I've been through you'd be craving one too." He struck the Zippo and moved to put the flame to the tip.

The child's tone grew harsher, "You will *not* smoke in here!"

Xander looked at the boy who, though he was much shorter, suddenly seemed to look down on him.

Do as he says, Trepis warned.

Frowning, Xander flipped the Zippo shut and put the cigarette back in the pack and pocketed it, "Happy?"

The boy nodded once.

"You got a name besides 'Sensei'?" he asked.

"I'm sure I did once, but one loses track of such things."

Xander sneered, "So what you're telling me is you're so ancient that you've forgotten your own name?"

"I have put out of my mind a title that was unnecessary for my journeys, yes," Sensei's calm voice was unwavering.

Xander frowned, not sure he fully understood. Though he'd learned a great deal about vampires from Marcus and Sophie, they hadn't said much about the aging process, just that they aged differently than humans. Could Sensei simply be a vampire child? Or was he a special sort of...

"You question my age," Sensei smiled and took another sip of his tea.

Xander chuckled, "I'm actually questioning my eyes."

"The eyes you look through do tell many lies, but I am what I appear to be," he smiled, "but, at the same time, not."

Xander sighed impatiently and, finally able to do so, rolled his eyes, "I understand that you're older than you look. I'm just wondering how old."

"More than seven centuries," Sensei answered.

Xander nodded, though it only arose more questions, "Fair enough. So why do they call you 'Sensei'?"

He shrugged and took a sip of his tea, "It is just a title."

Xander sighed and motioned towards the teapot, "You mind?"

Sensei smiled, "That is why it is there."

Xander reached for the pot and poured himself some of the steaming green tea into a mug and took a sip, "When I— we—first came in, you said it was good to see me *again*. Have we met before?"

Sensei put down his tea and stood up slowly, "No, Stryker-San, this would be our first encounter."

"I don't understand," Xander said, frowning.

Sensei looked up from his tea, his eyes wide with

surprise, "You mean you do not know? They have not yet told you?" he shook his head, muttering to himself before finally looking back at Xander and smiling, "I was talking to your father."

Xander cocked his head in confusion, "My father?"

Sensei nodded, "Mmhm. It's been quite a while since I had last spoken to him."

Xander clenched his teeth, "My father is dead!"

Sensei ignored both his anger and his words and began humming as he walked towards a sliding door between two wall scrolls, "Did you name the voice in your head 'Trepis' yourself or have you always known him by that name?"

"What does that have to do with my father?" Xander shouted, jumping up to his feet.

Sensei turned and faced Xander, unwavering, "I would suggest you calm yourself, Stryker-San, and listen to what I have to say. Your father—"

The burning rage gripped at Xander and grew in intensity at that, "MY FATHER IS DEAD!" he screamed, pulling back his fist and preparing to...

And then he was on his back.

The image of the bald Asian boy's head came into focus as Xander gasped and heaved on the floor.

Sensei squatted down and looked him squarely in the eyes, "The death of the body is not always the death of the mind."

Xander looked up, finally breathing, though it came in small bursts, "But Depok said..." he stopped, unable to fuel any more words.

"Depok knows many things, but he is sadly out of touch with the spiritual side of the world," Sensei answered.

Xander rolled over onto his stomach and slowly began

to push himself up, pausing to catch his breath, "My father…"

"… 'is dead'," Sensei finished, shaking his head, "His body is long since passed, yes, Stryker-San, but there is more to a person than simply the body. There is the fuel: *Chi*. It is one's essence that drives them, and when that life ends, the essence usually—*usually!*—leaves to become a part of everything. When your father was murdered, he pushed beyond the very limits to find you; and he succeeded. He found you before you'd ever seen the light of this world." Sensei smiled, "And he's been a part of you ever since."

Xander's eyes widened, "Trepis is…"

Sensei nodded, smiling, "He is your father."

A rock formed in Xander's throat and, despite how hard he tried to swallow it away, it began to grow. His eyes shut as he felt tears well inside of them and the corners of his lips drew back against his will. And there, on the floor, in front of a nearly seven-hundred year old prepubescent boy, he began to cry.

Sensei gently touched his shoulder with his right hand and Xander felt a familiar calming sensation. With renewed stability, he rose and looked down, choking on a sob.

Sensei, again, walked towards the door, "Would you like to meet the real Trepis?" he asked.

Xander looked up, "The real…"

Sensei slid open the hidden door.

"HOLY SHIT!" Xander fell backwards in a clumsy heap, trying to distance himself from the massive white tiger that stepped out.

"Be calm!" Sensei called out, but Xander wasn't listening. Sensei spoke again, this time in Xander's mind, *Relax! Trepis will not hurt you.*

"T-Trepis?" Xander stuttered, "How is *that* Trepis?" still trying to keep his distance from the mountain of a cat that stood before him, he began to push himself to his feet.

"He was your father's close friend for a long time. The night your father was killed, Trepis was there, trying his best to defend him." Sensei gently ran his finger along the side of the tiger's left ear, where there appeared to be a piece missing, "After your father passed, Trepis disappeared for a short time." There was a look of pride on his face, "You see, Trepis *always* knew where to find your father," Sensei explained, patting the big cat on the top of its massive head. "We always joked that he was a bit of an auric himself, and I never believed that more than when I found him standing guard over your mother's home while she was still pregnant with you," he laughed. "I can't imagine how she would have reacted if she had found him sitting on the back porch. He probably would've stayed there forever, but I told him that he had to let his friend go."

Xander looked at the tiger, "You told him?"

Sensei smiled, "It's one of the perks of being an auric."

"You can talk to animals?" Xander raised an eyebrow.

"I can express basic thoughts and emotions through the mind with them, yes."

Nodding, Xander looked up at the tiger; at the real Trepis. Slowly, he reached a hand out towards the animal, which stretched its neck slightly to give it a quick sniff and, to Xander's surprise, stepped around him and rubbed its side along his leg and stood beside him.

"Does this mean he's going to follow me around now?" Xander asked.

Sensei nodded, "He will be loyal and loving to you, as he was loyal and loving to your father."

"My father…" Xander chewed his lip and looked down, "Do you think maybe I could…"

Sensei nodded, "Of course. I was going to brew some more tea anyway." He bowed and turned, grabbing the teapot as he did, and stepped out of the room, pulling door shut behind him and leaving Xander alone with the two Trepises:

A purring tiger…

And the lingering remains of his late father.

It was a long, silent while of deep thought before Xander, taking a deep-yet-unsteady breath, finally reached back into his mind to talk to his life-long companion:

"Did you know?" he asked, unable to think of any other way to start the conversation. He couldn't help but think that, even if he'd had all his life to prepare for this moment, he would still not have known what to say.

I… Trepis paused. Then: *No. No I didn't know; not like this, anyway. I just always felt that I needed to be there for you.*

Xander chewed at his lip and began to pick at a strip of leather on his boot, "Do you feel like a father?"

Honestly, I don't. I've only ever felt like a friend to you.

Xander clenched his teeth at that and looked down, "What am I supposed to do now?"

You're supposed to make a choice.

Xander thought to himself for a moment, "I think the only choice now is how deep I'm willing to dig into this world."

You've already made the choice to stay then?

Xander nodded. "I've been crawling towards this world my entire life without even meaning to," he answered, wanting a cigarette more than ever. He sighed, "Yes. I've already made the choice to stay."

If you'd already made up your mind then why did you ask me what you should do?

Xander smiled, "Just making sure you're still with me."

I always will be.

The tiger, which, up till that moment, had been silent—aside for its heavy breathing—yawned loudly then as it lay down. Xander looked down and smiled at the animal and scratched it behind the ear, "Do you remember anything about this guy?"

I don't remember a thing. Trepis sounded upset about that fact.

"He must have meant an awful lot to you for you to remember his name after your death rather than your own."

I suppose he must have.

Several minutes passed in silence. Tiger-Trepis fell asleep and Xander watched the animal's midsection rise and fall with each breath. Finally Xander was able to muster the courage he needed to ask the one question that he'd always told himself he'd ask his father if given the chance:

"Trepis,"—he watched the still-sleeping tiger's ears perk at the sound of his name—"are you... I mean, do you think my father would have been proud of me?"

I believe he would be, Xander. You've grown up strong and intelligent, and I see you heading down a path now that I believe he would have applauded you for.

A single tear rolled down Xander's cheek as he nodded, "Thank you."

CHAPTER SIXTEEN
DOCTOR RANGE

"YOU'RE A DOCTOR?"

"Of sorts."

Xander laughed a little, "You really don't strike me as the doctor type."

"I know. My magazines are new."

Xander didn't get the joke in time to join Range in a roar of laughter. Instead he smiled and followed him into his office.

The night before, Marcus—looking livelier than he had the past few days—had explained that before the ceremony Xander would first have to meet with Doctor Range.

"Oh, and Xander!" Marcus had called as he'd gone to leave. "I got some time off coming my way in a few days and I'm going to be out of town for a week. I should be coming back sometime after the ceremony, but don't be surprised if I miss a day of your new life before we start with your training."

Xander had found the idea of vampires taking vacations a humorous one but had, nonetheless, thanked his mentor and gone to bed. The next morning a handwritten note was delivered to him with information on when and where to meet with the vampire doctor.

Range led him into a room that was brightly lit with a combination of several reading lamps mounted on a dirty desk, a well-dated Lava-Lamp and a series of lights attached to a dust-coated ceiling fan. As he took in the rest of the office, Xander noticed that the interior seemed more suitable for a historian of some kind rather than a physician.

Even if he was only a physician "of sorts".

Questioning the office décor, however, seemed foolish given the appearance of the doctor himself. Where he recalled the stereotypical white coat with salt-and-peppered haired Caucasian man in his late forties that seemed to fit the mold for all who practiced medicine, Xander was now face to face with a tall, lean black vampire with large brown eyes and an eerily captivating smile. A pair of off-green flip-flops and a casual, Hawaiian-style shirt over khaki shorts only distanced him even further from the cliché.

Xander took a seat in an artsy blue chair that Range motioned to and was startled by the amount of give the cushioned seat gave. Range, smiling at Xander's surprise, navigated around the desk to his own seat and plopped down.

"Stryker's kid in *my* office," Range said, shaking his head in disbelief, "Truly an honor, I must say."

"I've been hearing that sort of thing a lot."

Range leaned back in his seat, "I'm not surprised. Your father was a good friend to most in this clan, myself included. You're almost like family to us. Anyway,"—a clap of his hands brought emphasis to the subject change—"let's get to business."

"And business would be…"

"What do you know about vampires already?"

"Uh… life-feeders? I know that they—"

"I see you've been talking to Sophie," Range said with a laugh.

Xander blushed, "Yea. I—"

"Then I'm sure you know a lot about how aurics work and such. What about sangsuigas?"

Xander shrugged, "I know that they drink blood."

Range laughed again, "That's hardly a start." He reached into his desk and stood up, revealing three small, empty cylinders, an elastic strip, and a small white pouch. Maneuvering around the desk, he stepped beside Xander and tore open the pouch and removed something small and shiny, "I know you're going to hate me for this, but it's procedure."

"What is?" Xander asked.

"I have to take some blood," Range answered.

Xander relaxed a little, "That's it?"

Range, looking skeptical, shrugged, "Most aren't as comfortable with the idea."

"People are too afraid to bleed," Xander smirked.

Range laughed, "Too true."

The small and shiny something turned out to be a needle. Range, holding this in one hand, expertly tied the elastic around Xander's left arm with the other and tapped below the inside of his elbow until he'd found a suitable vein; the doctor's lip twitching as he did. Then Xander watched as he slid the tip of the needle under his skin and felt a slight pinch as the vein was pierced. For a moment, Xander felt nothing, as if the momentary pinch from the needle had vanished, but then Range attached one of the three empty cylinders to the opposite end of the needle and the air-tight vacuum began to draw blood. There was a slight tickle and Xander watched the red fluid begin to fill the container. When it was nearly full, Range replaced it with another, and then the last one when that, too, had become filled. When he was done, Range took the three vials of blood and started to label them.

"So what's the blood for?" Xander asked.

Range smirked, "I missed lunch."

Xander's eyes widened.

Range laughed and shook his head as he sat down again, "I'm just messing with you! It's a standard procedure for any who are going to be turned: ID, Social Security, and Mother's milk."

Xander stared at him for a moment, "You don't seriously expect me to understand what that meant, do you?"

"No, but it's fun to watch the human initiates squirm with confusion when I say it," Range said with another laugh, "Whenever the clan takes a human as a member, which *is* rare, they create 'files' of that person before they're changed. One of these"—Range held up a vial—"will be stored and recognized as your human blood before you were changed. Another will confirm that you are who you *were* in the event that such need arises. And the third is going to be your first meal when you've completed the change. Like I said: 'ID, Social Security, and Mother's milk'."

"You think that one up all by yourself?" Xander asked with a grin.

"Actually I have a team of writers," Range let out another laugh before putting the three vials in a small refrigerator behind his desk.

Xander leaned forward when the laughter had calmed down, "You were going to tell me more about sangsuigas."

Range nodded, "Yes, I was! I believe that if you're going to be turned, it's important to know what it is that you're getting yourself into." He grinned at Xander, "In this case, a little more than what we consume to survive."

Xander felt his face redden again and he nodded.

"Blood supplies nourishment for a sangsuiga not simply through the fluid itself, but also through the life-force that it contains," as Range explained this, he turned away and opened a drawer in a cabinet behind him and pulled out a squealing rat by the tail, "As you already know, like any other animal, this creature has blood coursing through its veins. It is real, it is physical, and"—he licked his lips—"it is tangible. However," he shook the rat gently by the tail, eliciting a series of panicked squeaks, "if we were to consult an auric, one who can 'see' the energies that living things give off, they would tell us of what else was coursing through the veins along with the blood." He looked up, "You met Sensei yet?"

Xander nodded.

Range laughed, "Yea, he's a strange one, too, always ranting about the fact that the Japanese word for blood is *chi* and... you speak Japanese?"

Xander shook his head.

Range nodded, "Yea, I tried to learn once, but it was too hard. Anyway, he's always pointing out that the Japanese word for 'blood' and 'energy' are the same."

Xander nodded, "*Chi*, right?"

Range smirked, "So he *did* mention it?"

"He said something about *chi*, I put the rest together," Xander shrugged.

Range nodded and eyed the rat for a moment before putting it back, muttering about manners. When he spun back around he rested his hands on his desk, "Well, as crazy as he seems, he's got a point!" He looked sternly at Xander, "Sangsuigas do not just drink blood, they drink a being's life essence. That, more than anything, is what sustains us.

"Anyway… since you're going to be one of us, I figured you might also want to know about what to be careful of and what to be ready for."

Xander nodded, "Alright."

Range smiled, "Okay. The popular myths have some truth, though most of them are bullshit." He chuckled, "Sunlight has always been one of my favorites. When you are changed, you *will not* melt or explode if exposed. However, your skin will become highly sensitive to heat energy. You see, sangsuigas are so well built for being predators that even our flesh is ready for the hunt; each cell taking in information from the air around it, looking for changes in heat to signify if an area is inhabited by potential prey. Because a sang's skin is so highly prepared for trace amounts of heat radiation, the rays from the sun actually overload the cells and begins to destroy them. The effect is you end up with a very bad sunburn after about an hour, your skin blisters with second degree burns after two or three, and by hours four or five…" he shook his head.

Xander nodded, "So sunlight *does* kill you."

"Oh sweet Jesus, yes! I just said it wouldn't melt or ignite you."

"What about aurics?"

"What about them?"

Xander frowned, "Do aurics react the same way to the sun as sangs?"

Range nodded, "Despite the obvious differences, all vampires have descended from the same primary species. Aurics are, like us, unable to tolerate sunlight for very long."

Range jumped back into the previous topic: "Next myth: garlic. The myth says that vampires are allergic to the stuff, but really I just think they were talking about the vampire's girlfriend."

Xander stared at him.

Range chewed his lip and cleared his throat, "Yea, I know, that one sucked... Anyway, garlic, despite all myths behind it, is an anticoagulant. That means that it helps keep blood flowing smoothly and keeps it from clotting. It is for this reason that it is actually *better* for a sangsuiga to consume garlic in some form. You see, because sangs can't usually feed on a set schedule and many times the blood running in their veins is several days old, it is not uncommon for it to clot, and you can't expect the heart to pump blood when it's all scabbed up." He smiled, "It actually provides extra mileage, so to speak."

Xander cocked his head, curious by these new facts, but nodded nonetheless.

"Once you've been changed, it's important to keep feeding, however. You will still be able to eat and drink normal foods like a regular human, but none of that will give you the energy you need to stay alive. Your body will break it down but your new system will have nothing to do with the components and you'll expel them. A lot of us stop eating regular food altogether after we're changed, others just incorporate blood into their meals—be it blood mixed in with their food or simply as a side."

Range took a deep breath then, "Moving right along: turning into a bat or wolf or whatever: can't happen. Flight: forget about it. Hypnosis: unless you're half auric don't hold your breath. Crosses: only as powerful as the person wielding them, which, most of the time, amounts to jack-and-shit. Silver: well, that myth started from the belief that the substance fights infection. Problem is the vampire gene isn't an infection; it's more of a cure—"

"Are vampires really dead?" Xander blurted, not seeing that particular myth coming into the limelight very quickly.

Range laughed again, "Nothing that feeds is dead, it's actually the other way around: eating is what keeps it from dying. The human body must die to allow the mutation to take place, but when the transformation is complete the system jump starts and new life begins."

Hearing the answer reminded Xander of one of the more pressing questions he'd been contemplating: "And how will I be changed?"

Range nodded, "That is the biggest question. The ceremony will take place in two days at midnight." He grinned.

Xander raised an eyebrow, "Is it always performed on the initiate's birthday?"

Range shook his head, "No, it just happened to work out that way. When that time comes you will stand before Depok as he reads the initiation to you and you will meet the pure-blood who will bite you—"

"Pure blood?" Xander asked.

Range nodded, "Only a born sang has the right glands to produce the mutagen that is responsible for the change."

"Mutagen?"

Another nod, "The fang of a sangsuiga vampire is hollow, like a snake's, and contains a combination of toxins, which puts the victim into a state of paralysis during feeding, a hormone to stimulate a healing process in the victim—"

Xander leaned forward, becoming more and more intrigued, "Healing?"

"Mmhm. Evolution seemed to have given us a nifty little way of hiding our feeding habits. A human who is fed off of will only show the puncture wounds briefly before a hyperactive healing process is activated from the hormones and the bites heal over completely with the remaining life the victim has. Without the puncture wounds at the site of the bite, whoever finds the body would figure they had died of natural causes."

Xander frowned, "But those who are made don't have any of those abilities?"

Range shook his head, "The change doesn't hollow out the teeth or completely form the glands."

"So they can't change a victim, then, can they?"

Range shivered at that, shaking his head, "Oh they can! The mutagen of a made sang doesn't allow for a *complete* transformation. The victims of their bites make haphazard changes and come out of the process as insatiable monsters. These third-generation sangs are commonly referred to as 'freaks'."

Xander did his best to fake a laugh, assuming it was another one of the doctor's jokes.

Range frowned, "I'm serious, Stryker! Those things are not to be taken lightly! They'll feed on you as quick as they'll feed on a human, and that sort of mindless killing results in secrets that have been kept for thousands of years being spilled. Any made sang caught making those things on purpose is hunted down and exterminated—no questions asked. So anytime you feed, be sure to break their necks or take off their heads to make sure they won't be coming back!"

Xander, still feeling foolish for laughing, cocked his head, "A broken neck stops the change?"

Range shrugged, "Can't start a new life without an intact nervous system."

Xander nodded, chewing his lip through the awkward silence that followed for a moment, "Anyway,"—he forced himself to sound upbeat as he changed the subject—"about the ceremony! You were saying I would meet my pure-blood…"

"That's correct," Range nodded, "At that point you will be bitten within the chambers of the 'Changing Hall'."

Xander couldn't help but laugh.

Range rolled his eyes, "Yes, I know. Whoever was making up names that day was having an off moment. Afterwards, you will die—pause for dramatic gasp—and, for three days, your body will undergo a complex metamorphosis."

Xander ran a tongue along his upper jaw. "So I'm going come out of all this with fangs, too?"

Range nodded excitedly, "Absolutely! Part of the change is the losing of your human canines. This will happen soon after you are bitten. From there, a complex, hollow, bone-pocket will form in the gums to sheathe your new fangs." He peeled back his upper lip and rubbed a slightly bulged area in his gums right above his elongated fangs. "This allows them to extend and retract while also providing enough rigidity to keep them from snapping out when you bite something."

Again Xander's tongue probed his upper jaw, caressing both of his canines before he nodded again.

"When the three days are up, you will awaken and feed for the first time"—he motioned towards the refrigerator behind him that contained the vials of blood—"and you will emerge as your new self and be greeted by the clan as one of us."

Xander smiled. The idea that he would finally be accepted was a euphoric and long since abandoned hope that was becoming all so real for him now, "Then what?"

Range shrugged, "Stryker's offspring is already the thing of legends. Once you've been changed and are a part of the Odin Clan..." he let out a long breath, "... well, after that we're treading in new waters."

"How so?" Xander asked with a frown.

"Xander," Range's tone became cold and serious, "there are already plenty out to kill you. Once it becomes known that you've been initiated, there's no telling what will happen."

CHAPTER SEVENTEEN
HAPPY BIRTHDAY, XANDER

XANDER RECALLED THE ANTICIPATION

he used to feel when his birthday approached; how he'd count the days remaining as his mother marked off another spot on the calendar. There was a great deal of magic and excitement in the thought that he would be celebrating his birthday *and* dressing up to go door to door for candy on the same day, and for the longest time he was sure that his was, by far, the best birthday.

Then, when Kyle arrived, Xander found himself marking

the calendar on his own, and the magic seemed to disappear. The years following, he stopped marking the calendar altogether. With Kyle in the family, he became used to riding life's torturous train straight through the last day of October without ever being reminded that it was his to celebrate.

The memory saddened and enraged him as he sat on his bed with a smoking cigarette pinched between his fingers. He'd been thinking about it for some time, and each time it started to hurt too much he'd light up a fresh smoke. Finally, crushing the fifth one that hour in an ashtray, he reached out to pet Tiger-Trepis, who had become a nearly permanent fixture inside his room when he was occupying it.

After moving in with his grandma, his birthday had again become something worth caring about, though he'd never fully gotten back into the habit of anticipation or celebration. This thought, while a forced attempt at making him feel better, only served to remind him of his recent loss and the need for another cigarette ached within him.

He sighed, looking at the clock as he lit up number six and ran his fingers through the length of the tiger's fur. After all those years of simply letting his birthday pass as another meaningless day, it seemed he was feeling all the added anticipation press down on him with every moment he was now forced to wait.

First time I've ever seen you actually eager to live for something in a while. Mind-Trepis said, startling him to the point of almost dropping his cigarette.

He smiled and nodded after he'd regained his composure, "I know. It's been a long time, hasn't it?"

It has. Maybe you should have some breakfast before the big event.

It was strange that the word 'breakfast' was being used at nearly eleven-thirty at night; even more-so that Xander was getting used to the idea. Regardless, he *was* hungry and wondered how long it had been since he had last eaten. Earlier, he'd gotten another two packs of cigarettes—a foreign brand, this time—from another charitable clan member and spent the rest of the time since his meeting with Range sitting in his room contemplating the upcoming event and smoking like a wild fire. He looked down at the tiger with pity, realizing that the animal hadn't eaten in a while either and decided that he owed it to both of them to take a trip to the dining hall.

The rest of the mansion was already awake and the clan's members were bustling about when he stepped out of his room. All of his life Xander had been uncomfortable around large crowds, and though he was in a place he knew he was accepted, it was hard not to feel the familiar shudder of insecurity travel up his spine and spark electrically in the back of his mind.

We don't need an anxiety attack in this place. Trepis scolded.

He sighed and nodded, taking a deep breath to calm himself and heading down the steps—Tiger-Trepis not far behind. It was a funny thing to see a full grown tiger walking about freely in a mansion without its occupants seeming to care. A few of the more familiar clan members even stopped to give the animal a pat on the head as they passed!

Arriving at the dining hall, Xander wasn't surprised to find that it was already crowded with clan members; some eating normally—as Range had described—with tall glasses of blood close at hand while others seemed content without the food. Several, Xander noticed, sat with neither food nor blood and simply conversed with their neighbors. These, he assumed, were auric members.

Heading towards the kitchen, he grabbed a miniature

box of Raisin Bran from the pantry that contained the more recognizable groceries and prepared a bowl before visiting one of the clan's kitchen crew and getting a large cut of steak for the hungry tiger. Afterwards, he found an empty corner table, politely declining the enthusiastic invitations to sit at other, more packed tables, and dropped the hunk of meat in front of his animal companion before starting on the cereal. As he scooped up a spoonful, he couldn't help but realize that it would be the last meal he'd eat as a human being.

Out of the corner of his eye, he saw Sophie enter the room and walk straight to his table with a purposeful stride. He frowned. That sort of walk was never followed by casual banter, and he knew that she intended to discuss something that he would rather not. However, as he watched her approach he felt his troubled mind suddenly calm and smirked at her, shaking his head. Though he still hated the idea of having someone besides his life-long friend poking around in his head, it was hard to feel angry when she was putting forth so much of an effort to keep him calm. Seeing his smile, Sophie's own lips curled upward as she pulled back a chair and sat down.

"Finally using *real* chairs, I see," Xander said as he poked at a sugar-coated raisin.

Sophie shrugged, "Can't show off all the time."

Xander nodded, "I suppose not."

"So... you ready for the ceremony?" she asked.

"Ready as I'll ever be, I suppose."

Nodding, Sophie looked down at the bowl of cereal, her lip twitching slightly at the sight.

Xander frowned at her reaction, "You don't eat?"

Sophie grinned, "I *am* eating."

Xander nodded and chuckled. Of course; the entire

bustling room was practically a buffet for a mind-feeder! His eyes scanned the room before stopping on a clock hanging on the wall.

It was nearly time.

The growing anxiety formed into a lump in his stomach and he pushed the cereal away.

Sophie looked at him, "I don't like to act like a therapist, but it's hard *not* to see your fears and concerns."

Xander frowned, the feeling of invasion suddenly returning, "I'm not—"

Her hand went up to stop him before his pride started an inappropriate monologue, "I hate discomfort, Xander; it tastes foul. I step into this room—hell, this *level*—and I can taste yours like spoiled milk. I can see that you're eager for this to happen, but I want to see you step into your new life with at least some confidence."

Xander's face reddened. Though the words were kind, he didn't like being analyzed—especially when they were accurate. "You play therapist pretty well for someone who doesn't like the game," he grumbled, staring down at his increasingly unappealing meal.

Sophie was scowling before he'd finished his sentence. "I know, and I'm sorry for making you feel"—she clucked her tongue—"weak by doing it. But it's easy to see for those like myself that your entire life has been spent in unease and fear. Whatever it takes, do what you need to enter that ceremony in the right frame of mind."

There was a pinch in the back of Xander's mind that rose into a flame of concern, "Do you know something? What's going to happen?"

Sophie's features gave her away and her sadness leaked through, "Nobody can see the future, sweetie, but it's important to stay strong… no matter what happens."

He wasn't sure if it was the power of her words or the power of her mind, but he suddenly felt empowered and, moreover, motivated. He nodded and got up, tossing the half-finished bowl of cereal into the garbage and turning to leave.

"Hey, Xander!" Sophie called out.

He turned towards her, almost afraid of whatever closing remarks she might have, "Yea?"

Though her face had moments ago been sad and concerned, her fresh smile was warm and sincere, "Happy birthday."

Xander smiled faintly as he turned and headed towards the stairwell to make his way to the ceremony room. Somewhere in the distance, a large grandfather clock struck the hour and the new day—his birthday and last day as a human being—began.

When, at last, Xander had found and entered the ceremony room, he saw that most of the square-footage was occupied with red and black candles that supplied the large area with all of its light. A figure stood before him in a red robe with a hood pulled up over its head and as Xander approached, it turned and faced him, bowing. As Xander drew nearer, the figure pulled the hood back and revealed itself as Depok, who smiled and guided him towards an altar that rested in the center. As they arrived at the massive stone surface, Depok stepped away and positioned himself over a nearby podium that held a large, leather-bound book.

While Xander looked around the room, Depok lifted a

small bell from the podium's surface and shook it three times. Just then, two figures in matching black cloaks emerged, one carrying a red bundle tied with a length of thick, black rope. Depok nodded once to them and the empty-handed figure began to help Xander out of his clothes. He was compelled at first to struggle against the invading hands, but held back the urge and allowed the mysterious vampire to continue with the task. The second figure, standing a short distance away, began to untie the bundle it carried, revealing a long red robe— similar to Depok's own—and helping the now-undressed Xander into it. Before leaving, the figures tied the black rope that had held the bundle together around Xander's waist and stepped back, bowing in unison and leaving with the same speed and silence as when they'd entered. When they were alone again, Depok motioned to the altar and Xander nodded and sat. Even through the fabric of the robe, the stone slab sent a chill up Xander's spine.

"Are you ready?" Depok asked him.

Somehow feeling it would interfere with the significance of the event, Xander opted to nod rather than speak.

Depok looked down at the book and began reading in a low tone. The language was not one that Xander recognized, and instead of trying to decipher the words he let the melody the words created lull him into a trance; feeling his mind calm until no thought existed.

At the other side of the room, the sound of a door squealing open and shutting soon after snapped Xander from his trance and he shifted his eyes to see who had entered.

"Xander Stryker," a thick, rich voice filled the hall. The speaker stopped at the altar, standing in a blue robe. His thick brown hair was slicked back and tied in a small ponytail in the back and his solid blue eyes—matching the shade of his robe—shifted from one to the other.

Xander blinked several times, clearing the grogginess from his mind, and began to sit up, nodding his respects at the newcomer.

"My name is Ronen," the newcomer said, bowing his head as he took a step towards him, "and it will be my pleasure to guide you through the change." He stopped for a moment, smiling warmly, before lifting Xander's left arm. Pausing, he locked his gaze on Xander's own, "You are sure that this is what you want?"

Xander nodded.

There was a sharp sting then as Ronen bit into his wrist and Xander flinched before a warm rush made the pain subside and the room began to spin. Thrown off kilter, Xander felt himself start to fall as the poison seeped into the veins of his arm and, after a long, lingering moment, crawled past his shoulder and into his chest—into his heart—where it suddenly exploded into a full-body inferno.

He was burning to death!

When he was certain that he was on fire there was a sudden cool rush; a wave of ice that ran through the length of his body and seeped into his core until he found his eyelids and pried them open. The image of Depok and Ronen came into focus and he was vaguely aware of Depok's left hand on his shoulder as the pure-blood pulled his fangs away from his wrist.

Mind still reeling, Xander noticed, not without a bit of shock, that he was still lying on top of the altar. A moment later, his eyes rolled back in his skull and the lights from the candles melted into a solid glow that swallowed him and faded to black. As Death swooped down and enveloped him, he heard Depok's voice in the distance:

"Welcome home, Xander."

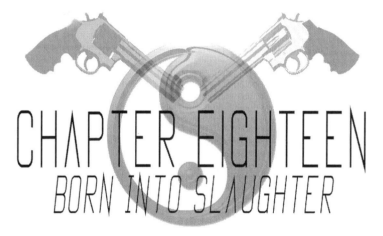

CHAPTER EIGHTEEN
BORN INTO SLAUGHTER

THE DARKNESS SEEMED TO STRETCH

on forever. It encased and bled into Xander, making him
blind even to his own thoughts. As he tried to focus, he
became aware of a distant sound, followed by another, and
then again by another—each time becoming louder. Ahead of
him the darkness rippled as a figure emerged, and the red
fabric of Depok's robe became visible as he stepped into an
invisible source of clarity. The darkness unveiled Depok's
smiling face and Xander couldn't help but return the smile as

he hurried towards him; the clan leader's arms opened to him.

He continued forth, beginning to feel at last like he belonged, when suddenly a portion of Depok's face peeled off and fluttered to his feet. Watching in shock, more bits of the still smiling—still waiting—vampire fell away, until Xander finally recognized the strips as paper; pages from the library's dusty books! He looked up, horrified, at Depok moments before he suddenly burst in flames.

Startled, Xander fell back and watched as the clan leader's face—still wearing the same caring, welcoming smile—melted away and exposed a grinning, chattering skull. His arms were still held open in an invitation as more and more sheets of burning paper fell. Xander rose to his feet to flee, and, before turning away, caught sight of the vampire elder's dwindling arms as they snapped and fell from his body.

As he hurried away from the all-consuming fire, Xander could suddenly hear the blood chilling screams.

The darkness went on forever! No matter how far he ran there was nothing but infinite blackness surrounding him.

And the screams…

No matter how far he went—how hard he tried to escape them—they followed!

Finally the shrieks and wails caught up to him, knocking him off his feet and drowning him in a thick, red noise that turned sticky and warm and seeped into his core.

He tossed and shook, trying to free his body from the weight of the tragedy that was creeping into him. When he saw there was no salvation from the cries he looked up at the source—into the void above him—and saw them.

His clan!

His grandmother!

And there, in the abyss, Xander saw his mother.

All of them were crying; weeping bloody tears that fell onto his face and dripped into his open, horrified mouth.

And then he felt the hunger.

It was agonizing! He'd never felt so empty; so devoid of nutrition. Desperately he began thrashing within the suffocating darkness. There had to be a way out, had to be some way to find something—some*one*—to eat.

Xander? The voice in his head seemed distantly familiar.

Something skittered and made a noise by his ear.

Noise.

Meaningless noise.

He ignored it.

He had to eat! Had to find a way out! A way to escape the haunting nightmare! Damn it, he could still hear their screams!

His searching hands found something in the darkness; something long and smooth. He was about to throw it until he smelled the sweetness. Such sweetness. He pulled the prize to his nostrils and inhaled. The sweetness was contained within it; inside the cylinder. Blindly examining with his fingers he found a lid on one side and eagerly twisted it off and poured the contents into his mouth.

The taste of blood was not foreign to him.

Whether it was an innocent drop on his tongue after prying a loose tooth free or something more violent, he was more than used to the sickening, metallic taste. But this time was different. This time it was more than just the taste. His entire body seized as he emptied the contents of the cylinder into his mouth. Invigorated, he swallowed the small mouthful, the blood traveling down his throat and pushing a groan from his esophagus. As the rich substance sank into him, a jolt of life flooded over him.

Xander!

He shook his head as his mind returned to him.

"Trepis?"

Freak out much there, spaz?

He frowned, remembering the past few minutes in horrified detail, "Shut up."

The familiar sensation of Trepis' laughter tingled in his head.

Finally sated from the intense hunger, Xander was able to put his mind towards more important things, like finding a way out of the darkness. Wherever he was, he realized, he was lying on his back and, for a moment, feared that someone might have buried him while he was undergoing the change. This fear was put to rest, however, as his previously-blurred vision focused enough to allow him to make out an outline of light at his feet. Already growing impatient and more than just a little claustrophobic, he drove his feet against the door again and again until it flew open.

A bright flood of light overtook him and he was momentarily blinded. As he pulled himself out into the open and stood on his still-shaky legs, he found himself inside a large, circular room with metallic drawers built into the walls and soon realized it was from one of these that he had just excavated himself. He turned back to glance inside the drawer that had served as his tomb and saw the empty blood cylinder that had, moments ago, provided him with his first meal.

He smirked, "Mother's milk."

For a moment he stared into the depths of the drawer before starting to turn away. As his body shifted, however, some light was allowed through and illuminated something else that rested inside. Looking closer, Xander saw that there were actually *two* of the small, white somethings and he carefully reached in and retrieved them. He inspected them, rolling the two small objects in his hand, noting one side that was somewhat jagged while the other caved in and was pinkish on the inside. After several moments he sneered, realizing that he was holding his human canines in his palm.

Instinctively, he began to probe his mouth for any gaps but found none. Instead, along each side of his upper jaw, his tongue rolled over a spot on each side where his gums felt thicker; more muscular. After dwelling on this a bit longer, he clenched his palm with the teeth inside.

He frowned as he looked around the empty room again, "I would have thought there would have been more people down here."

You mean others who were changed? Trepis asked.

He shook his head, "No. I just thought that at least Depok would be down here to..." he looked down sadly.

Maybe there's a surprise party waiting for you. Trepis offered.

Xander frowned, doubtful, "Yea. Maybe."

As he made his way towards the only door in the room, he saw that the clothes that he had been stripped from before the ceremony had been washed and folded and were waiting for him. He smiled slightly at the favor and changed—glad to finally be in something other than a ratty, old robe that reeked of dust and death—into the far-more-comfortable black jeans and red tee before opening the heavy door.

The sweet smell hit him instantly!

It was faint, but Xander already recognized it.

"Blood!"

Told you! They're waiting for you!

"I'm not so sure..."

Stepping out into the hall, he was greeted by only a

staircase. As he began his ascent, he became aware of not only the scent of blood, but that of smoke as well!

Xander!

"I know!" his slow steps became a full sprint, "Something's wrong!"

Taking the steps four at a time, he finally reached a brick wall; a damned dead-end! A moment was spent looking for a latch or a knob that would let him through before he started clawing and pounding at the stone. When this didn't work, he drove his fist into the center as hard as he could. Something sounded then and the barrier slid open, exposing a familiar winding staircase ahead of him and the entrance to the library to his right.

Xander's nostrils burned as he approached; the pungent stink of gasoline and the choking smell of smoke almost too much to bear. Slowly, with each agonizing step forward, his worst fears were confirmed: Depok's library was on fire!

The doors, ripped from their hinges, lay in the center of the giant room along with the antique wooden desks and chairs, all of which fueled a massive inferno within the stripped room. Bits of torn paper and ash rocketed upward on billows of thick, black smoke only to come back down again like a twisted snowstorm. The books, all torn and shredded, were left in tatters on the floor and the artwork that had lined the halls now lay in broken, twisted heaps amongst the rest of the burning treasures.

All of this, horrible as it was, was quickly forgotten as Xander's eyes fell upon the centerpiece.

There, hanging over the hellish bonfire, Depok's body swung; his limp, dead feet scraping the burning pile with each pass. The flames had caught and begun their climb up his robe. As Xander watched in horror, the rope that suspended the clan's leader snapped and dropped him onto the inferno; the flaming pyramid toppling under the weight and forcing it to spread across the floor.

Xander, speechless, couldn't grasp what he was seeing. He had only just woken up into this new world; *his* new world! How could he come into being like this?

A gust of warm air passed, coming down from the upper levels and carrying with it the scent of blood. Lingering on the all-consuming fire a moment longer, Xander shuddered at what could possibly be awaiting him.

He turned, the floor squeaking under his heels as he rushed for the staircase. As he took to the steps again, Xander was startled by a fleshy mass that lay in the center of the steps. The face that stared up at him was frozen in fury and smashed in, rendering it unrecognizable. Stepping over the body, he paused a moment to look down at what should have been a comrade before beginning to race up the stairs again; tears growing in his eyes.

"The dream…" Xander panted as he dashed—moving faster than he'd ever thought possible—past several more discarded clan members' bodies.

Do you think… Trepis began.

Xander came around the last bend to the first level and stopped in his tracks, "Oh my…"

The dark-skinned body of another clan member lay in front of him. Whoever was responsible had stripped the poor vampire naked and carved "Stryker" all over her torso. Looking past this, Xander could see more like her: stripped and tagged with his name. All of them had been strewn about, their bodies littering the ground.

As he moved forward through the aftermath of the massacre, the fiery rage grew inside him, spreading from his chest to his arms and legs, making his muscles twitch and jolt with a strange new energy and he felt a pain in his gums. He frowned at the new sensation—not unlike a throbbing toothache—and ran his tongue across the long, pointed fangs that now protruded from his upper jaw.

The rage that he had lived with his entire life seemed to fuel his new vampire body and, pushed onward by his rage and a new sense of power, he stepped further into the blood-splattered walls of the destroyed Odin mansion.

Bodies hung from rafters and lay in decrepit heaps. Forms that had once been natural were now contorted into grotesque abstractions. Most of the corpses had been treated the same way: stripped and tagged with Xander's name, further reminding him of the reason why they had died.

Walking amongst the gore, an even more horrifying thought came to him, "Trepis!"

Yea? The voice of his old friend was heavy with sadness.

"No, I mean… can you still sense the tiger?"

There was a long, excruciating silence as Mind-Trepis probed the building for the animal's unique energy pattern.

Sensei's dojo. He finally responded.

Xander wasted no time in getting there, encountering more and more of the carnage until he finally slid open the tattered bamboo doors. At the other side of the room, he could see the body of the young boy that housed an ancient mind.

"Oh no…"

He stumbled across the room, which had been decorated with Sensei's insides as well as the battered bodies of those who Xander assumed had been the first to try and take him down until he was standing in front of the body. Sensei's bald head had been cracked open and held in place from the final blow: one of his own short swords that had been driven through his skull and pinning it to the wall. The dead vampire's neck stretched from the weight pulling downward on it and Xander shuddered as he, after several hard tugs, was able to yank the weapon free. With this done, he carefully lay the body down on the floor.

"Is he in here or not?" Xander demanded, his breathing coming out in jagged bursts.

The back of his mind crackled before Trepis finally answered: *Behind the wall.*

Xander recalled the secret door and rushed over to it, throwing it open. Though the room on the other side was pitch-black, his new eyes were quick to adjust and he could see inside almost as well as he could see inside the brightly lit dojo. Stepping inside, he began to look around, noticing various stuffed animals that showed evidence of tiger-play. On the far wall was a picture of a man with clean, well combed black hair and piercing hazel-green eyes, and though Xander had never seen the man before, he knew exactly who he was looking at and fought the tears that pushed at the corners of his eyes. He lingered on the photo, feeling his throat tighten as he fought the flood of emotions, and was startled by a soft growl that issued from his left. He turned, grateful for the distraction.

"Trepis!"

The tiger stood and hurried to his side, panting nervously. He began rubbing his head against Xander's hip, happy to have somebody alive and on his side. This time Xander could not hold the tears back and crouched down, dropping the short sword to the floor and beginning to pet the still-terrified animal.

"It's alright, buddy," Xander whispered, "It's al—"

The sound of approaching voices echoed down the hall and Xander turned towards the noises, smelling a combination of gunpowder and blood. Instinctively, he peeled back his upper lip, allowing his fangs to show in their entirety, and let out an angry hiss as he scooped up the short sword.

"Stay," he whispered to Tiger-Trepis, hoping the animal would understand.

Peeking through the open doorway, he saw that the speakers had not yet reached the dojo's door. The rage within him flared and he tightened his grip on the sword's handle. Despite their distance, his sensitive ears could make out their words as they approached.

"It came this way!"

"What? Another fuckin' vampire? I thought they were all dead! God dammit, he said they were all dead!"

"I don't know what it was! It looked like a shadow or something… only it was red."

"Well why the fuck didn't you shoot it? What do you think this guy is paying us for?"

"Are you fucking kidding me, man? I'm scared shitless enough just walking around all these *dead* blood-suckers. Last thing I want to do is go poking my neck around a **live** one!"

The shadowed outlines of the speakers came into view on the other side of the dojo's paper walls and Xander felt another surge of rage.

It was silent as the two humans approached the entrance, each one shivering as they pointed their guns back-and-forth. Tiger-Trepis snorted nervously at the sound of their approach and moved back to his hiding place, stepping on a loose piece of bamboo in the process.

The two men stiffened at the sound, pointing their guns

in unison towards the dojo.

"You know, I think this area's clear, actually," the first said, his head quickly darting from one direction to the next as he backed away. He laughed—a nervous, forced sound, "Your red shadow was probably just a fox that came in to scavenge on these dead fuckers."

His partner followed suit, backing away, "Yea, you're probably ri—"

Xander startled even himself at how fast he struck. One moment he'd been crouching and the next he was a blur. He smirked. He *was* a shadow.

A crimson shadow!

His hands clamped on the shoulders of the first, a fat man with a receding hairline. Yelping in surprise, he stumbled back into Xander, who swung the short sword in an arc, imbedding it in his shoulder and groaning at the smell as fresh blood was spilled. Ignoring his urge to feed, he roared out, hurling the screaming man down the hall and leaping onto the other. His new victim, far younger and thinner than the first, was too light and was thrown off his feet from the blow and hit on the ground hard, shattering his nose upon impact and sending a river of blood into the floorboards.

More sweetness filled the air!

Xander grabbed the back of the thin man's blonde hair and smashed his already battered face into the stained floor again and again. Blood splattered against the walls and speckled his face as he continued until the man's features had become a broken, flattened mess. The two's combined guttural screams of pain echoed through the hall and Xander snarled.

The smell!

It was everywhere!

That vial had carried him only so far and already he felt like he needed more. Losing himself to his new instincts, he twisted the mutilated man's head to the side and lowered himself to his neck, piercing through the flesh and letting the blood fill his mouth. His victim cried out and began flailing; bucking and writhing and trying to free himself from Xander's hold.

Getting his fill, Xander rose and wiped the blood from his chin and licked his hand clean as the human gurgled and thrashed about in his dying moments. Filled with rage and disgust, Xander balled his fist and drove it through the back of the man's head, decorating his hand with bits of skull and brain. The fat man at the end of the hall, still trying to pull the sword from his shoulder, whimpered and worked his good arm to drag himself away from the horror in front of him. Xander smirked, lost in the lust of his first feed, and shook the gore from his hand as he rose to his feet.

As he fed on the second man, a rhythmic pounding grew louder and louder until he could no longer ignore it and finally looked up. Glaring at the newcomer, Xander showed his fangs and hissed. The figure, concealed by a shimmering wall, stood a short distance away as the sound of static grew louder and louder until it filled the hall. Squinting against the barrier, Xander barely had time to register the rippling wave of energy as it shot at him and hit him like a runaway train.

CHAPTER NINETEEN
TOYING WITH MAGIC

ESTELLA SIGHED IN UNISON WITH THE
jingling brass bells as she pulled the library doors closed
behind her. A large, pale moon hung behind several bare
trees, providing just enough light for her to find the keyhole
so she could lock up.

Miss Leon, the head librarian, had offered to put the last
of the returns away so that she could go home early; the
middle-aged woman's concern for her wellbeing proving to
Estella that her attempts at hiding the stress that had been

plaguing her had not been successful. Refusing her boss' offer, she'd lied and told her that the family dog had not been feeling well and, at the same time, sent out a wave of positive energy as well as forcing a smile to her face. Estella found it funny that casting the spell was easier than making the phony gesture, but that was just the story of her life. Though she had been positive that it would fool no one, the magic had obviously secured any lingering doubts that Miss Leon might have had and she smiled warmly in return and wished the family pet a speedy recovery.

The reality was that Zip, the Manning family's black lab, had passed that previous year and they had yet to find a new pet. She had felt guilty for lying and it still lingered as she headed towards the woods at the other side of the parking lot. Though it was a shorter walk to just keep to the road until her street came up, she often preferred the quarter-of-a-mile horseshoe path through the woods—especially when she wanted time alone to think.

And she had a lot of thinking to do.

She didn't allow Xander's name to surface in her mind until she was deep within the depths of the forest; surrounded on all sides by the fall-stricken trees with their discarded leaves crunching under each step. Off in the distance, a string of orange and black lights were visible from a nearby home that had yet to take down their Halloween decorations. She frowned at the sight and allowed her tiny body to fall against the trunk of a nearby oak. Thinking of Halloween only served as another reminder of Xander. He was another year older…

Or so she hoped.

News of Xander's house burning down had spread through the school like the fire itself, and though Estella had been saddened by the news it still came as a relief that he had not been found amongst the remains. Others at school had joked about what a shame it was that the fire hadn't taken him, and though Estella had never before felt more compelled to cast a curse on her peers, she could not muster the will to bring harm to another living being.

An even more unnerving thought was that Xander had finally succeeded in killing himself and she shivered at the thought as she pulled herself away from the tree. As another shiver wracked her body she recalled the sensation of the gun pressed against his temple the last time she had cast Other's Sight. She'd sworn at herself for ever having been curious enough to use such a powerful and invasive spell on her old friend during what she had discovered was his nightly ritual.

Was she *really* ready to attempt that spell on him again?

Nostalgia swept over her and she couldn't help but think back to their earlier years—their happier years—when they had actually shared their secrets with one another. Those years, like most Estella realized, had been rough on Xander, and while it was clear that he suffered what surprised her most was how much he had held back; how much he *had* kept secret. This was never more evident than the day that he had accidently introduced her to the world of magic.

It had started like any other day, but at lunchtime Xander hadn't been as quick in taking his normal seat across from her. For ten minutes, her tiny head had swiveled from side to side, scanning the densely populated area for her friend. It was only when her eyes felt so worn out from searching that they might roll from their sockets that Xander had finally entered the cafeteria.

She had known instantly that something was wrong.

His solemn face hung so low that his features were

hardly visible under the curtain of black hair. His steps were slow and uneven, and Estella had winced at the realization that her friend was limping. As he made his way to their table, he had been bumped and shoved by the other students, who had shown no mercy despite his obvious pain. Nearby, a teacher who Estella remembered had once called her friend a "freaky little bastard" when he thought nobody was listening had looked away, pretending not to notice the bullies' antics.

When he'd finally reached their table, Xander had barely looked up and instead simply nodded a greeting.

Estella, almost driven to tears from her friend's obvious distress, had been frantic, "Are you alright?" she'd demanded. She had noticed then that his hands were shaking. Frowning at this, she'd looked at his face, trying to see through his bangs to his eyes, "What happened?"

Xander's face was twisted in a scowl as he turned his head towards some kids who were still laughing at him.

"Xander..." Estella's voice, she remembered, had been a meek whisper and she'd tried to reach out to him.

Hearing his name, he turned and parted his lips. "I told the principal to 'fuck off' and he took me to the office," he'd finally told her.

Though he'd seemed to swear a lot since his mom had gotten remarried, it still made Estella feel rotten whenever she heard it and her cheeks had gone hot at the F-word.

Xander, noticing her reaction and recalling her aversion to cursing, frowned and looked away. "Sorry," he'd grumbled.

Estella had smiled and nodded her appreciation. She'd known that Xander didn't like to say he was sorry, but for her his apologies were always genuine.

A brief silence took place before she had decided to try and find out again what was wrong, "So what happened?"

she'd asked.

Xander's frown had returned and he pulled his still shaking hand out from under hers. "I don't want to talk about it," he'd answered.

Estella wasn't sure how to respond, and after a moment of thought a slight grin pulled at the corners of her lips, "Does Trepis want to talk about it?"

When they had first met Xander had told her about his friend, Trepis. Since then, the two of them—or, rather, the three of them—had spent most of their time alone, talking amongst themselves. It had seemed that if ever there was something that Xander didn't want to talk about, Trepis would be more than happy to offer the details.

A blank look had crossed Xander's face as it often did when Trepis was about to talk for Xander. Before he'd said anything, however, Xander had shaken his head angrily and looked away, "*I* don't want to talk about it!" he'd repeated.

Estella, for the first time, felt nervous for Xander and her throat tightened as her jaw trembled, "B-but…"

Xander was on his feet before she could get the whole word out. "I need to go," he'd said in a low tone.

He had been halfway towards the exit when one of the older kids stuck out their foot, snagging him in mid-step and sending him sprawling to the ground and the cafeteria erupted in a roar of laughter. Xander was slow in getting back up, his body shaking so hard that Estella was afraid that he'd been badly hurt. While everyone stared down at him, cackling, Estella had watched as the bully's lunch tray began to shake on the table.

While nobody else seemed to notice this phenomenon, however, Estella watched intently. Xander, though slow to do so, had risen to his feet and narrowed his eyes in anger. As his rage intensified the tray's quaking seemed to become more violent and Estella realized at that moment that Xander was responsible for what was happening. Suddenly, it shot forward from the table's surface and struck the still-laughing bully, smearing its contents all over his back. The boy quickly turned then, enraged, and demanded to know who had thrown his lunch at him. Looking around and confirming that nobody had seen what had happened, Xander was quick to turn and leave.

That day had marked the beginning of her path into the world of magic; a path that she blazed through over the years—studying and practicing until she'd nearly perfected the art. Knowing from day one that Xander didn't want her to know the truth about it, she never approached him with the subject.

Estella sighed as the living room lights from her house came into focus between the rows of trees. Despite the sadness from the memories, it felt good to be able to recall the times she had had with her best friend. Knowing that her journey had come to an end, she stepped past the threshold into her backyard and headed towards the patio door. Finally inside, she hurried through the living room she called out "I'm home" and "Goodnight" to her parents before making her way up two flights of stairs to her bedroom in the attic.

Though they had remained friends for some time after that, their secrets had put a dent in the friendship. She hadn't been happy about lying to Xander, especially since doing so only seemed to put more and more secrets between them until their friendship was dry and brittle.

But it had been the death of Xander's mother that had finally shattered it.

The lingering scent of Dragon's Blood incense hung in

the air as she entered her room and she breathed in deeply before taking out and lighting a fresh stick. With the aromatic silver smoke coiling and churning about the room, she went about looking for the old birthday card. She thought of the hand-made gift in her mind, hoping the energies they invoked would help lead her to it; she pictured the plain white paper folded in half with the picture of the two of them glued to the front that had been taken on Xander's one visit to her house. Remembering the way it looked the last time she'd used it for the spell: the paper faded and beginning to turn a slight yellow shade. Then she thought of what was written inside:

"Whenever you need a friend"

Xander had never been sentimental and he was most certainly not the poetic type, but those five words had meant everything to Estella and, thinking back on it, they still did. Despite it being all that Xander could give her for her birthday that one year it had been Estella's greatest gift— both then and ever since.

She had never felt more loved.

A spark caught her attention at that moment and she turned towards her closet, suddenly remembering the shoebox and went about digging until she found the small pink and white box therein. Extracting it, she shook off some of the dust that had collected on the lid before pulling it off and exposing an ancient pair of pumps and, beneath them, the birthday card. The familiar picture stared up at her as both a reminder of her lost friendship as well as the last time she had cast this spell—the same shiver from before seizing her in the middle of her spine. Taking the card into her palms as though it were a living thing that might die at any moment, Estella lingered on the image before turning and taking it to her bed.

Estella frowned as she gently held the birthday card tightly. She had been so ignorant; so utterly stupid! She clenched her teeth as she traced a finger lightly down the image of young Xander's cheek in the photograph.

"How could I have been so blind?" she whispered to it.

All of Xander's anger and pain had been his stepfather's doing. He was the one person who was responsible for all of the hurt that Xander had felt in his life, and she hadn't seen it in time. She never even had any suspicions until the night she'd gone into his head and seen flashes of his memory as the shaky gun barrel shook against his teeth. It was his name that had, over and over again, flooded his mind as he mustered the courage to once again pull the trigger.

Kyle…

It hadn't been unusual for Xander to miss a few days of school—it was actually a rare event if he made it through a full month. Estella had been, of course, upset to be without her friend whenever this happened, but there was little she could do.

The worst of the absences was when he had fallen down the stairs and landed himself in the hospital for several weeks. Though it was out of the way, Estella had visited him every day during his time there.

It was during one of these visits that she'd met the monster.

She had been leaving Xander's hospital room, his mother having just arrived for her own visit. Though Xander always put on a strong act during her visits, Estella had been able to see the obvious pain of his injuries each time he shifted in bed and it had been all she could do to hold her tears in until she was out of the room. She had been halfway down the hall, working on collecting herself so that her mother wouldn't see her crying when a strange and sudden cold had overcome her. As the frigid sensation came to rest at the base of her neck, Estella had nearly collapsed under the weight of a heavy dizziness. When at last the dizziness had begun to fade, she looked up and noticed Kyle sitting in the waiting room; staring at her with a sadistic grin.

A hot blush had taken to Estella's cheeks as she fought her natural urge to look away. She'd seen Kyle before in passing and recognized him as Xander's stepfather. Though she felt uneasy maintaining eye contact with the man, she knew that to look away would be rude and as she stood there, fighting the fear that Kyle seemed to instill, the dizzying cold returned and caused her to flinch.

"Cold, aren't they?" he'd said, still staring; still grinning.

Estella's jaw had felt too stiff to speak, "H-huh?"

Kyle's grin had widened and she'd felt bile rising in her throat. "Hospitals," he'd clarified, "they're always so cold." His face turned serious, and Estella shivered in her bed as the still-vivid memory played out. "That was why you shivered, right?"

The question had seemed more like a demand.

Estella had been unable to respond, her jaw too taken in whatever fear-born paralysis it had been in. Eager to get away, she'd finally pulled her eyes away from Kyle's gaze and nodded, hurrying past.

"Probably trying to keep all those uncomfortable patients tired," he'd continued as she scurried off, "All that pain. All that discomfort. And all in one place."

Pushing through the coldness and dizziness, Estella hadn't looked back until she was through the hospital doors and in the parking lot. Seeing her in such a state, her mom had demanded to know what was wrong and she had eagerly told of Xander's stepfather and what he had said.

Her mother had listened, though Estella still believed that she'd never heard a word, and had sighed when she'd finished, "That poor man, he must be so worried. Just imagine what it must be like to have someone you care about in that state: hurt and scared in a hospital room. He's probably just upset."

Estella had known, even then, that arguing would be pointless, and she had nodded and apologized for being so rude. Kyle had made one good point in his ranting though, Estella had noticed: the hospital had been filled with the pained, the sick, and the dying. All that fear and sadness must have been what overpowered her heightened receptors of energetic forces. Though for a long time she had wanted to believe that, somehow, Kyle had been responsible for the dizziness and the inescapable cold, the truth was that she had let her guard down and all that pain had gotten in.

She shook her head at her past self.

No, Kyle wasn't some sort of magic monster. He was just an everyday monster preying on his stepson. But Estella hadn't seen that until later.

Until it was too late.

It had been the night of Xander's mother's death that she had seen Kyle for the monster he was. Something dark had been in the air that night all those years ago. Something that refused to let Estella sleep for very long, and what sleep she was granted was haunted by shady, grisly images and horrible screams. That night had been the first time she'd cast the spell of Other's Sight; the first time she'd been able to leave her body in an astral form and see through Xander's eyes.

It was a spell that had broken her heart twice already.

One that she was about to cast again.

She sighed as she lay down, holding the card across her chest to help direct her emotions and energies in the right direction. She thought for a moment of the past two times she'd cast this spell: once by accident in her dreams and then again to see if her old friend was alright. After the second time Estella had cast the spell and caught Xander in the middle of his suicidal ritual, she had tried to approach him in an attempt to rekindle their lost friendship and give him a sympathetic ear to all the problems that he clearly was keeping inside. Before she'd had a chance to finish, however, Xander had begun to storm away. Seeing her chance at redemption slipping away, she'd made one last effort:

"W-what about Kyle?" she'd stammered, "Is he in jai—"

Xander turned so quickly that she had nearly fallen back; his fury-filled face so close she could feel the heat radiating from him, "Kyle is dead!" he'd spat, his eyes shaking in his rage, "He's dead," he repeated, his clenched teeth turning his words into a growl, "and that's the only good thing he's ever done with his life!"

After that day, Estella had realized that nothing could be done to reverse the damage and stopped trying to talk to Xander for his sake. Despite this, she'd never stopped caring for him, which was why, once again, despite all the previous times she'd done it, she was going to cast Other's Sight on him again.

She carried this final sentiment with her as the emotions became a warm energy that she held tightly to and wrapped around herself. She concentrated on Xander, fighting away any other memories that would distract her. She envisioned his face and was momentarily saddened that the only images she could pull up were ones of him either upset or hurt.

Shaking off the inhibiting emotion, she allowed herself to further fall into a comfortable trance, imagining herself as lighter than air as she quietly mouthed Xander's name over and over like an obsessed lover in an attempt to keep herself focused.

"Xander Stryker... Xander Stryker..."

A light pull tugged at her that she had come to associate with her mind separating from the solid world and her sight began to fade. Ignoring her blindness, she focused harder, pushing forth an energetic zip-line that was meant to latch onto Xander's mind, but it couldn't seem to get ahold of anything. Beginning to fear the worst as her efforts to connect with his mind were met again and again with failure, she doubled her efforts.

Had he actually been caught in that fire?

Or, worse yet, had he finally killed himself?

"Xander Stryker! Xander Stryker!" her distant voice echoed within her.

And then she felt it! A sudden connection on the other side and a blurred scene appeared before her as she entered Xander's mind.

Casting the Other's Sight spell usually meant a front-row seat to the sights, sounds, smells, thoughts and sensations of whoever the spell had been cast on. Usually, these senses came in crisp and clear, so much so that the second time Estella had cast it on Xander it had taken her hours to convince herself it hadn't been her own hand on the trigger.

This time, however, was different.

Rather than a clear view she was instead treated to a shaky and distorted show that kicked in and out of focus. One moment, she was looking at what appeared to be a bloody corpse and feeling horrible sorrow and fury and the next she was blind, left only with the lingering rage.

Was this truly Xander?

The rage felt familiar, but something was different about whoever she had connected to...

Sight returned then: a shaky rollercoaster ride ending face to face with a white tiger and a feeling of relief, then darkness again. Estella fought to strengthen the connection and was rewarded with several voices in the darkness accompanied by a murderous need and a powerful thirst.

Suddenly there was a scream, and a nanosecond later her vision was filled with a man's face—pudgy and smeared with blood—as he screamed in horror and agony. The hunger grew more intense as Estella watched the blood seeping from the man and somewhere in the distance she felt her body, still lying in the bed, shudder with disgust.

But it smelled so good!

And she was so hungry!

She stopped herself. She needed to remember that she was riding someone else's experiences and that she could not allow herself to slip again and believe that she was them. The image flashed and grayed before wavering and cutting out again, but the rage and hunger stayed a moment longer before it also disappeared, leaving only the taste of blood.

Estella was distantly aware of her heaving and was vaguely aware of throwing up on herself. She worried for a moment that she may have made a mess all over the card and felt herself begin to get dragged back towards her own body and pushed away the thoughts in order to keep herself focused.

"Xander Stryker! Xander Stryker! Xander Stryker!"

The picture returned—this time without any color except for the red blood smeared everywhere. There was another distant heave and Estella tried to keep the reality from her mind as she held her focus. The thought patterns were too familiar for her to be seeing through the eyes of anyone else but Xander, but there were elements that had not been there before, and Estella couldn't get a complete grip on his mind because of them.

There was a spark of alertness and the view skewed as they turned to face a set of approaching footsteps. When the image was still again, it was fuzzy and blurred and Estella struggled to come back into focus briefly before realizing the blurriness was not a result of a weak connection; it was coming from the other side…

There was a loud, electric whine and Estella screamed out in agony from her bed as she fought with everything she had left to stay connected. Suddenly, the distortion became nearly solid, looking like a shimmering wall of glass filled with lightning that became closer and closer, shooting at them like a missile.

Fearing whatever was about to collide with them and what would happen to her if her mind was still connected to his when it did she severed the link and concentrated on returning to her body. Despite this, the static shriek seemed to follow her as she felt the pull back to her own body.

Falling back into her vomit-covered body, she was still distantly aware of the sound and suddenly very aware of an excruciating pain in her right eye.

The reintroduction to her body caused her chest to heave from a lack of oxygen—she'd yet to figure out how to control her breathing when outside her body—and she quickly rolled to her side as she heaved and threw up once again.

No longer held to her host's thoughts and desires, the

realization of what she had seen pulled a terror-fueled shriek from her lungs and her thrashing body fell from the bed.

A moment later her mother's voice issued out along with her approaching steps as they ascended the stairs, "Stella? Honey, is everything okay?"

Estella looked down at herself—sweat-and-puke-drenched and beat-red from heaving for air—and realized she did not want to be walked in on.

Some things, she thought as she pulled herself up, *are just beyond explanation.*

Throwing herself against the door and propping it shut, she tried to muster enough air in her lungs to speak, "I-I'm fine, Mom! Just had a bad dream."

The rushing footsteps slowed to a reluctant stop a short distance from her; Estella could hear her mother's worried breathing through the door, "You sure? You were screaming bloody murder!"

Estella held back a nervous laugh at the irony of her mom's statement, "I know, Mom. But I'm okay. Really."

An uncomfortable silence followed, and although Estella's lungs still ached, she held her breath and waited for the sound of her mother's footsteps going back down the stairs. Once she was sure that a trip through the hall would be unobserved, she hurried down the stairs and into the bathroom, locking the door behind her and turning on the shower to the hottest her skin could tolerate. The running water served to mask her sobs as she let her body sink into the tub.

"Xander…" she whispered, "What's happened to you?"

CHAPTER TWENTY
SEEING RED AGAIN/THE HARD GOODBYE

THE MUSIC WAS FAR TOO LOUD AND

added to Xander's already throbbing head. He cringed at the melodic invasion and dug himself deeper into the cushioned surface he found himself on in an attempt to drown it out, groaning in pain as he shifted. A drum solo kicked in and he cried out in pain.

"Xander? You awake, buddy?"

He groaned again as he shifted his body—careful to move slower in an attempt to avoid any more aches—and felt his arm drop over the edge of whatever he was lying on. As gravity tugged at his injuries he let out another pained moan.

The music silenced then, plunging the swirling darkness behind his eyelids into silence. Finally able to hear himself think, he wondered why his eyes hadn't opened yet.

"Hey," a familiar voice called out again, "c'mon, Stryker! Show me you're still alive!"

Xander whimpered in response as he pulled his arm back to his chest and turned around; he didn't care where he was, how long he'd been out, or even how he'd survived being hit by what had felt like a bomb—especially since it felt like he'd taken almost all the impact solely on his head. He just wanted to slip back into unconsciousness until the pain was something close to bearable.

"Come on, Xander!" he finally recognized the voice as Marcus', "Open your damn eyes and tell me you're at least not blind!"

"That's... not... funny!" Xander took in a deep breath to try and combat the agony in his chest as well as the Antichrist that was birthing itself through his skull.

"It's not supposed to be, bud. Now open wide and tell me what you see," there was a faint slurping.

Xander sighed and strained his eyelids to open and cried out in pain.

Marcus sighed, "Yea, Stan said you'd be hurting for a while. He did all he could on you, but there's only so much that magic can do." Xander noticed his voice get louder as he approached, then another brief slurp, "All things considered, it's a damn miracle that you're even alive!"

Xander frowned at that and gently turned his head towards Marcus' voice and tried to open his eyes again. There was another pinch at his temples as he did, but he held them open through the agony and looked up at Marcus, who stood over him with two medical bags of blood, one of which he had opened and was sipping from with a crazy-straw. He started to laugh at the sight but a sharp pain in his spine stopped him.

"Stan?" he gritted his teeth and rode out the sensation, "You know him?"

Marcus scoffed, "There aren't many in the Odin Clan who don't—" He frowned, "… Who *didn't* know of Stanly Ferno. I'm surprised you didn't know."

Xander shook his head. "Depok said something…" He sighed, "What was Stan doing at the mansion anyway?"

"I've learned better than to question Stan and his methods," Marcus answered, "Either way, he saved your life; though we were both concerned about your vision."

An itch in Xander's right eye distracted his thoughts and he tried to blink it away, noticing that his vision *was* slightly blurred. As he tried to focus, he looked back up at Marcus, frowning as he noticed a bluish, fluid-looking haze that surrounded him.

"I… I can see just fine," he lied and pulled himself to a sitting position, riding out the resulting pain with a deep exhale. "So what was with that insanely loud wake-up call?"

Marcus frowned and plopped the spare bag of blood on the coffee table in front of him. "Sorry. Stan said you'd be out for a while and that it'd take the apocalypse to wake you," he shrugged and sat in a nearby chair that had clearly seen better days. "Figured I'd be able to relax for a bit without bothering you."

Xander scoffed, his vision beginning to clear but the shimmering blue outline remaining around Marcus, "Heavy metal relaxes you?"

"So I've changed some with the times. What? You gonna tell me I'm too old to like that kind of music?" Marcus challenged.

"Well, no," Xander shook his head, "But it *relaxes* you?"

Marcus frowned. "Well if *that's* the way you're going to be, would you rather listen to Britney-fucking-Spears or something else that parallels your insatiable teen angst?" he glared and took a sip of blood.

Xander couldn't argue, though he still felt that, when one was suffering from the King Kong of headaches, perhaps calmer tunes would suffice. He rubbed his forehead and let his eyes close again, "What happened anyway?"

He heard Marcus shift in his seat, "Somebody came gunning for you while you were undergoing the change." He sighed and slurped again.

"Do you know who?" Xander asked, moving his hand up to rub his itchy right eye.

"WHOA! HEY! NO!" Marcus shot up and grabbed his hand so fast Xander didn't see him move from his seat, "Stan said it'd be best if you didn't touch that eye for a while."

Xander frowned, thinking back as far as he could. The last thing he remembered he was drinking from the two humans near the dojo… and then the blurry figure.

He looked up at Marcus as he sipped again from the nearly empty bag of blood and then eyed the other one that had been put in front of him. Though his body urged him to reach out and take the offered blood, there were more important things at hand.

"So do you know who's responsible for what happened?" he asked again.

"We're not sure," Marcus looked away. "Whoever it was knew enough to cover their tracks, and cover them pretty damn well, too! Stan tried to scan the history of the place—whatever the hell that means—but came up with nothing. Apparently there were psychic blocks set up."

Xander looked down and tried to remember more, but aside from the sharp impact from what could only have been a flying brick wall he couldn't recall anything. As he pondered his last moments in the Odin mansion, Marcus rose to his feet and stepped over to a bookshelf and pulled something from the top shelf. Xander looked away; still irritated by the ghostly blue outline around Marcus.

Though the blurriness had faded, it still remained...

"Where am I?" he asked.

"My apartment," Marcus answered, "I told you I was taking some time off, remember?" He scoffed and shook his head, "Guess I should consider myself lucky."

Xander bit his lip; something in Marcus' voice sounded regretful and he wondered if the vampire would have rather died with his comrades.

Marcus lingered a moment longer at the bookcase before he turned back and headed towards his chair again. "I hated the formality of the mansion," he explained, "So I asked Depok a while back if I could be excused from the cushy room they had given me." He set a familiar wooden box down beside Xander's still-untouched bag of blood, "Stan said these are yours."

Xander reached out and pulled the box towards him, feeling the instinctual rise of fear and sadness in his gut that he'd had each night he pulled it out from under his mattress back at home. The silver clasp that held the lid shut felt cool to the touch as he flipped it open and he pulled back the velvet sheet that served to protect the twin revolvers and, for the first time since the day he was dragged into the new world, he looked down at Yin and Yang.

They looked the same as they had the last time he'd seen them and, startled, he looked up at Marcus, "How were they not destroyed in the fire?"

Marcus shrugged. "Like I said: don't question Stan," he smiled and looked at the guns, "Pretty sweet pieces. They would've served well in battle."

Xander narrowed his eyes as he hoisted Yin from the velvet lining and realized that it felt lighter; the cold handle feeling more at home in his grip than ever before. He inspected the modified eight-round chamber, finding that it still held the same one bullet that, time and time again, had refused to take him. He thought about what he'd seen in the mansion; the massacred and vandalized bodies of those he had met.

All because of him.

He set the black revolver back down in the case. They still might serve him well...

"Stan said he wanted to see you at his place when you were up and ready to move around again," Marcus said after a long silence. He chuckled and shook his head, looking Xander square in the eye, "Crimson Shadow."

Xander looked up at that, "Huh?"

Marcus' grin widened; the strange blue haze around him bubbling and turning brighter. "Stan 'heard' your thoughts when you made your first kill," he nodded slowly and said it again: "The 'Crimson Shadow'. I like it." He chuckled again, "Suits you. I guess 'Xander' wasn't a badass enough title, huh?"

Xander felt his face redden and rubbed at the back of his neck.

Marcus continued to laugh as he leaned forward in his

seat, "So to Stan's then?"

Xander nodded; it would be a refreshing face to see after all the things that had transpired. He locked up the case and, feeling an itch welling up, went to rub his right eye again.

"Dude! Careful! Your eye is pretty fucked up! I'm not sure if you should be touching it!" Marcus barked at him.

Xander growled in aggravation. "What in the hell is the matter with it anyway?"

"Chill out! After the hit you took, you're lucky to still have a head attached to your shoulders!"

Xander bit his lip in confusion. "The hit?"

Marcus nodded, "Most of the ones that swarmed in and dusted the place left after a few hours, but I guess you were lucky enough to meet a straggler." Xander stared at him and Marcus sighed, "It was a very powerful auric; one that threw quite a lot of mind-popping shit at you!"

Xander looked at him, still confused.

Marcus shifted. "Look: what I'm trying to tell you is that the energy blast that you took should have killed you, or at the very least landed you in a padded cell with a bib for the rest of your life."

"That doesn't explain my eye," Xander countered.

Marcus growled, shaking his head, "God you're an asshole! Being your father's son, you were born with"—he frowned and smacked his lips—"well Stan had some cute words for them. Let's just say 'parts' that weren't 'turned on'. When the auric attack hit you, instead of shutting everything down, it flipped the switch on them."

Xander glared, "So some auric 'turned on' my 'parts'? You're not making any goddam sense! And you still haven't told me shit about my—"

Marcus shot a look, "Listen, the machinery of your brain

jumpstarting gave you quite a tremor. Stan said when he found you your nose and ears were bleeding all to shit and your right eye..." Xander leaned forward, eager to have an answer, "... well, you flood the head with enough blood and I guess there's going to be some staining," Marcus finished with a nervous laugh.

Xander frowned and got up abruptly, "Where's your bathroom?"

"Down the hall to your left; hall light's busted, not that it makes a difference to us anyway."

Xander realized shortly after that he was right. Despite the 'L'-shaped hallway having no source of illumination, he had no problems finding the bathroom door. Though he had just realized it was unnecessary, he flipped both of the light switches on the wall, flooding the room in light.

Steadying himself in front of the mirror, he saw for the first time why his right eye was so itchy. Leaning in close to the glass, he could see that it was completely—as Marcus had put it—blood-stained. The whites of the eye had turned completely red and his hazel iris had been buried as well and only shone through slightly.

His entire right eye, except for the pupil, had turned blood-red!

"What. The. Fuck!" Xander whispered as he stretched his lid open to fully inspect it. When he had had enough of the ugly truth, he went back to the living room and snatched the bag of blood from the table and downed it in several gulps. As he finished the last drop of the uncomfortably cold fluid, he licked his lips and grabbed his guns. Turning to Marcus, he frowned, seeing that the blue haze still surrounded him. Discomforted by this, he looked away again. "So are we going to Stan's or what?"

Growing up without a father, Xander had grown close to his mother, which, until the emergence of Kyle, had gotten him labeled as a "mama's boy". When the terror known as "Kyle" entered the household and took his mother, he became reliant on himself. Not playing with his classmates stirred up concern from the teachers, who began to think he was "special", while the kids just called him "weird". As he grew up with the views of his peers making him feel less and less a part of the world, Xander began to resent and eventually hate them, and "special" turned into "psychotic" and "weird" turned into "freak".

Walking into school each morning with fresh bruises made him a "klutz" to the kids, and a fear of physical contact got him labeled as "socially anxious" with the faculty. When he missed the bus on purpose to not go home and instead stayed in the playground, talking to himself when he was sure nobody was looking, the teachers began to write "runaway" in their notebooks and asked him if his mother hurt him. Kyle had always warned him about discussing "family matters" outside of the home, and when questions like those arose, he could only sob and swear that he'd given himself the bruises. Then the teachers wrote bigger words in their notebooks that put him in the school shrink's office.

After an entire childhood filled with labels, Xander hated the idea of judgment. Even more so he hated the feeling of being a hypocrite by passing judgment. Despite this, he felt that a top warrior for a once powerful vampire clan would drive something better than a rusted-out white Subaru circa nineteen-why-the-fuck-is-it-still-running.

Nevertheless, it *was* a car and it *was* taking them where they needed to go.

Stan lived in the ritzier part of town, which just happened to be a thirty-minute drive from the city where Marcus had decided to rent the two-bedroom apartment in a complex across the street from an adult bookstore and an Asian market.

Xander was still working out which was weirder: the vampire warrior that had a room in a mansion deciding to live in a ratty apartment, or a single, public school teacher living in a three-story home in a neighborhood where the biggest recent crime had been when the Swansons had accidentally opened their neighbors mail after a delivery mix-up, when they finally pulled up to the light blue house.

Marcus laughed. "Strange crib for someone who's been called a 'devil'," he muttered as he threw his shoulder into the driver's side door to get it open.

Xander figured he'd keep the ever-growing list of comments he had concerning Marcus' car and apartment to himself and instead followed after with the case tucked under his left arm.

The patio light was on, and, standing on the front porch, Stan was already waiting for them. Xander couldn't help but smile at his friend as he walked in and headed over to the living room where he and Stan used to sit and play chess. There he found his tiger companion sprawled out on the floor in front of the fireplace as it warmed the house against the fresh November chill. He smiled at the sight, glad that he was safe.

Stan took his time in closing the door and turned to Marcus with a grin as they both said in unison, "Got any decent beer on tap?" and exploded into laughter.

Xander frowned, feeling that he was missing a good joke.

After their laughter had died down, Marcus came in and took a seat on a nearby chair while Stan strolled into the kitchen, returning shortly after with three beers. Xander was surprised to see that his friend had brought him a bottle and eagerly accepted it as it was offered to him.

"Thanks. Don't suppose you got any cigs on you, though?" he looked up and smirked.

Stan frowned and shook his head. "You know I don't smoke."

Xander nodded. He didn't mind so much that he couldn't smoke since he had not felt the tugging urge since he'd been changed. Instead, he looked around the house, noting the small changes that Stan had made in the décor and took a sip of the beer. He'd been surprised that, despite the entire bag of blood that he'd emptied into himself earlier, he'd felt hungry again soon after. Marcus had explained in the car that his body had used that meal to work on healing the wounds he'd sustained from the attack and that he'd need more soon.

Stan, taking a long sip from his own beer, crossed his legs as Marcus rolled the neck of the already-empty bottle between his fingers and let loose a belch that made the tiger jump.

"It's been a while," Stan finally said to Xander, "Lots of very, *very* new things to talk about."

Xander nodded and set the beer down on his wooden box before having second thoughts about it and rested it instead on his lap. Marcus stood up and signaled towards the kitchen and headed, without acknowledgement or permission, towards the fridge.

Stan rolled his eyes after him, though it didn't make a difference at that point, and turned to Xander. He smirked as his gaze locked on his eye and he shook his head, "I have to say, the look suits you."

Xander scowled and raised a gentle hand to it. "Yea. I still don't get it though," he sighed and let his hand drop as he took a sip of his beer. "I mean, this can't be natural."

Stan shook his head. "Not for humans, it's not."

Xander looked up with a scowl. More riddles; just what he didn't need, "So this is *normal* for vampires then?"

Stan shook his head again. "Not exactly," he leaned forward, "Look, you had *just* come back from the dead, Xander! You're body had been making some very massive changes; changes that were still in their final stages! I mean—Hell!—you were still metabolizing your first meal when the auric attack hit you."

"Final stages?" Xander frowned.

Stan nodded, "Like a baby's skull not being completely formed at birth a vampire doesn't emerge from the transformation fully changed. It still takes a few hours, sometimes a day or two. In your case, all the hemorrhaging to your eye was incorporated with the final stages of the change."

Xander stared in silence, not liking the new explanation any more than the old one.

"So," Stan changed the subject, a broad smile spreading across his face, "can you 'see' them?"

Xander raised an eyebrow, "'them'?"

Stan nodded and smiled, "Auras, man!" He motioned towards the kitchen, where Marcus was still raiding his fridge.

Xander's frown tightened, "Auras…" he looked back towards Marcus and the strange blue haze that still surrounded him. At first he'd passed it off as an annoying after effect of what had happened to his eye, like the similar outline he'd seen around people when he'd gotten too much chlorine in his eyes at the public swimming pool. But, studying Stan, he noticed that there was nothing surrounding him.

Stan smirked, "You're not going to find one around me." He took a sip of his beer, "Like an auric vampire, I've *absorbed* my aura. I've become a part of it—or rather it has become a part of me."

Xander nodded, not completely understanding, "So that strange blue thing around Marcus is…"

"His aura," Stan finished for him. "It's his energy signature. They're not all blue, though. The color is unique to the person; nobody's aura shines the same, so don't trust the colors as some sort of code." He grinned and nodded towards the kitchen, "Blue just happens to be one of the more common shades."

"You guys talking about me in here?" Marcus stepped between the two before sitting down with several new beers.

"Just seeing where the boy is in his development," Stan replied.

Marcus nodded before turning to Xander with a grin, "You've barely touched your beer!"

Stan smiled and nodded, "Yea, drink up! I stocked the fridge so you'd have something to take the edge off!"

Xander frowned. He knew that a lot had happened, but the way Stan had said it…

"What edge are we talking about, exactly?"

Stan had the bottle to his mouth when he froze and looked over at Marcus with an angry glare, "You didn't at least mention it?"

Marcus rubbed his neck, "I just figured enough shit has hit the fan that I didn't need to squat a fresh batch on him just yet."

A heavy sigh escaped Xander and the two turned back to him, "I'm really in no mood to listen to your side conversation. So why don't we all take our heads out of our asses, turn them towards me and tell me what we're taking the 'edge' off of!"

Marcus sighed and tossed Xander his reserve bottle.

Xander, catching it, still glared at the two but nodded his appreciation as he chugged the contents of his first bottle before opening the new one.

Stan frowned, looking down. He'd known from experience that it was best to be straightforward in this kind of situation, "The psychic attack you suffered awakened the auric potential inside of you. The process was a violent one, and the…" he paused, "… the 'container' that was holding all of it ruptured, spilling all the abilities that you should've been born with back into you."

Xander stared at him.

Stan frowned and looked down sadly for a moment before looking back up at him, "Listen: you were born a half-auric because of your father, but, as you already know, your father attempted to contact you at the time of his death. Most of who he was got stripped away during the process of reaching out to you, but what *did* get to you—what was left of him—needed to find a way of staying intact so it could watch over you. So it wrapped itself in an auric bubble in your mind, using most of your own auric energy to sustain it." Stan frowned and glared at Marcus again for not having said something about this sooner, "A lot of your untapped powers were in that orb and when you were attacked the orb burst, flooding your head with the 'borrowed' auric energy as well as the entity, which, when unable to sustain itself, simply diffused into your mind."

Marcus sighed and turned to Stan, "Why do you have to make it so hard?" he turned to Xander, looking exhausted, "Xander, you absorbed Trepis."

It was then that Xander realized that he hadn't heard a word from his life-long friend since he'd awoken on Marcus' couch. He saw his own aura at that moment—a red and black, semi-translucent tendril that whipped out from his chest. He opened his mouth to say something but a choked sob emerged and he shut it to prevent a repeat. He looked at the tiger, the *real* Trepis that had shared the link with Mind-Trepis.

He hadn't looked at him once since he'd sat down!

Suddenly, despite all the company, Xander felt more alone than he ever had in his entire life.

CHAPTER TWENTY-ONE
THE TRUTH

IT WAS A FOREIGN SENSATION...

albeit a familiar one.

"Xander! Put it down!" Stan repeated.

Cold metal.

Hot tears.

The hope of no future.

No way out but through the squeeze of the trigger. To think he'd reached a peak in life where this ritual seemed unnecessary. How could he ever have trusted life so much to let his guard down?

The tiger—the only Trepis left—had slinked away and was curled up in the corner, his tail darting back and forth in nervous protest at the chaos.

Marcus stood beside Stan with a frown that showed more than just a little nervousness, "STRYKER! CUT IT OUT!"

He ignored them. They were just more noise; noise that would be turned to blissful silence soon enough. That round had sat in the chamber long enough! It belonged in his skull once and for all!

He looked at Stan through teary eyes and the red and black cloud his protruding aura had become. As if following the cues of his eyes, the dark mass stretched towards his old friend as it sparked and spiked violently, mimicking the muscle spasms of his over-tense body.

"Do you think it will take me tonight, Stan?" he asked in between sobs.

Stan furrowed his brow for a moment before all visible tension left his body, "I know that it won't, actually."

Xander shut his eyes against the answer. It wasn't the one he wanted; wasn't the one he needed! He felt his jaw tighten and the burning started at his back and wrapped around to his shoulders. His tear-welled eyes opened briefly and he could see it; saw the rage-fueled auric tendril as it coiled tightly around him like a neon red serpent. It was what was burning him; what had *always* been burning him! It stretched and grew until it all but consumed him. As the streak of anger came to coat his entire body Xander felt the heat spread and overcome him.

Stan watched this happen and steadied his footing on the floor, "Xander!" his voice was calm-yet-stern, "You *have* to relax!"

Noticing Stan secure his footing, Marcus narrowed his eyes at Xander and took an uncertain step back, "What is it? What's he doing?"

Stan couldn't *know*.

Not like that.

He'd said it himself: nobody can see the future! It was nothingness; an unwritten book!

He was bluffing, and Xander was going to prove it.

The tightness of the revolver's trigger was the only resistance he faced as he pulled the trigger and finally fired the weapon.

For many years he had held Yin to his head and pulled its trigger. Every time he was fully prepared for the blast, wanting it more than anything.

He'd never expected it to be so loud, though.

His body was blind and frozen, waiting for the final tug away from his horrid existence.

But he could still feel his heartbeat...

And he could *hear* Stan's and Marcus'—hell, even the damn tiger's—hearts!

There was a metallic clink on the floor and Xander thought of a dropped coin and paid it no mind. The hammer had finally fallen on the one round!

And he was still alive?

"But... how?" he frowned and looked at the gun in his hand, the barrel still smoking from the recent firing. He glared at it and then up at the two non-humans in front of him.

One of them had to responsible!

Stan hadn't shifted into a relaxed state yet, and Marcus stared in shock and awe, as eager for answers as him. So much was not adding up: if the gun had fired, where was the death that should have followed?

Even a vampire couldn't survive a shot to the head! Marcus' bewilderment told him that much.

But Stan…

Why was he still tense when nothing had happened?

He'd known!

He'd known and that wasn't possible and Xander hated him for it!

The rage-serpent that had constricted him and burnt him sparked violently, "WHY?" Xander roared at him. His aura whipped forward with the scream and crash into the two in front of him.

Marcus cried out as he was tossed back to the end of the room where he landed crookedly in the fireplace. He rolled quickly away, slapping out the flames that had caught on his legs before looking up to see if Stan had met with a similar fate. A look of disappointment spread across his face when he saw that he'd been the only one affected.

Xander dropped to his knees, breathing heavily as Stan finally relaxed his stance and approached, kneeling down and picking up the bullet that had dropped to the floor.

Xander looked up at him, suddenly exhausted, "How could you have known?"

Helping him to his feet, Stan shook his head and handed him the bullet, "Because this was never yours to begin with." He turned and sat down on the couch and lifted the bottle that rested nearby, "and a part of you has always known that."

Marcus sighed and shook his head as Stan sipped at his beer. He dragged himself to his feet, the burns on his leg already beginning to scab over.

Xander's aura—showing the same exhaustion that his mind felt—rippled and receded back into his chest, "Not mine…"

Stan sighed and shrugged, "Consider that the poet's explanation." He let his head fall back onto a couch cushion and paused, "How many times have you pulled that gun on yourself?"

Xander frowned and looked away, feeling his face turn red. "Too many times," he shrugged, "At least that's what you'd tell me, right?"

"'Too many times'… and to never land a single shot? A one-in-eight chance taken day-after-day for so long and yet here you remain. Even Trepis could have taken control any one of those times and put the weapon away, but he knew something I didn't realize until now: you *didn't* want to die!"

Xander glared at the preposterous statement.

Stan ignored him and continued: "You've had these powers your entire life, but while you've been using them to do parlor tricks and throw hissy fits, they've been getting stronger. How easy it was for your mind to make sure that that one chamber wasn't fired *once*! And just now, in that stunning display, your own mind played tug of war with the decision of whether or not to die.

"Sure, you finally fired the one bullet, but your aura— your own goddam aura!—stopped it in the barrel before it could even touch you! Your own subconscious is telling you to cut this shit out." Stan smiled, "Joseph Stryker's bloodline will not go out that easily, Xander! You've got too much to do with your new life, and a big mess to clean up from your old one."

Xander frowned, "A mess?"

Stan nodded, "A big fucking one! And even though you

don't know it, your auric powers can sense it; could *always* sense it!"

"Sense what?" Xander bit his lip.

Stan frowned gravely and handed the bottle back to Marcus and leaned forward, resting his arms on his knees, "It's time you finally know the truth:"—Stan paused for a moment—"he's still alive."

Xander frowned, considering his words before looking again at the gun. After a moment he set it back in its box, slumping down in one of Stan's chairs. His eyelids were heavy then, and he fought the urge to close them.

He didn't need to ask who he was talking about; Stan was right: a part of him knew already.

Xander watched his aura seep out from his chest. Tiger-striped bolts of red streaked through the blackness as it came to hover in anticipation around him. It felt like fear and hatred and tasted like a dream come true. It stretched across the room then as Stan's own greenish-orange aura extended out as well. As the two met, Xander could suddenly "see" into Stan's mind—read his thoughts as if they were his own.

They talked for hours in the span of seconds before Xander finally pulled himself away and separated the link.

Clenching his teeth, Xander reached up and clutched the charm on his mother's necklace until he felt the corners digging into his palm. He shut his eyes and bit his lip, allowing his fangs to cut into him. The two tiny wounds bled for a moment before his superhuman body healed them. Then he did it again… and again, repeating the process until he'd finally mustered the courage to say the name:

"Kyle."

CHAPTER TWENTY-TWO
MOTIVATION

XANDER WAS ONLY EIGHT YEARS OLD

when his mother met Kyle. He remembered little of the early years; whether that was normal or if he had repressed the memories was something he never let himself dwell on long enough to decide. Despite this, some memories refused to be forgotten.

Memories of times that he'd sooner wish to forget than reflect upon...

Like the memory he had of Kyle forcing his young, frail body to the stove-top and pinning his back against the electric burner. The act left him with a dark, spiraled burn scar in the center of his back that had warped and stretched as he'd grown.

How many scars had he been given that he'd never be able to identify?

How many torturous memories had his mind let slide into blackness?

But it would never let him forget *the* most torturous one of them all.

It was nearly a month before his thirteenth birthday and he was sitting in the living room where Kyle had told him to wait for a surprise. Xander hadn't wanted the surprise; Kyle's surprises were always painful and humiliating. But his punishments were far worse. So Xander did as he was told and stayed quiet, pulling out his Batman action figure and trying his best to play.

After a short while there was the roar of a car engine as it pulled into the driveway followed by a moment of calmness before Xander heard the car doors open and slam shut. The voices of Kyle's friends picked up and faded as they passed by the window, heading towards the front door. Then the doorbell rang.

Xander, already nervous, had turned towards the hall that led to his mother and Kyle's bedroom. He could hear fragments of their voices—of Kyle yelling—and then the distinct and familiar sounds of Kyle hitting his mother.

The room had gone silent and the doorbell rang again.

The caped crusader figure was held in mid-attack—frozen in imaginary time—as Xander listened to all of this, wishing beyond wishes that he had the strength of Batman;

the strength of a hero. He wanted so badly to be stronger so that he could help his mother and chase his stepfather and his awful friends away.

The doorbell rang several more times, demanding an answer and Kyle's steps sounded across the floor.

Kyle's boots had always warned Xander of his approach. It was the sign to stop if he was doing something he shouldn't—like playing with his action figures, which Kyle had said were only for infants and retards. His stepfather's footsteps were always quick and purposeful, rarely giving him enough time to react. On that occasion, Kyle had moved especially quickly, and a panicked Xander was forced to hide the toy under the couch before he was seen and beaten for being a "doll-loving faggot".

Instead, Kyle's boots traveled passed the living room and down the hall to the front door and Xander listened as the voices of his stepfather's friends became clearer as they entered. Then Kyle's footsteps returned, now with several others following behind him.

There were three lights in the living room: one of which had burnt out and another that had been rendered useless when Kyle had out yanked out its cord to use as a makeshift whip to punish Xander and his mother for taking a walk without his permission. The remaining source of light clung to the ceiling and collected dust. This sole source of illumination was blocked out as the men entered and towered over Xander.

Though he always tried to be brave, he couldn't help but trip on his breath as he turned around and saw the men grinning down at him. Kyle held his hunting knife—a tool that he'd used many times in the past to scare Xander and his mother—in his left hand, pinching the black handle between his thumb and middle finger and tapped his index along the guard. The room seemed to go suddenly cold then as the shadowed forms of the men moved towards him until Xander felt like he was being swallowed up by the darkness.

Kyle, flipping the knife in his hand so that he could grip it by the handle, had plunged it into the arm of the couch. The sound of the fabric ripping under the assault had made Xander jump as the furniture was slashed and a clot of its stuffing exploded out from the wound. Xander shivered and Kyle, as he had so many times before, smiled at his stepson's fear and inhaled deeply.

"Ready for a good time, son?"

One of the men stepped forward, pulling out an old shaving razor in his right hand and swinging it casually on its hinge as he looked at Xander; his wiry brown hair and fierce, dark eyes like that of a feral animal. Another—a fat man who wore a leather jacket—called the quivering child a "li'l faggot" as he cracked his thick knuckles and licked his lips while a bony Latino leaned against the butchered couch, rubbing his crotch over his tight jeans and laughing wickedly at this comment. The last, a blonde man with an earring, stood in the back and lit a cigarette.

Kyle had ignored the others, letting them carry on as they pleased, and stepped around them to get close to his stepson and looked down at him with a grin, making Xander feel smaller than he already did. In the past, whenever Kyle's friends had come over, he had entertained them by making a show out of abusing Xander.

He'd been certain that this occasion would be no different.

On that night, however, they seemed to have other plans.

"I mean, they're only paying us to do the brat in. They never said nothing about having some fun with him first," the blond had said around his cigarette.

The Latino had nodded excitedly, rubbing his crotch harder, "Shit yea, bitch! We don't need to scrap him straight up! Let's play around with him and *then* peel him like a grape! We're getting paid one way or another; long as they get the body!"

"Whoo!" The fat man hollered, his gut rolling under the leather jacket, "Enough fuckin' cash to keep us rollin' for *TEN* lifetimes!"

It took several minutes of talk like this—talk that, though he hadn't understood, he still crept away from—before Kyle finally shrugged and began to undo his belt. Seeing this, the men all laughed and cheered and circled around Xander to watch the beating.

The Latino, giggling like a little boy, pushed Xander into Kyle, who caught him in his left hand and brought the belt down with his right. The strike connected with his chest; the large metal buckle sounding off as it drove into soft flesh. A cry of pain shot from Xander's mouth and the men all laughed and cheered Kyle on.

"Hold him down!" Kyle had ordered.

All the others kneeled down to hold the squirming child to the floor as Kyle repeatedly brought his belt down on his torso. Xander screamed and squirmed to get free but only succeeded in hurting himself more as the tight grips of the men dug into his wrists and legs. As the beating continued, the man with the razor let go of Xander's left leg for a moment before the fat one, already holding his right, pressed his bulk down on both. With his hands free, the man pinched the blade with the fingers of his left hand as he held the handle with his right and chuckled. After a moment of teasing, the razor was brought down, slicing carefully through the fabric of the nice blue shirt that Xander's mom had recently bought for him, exposing his already bruised chest. Then, as the chuckle evolved into a heavy cackle, the man carefully traced the edge of the blade across Xander's chest, threatening to cut him and making him cry out even louder; tears pouring down his face.

Too much terror.

Too much commotion.

Too much going on for anyone to notice as Xander's mother emerged from their bedroom. Xander saw her as she approached; noticed her red, puffy cheek and bruised eye as she charged the group; her eyes filled with fury.

"Leave him the fuck alone, you bastards!"

The slap landed and the entire room had hushed as Kyle had turned to face his wife, shock and anger shooting from his eyes. His friends all stood and stepped away, giving Kyle room enough to approach his wife and take her by the throat and spit in her gasping face.

Her eyes danced in a ballet of terror until they had landed on Xander, who stared back in mirrored fright, his lower lip—torn slightly and pumping blood down his quivering chin.

"Xander!" she called to him. "Run away! Hide! It'll be—" Any other words she had planned were cut short as Kyle's grip tightened around her throat.

But he couldn't run.

He couldn't look away.

Couldn't do a damn thing to stop it.

Kyle looked over his shoulder at his friends as sadistic inspiration struck, "What do you say we have a little 'down time' with Emily here before we get to business?"

His wife's eyes widened then as the men, grunting and chuckling, approached and began undoing their belts and pants. She struggled harder against Kyle, who finally threw her down onto the floor and began to unzip his pants, as well. With her throat free of its restraint, a hoarse groan escaped her mouth, slowly growing into an ear-splitting protest and howls of pain as the men began to pummel her to accommodate their desires.

Kyle stood over the mass, casually watching as his friends beat and raped his wife. As her screams grew louder and more desperate, his smile broadened and he let out a euphoric sigh, "This *is* the life, ain't it?" he'd called over to his stepson.

Xander hadn't been able to drag his gaze from the sight as he took small, shaky steps away until his back found the far wall. Realizing he could go no farther, he whimpered, his eyes blurred with tears and a painful knot formed in his throat.

From the heap of men, he saw ripped pieces of his mother's red and purple dress as they were torn from her body and tossed aside. A shriek of pain shot out and a fist-full of black hair flew straight up like confetti from the writhing mound. Somewhere in the chaos the Latino slapped his victim, cutting off her screams for a moment.

The men continued; twisting the one good thing in Xander's life to accommodate their perversions. He clenched his eyes from the sight and began shaking his head, screaming obscenities he'd only ever heard Kyle utter. Though the words were useless, they were his only weapon.

For the first time Xander was yelling at Kyle, begging to be the object of their torture. Despite this, they ignored him and only pushed harder, cut deeper, and laughed louder.

Crushed and defeated, his knees buckled and he felt himself slide down the wall into a crumpled heap.

As each of the monsters sated their lust, they turned to simply beating their victim. A vase that held fresh flowers was snatched up from the counter and brought down on his mother's skull, spilling daisies and water and blood all over the carpet.

Despite the severe beating, she somehow stayed conscious—somehow stayed alive!—and called out again and again, telling Xander to run away and hide.

But he still couldn't move.

Kyle smiled at her desperation as he pulled the knife out of the couch and spun it in his hand, grinning as he held it over his wife's heaving chest. As if suddenly remembering about the screaming child behind him, he turned to look at Xander with a smile.

"Perks of the job, eh son?"

And then the blade dropped.

And dropped.

And...

Xander found his legs then and turned and ran. He was not a hero. He was not brave. And he had failed the only person he cared about.

In a panicked sprint he collided with the wooden doors of the coat closet and fell back, too scared and determined to hide to even begin to think about the pain. Rolling to his hands and knees, Xander had crawled into the closet and dug further and further through the mounds of coats and shoes until he'd reached the vacuum cleaner at the back and hid behind it, pulling all the coats on top of him to hide from the last dying cries of his mother.

The remainder of that night was spent in hiding as he

shook in fear and, more than that, hatred of himself; listening to his stepfather and his friends as they cursed and ransacked the house looking for him. The one time someone thought to check the closet, he flattened himself and held his breath, ignoring the pain—feeling he deserved every moment of it—that came from his contortion. After a moment, a series of curses was uttered and the closet was slammed shut.

The next morning, he had been dragged—screaming and crying—from his hiding place by the police. The neighbors, it turned out, had made the call, reporting a possible break-in when they'd seen a group of men leaving the house with the television and several other valuables. In the end, it took four officers to drag the kicking and screaming boy out of the house.

Recalling the events, Xander clenched his fists and held back the tears that welled in his eyes. His grandmother had promised him long ago that Kyle was dead; that he had died and could never hurt him again.

She'd lied to him!

He looked down at the open box containing his twin revolvers. He had only ever held Yin, entertaining the dark fantasy of suicide from the solid black revolver. As he thought about it, he realized he had never even *touched* Yang. The irony of using a twin set of guns called Yin and Yang in an uneven fashion only made him feel more compelled to use them together.

And now he had a loose end to test them on.

He looked up at Marcus and Stan. They had sat silently for some time, sipping their beers and looking out the nearby porch door at a family of deer that passed through the backyard. How long had they been waiting for him to say something? He looked once more at the guns; weapons that had been his father's when he had been a warrior for the now-destroyed Odin Clan. Finally, he nodded in understanding of what had to be done.

"Kyle needs to die."

CHAPTER TWENTY-THREE
THE PLAN

WAKING UP THE NEXT NIGHT, XANDER

pulled himself out of Stan's guest room bed and looked out
the window in time to see the last few rays of daylight
disappear. He lingered on the sight a moment until the sky
had lost all traces of orange and turned to a dark purple.
Pulling himself up, he stepped out of the room and padded
down the stairs and into the kitchen, heading straight for
Stan's fridge. As he opened it, he realized that the once well-
stocked fridge was down to only three beers.

He'd known before going to bed the night before that Stan and Marcus would stay up and make plans on how to train him, but, seeing the damage that had been done to Stan's supply, he had to wonder just how long they'd been up...

"Last two are mine, in case you're wondering," Marcus called out from the living room.

He heard Stan scoff, "Like hell!"

Xander turned and walked out of the kitchen to join his friends, biting his lip for a moment when Tiger-Trepis slunk away upon seeing him enter.

"He still doesn't like me..." he sighed, turning away from the nervous-looking animal.

Stan gave him a reassuring smile, "Give him time. So how are you feeling?"

Xander frowned at the question and shrugged, "Can't you read my mind?"

"I could," Stan nodded, "but that doesn't mean I *want* to."

Marcus smirked and chugged the last of his beer, letting out a sizable belch before pointing to Xander with the empty bottle, "How bout I give it a shot: you're scared... *and* you need blood."

Xander glared, "I am not—" The two stared at him skeptically and he sighed, letting his shoulder's sag in defeat, "How'd you know?"

Marcus, still smirking, shrugged, "I can hear it: you're heart-rate is high and your stomach is growling."

Xander shook his head and plopped down on the couch next to Marcus. He recalled the previous night when, in the midst of the chaos, he too had been able to hear the three's heart beats. He tried to listen for them again, but found it difficult to focus his hearing to that degree. Turning to Stan, he raised an eyebrow, "So what do you 'see'?"

Stan frowned, "You *really* want me to?"

Xander shrugged, "Doesn't matter much now, I suppose."

Leaning back, Stan reached out with his aura and wrapped it around Xander's head, "You... dreamt of your mother again," he bit his lip and looked down as he "saw" the dream, "and you're thinking of all the ways you'd like to torture and kill Kyle."

Xander nodded as Stan's aura withdrew, "I know that both sangs and aurics have different abilities that help them to hunt and feed, but which of the two is more powerful?"

Marcus shrugged, "As much as I hate to say it, that's an unanswered question. I mean, I've seen sangs that could move so fast that an auric couldn't read a full thought before they'd been brought down."

Stan nodded. "And there are aurics with such spectacular control that a sang didn't have time to react before they'd been drained and killed," he added with a chuckle.

As the two continued their back-and-forth, Marcus smirked wide, exposing his fangs as they extended from his gums. Not about to be outdone, Stan once again reached out with his aura and snatched Marcus' beer out of his hand; beginning to spin it in midair. Though there was a substantial amount of fluid still in the bottle, the speed that he spun it with kept any from spilling out.

Xander smiled at the exchange and looked down at the coffee table, where he had left Yin and Yang the night before, only to find the spot barren.

"Where are my guns?"

Stan looked up at the question, becoming distracted, and

the bottle slowed in mid-spin, bringing the force of gravity back into effect and spilling the contents all over his shirt and pants, "Ah! Son of a bitch!" he shot Xander a glare and got up to wipe himself off.

Marcus laughed at Stan's blunder and smiled at Xander, "Thank you for that."

Xander ignored this and narrowed his eyes at Marcus, "Where are they?"

"I brought them to a friend of mine," he said with a shrug.

Xander scowled, "You *stole* my guns and brought them to somebody I don't even know? What for?"

Marcus leaned forward, stealing Stan's bottle and taking a sip before shaking his head. "Chill out! They needed to be cleaned and inspected," he looked up at Xander, who was still glaring at him. "Stan told me you don't know how to do *either*," he took another sip and stood up, "They also need to be loaded—over and over and over again—I might add. Three bullets just ain't gonna cut it, and unless you intended on killing your enemies by poking them to death, I figured you might want some ammunition. Now wipe that fucking glare off your face, or I'll teach you right here and right now how to take a punch to the teeth."

Xander bit his lip and recoiled as his extending fangs tore his lip. He took a breath to relax and thought about what Marcus had just said. *Three* bullets? He'd known that Yin had had the one round in it for all those years but…

"There were bullets in Yang?"

Marcus shook his head. "Are you kidding me? You didn't know?" Marcus shook his head, "Look, you need to learn to know your weapons inside and out. If you're on the field, you'd better know how many you got before you find yourself pulling the trigger of an empty gun!"

Xander nodded, beginning to turn red, and looked back up to Marcus, "I take it training's begun then?"

Marcus nodded, "With me it has." He sighed and looked down, his voice becoming serious, "Listen kid… when you're done, you're going to be taking to the streets with no clan to back you up! You had better be ready to defend yourself!" He shook his head and gulped the rest of the beer and set the bottle next to four others by the fireplace and let out another belch, "I've trained fledglings before. It's a long and hard process that takes several months to fall into and almost a year to complete, and Devil-man there"—he motioned to Stan, who was returning wearing a new pair of pants and a tank-top—"and myself have decided to each take a month to get as much as we can in your head. Now Stan tells me that should be plenty of time since your noggin's filled with all of your old man's combat training as well as the…" he frowned and looked at Stan.

"The awakened auric potential," Stan finished for him as he sat down on the couch beside him and patted his shoulder hard enough to send him lurching forward with each slap, "I told you to have more faith in the boy," he said, finally turning towards Xander. "You've got forces on your side. Though the voice you grew up with has been silenced, Trepis is now more a part of you than he ever was before, and soldier-boy and I believe we can drag those instincts out, as well as refocus your rage into something more…" he smiled, "… productive."

Xander looked between the two before nodding, "Alright, then!" He stood up, smiling excitedly, "Let's make me a warrior!"

CHAPTER TWENTY-FOUR
TRAINING WITH MARCUS

XANDER HAD VISITED THE PARK

often with his mother before Kyle had come into his life. He used to spend hours on the swings, watching in fascination as the sight of the earth below him quickly changed into the beautiful sky above. Later on, when his mother got married and trips to the park became less and less frequent, he started dreaming of being on the swings, looking down at Kyle as he beat his mother and then swing upward and see...

But he always woke up before it finished.

It was close to midnight, and all of the families and romantic nighttime couples had long-since left the sight of the moon and its reflection off of the waters of the lake. Unpopulated, the area seemed much larger than Xander had ever thought. The only occupants that remained being several late-season squirrels, some lazy birds…

And a twig of a man who sat by himself on one of the benches.

He had a bowl-cut that left only the very top portion of his head covered in muddy-looking hair, and his dark, sunken eyes moved too fast and too often, never focusing long enough on anything before darting to a new target. He wore a windbreaker that flapped loosely over a button-up shirt that was missing half its buttons and his pants were torn, and stained and held up by a section of rope that had been cut to fit the purpose. What Xander thought were brown leather boots he soon realized were actually the man's bare feet after he began to wiggle his toes against the frosted grass. Appropriately enough, the entire package was surrounded by a puke-green aura that lurched and spiked spasmodically.

Xander and Marcus stood in the shadow of a large oak; invisible to the man as they watched him.

"I've seen him before," Marcus whispered, his words coming out in pale plumes that hovered in the November chill, "Hangs out around the Elementary school a lot."

Xander looked at his mentor and then back at the man, wondering what sort of diseases and infections he might be carrying, "Does feeding from something like that have any effects?"

Marcus kept his eyes on their prey and shook his head, "Only the ones you want. Your system will take only what it needs from the blood; diseases, impurities, anything at all that won't help strengthen you and keep your cells from breaking down will be sent off as waste."

Xander nodded, keeping his eyes locked on his prey.

"I know that you've fed before," Marcus smirked. "Stan said you were quite a sight, too. But to act like that out of rage is something that even a human is capable of."

Xander frowned and looked up at his mentor, "You think I won't be able to do it again?"

"I think," Marcus sighed, "that you're going to have to show me what you can do."

"Now?" Xander whispered.

Marcus nodded once.

Xander wasted no time in sprinting out from behind the tree and started to close the distance. Darting around a bench that separated them, he smirked when he saw that the creep was too scared to even move! He sat there, staring out towards Xander as he closed in on him. When he was finally close enough, he lunged at the man and wrapped his arm around his prey's shoulders, holding him in place as he yanked his head up and exposed his throat. The man suddenly jerked—the instinct to survive taking over—and he grunted in confusion and tried to pull away. The motion twisted his neck as Xander went to bite down on it and when his fangs pierced through the flesh he found that it wasn't a steady flow like Marcus had explained, but an *explosion* of blood. He was startled long enough to let the geyser spray his face, but as the taste seeped past his lips, he no longer worried about what had gone wrong and brought his hungry mouth down on the wound.

The flavor was exquisite: sweet and metallic; just as he remembered from back at the mansion. He gulped, emptying his mouth as quickly as possible for the next mouthful. The blood smeared his lips and cheeks, running down his chin, and he pulled away long enough to lap up what he could before returning to the man's throat.

When he felt the current begin to slow, he instinctively bit down again and again, only to get a quick spurt and nothing more. Despite wanting more, he could sense from the rapidly dimming aura that the man had nothing left to give. He scowled and finally straightened himself, wiping the excess from his face as he turned towards Marcus, who had come out from hiding and stood in the moonlight, applauding.

"That was fucking beautiful!" Marcus cheered, still clapping, "I've never seen a fledgling jump into overdrive so smoothly; so quickly!"

Xander frowned, "Overdrive?"

Marcus nodded, "Yea. Well, that's *my* word for it, but it works. Some have referred to it as 'flitting' but…" He stopped suddenly and frowned, "Wait, you didn't know you were doing it?"

"Doing what?"

Marcus' clapping started up once more and laughed, "My star pupil in the making!" He calmed himself and approached, "Didn't you notice our friend here made no attempt to get away? Didn't even fucking *move*?"

Xander frowned, "I just thought—"

"Well you thought wrong! The truth is: you were moving so goddam fast he didn't have *time* to react; he didn't even *see* you coming at all!"

Xander shook his head, looking back at the corpse, "But he struggled!"

"Well yea," he laughed "You *were* tearing into his neck,

after all!" Marcus nodded towards the corpse, "You dropped out of overdrive right after you grabbed him. It'd be pointless to try and drink when you're moving that fast; the blood would flow like frozen molasses!" he laughed at his own joke and clapped once more. "Look, the guy was sitting by himself when suddenly there was some*thing* grabbing at him and he freaked!"

Xander nodded slowly and looked at the corpse, now twisted awkwardly on the bench. "He couldn't see me at all?"

"Nope," Marcus shook his head, "From where I was standing it looked like you'd *teleported* from the tree to him. There was nothing in between."

Xander frowned, "I was moving *that* fast?"

Marcus nodded, "Have you ever seen a humming bird's wings in flight?"

"Well, no. I guess not really."

Marcus smiled, "When a sang kicks their ass into overdrive, they're moving *faster* than those wings. And, since you're not repeating the same motion over and over, you don't even register as a blur to the human eye!"

"I see," Xander nodded and looked down at himself, taking in for the first time the gory mess his meal had left on his shirt. Marcus had mentioned before they left that he may want to wear something he didn't mind getting dirty, and he was glad that he had listened, "That was like trying to drink from a fire hose!" he said, still sneering at his ruined shirt, "Did I do something wrong?"

Marcus cocked his head and turned to look more closely at the corpse before shaking his head, "Well, you fed, so technically no. But when our friend here decided to start jerking around you missed your mark and hit his jugular. Bite like that makes quite a mess. Still, it gets the job done." He

214

crouched down and continued to scan Xander's kill, "Your vampire instincts are stronger then I would've thought."

"Instinct? If I did that on instinct alone then why bother training me at all?" Xander snorted.

Marcus looked up, "It's a matter of control. Overdrive consumes a great deal of energy. The training isn't—or it won't be—so much about teaching you *how* to do it, but *when.* I was just surprised at how well you transitioned." He shook his head, beaming, "Instinct or not, newbies aren't always so slick."

Xander smiled at the compliment.

Marcus nodded, "Just one thing left to do."

Xander watched in morbid fascination as his mentor pulled the dead man's head back and twisted it quickly to the side. The sound of its neck breaking was louder than he would have thought and he flinched. When the job was done, he knelt down to take a closer look at the body.

Marcus sighed, "C'mon, numb-nuts! You have to dump this thing! I'll be in the car. Try not to take too long."

Xander sighed, watching as Marcus disappeared from sight—finally getting an idea of what "overdrive" looked like—before staring down at the corpse and lifting it from around the waist and hoisting it over his shoulder, startled at how easy it was.

After flinging his victim into the lake, he spent a moment watching the rippling water distort the moon's reflection. Before turning back and heading to Marcus' car, he dipped his hands into the frigid water and washed his hands and face.

After nearly a week of feeding and basic combat training, Marcus once again surprised Xander by taking him on a trip into the city.

As the two walked down the sidewalk and around a bend, they collided with a pod of teenagers. Marcus stepped around the group, putting them behind him in one fluid step and leaving Xander stuck in front of the crowd. He tried to move out of their way but was caught off guard when one of them—decked out in leather and sporting a purple Mohawk—puffed out his chest and stepped forward, smirking.

"That is an excellent contact lens, dude! Very realistic!" he remarked, putting unneeded California-esque emphasis on "excellent" and "dude".

Xander frowned, not feeling the compliment, offered up a "Yea, thanks" and shoved through the group and caught up with Marcus.

"YEA? WELL, FUCK YOU TOO, ASSHOLE!" The kid shouted at Xander's back.

Frowning, Xander stuffed his hands in his pockets, "Please tell me I can feed from him."

Marcus couldn't help but smile, "Not really the social type, are you?"

Xander scoffed, "What gave it away?"

Marcus laughed and gave his shoulder a rough pat which Xander countered with his own.

Marcus flinched.

Xander noticed and smirked. There was no denying he was getting stronger; their sparring match earlier that night had proven that he was advancing more quickly than expected, and, though Xander had never been trained before, he was learning quickly. While Xander was proud of his progress, none was more surprised by it than Marcus, who had nearly left their last sparring match with a dislocated his arm.

Xander *would have* felt some pity for his mentor if it weren't for the similar treatment he'd seen in previous sparring sessions. Several days earlier, upon finished a sparring match, Xander had gone into Stan's house with a broken collarbone, two cracked ribs, several fractures in his left arm and a great deal of heavy bruising all over his body. Stan had been available to mend most of his injuries, and a bag of blood had been there to heal the last of his wounds.

"So when's the fun start?" Xander asked as they put the teens further behind them.

"Soon," Marcus answered, preoccupied, as he glanced around for any onlookers before stepping between two buildings. The space was wide enough to fit a bus into and twice as long; the far side coming to a dead-end with a dumpster. Satisfied with the location, Marcus turned towards him, "You've been feeling it lately, right?" he asked.

Taken aback by the question, Xander looked up, "Huh?"

Marcus rolled his eyes, "The strength! You've fed like it was fucking vampire-Thanksgiving night after night for nearly a week! You must feel like the goddam Hulk by now!"

Xander frowned as he thought of this. Along with the kill in the park he had been supplied with a nearly endless supply of bagged blood, and he *was* feeling stronger, "I guess."

Marcus shook his head, "Your enthusiasm inspires me." He looked up along the length of the buildings that rose up into the night sky and then back at his pupil, holding out his hand. Xander wasn't sure when he had grabbed them, but, staring into Marcus' palm he saw three rings.

Marcus clenched his hand again, concealing the jewelry and bringing Xander's attention back to him, "These were going to be a gift from Depok when your training was complete, but we both know how that ended. *I* don't know what they mean, but Stan said he'd tell you when it was his turn to train you. He does, however, want you to have them by the end of tonight. I've decided that instead of simply *giving* them to you, though, I'll use them as an incentive. So, to get them you'll have to perfect your strength and..." he tossed all three rings into the air and caught them each one at a time, "... your agility." When he had finished his speech he walked over to the dumpster and threw one of the rings underneath. Xander's jaw dropped in astonishment. "You know," Marcus teased, "I've seen the trucks actually start to tilt from all the weight when they're *this* full!" He smirked at Xander before jumping several yards straight up to the first of a series of fire escape platforms and looking back down at him, "You can get started with that project before a rat makes off with it." With that he turned and launched himself across the gap between the two buildings, landing on the next fire escape platform and climbing to the one above it.

Xander forced his attention away from his mentor despite the awe of the superhuman spectacle.

The dumpster was old—not very, but old enough to have accumulated rust and other forms of nastiness. He was relatively sure working up the nerve to actually *touch* the dumpster was a test in and of itself. He looked again to the fire escapes, where Marcus continued to leap impossible distances only to pause and do it again. When his mentor caught him peeking he glared.

"Don't waste time watching me, kid. You got a present to open!"

Xander frowned and turned towards the dumpster once again. Closing his eyes and pretending it wasn't what he knew it was, he grabbed it by the bottom corner and pulled up as hard as he could.

Nothing happened.

He put his mind into focus, pushing himself as he had all those times he had gone into overdrive. His muscles throbbed and he heard the front end of the dumpster begin to creak as it lifted off the ground. But it still wasn't enough.

"Better hurry up, Stryker!" Marcus shouted down, "I'm going to start the second task without you, and it's *timed!*"

Xander sighed in frustration. He knew that Marcus would make him repeat the process over and over; even if the sun came up—he was sure that his mentor would turn the threat of sunlight into a lesson of its own. He struggled once more with trying to lift the obstacle and finally released it, the front end crashing down loudly.

He groaned in disgust and shook his head, "Gross" he muttered as he pulled back his fist and drove it into the side of the dumpster, which indented deeply, leaving a somewhat well-formed outline of his fist. Looking at the damage he'd inflicted he smiled, hatching an idea, and pulled his arm back and threw his fist again and again into the dent until it tore open and formed a hole the size of his head. The side of a garbage bag rolled and tried to spill out but got stuck and spewed some of its contents at his feet. He felt himself wretch and then composed himself, gripping the corners of the hole and pulling it open, widening it until he could crawl inside. Completely submerged in filth, he dug blindly downward to the bottom and began to repeat the punch-and-tear process until he'd revealed the ring on the pavement below. Grabbing his prize and sliding it onto his finger, he hurried in pulling himself out and began wiping away the grime.

Marcus' familiar applause sounded and he looked up at his mentor, who was sitting—feet dangling—on the edge of the building on the left, "You know that Stan will never let you into his house looking and smelling like that!" he laughed.

Xander considered screaming some obscenity up at him, but figured it would only lead to further torment, "Just tell me what the next task is!"

Marcus kicked out his legs and clucked his tongue as he surveyed the fire escapes he'd just scaled before answering: "Task two: a test of speed, reflexes, and observation under pressure. You saw how I got up here and now all you have to do is the same thing. There are thirty-eight platforms between these two buildings, and each one has something on it resembling a ring. I'm going to give you a break and give you ten seconds to retrieve everything and put all the decoys in this:" he held up a coffee can. "Your final prize will be waiting beside it." He grinned as he rolled the final ring between his fingers, "It's really too nice to be tossing under dumpsters and leaving on rusted fire escapes."

Xander frowned, "But how do I jump like that?"

"It's just like overdrive, kid," Marcus answered, "Just *do* it."

Xander nodded and paced for several moments before signaling that he was ready to begin.

Marcus waved a stopwatch, "I press this and you start, it will be by the coffee can when you're done. I'll let you stop it yourself to ensure accuracy." He held his arm up.

Xander held his breath.

The beep of the watch sounded and Xander jumped into

overdrive and went to jump to the first platform and cleared several feet of air before landing on the alley floor again. He frowned, realizing the clock was ticking and he'd just screwed up. Desperate to make up for lost time, he ran at the opposite wall and jumped, pushing off of it with his right foot and using the momentum to carry him to the first platform where he found a washer. This he snagged and used his arms to throw himself over the railing to the next fire escape platform: a marble?

After the third jump to the next platform—a cheap, vending machine ring—he realized that he was getting the hang of it. His landing at the next platform was shaky and he teetered and began to fall. Regaining his composure at the last moment, he scanned and finally found the second ring! He took the prize, not stopping to admire it before sliding it onto his left middle finger and next to the one from the dumpster.

He continued to collect the fakes, knowing well that Marcus would make him do the whole thing over again if he didn't. When, at last, he reached the roof he found Marcus, seemingly frozen in time. Suppressing the urge to use the opportunity to his advantage and pop his mentor a much needed punch to the face, he dropped the fake rings—or at least released them and let them hang in midair in a super-slowed descent—into the coffee can and scooped up the last of the rings. With the task completed, he snatched the stopwatch from Marcus' hand and stopped the timer; dropping out of overdrive as he did.

The digital reader paused at 13.27 seconds...

Xander's shoulders slumped as Marcus stood up and read it, nodding his head, "Good job."

Xander sighed and handed the stopwatch back to him, "Good job? But you said *ten* seconds!"

Marcus shrugged, "For a first timer you did just fine."
He smirked, "Though you *will* be punished for lagging."

Xander frowned, suddenly feeling weak and exhausted,
"How?"

Marcus pointed off towards the left, "Stan lives in that
direction."

Xander glared at him, "I have to *walk* home?"

Marcus sighed and shook his head, "You will *not* walk!
You will *jump* from rooftop to rooftop until you're out of the
city, then you'll finish the trip in overdrive." He gave him a
smirk then, "By the way, that lagging sensation you're feeling
is normal; comes from being in overdrive for so long, so I
suggest you don't lag this time". With that he turned and
walked towards and over the edge of the roof, dropping the
full distance before landing on his feet. Brushing himself off,
he looked up towards the rooftop, "I'll have a meal waiting
for you when you get there. And be sure to hose yourself off
before you come in!" With that he turned and headed
towards his car.

Xander took a moment to catch his breath, shaking his
head and cursing Marcus' name, before he looked down for
the first time to admire the rings. The first bore an intricate
inlay design that traveled around its length while the second
had a strange symbol etched onto one side. The last—a small,
silver band with a tiny ruby on top—he had trouble fitting on
his pinky and he finally resorted to licking the length of his
finger before successfully sliding it on all the way. Staring at
them all he marveled at how, though they were each different
and seemed in no way related to the others, they seemed
appropriate together.

He sighed, dragging his eyes away from his prizes, and
looked off in the direction that Marcus had pointed him in

and cautiously stepped up to the edge of the rooftop, mentally gauging the distance between his and the neighboring building. Before taking the first leap, he looked once more at his left hand and his newest treasures.

CHAPTER TWENTY-FIVE
NO TAG-BACKS/A LOVER SCORNED

IT HAD BEEN A LITTLE MORE THAN

two weeks' worth of searching, and Erika had finally tracked down Brad's killer. It had taken a great deal of planning and snooping around, and she had been forced to call in a few favors from a few of her closer friends, but the time had finally come that she would have her revenge.

Despite all her efforts, she knew little more about her target beside the fact that he was driving a beat-up Subaru through the city at two-in-the-morning...

… and that he was about to die!

All the vengeance that had been welling up within her leapt through her throat at that moment and stuck, choking her up and bringing tears to her eyes.

"I love you, Brad," she whispered as she watched her prey drive by.

She had chosen an all-black outfit for the task—wearing loose-fitting sweats to keep away the cold and allow her to move freely. While it wasn't very stylish, it was effective. Coupled with the fanny-pack at her waist, she looked like nothing more than a late-night jogger.

When she was certain it was safe to do so, she allowed her body to slip into the next phase of motion, and rocketed like a bullet after her target. She rarely had found a use for flitting—an ability that, until then, she'd seen as unneeded for a modern-day vampire—but, now that it was about to help her get her revenge, it meant the world to her. As she followed after her target, she circled once around the bastard's piece-of-shit car as it sat—seemingly still—in the middle of the street.

Once in position, she reached down, tugging the zipper of her pack and growling as it snagged. Her aggravation grew and she yanked it harder, tearing the fabric and finally retrieving her stolen Glock.

A year-or-so back, an asshole sporting a hard-on had decided to try and take her by force. At first, it had been difficult to discern the gun from his prick, so she had torn both free from their respective grips, winning two prizes at once and walking away as the man dropped to the ground behind her and screamed over his broken fingers and lost manhood. The penis she'd discarded soon after in a garbage bin, but the gun was too sleek and sexy to toss.

Pleased with her position, Erika aimed carefully—taking her time and savoring the moment—and pulled the trigger before returning to normal speed. The bullet, from her perspective, went from a slow-moving joke to an untraceable blur that blew out the front passenger-side tire and sent a chunk of black, stinking rubber flying down the street. No longer balanced, the car fell at an awkward angle and screeched loudly, throwing sparks all over the road.

Erika watched the delicious chaos for a moment before flitting once again—watching as the car froze in mid-swerve—in order to take her second shot and returning to normal again at a safe distance. The second bullet tore the opposite tire to hell and dropped the front-end of the car and sent it skidding until it collided with a nearby light post.

She smirked, playing with her grip on the gun's handle. She *could've* simply put a bullet in her target's head…

… but then he'd never get to see his killer's face.

Smiling triumphantly for a moment, Erika leveled the gun at her target as he tore a hole in the roof and climbed out through his home-made sunroof. The murderer—"Marcus" Brad had called him—looked up at her and, seeing the gun, disappeared in a blur just as she squeezed the trigger. A moment later he appeared a short distance away as the bullet flew harmlessly over the roof of the car.

Marcus heaved from the sudden jump in and out of overdrive. Like training the kid wasn't exhausting enough, now he had to deal with some psychopathic rogue?

Realizing that his clan-issued Berretta was still in the car, he tore the passenger-side door off its hinges and flung it at the shooter to throw them off while he fetched it from the glove-box. The gun—a nine-millimeter M9—had yet to let him down in a time of need and he hoped that this occasion wouldn't be an exception.

Erika hoisted herself from the ground after jumping clear of a flying door and caught sight of the asshole as he drew his own weapon and pulled the trigger repeatedly. Once again forced to flit out of range, Erika easily evaded the shots and returned to normal speed several yards away and returned fire. Three shots were fired and another furious pull of the trigger was met with...

Nothing?

Shit!

She'd been carrying a piece for more than a year only to have it not be fully loaded?

She had convinced herself that her love for Brad would carry the bullets through the asshole's head before a reload had been necessary. She growled and cursed her overly poetic mind and the falsities of romantic mysticism as she tossed the weapon aside and charged at him; her fangs fully-extended.

At least she'd been smart enough to establish some backup if the situation turned ugly.

"Fuck!"

Marcus cursed and dove to the left, dodging the psycho bitch-rogue and landing painfully on his already-sore shoulder and rolling clumsily to his feet. He listened as his gun hit the pavement and skidded across to the other lane.

The bitch was fast, he'd give her that much, but she was sloppy. Either that or she had never been in a fight before. He watched as she stumbled, trying to get a fresh grip on the ground to try and charge at him again.

She'd missed, but her target had hurt himself in the process of avoiding her. She couldn't be sure how badly, but his left shoulder was sagged and he was clutching it as he glared, awaiting her next attack.

He moved into a wide stance and narrowed his eyes at her. She knew little of fighting, but Erika had watched enough crappy interpretive dance routines to know when somebody was preparing to jump without knowing at that moment what direction it was going to be in.

He was *expecting* her to charge again.

She snarled and, instead, pushed off the ground—springing into the air like a cat and coming down hard on the fucker as he tried to compensate for a faulty strategy. With revenge so close at hand, Erika thought of Brad. She thought of his face and how he'd made her feel just with a simple stare. The warmth that she used to feel when he touched her swelled under her skin and turned to rage as she spotted Brad's murderer. Feeling her fangs begin to extend, she hissed and swung her right hand. The attack caught him in his throat and reminded her how hungry she was to both see and taste his blood.

"Dammit!" Jurek rubbed his arms with his palms. The network of fibers that made up the fish-net top he wore stretched and relaxed with each rough pass, "It's fuckin' cold out here!"

Derryl shook his head and glared, "Did you honestly expect that… thing you're wearing to keep you warm?" his voice rang out harshly as he shoved his hands into the pockets of his fur coat. "Seriously, you're out of your mind! At least Erika had the mind to wear something warm."

Jurek scoffed and shook his head in disbelief, "You're *glad* that she's all covered up? Fag!"

The two grew silent, as they often did when Derryl's sexuality came up. They shifted, looking away from one-another and peering over the edge of the rooftop Erika had asked them to wait on. Another breeze kicked up Derryl's coat tails and Jurek shivered and swore again.

"I mean, maybe we don't even need to be here! Huh? She's kicking the shit outa that blood-sucking bastard down there! What the hell does she need us for?!"

"We're here in case something goes wrong. Yes, she's got the situation handled, but things can go awry and she's asked us to wait here for her in case they do."

"*You're* here because you were best friends with Brad and are just as interested in seeing the leech dead!" Jurek spat, not turning away from the battle in the street.

"If it's so miserable for you to help out"—Derryl shot a glare at his companion and grinned as a hard shudder crawled up his spine—"then get lost!"

Another silent moment was shared.

Jurek looked up at his friend, still slightly shaken, and heaved out a foggy sigh. "Just said we didn't *need* to be here," he mumbled, "Didn't say anything 'bout leaving."

Marcus could feel his pulse in the spot the rogue had hit him, and it felt like the throbbing might wrap around his throat and choke him.

Looking up at her, he bared his fangs and hissed. She clearly wanted a fight, and he wasn't about to lie there, gasping for breath while the bitch got her way. He smiled with satisfaction as she recoiled and he jumped up, catching her at the waist with a hard kick and bringing her crashing down to the street. He pulled his fist up and brought it down to where her head had been a millisecond earlier.

The fucker was trained!

Brad's killer wasn't some art thief or bitter rival come to get some trophy. He was a fucking professional!

She saw his fist coming and rolled her neck to the side at the last moment, screaming in surprise as the force chipped the road and sent bits of it into her face. If she lived through this, there'd be scars. She shook her head, ridding herself of the thought. It would be worth it. Beauty had died in Brad's bedroom…

It was time for the beast!

The fury in her grew and her knee pulled up instinctively, bringing it squarely into his chest and forcing bloody breath from his lungs. He roared out in animalistic fury and jumped to his feet, gulping in air and stomping down.

Rolling free, Erika did a back-handspring—recalling her

time spent in gymnastics—to her feet and charged him again. The hunger was eating away at her. Never before had she put so much effort into anything and her body was beginning to argue with her demands. Though it felt like they'd been fighting for hours, barely a minute had passed.

She gritted her teeth and breathed heavily; this only meant she was putting her all into killing him.

Marcus had been holding back, thinking that the bitch might tire herself out and then simply high-tail it and he'd have a story to tell the kid as a lesson in being prepared, but there seemed to be little hope in her wising up anytime soon.

Still, she did look familiar; old girlfriend?

She started throwing punches at him with both hands in a fashion that made Marcus think that maybe she'd watched too many Kung Fu movies. They were easily evaded, but the few that landed did more-than enough damage. A fist slid by his defenses and he felt a sharp pain in his right arm as something broke.

Block. Block.

Broken collarbone.

Block.

Torn lip.

Block. Block. Block.

The pain caught up on him and he stumbled and soon all of the attacks began landing. His worn-out body slipped out of overdrive and he felt the individual punches turn into an unbearable force that simply pushed down harder and harder. He couldn't see her arms anymore, just a woman standing over him and blurs extending from her shoulders.

Her face was so damn familiar!

He stared, trying to ignore the pain of a thousand simultaneous punches. It was beyond even trying to block them anymore; at her speed it would have been trying to stop a bus with a spit bubble.

She *was* pretty, he had to admit it, but more hippy-esque then he was usually attracted to.

Hippy?

Brad!

He frowned and felt that his nose had broken and wondered how many punches ago that had been.

He frowned and tried to ball up to protect his organs. He had done his job! A simple mission! He didn't want to think of Brad being killed by one of the others of the clan… so he had taken it. And now his mission's angry girlfriend was taking her revenge.

He stared up again at her as tears streamed down her face, her fists still pounding him with inhuman speed. Almost at once he felt several of his ribs break and his eyesight dimmed. As he questioned whether or not he felt remorse for taking the Brad-job, Marcus saw the shaggy black hair and the fierce red eye rushing towards them.

Remembering how exhausted he'd felt after his training in overdrive, Xander had decided to save some energy and rest for a moment.

There was still a long distance to be traveled and he was thinking of moving on when he heard gunshots and a crash several blocks over. Curious, he turned away from the path to Stan's house and instead followed the sounds.

At first he saw nothing; just some wrecked car that had gotten itself wrapped around a streetlight. As he continued to stare, however, there was a sudden shimmer near the wreck; a shimmer that he recognized as the movement of a vampire in overdrive. He frowned, looking back at the totaled car and suddenly realized that it was *Marcus'*.

Concern rising, he watched more intently; the shimmering blur slowly falling into focus.

Marcus' body appeared on the street and began morphing in front of his eyes into a broken and bloodied heap. After a second another individual shimmered into view: a woman with a dark yellow aura—her arms moving in a blur as she dealt more and more damage to his mentor. As he watched, Xander saw Marcus' usually bright and lively blue aura start to dwindle and dim.

Scanning the streets for anything he could use to turn the tides of the fight, he saw a discarded handgun. Though he wasn't sure whose it was, it mattered little at the moment and he jumped from the rooftop and hurried to retrieve it.

"Who the hell is that?!" Jurek demanded, thrusting a long finger in the direction of a figure that dropped down from a shop across the street.

Derryl shook his head. "He's not with us," he said as his feet slowly lifted off the rooftop, "And that can mean only one thing!"

"This mean we finally get to see some action?" Jurek asked, suddenly seeming unbothered by the cold.

The fur-clad auric didn't respond as he flew off the roof like a human cannonball and hurtled towards the scene.

Jurek's smiling face tightened as he groaned in pain, his jaw twitching and snapping forward. His body seized, his joints tightening as his muscles bulged under his skin and he felt himself sway unsteadily for a moment as his six-foot frame became a nearly eight-foot one. A hot wave swept over him and he grinned, letting out an excited chuckle, as a patch of nearby ice melted and evaporated from his body heat. The all-too-familiar sensation of his bones breaking and reshaping cut his laughter off and he threw his head back and howled in both pain and exhilaration.

It hurt like a motherfucker, but something in the release from the filthy human form compensated for it.

Xander ran towards his mentor and the female vampire attacking him; fumbling with the retrieved handgun. When he was sure that his grip on the weapon was firm enough he took aim.

Only to have it ripped from his hands by a bright purple aura.

The young vampire was bold, Derryl noted, but he was also very, *very* clueless.

Grinning, he brought the stolen Beretta closer to himself, disassembling the weapon as he did until all the separate pieces floating in his aura resembled a metallic grape Jell-O mold. Finally, with the gun rendered useless, Derryl pulled his aura back into himself and let the various components fall to the street.

Jurek's energy signature grew stronger as he jumped down from the roof and his heavy steps approached from behind.

The auric that had taken the gun *had* caught Xander off guard, but it was the approaching monstrosity that *scared* him! He stared, slack-jawed, as the beast—looking like an eight-foot tall, bipedal pit bull with a steroid problem—stopped beside the smirking auric and looked Xander over. Its aura, the same color as October leaves, writhed around its bulking form like a nest of snakes, rolling out with each heavy breath. It grunted, looking towards the auric beside him—heavy clouds of breath wafting from its gaping jaws.

Its companion shrugged, pulling his hands from the pockets of his long, brown fur coat and pinching the end of his chin as he looked at Xander for a long, silent moment. In the distance, the sound of Marcus' beating continued, and Xander frowned and looked away long enough to determine that his mentor wouldn't last much longer.

"He's a fledgling," the auric said in a silky, feminine voice; the tone ringing as though he was analyzing a painting in a museum. He stared a bit longer before shooting a glance to Marcus and nodded slowly, "He intends to save the murderer."

The monster let loose a rumbling cackle that sounded like a demonic hyena and curled its lips back, displaying its horrifying array of teeth.

A shudder seized Xander as a deep instinct overtook him and his fangs extended like daggers and an angry hiss shot from his throat.

The blows had begun to land less frequently as the bitch-rogue tired. Despite this, Marcus' defenses were too weakened and he was sure even a human could take him on in the state he was in.

Xander's sudden arrival seemed both a blessing and a curse, though the familiar growing odor didn't bode well.

Even through a broken nose he recognized *that* smell. Therion!

His attacker let out a sob as her arms came into focus, her face twisted in a bizarre combination of rage and what appeared to be sorrow, "WHY WON'T YOU DIE?" she demanded, tears rolling down her cheeks.

Her growing emotion made her sloppy, and her next swing came into view.

Marcus, seeing his chance, deflected the blow with his good arm and grabbed her wrist and pulled her towards him as he threw his bruised and broken face forward in a head-butt. A flash of pain erupted from the impact and as the bitch stumbled back, clutching her lower jaw, Marcus rolled to his side and spit a mouthful of blood onto the street.

If he survived this, he was going to drain the first thing with a pulse he came across.

Both Xander and the two mythos turned their attentions to the sudden cries of Marcus' attacker as she staggered back.

Xander watched his mentor as he pulled himself up on unsteady legs, his right arm dangling like a piece of dead meat. He started to take a step towards his mentor but stopped and watched in horrified astonishment as the monster shot forward—rocketing itself on all fours—and crashed into the still staggering older vampire.

Marcus had barely enough time to celebrate his freedom and find his center of gravity before the reeking therion crashed into him. Forcing him back a ways, the two slammed with an explosive force into the brick foundation of a nearby building, sending chunks of the structure raining down on them. Razor-sharp teeth embedded in eager jaws snapped inches from his face and he grabbed at its throat with his good arm and used what strength he had to hold it back.

The therion reared back and swung a massive, clawed hand into his dislocated shoulder, sending a sharp pain shooting throughout his torso. With his grip weakened, the therion grinned hideously and lifted him off his feet, holding his arms at his sides.

Marcus' vision blurred as his foe continued to keep a firm grip on his bad arm. Determined to put some distance between him and the ugly beast, he pulled both legs up and drove them forward into its chest, sending it hurling back.

Xander rushed towards Marcus, determined to do whatever he could to get the giant beast off of him. He'd barely cleared a quarter of the distance before a transparent, shimmering-purple wall appeared in front of him. He recoiled and turned to face the source: the still-grinning auric.

Scowling, he took one quick look in his mentor's direction before squaring off against his opponent as he'd been shown.

"Cute trick," he glared.

"You like that?" the auric asked, his face turning hard, "I've got plenty more where that came from!"

Before he was even finished talking, the wall of energy shot forward and curled around Xander, snaring him. A startled cry escaped him as the auric net whipped him and he was hurled down the street, skipping several times before skidding to a stop nearly half-a-block away.

Battered and disoriented, he barely had time to recognize that the hellish trip down the street had ended before his vision went purple again and he was lifted, struggling, into the air. Without warning, the aura he was trapped within separated into four parts—one holding him at each limb—that began to pull in opposite directions. The pain was so sudden and intense that Xander's gaping mouth didn't have the time to scream.

Finally free of the therion's grip, Marcus dropped to his knees. Struggling to get to his still-shaky feet, he began to scan the area for Xander. Though his skirmish with the beast had been a brief one, he knew all too well the trouble that even a stolen second could bring…

And the kid wasn't nearly ready for this kind of action yet!

He was surprised to find his pupil floating in the air a short distance above the fruity-looking auric vampire. Seeing the pained look on Xander's face, he could tell that he only had a short time before he lost him.

Some of the more minor injuries he had sustained from the bitch-rogue's beating were starting to heal—some of the lesser fractures even beginning to knit and reform. Taking this as a sign that he wasn't out of the fight just yet he grabbed several large chunks of the wall he'd been smashed through and began heaving them at Xander's attacker with all the strength he could gather.

The auric bastard was sure taking his time in killing Xander!

He let out a breathless groan as he felt something in his shoulder start to tear; hot tears running down his face and his groan of agony extending into a croak.

Then, as suddenly as it had started, he was plummeted to the street below where he crashed painfully. He heaved, taking in as much air as he could, hoping the cold might soothe at least some of the burning pain inside of him. Curling up, he pressed his forehead to the street until the pain finally subsided to something bearable. With his curiosity as to why he had been spared outweighing his desire to remain balled up on the chilled concrete he glanced up at his would-be killer.

The once calm and composed auric who had, moments ago, been gleefully torturing him now clutched at the side of his bloodied head and cursed. His purple aura—now a darker, angrier shade—whipped about and tore a newspaper dispenser from the sidewalk as the still-forked tendrils slowly recessed back into his chest.

Positive that his survival had something to do with Marcus, Xander counted his blessings and got to his feet. The scene on the street had become a chaotic one; both sides injured in some form or another—though he was sure that his mentor was still in the worst condition amongst them.

Marcus looked at him from the distance—his eyes scanning his body for any sign of injury—and Xander nodded back that he was alright. The gesture seemed to take some weight off his mentor's shoulders and he began to approach.

Stryker was alright, and, for the time being, that was what mattered most. Satisfied, Marcus paused in mid-step to glance in the direction of the injured therion. The beast was beginning to change back to its human form to heal the broken ribs Marcus had given it; though, judging from the way it twisted in agony, clutching its chest, it still had a ways to go before it was fully healed.

"Teach you to fuck with me!" Marcus said in its direction.

The auric he'd clobbered with the brick continued to bitch and moan, gripping his injured head and Marcus smiled at the sight.

He was only a few yards from Xander when an angry shriek shot out and the bitch-rogue dropped out of overdrive right in front of him. Marcus' eyes went wide as he was swept off his feet and sent into a dizzying flip that landed him on his right side. A hurricane of pain consumed him and he cursed between clenched teeth.

The woman from before had come out of nowhere,

appearing in front of Marcus and kicking his feet out from under him.

Before Xander had a chance to react, the woman turned to face him. Though there was caked blood under her nose and around her eyes from Marcus' head-butt, it was the shiny, recently-shed blood that decorated her lips that caught his attention.

And then he noticed her aura: brighter, more vibrant than before! He sneered, infuriated. She'd run off somewhere to feed and rejuvenate while her backup kept them busy.

"Bitch!"

"Did you come to help *that*?" she growled, ignoring his insult and pointing back at Marcus.

Xander stood, his knees shaking. He'd seen what the vampire could do, and he couldn't help but feel that he wasn't ready to face off against a real threat just yet. Somewhere over the vampire's shoulder the monster—who had since turned back into a man—rose to his feet and began a purposeful stride to join them, kicking Marcus in the face as he passed.

"Teach you to fuck with *me*!" he growled.

The injured auric narrowed his eyes at the fallen Marcus and smirked; throwing his aura out and ensnaring him. For a moment nothing happened, then the purple energy signature started pulsing and Xander saw Marcus' own aura dim as his life force was consumed.

"GET THE FUCK OFF HIM!" Xander screamed, taking a step forward only to be knocked to the ground by a swift slap delivered by the woman.

"This doesn't concern you, kid," she said softly, looking down at him, "You could walk away right now and no one would stop you."

Xander glared up at the woman, who turned her attention to the auric. He followed her gaze and saw that the once-injured vampire was healing himself with the stolen energy. The woman smiled as she watched, licking her blood-smeared lips.

"Kill him," she whispered, "And make it hurt… a lot!"

As soon as the words were past her lips Marcus cried out in agony, curling himself tightly into a ball and hugging his head between clenched fists. The woman smiled at the sight and sound of Marcus dying and stepped in for a closer look. Before Xander could consider trying to help, the beast-man let out a deep growl as a warning.

C'mon, Xander! Fight! Stan's voice shouted in his mind.

Xander shook his head, confused by the sudden intrusion.

You're a Stryker, dammit! The son of one of the most powerful auric vampires I have ever met! You have the instincts! You have the desire! USE THEM!! The roar of his friend's voice was so intense that Xander clenched his eyes against it.

As the echo in his head died down the agonized sounds of Marcus dying once again rose and rang in his ears and he tightened his jaw. He was vaguely aware of the familiar hot rage as it coiled around him and he opened his eyes, watching as the red bolt of his aura snaked out from his chest.

Marcus' screams stopped suddenly as the auric turned his attentions to Xander; jaw gaping at the display.

"Why in the hell did you stop?" the woman demanded.

The auric only had enough time to point before Xander's aura whipped out like a scarlet whirlwind, throwing the looming monster-man and the woman into the air. The auric, though startled, had been given enough of a warning and stood his ground, his purple aura wrapped around him and protecting him from the attack. Xander locked eyes with him and their auras shot at one another, colliding in a violent explosion of neon-colored energy.

Marcus groaned.

There was no getting up; no use in even trying.

Something had sparked in the Stryker boy and his powers had saved them both. However, as he painstakingly rolled to his side to see what was happening, he saw that they weren't in the clear just yet.

To the naked eye, it appeared that Xander and the fruity auric were simply locked in a vicious stare-off, but he knew better. He'd been around enough aurics to know when a great deal of psychic energy was being pushed out, and though he couldn't see them, he was sure their auras were clashing like medieval swords.

Despite the chill of the season, the air around them began to grow warm and the faint crackle of excess static grew louder. A pile of newspapers that had spilled from the destroyed dispenser whipped about them in an invisible hurricane. Focusing on his pupil, he could see that Xander was beginning to shiver and sweat from the exertion and Marcus frowned, wondering how much more he had in him.

In the distance, staying out of range of the auric stand-off, the bitch-rogue and the therion stood, waiting out the two's battle. Marcus didn't need to guess what for; their companion was clearly more experienced and controlled. Though he knew that with a bit of time and training Xander would have easily wiped the floor with the fruity auric, there was no doubt who would win then and there.

Marcus took in a lungful of static-charged air, finding the task painfully arduous. It wouldn't be long before they were *both* dead…

Fat, blinding beads of stinging sweat fell into Xander's eyes and he felt his aura as it was forced back further; his focus wavering. The auric seemed unaffected by the effort he was exerting in the attacks, and Xander clenched his fists, enraged not only by the situation but by his apparent weakness.

This is what they're so excited about? Xander thought to himself as his aura was deflected and forced away once again. *This is their fucking legacy?*

The overwhelming sensation of weakness broke what little focus he had left and his enemy's aura shot at him and ensnared him, constricting around his entire body and once again crushing the air from his lungs. Trapped and suffocating, Xander was powerless as his captor approached, stepping with the confident stride of a homicidal super-model.

"'Legacy'," the auric scoffed, "*You're* supposed to be something special?" He stopped in front of Xander and eyed him skeptically.

There was no air for Xander to speak with, and his eyes fluttered as his suffocation continued.

In the distance Marcus groaned in protest as he tried to crawl forward, only to be kicked back again by the monster-man.

The auric frowned and turned, his aura flaring the color of a ripe bruise, "Your time will come soon enough, murderer! But until then you get to watch your fledgling die."

The woman seemed to enjoy the pained expression on Marcus' face from this and beamed. The auric nodded, turning back to Xander and tightening his hold, making him flinch.

"What do you say, Xander?" the auric taunted, "Are you ready to die *tonight*?"

The purple aura continued to grow tighter and silent cries of agony hiccupped from Xander's throat. Over the auric's shoulder, the blurred outlines of the woman and the monster-man grew larger with their approach.

"You and Jurek can do what you want with the boy," the woman's voice rang out, "But Brad's killer is mine!"

Xander didn't fully understand what the words meant as his mind glazed over from the lack of oxygen, but he knew that they weren't good for him or for Marcus. His vision continued to fade, distorting shapes and shades until everything melted into a shadowed grey.

And then all hell broke loose...

CHAPTER TWENTY-SIX
STAN'S WRATH

THE EYES WERE AS BIG AS PICKUP

trucks and blue like jewels. They appeared, opening from behind hidden lids in the sky and piercing through Xander's grogginess with sudden awareness. Though they appeared soft and caring, there was a wealth of power and rage that shone behind them.

As his vision began to focus once again, Xander smiled knowingly.

"Stan..." he forced the name out.

"What did he say?" the woman asked, surprised that he wasn't already dead.

The auric frowned and turned to face in the direction that Xander was facing. For a moment he appeared to see nothing, then the eyes in the sky narrowed and focused on him, "WHAT THE FUCK?" he cried out, stepping away and releasing his hold.

Finally free, Xander inhaled deeply, swallowing breath after breath in an attempt to satisfy his starved lungs.

The woman and the monster-man stared in bewilderment in the direction their companion was retreating from, but were blind to the shiny blue eyes as they drifted and touched down on the street in the distance and shimmered. As the image continued to waver a figure stepped from behind them and approached, hidden in the distant shadows. The form writhed and twisted as it moved—a sound like snapping bones echoing down the dead-silent street.

A streetlight flickered and dimmed as the liquid-shadow figure passed and, when the last of the dying bulb's light had faded, it raised its arm and pointed forward towards them, sending a wave of darkness down the street in their direction; snuffing out all light in its path. The curtain of blackness crept closer, coating the walls of the buildings on either side as it continued its path down the street; everything it touched turning empty and dark. The still-retreating auric whimpered as his companions, now seeing the approaching darkness, cursed and turned to retreat as well.

Xander cried out as Marcus, unable to move, disappeared into the expanding blackness, followed quickly by their retreating enemies and then, finally, himself.

For a long time there was no sound, just the darkness and the others, looking equally as stunned and afraid. Then, slowly at first, elements of the street's prior scenery appeared; streetlights, though still without illumination, appeared on either side of them as well as a fire hydrant and the tattered and torn newspaper dispenser that had been ripped from the ground. Deeper into the darkness Xander could see the bent and twisted streetlight with Marcus' mangled car still wrapped around it.

Beyond this, the blackness consumed the rest of the world.

In the distance, where the figure had been standing, the darkness shimmered and Stan appeared. His dirty-blonde hair waved fluidly and his blue eyes shone as the brightest source of light in his twisted shadow-world. Xander wasn't surprised that he was wearing all black, an element that made him blend and disappear into the scenery; his body becoming a part of everything around them.

The woman looked at him and scowled before turning her attention to Marcus, who was still curled up and breathing heavily on the ground. After studying her target a moment longer, she signaled to the others and motioned to Stan.

"Deal with that!" she ordered.

A wide, toothy grin swept over the beast-man's face as his body erupted once again into the towering monstrosity and let out an angry howl. The sound, though loud and intimidating to Xander, seemed drowned and compressed; an effect of Stan's manipulations, no doubt. As the beast took a step towards him the darkness shimmered and Stan's glowing eyes widened. The beast lunged forward then as a series of purple lightning bolts erupted from the auric's chest and lifted him off the ground, hurling him at Stan like an angry, violet storm.

Before Xander had a chance to leap to his trainer's side the scene before him froze and an infinite number of shining blue eyes opened up all around them, completely covering the strange shadow-world that Stan had cast upon them. This addition caught not only the woman off guard—causing her to step slowly away from Marcus and gaze about in awe—but the attacking mythos as well.

Still in mid-lunge, the monster suddenly reverted to his human form and he stopped and stared at his hands in disbelief, "H-how...?"

The auric, too caught up in his own attack to notice his comrade's predicament, made it slightly closer before his aura crackled and sparked, disappearing from under him and sending him crashing to the ground with a loud grunt.

The woman hissed, clearly fed up with the interference, and disappeared from Xander's sight as she jumped into overdrive, suddenly appearing in front of Stan and lunging at him.

As Xander watched, Marcus' totaled car—a short distance away from Stan—exploded into fragments ranging in size from as small as a bolt to as large as a tire. The pieces hovered in place, the three enemies staring in confused fascination at the eerie spectacle. Then, as Stan took a casual step aside, the car's components began to fly at them.

The beast-man turned to run only to have his left arm ripped from his shoulder by a hubcap. A pained cry shot out as more debris began to take him apart piece-by-piece. The auric, who had fallen back in surprise, shrieked before he was crushed under his own share of car parts.

As the carnage continued, Xander made his way towards a stunned Marcus.

"My... my car..." he stammered.

Xander nodded, refusing to look away from the scene, "Did… did you know he could do this?" he asked.

Marcus shook his head, though Xander wasn't sure if it was in response to his question or further disbelief of what they were witnessing.

The two watched as the woman kept her composure against the onslaught, facing off against Stan the whole time.

"Brad"—though the words were whispered they rang out like church bells in the shadow world—"I'm coming."

And then the whirlwind closed in and took her.

She didn't scream or cry out, and after several seconds of bitter silence the swirling car parts and severed limbs fell to the ground and faded into the blackness, becoming a part of the nothingness.

As soon as the last traces of car and corpses were gone, the darkness recessed. The once-dead streetlights came back to life one-by-one and the buildings' lights reappeared a moment before they came into view. As the last of the void was absorbed into Stan, the bent and beaten streetlight emerged—whole and new-looking—shining its light down on Marcus' fully restored car.

Xander stared at it for a moment and then turned to face Marcus only to be further shocked as his mentor rose, unhurt, to his feet, "But… how?" He looked back at Stan, who had begun to walk towards them.

Marcus grinned and took a deep, full breath and stretched his right arm, "Our man Stan: always full of surprises!" He laughed triumphantly and stared at his car for a moment, "Have no idea how you did that, though," he circled the Subaru, kicking a tire and shaking his head.

Stan stopped in front of Xander, his expression tainted by his obvious exhaustion. No words were spoken for a short while as the two studied one another. Though Xander had always been aware of his friend's powers, he'd never before witnessed the *extent* of his abilities. Finally, he turned away, scanning the streets.

"I…" Xander shook his head when he could find no evidence of the event and looked down, unable to think of what to say to his friend.

"You did well," Stan said, putting a hand on his shoulder and smiling, "It was a lot to take on your first time out, but you handled yourself with as much skill as would be expected at this point."

Xander frowned and nodded slowly, feeling that, despite the praise, there was more he could have done.

Stan shook his head and chuckled. "You always do this to yourself," he chided him, turning and walking back towards Marcus' car, "Come on. There are some things that we should discuss."

CHAPTER TWENTY-SEVEN
MONSTERS: OUTSIDE AND IN

XANDER SAT STILL ON STAN'S COUCH, ignoring the discomfort and trying not to seem unnerved by the drawn-out silence. A sudden *pop* from the fireplace startled Tiger-Trepis and the animal's raised head served as a distraction as he reached out and scratched it behind the ear. The tiger, which seemed to be warming up to Xander all over again, closed its eyes and purred loudly at the attention.

Stan smiled as he watched and took a slow, calculated sip from a fresh bottle of beer. He remained quiet, despite the change in atmosphere, and peered over his shoulder. As he did, his aura crept from his chest and extended in the direction he was staring in.

Soon after they had gotten back to his house, Marcus, though fully healed from the skirmish, had gone to the guest room and locked the door behind him; offering not a single word to the two as he did. Xander hadn't been too surprised by this, though. The early morning sun was becoming visible over the horizon and his mentor had faced a hard night. He knew that he, too, should be trying to get some rest.

But, at that moment, it was out of the question.

Though he couldn't see what Stan was "looking" at, he dared a quick peek over his friend's shoulder, hoping his newly awakened auric powers might shed some light on what had him so curious.

They didn't.

"He'll be fine," Stan said, his voice calm and his head still pointed towards the guest room. "He's just been through a lot," as he said this he reached behind him and pulled the zipper to one of the couch cushions and pulled out a ratty, old package and slid a crumpled cigarette from it.

Xander's eyes widened, "I thought you didn't smoke!"

Stan frowned and shrugged, "You'd be surprised what *real* fighting does to you." He looked at the tip of the cigarette and Xander watched as his aura extended and touched the tip of the cigarette, flashing suddenly and lighting it. Stan sighed as he took a drag, shaking his head, "I still don't condone it, though."

The smoke wafted by and Xander suddenly realized how long it had been since he'd last had a cigarette. The transformation *had*—as everyone had said it would— eradicated his addiction, but it appeared as he reached into his jacket for his own pack that the habit remained.

Stan frowned as he saw this but nevertheless extended his aura across the space that divided them and ignited the end of his own cigarette for him, "Got a lot on your mind now."

Xander nodded, though he knew it hadn't been a question. He looked down and blew out a cloud of smoke as he caressed the tip of his left fang with his tongue. Though Stan's magic had healed him, his body still ached with thirst, and the throbbing in his gums served as an ever-constant reminder. Try as he might, however, he couldn't convince himself that it was the only thing bothering him.

"You want to talk about it," another non-question.

He kept his gaze pointed downward and remained motionless, watching the ash lengthen at the end of his cig. The fire sounded again but only the tiger's tail twitched in response. Xander eyed the animal a moment and switched his probing tongue to the opposite fang, traveling its full, hungry length before letting out a breath and looking up, "What *was* that back there?" he asked, "What did you do?"

Stan nodded, clearly expecting the question, "I brought you all into my aura to better control the outcome. Once you were all a part of me, there was nothing that I couldn't control." He shrugged, flicking an ash from the tip of his cigarette and consuming it with his aura before it touched the floor, "It's actually more complicated than that, but there's no other way to explain it." He tilted his head, "But that's not all that's bothering you."

Xander frowned a moment before shuddering at a memory. "Who..." he shook his head and took the cigarette between his fingers, "*What* was that... that *thing* that attacked us?"

"Thing?" Stan teased his word choice. Xander noticed,

however, that his friend cringed slightly at the mention.

Xander sighed and rolled his eyes, "Yea, you know: the monster guy-dog... thing!" He sighed, "You know what I'm talking about!"

Stan raised his brow, "You noticed that, huh?"

Xander rolled his eyes and took the cigarette between his lips for a quick drag before once again pulling it away, "Don't play with me right now, Stan!"

"Well... I guess they *do* still have an effect on me after all these years."

Xander stared silently, waiting.

Stan scoffed at himself. "When I first moved here I was attacked by one of those 'monster guy-dog things' and saved by your father. Those particular mythos are called theriomorphs—though most have taken to just calling them'therions'—and they're the real-life, no bullshit, tear-out-your-heart-and-eat-it bastards who are responsible for all the werewolf legends." He sighed and took another drag off his cigarette.

Xander frowned, "You said they're mythos too?"

Stan nodded, raising an eyebrow at him. "You thought it stopped with just vampires?" he quipped.

Xander felt his cheeks redden and shot him a glare, "No! I just didn't think that there were things like *that* in the world!"

Stan rolled his eyes, "There's a lot of 'things' out there hiding from humans, Xander." He sighed and shrugged, taking another long drag off his cigarette, "Sensei once trained with a tribe of anaprieks to learn how to 'talk' to animals."

Xander raised an eyebrow, "Anaprieks?"

"You'll learn *all* about it, I'm sure," Stan peeked over his shoulder again before taking another sip from his beer, followed by a short drag from his cigarette.

Xander frowned, seeing how unnerved his friend was, "A penny for your thoughts, teach."

Stan shook his head, "You're not ready for that much bad news, kid."

Xander bit his lip and looked down. He couldn't go to sleep knowing there was something big that he didn't know about. "I didn't realize there was a limit for bad news tonight," he forced a weak laugh, "There's nothing to bring me down from."

Stan shook his head again and took another long drag followed by an equally long drink, "You really aren't going to just let the subject drop, are you?"

Xander shook his head.

Stan sighed, holding what remained of his cig upright and focusing his aura on it until it was completely burned away. When it was gone he waved his hand over his head, fanning away the smell of smoke.

"Stop stalling!" Xander barked, annoyed that he was being made to wait.

Stan frowned up at him and leaned forward. "I've been searching around the globe for traces of Kyle," he explained. "I figured if you were going to go after him then you should at least know *where* he was."

"And…" Xander's interest peaked and he dropped his cigarette into his own empty beer bottle.

"I found him easily," Stan confessed.

Xander clapped his hands, "Yes! That's great!" He frowned, shaking his head, "But… wait. How is that *bad* news?"

Stan gave him a serious look.   "I found him easily," he

repeated, "*Too* easily. There was practically a screaming red beacon telling me where to look. I saw into his head and"—he shifted in his seat—"saw what he'd done..."

Xander narrowed his eyes, sensing that there Stan's reluctance growing. "What is it?"

Stan looked up, "He's in Maine. He's doing to another family what he did to you and your mother. But it's *why* he does those things that's got me concerned!"

"Why..." Xander parroted the word and caught Stan's eye, "What do you mean?"

"Xander," Stan gripped his head in his palms, "He's... he's not human! He never was!"

"Not... human?" Xander frowned.

Stan nodded slowly, "He's an auric vampire."

Xander froze and stared at him in disbelief, not sure what to say to this news. After a long moment of staring, he finally stood and, without another word, walked out of the living room and went to the other guest room to think.

It made sense; that was for goddamn sure. As a mind-feeder, Kyle had been a culinary sadist! He *had* always seemed to get some twisted pleasure out of torturing him and his mother, and now he understood why: the whole time he'd been doing it for their emotions; *feeding* off of their torment.

It was nearly noon when Xander came to grips with this new information. By that time his relatively new pack of cigs lay crumpled on the floor and he stared at it, feeling a similar crushing sensation in his chest. With a sigh he leaned back, staring at the ceiling, and wondered how long it had been since the last time he'd been happy. The thought was bubbling through his head when the first knock hit the door. Though slow in rising and crossing the length of the room, he finally turned the knob and allowed Stan in.

"I know you hate it when I look in your head,"—his friend started, handing him a frosty beer,—"but I figure it's still something I should address."

Xander glared and took a swig from the offered bottle, "And what is it that you're seeing?"

Stan frowned and sat on the edge of the bed and lifted the cap of his own beer off with his aura and snatched it in his palm before he took a sip, "You've watched a lot of people die lately; people who were close to you. Even if I hadn't read your mind I could have guessed that you're feeling lonely and that Marcus and I alone can do little to mend it."

Xander frowned, "What is it you're trying to say, Stan?"

Stan sighed and looked at him, "Estella has been asking about you lately. She comes into my office at least once a day asking if I know anything or if there's any news about you and I'm running out of lies to tell her."

On top of teaching, Stan often went outside the parameters of his job and helped students with their troubles. Whenever somebody had a problem and needed to chat, they often ignored their guidance counselor in exchange for a meeting with him. While Xander had only visited his office to bitch about his day and talk with him about magic, he rarely ever went for actual relief for his distress.

But there *were* those who vented often to him.

Xander looked down, dumbfounded. Estella had been visiting his office? He bit his lip and ignored the pain from his fang, "Estella…"

Stan nodded, "Estella Edash. Old friend of yours, I believe."

Xander shook his head and sat down next to Stan, "A long time ago, yea. She couldn't care less about me now, though." He took a sip of the beer and swallowed it the wrong way and started coughing.

"Not what she's been telling me lately," Stan said, ignoring the coughing fit.

Xander fought to stifle his hacking, "W-what are y-y-you talking abo-bout?"

Stan smiled and looked over at him with a sly grin, "You think a girl will waste her breath asking about somebody she doesn't care about?"

Xander frowned and coughed one last time before looking down, "What *have* you told her?"

"Only that you're alright and that I'd tell you she was asking," Stan answered before taking a sip from his beer.

Thinking about his old relationship with Estella in their Elementary school days, Xander realized that she had never done or said anything to end their friendship. In silent astonishment and horror, he realized that he'd been pushing away an ally all that time.

He knew the direction Stan was taking this in, and he agreed.

He had to visit Estella.

CHAPTER TWENTY-EIGHT
A YOUNG THERION

A PART OF TYLER—THE PART THAT

still believed in the dreams—played with the idea of tearing Kyle apart as he tried his best to ignore the hollowed, pained groans and grunts that echoed down the hall of the floor above him. He knew better than to ever be curious about *those* sounds again, and his stomach turned at the memory of walking into their room and seeing Kelly and Kyle doing things that he and his friends at school used to joke about on the bus.

The mental image of Kelly's battered body bouncing lamely on Kyle made the fifteen year-old-boy shiver. He was relieved that Kelly hadn't noticed. The memory of seeing his foster mother and her husband engaged in the emotionless act had been far less disturbing than the horribly deranged grin that Kyle had bared to him at the time.

Shivering again, Tyler attempted to drown out the sounds and the memories they brought by turning up the volume on the TV.

The snow was falling again, and rather than watching the cartoon that flashed its brightly lit colors at him he let its exaggerated noises fill the room as he watched through the nearby window at the surrounding forest as it was buried deeper in layer after layer of powder. He watched, as a chorus of high-pitched cartoon banter fell on lame ears, for a short while before becoming both tired of the sound and upset by the sight and left both behind to sit in his room with his comic books.

Time passed as it usually did when he read: quickly and, thankfully, without any reminders of the real world and its constant pain. After a deep yawn, he looked at his alarm-clock and was surprised to see that nearly four hours had passed. He set down the comic he was working on and, despite his growling stomach, decided to get ready for bed.

Though he knew he was pushing his luck, the stale flavor of a meal he'd long since forgotten still lingered in his mouth and he slowly tiptoed from his room to brush his teeth. After a tension-filled and agonizingly-slow trek down the hall, he pulled the bathroom door gently shut behind him and let out a relieved sigh.

The string of neon-green toothpaste had barely begun its birth from the tube when the sound of Kyle's boots sounded across the hall and grew louder with his approach. Tyler, toothbrush frozen in hand with a wad of toothpaste hanging by a withering tail, shivered as his eyes shifted in his skull away from his terrified reflection to the bathroom door. A silent prayer formed in his mind, begging God that his psychotic stepfather didn't need to take a leak.

As he listened, the footsteps walked past the closed door and headed further down the hall until their distance assured him that he was safe and he turned back just as the wad of toothpaste fell free and landed on the counter. He cursed silently as he grabbed a length of toilet paper to clean the mess. The trip back to the sink was nearly completed when the door suddenly flew open and threw him back; his head narrowly missing the edge of the tub as he crashed to the floor.

Kyle smirked slightly, standing like a demon in the doorway for a moment before stepping inside and shutting the door behind him. Tyler, still dazed from his impact with the floor, turned towards his approaching stepfather, noticing his now bare feet as they touched down noiselessly on the light-blue tiles. Kyle's smirk turned into a beaming smile then, and he chuckled as he began to undo the clasp of his belt.

Knowing that his stepfather would most likely make the beating a long and hard one, he decided that he'd let his mind wander to try and alleviate some of the pain and humiliation. At first, he figured he'd recite some of his favorite songs to himself, but with the first sharp impact of the folded leather he felt the lyrics abandon him and leave him with nothing but the pain. Left with no other option, Tyler finally began to think about his dreams: the only thing he had that made him feel strong.

They were, as all dreams were, hazy. Despite this, one detail that never wavered was the always all-too-clear image of the creatures that were, as the doctors had put it, a "mental reconstruction of his parents coupled with an overactive imagination". More often he remembered the part in the dreams where he was running with them; the glorious scene of the wind-bent trees rushing past like careless memories as his father and mother led him through the wilderness.

He vaguely remembered parts in the dreams where he would hunt—stalking baby rabbits with others like him to bring home to their parents like trophies. He remembered the intimidating, predatory faces of the other members of the pack when they hunted, as well as the soft human faces they took when they didn't.

And he remembered where the dreams became nightmares...

The vague recollection of a conflict between his "parents" and the other members of the pack always— though he knew it was stupid to cry over dreams from so long ago—brought tears to his eyes. The scene of the ravenous creatures that had burst forth so violently from such soft human skins to rip into them made Tyler shudder harder as Kyle continued and grunted in angry exertion as if he knew he didn't have all of Tyler's attention.

. And then he remembered the end of the dream; a simple, common nightmare: falling.

His first *real* memory was of waking up in the hospital, finding himself hooked up to beeping machines; half his head wrapped in bandages. He remembered doctors shuffling in, filling the small room quickly with their questions on his wellbeing as well as the incessant and ridiculous question of who he was and if he remembered his name.

They *would* have been ridiculous if he had actually remembered.

When their questions went unanswered, the doctors

began to shuffle out, leaving one particularly round doctor with an equally round brown mustache standing in the room. The doctor had scratched some notes onto a yellow pad and slapped it shut before leaning forward and asking more questions about what he *had* been able to remember.

And so he told the round man about his hazy dreams. The story poured out as smoothly as quickly fading dreams do, and the doctor had patiently listened. When he was done, the doctor had nodded and stood up, telling him that they had found him in the woods at the base of a tall hill, which, he told him, explained his memory of falling.

Though the last parts of his dreams he was willing and eager to pass off quickly, he had been reluctant to accept that the parts—the wonderful, all-too-real sensation of running through the woods as something more-than human—had been nothing more than a dream. The doctor had been insistent, however, and desperately worked against any grips that he had on the fantasy.

It wasn't long before he demanded to have a name. At first, the hospital staff had been uneasy with the idea, but a nurse who had been making her rounds suggested that they call him "Tyler"—her late father's name. Eager for any sort of hold on reality and afraid that at any moment he'd wake up and have to go through the entire process all over again, he'd quickly accepted the name as his own.

After the third week Tyler was left with little more than some bumps and scabs, but still no memory. The doctors, at that point, could do little more than file the necessary paperwork and put him in a foster home, assuring him that he would be adopted and become part of a stable household in, as they'd put it, "no time".

"No time", Tyler thought as Kyle's belt struck again, had

turned out to be several years.

While he was in the foster home, he'd done his best to be friendly with the other children, often struggling against the desire to instead run around on his own. On days when potential foster parents came to eye the children like hanging meat, Tyler did as the others had suggested and tried to look happy and playful while at the same time lonely and depressed. However, despite his best efforts, the potentials never gave him a second look, often muttering about how he was "too old".

Several months after his eleventh birthday, a young couple had come in and, once again, all of the children took their positions in hopes of being selected. Tyler, who at that point barely adhered to any hopes of being chosen, remained quietly seated in the back of the room with an old, tattered copy of Goosebumps.

They were like all the others and were unnaturally hasty and had stepped out of the room without choosing any of the children. As they discussed their options, a thirsty Tyler had excused himself to get past them to get a drink at a nearby fountain.

The woman—a beautiful, fair skinned blonde with soft features and wide brown eyes—looked down at the passing boy and gasped in surprise. Tyler later found out that her reaction had been in regards to his appearance, as he bared a strong resemblance to her younger brother who had been killed several years earlier by a drunk driver. After several moments of awe-filled staring, the woman had whispered something to her husband before turning back and asking Tyler his name.

Having rarely been talked to by potentials, he'd looked at them and stammered out "Tyler" before looking down at the floor in embarrassment at his stuttering. The husband, a sharp-featured man with well-cut brown hair and narrow, sharp eyes, had smiled warmly and patted him on the shoulder, telling him not to be so nervous.

After talking amongst themselves, they asked about his past. He'd once again blushed and answered that he'd spent what portion he could remember in a hospital healing from a fall before being sent to live at the foster home. When asked if he could remember his parents, he was reluctant to answer, though finally sighed and shook his head.

Kelly and Robert, as they'd introduced themselves, were quick in choosing Tyler after talking with him a bit longer. Both had agreed that, despite his age, he was remarkably mature and well-spoken—both of which Tyler had his compulsive reading habit to thank, though he couldn't remember where he'd learned how to. After some talking between the adults and a long line of paperwork, Tyler finally found himself preparing to go to a new home.

Though the ride had only lasted forty minutes, the trip seemed to take forever. When their car had finally turned off the main road onto a long, unpaved stretch surrounded by trees, Tyler had found himself instantly drawn to the sight and had pressed his face against the window to watch the forest rush past. The sight seemed oddly familiar, like careless memories.

Kelly had smiled at their new son's enthusiasm, turning around in the passenger seat and ruffling his hair. "Do you like the woods? My father *loved* the woods. He spent a lot of time just looking for the perfect place to build our house," her smile had grown so wide that it had made Tyler's cheeks ache just to watch.

Tyler remembered the first time he'd seen the house and,

despite the perpetual pain from Kyle, he felt his cheeks give way to a smile at the memory just before the belt bit into his lower back again and he cried out.

The house was like a castle—a towering three stories tall!—with the corner of an in-ground pool peeking around the back and a large swing that hung on a tall, old tree in the front. The sight had made Tyler's smile match Kelly's, and his cheeks began to ache even more.

It was the first, genuine smile he remembered having.

Kelly had nodded, looking at the house as if for the first time as well, "Do you like it?"

Tyler had nodded as he continued to gaze at his new home. "Better than I could have wished for," he'd told her.

The new family was extremely happy together. Though the summer was not yet through, Kelly's eagerness to get Tyler enrolled had the young man excited at the idea of finally attending a real school. On weekends, Robert had taken him deeper into the woods, stopping only when the thickness of the trees had finally blocked out the sight of the house, and they'd camped—spending the rest of the sunlit hours playing catch and most of the night telling scary stories and roasting marshmallows.

Kyle growled in frustration again, bringing the belt down harder. He shrieked in agony and the familiar chuckle sounded as his stepfather continued.

Desperate to escape the pain, he continued to try to remember...

But Kyle's poison had seeped beyond the flesh and even his memories turned painful.

Robert, who had always been what Kelly had called "overly friendly" had met and befriended a newcomer to the area while out shopping. After some small-talk in the check-out line, the man introduced himself as Kyle and invited Robert and his family to a barbeque at his house. Robert later speculated, as he'd discussed the event with them, that he'd never mentioned his family, but figured that he "just had that charm".

Both Kelly and Tyler had been unsure about Robert's new friend but had both been quiet and polite during the outing. Afterwards, much to Tyler—who had felt an aching discomfort the entire time he'd been in Kyle's company—and Kelly's dismay, Kyle had scheduled another outing with Robert. Kelly, on the car ride home, nervously confessed that she hadn't liked the way Robert's new friend had looked at her. Robert had passed it off, telling her it was the anxiety of meeting a new person.

Shortly after the second meeting with Kyle the fighting had begun. Tyler noticed the sudden shift in their nearly perfect relationship immediately. Equally as painful, their regular weekend camping trips became less and less frequent until the day finally came that the outdoor gear was thrown out.

It had seemed that the only person at that point who got along with Robert was Kyle, who always insisted that he bring his family with them to their outings. The events, which had become as frequent as three nights a week, became harder on Kelly, who had finally told Robert that she couldn't handle being around Kyle anymore and demanded that she and Tyler be kept out of any future plans, leading to one of the worst fights that Tyler had ever heard. He could still remember the tear-filled call that Kelly had made to her sister explaining how she felt like Robert was a whole different person.

Several days later, Robert left them.

Though the event was hard on Kelly, Kyle had been sure

to make himself available as a source of support, and Tyler was shocked to see that his foster mother was quickly becoming more and more attached to him with each visit.

It wasn't long after that that Tyler had found himself with his new abusive stepfather and a perpetually terrified foster mother.

His perfect family had turned to anything but.

The final crack of the belt always stung the most and Tyler shook, his teeth clenching painfully, as he felt his hatred for his stepfather grow. Kyle let out a satisfied sigh and rose to his feet before starting out.

"Goodnight, son," he called over his shoulder.

Tyler had always hated it when Kyle called him that, and he knew that the bastard knew it. Though he'd spent a lot of time under Kyle's belt, something about feeling the hurt while remembering his past made him so angry that his blood seemed to boil in his veins. Though his exhaustion outweighed any ability to do so, he felt compelled for the first time to fight back.

Despite the recent blizzard the night was hot and restless; filled with the warped and terrifying faces of the creatures from his old dreams. In the middle of the night he shot from bed with a violent stomach ache, barely making it to the bathroom in time. Finally, when the vomiting had ceased and the need for sleep once more had become a pressuring force, he drew his head from the toilet and, overcome by aches and dizziness, passed out.

When he awoke the next morning, Tyler was met with the realization that he was covered in puke and sprawled in the tub. With this burden set aside in the "bad start" bin, he pulled himself to his feet and ran the shower for a moment to rinse both it and himself off. Finally, mouth filled with the lingering taste of vomit, he stumbled to the sink to brush his teeth.

The illness of the night before faded as he finished and went on to wash his face, leaving behind only the burning hatred that Tyler felt for his stepfather. For the first time, however he felt strong and, moreover, no longer afraid.

Shocked by his newfound braveness, Tyler looked up at the mirror as he finished washing up and jumped back in surprise. The face staring back at him did so with hard, foreign eyes; eyes that made his soft, sad own look weak in comparison. As he studied the rest of his reflection, he was only filled with more shock and confusion: his entire face was stretched and his jaw was jutting out. When he opened his mouth he saw that his teeth were irregularly spaced and, more surprising, longer and sharper!

He shut his eyes then, blocking out the reflection.

"It's not real," he whispered, "You're angry and you're sick... and you're seeing things that aren't real!"

He shook his head again, concentrating on waking up from the illness and rage-induced hallucination. There was a sudden pain then that forced his eyes to shut tighter until it passed and when he finally opened them he was himself again.

And he was hungry!

Confident the episode was a lingering effect of the previous night's illness and driven by his hatred, Tyler made his way to the kitchen and threw open the fridge. He let his eyes roam through the contents before moving down to the shelf that Kyle had set aside specifically as his own; the "forbidden shelf" as he called it. Tyler scoffed at the thought and yanked a package of steaks and several bottles of beer from this before slamming the door shut behind him.

When the frying pan he'd put on the front burners of the stove was hot and ready, he threw two steaks on. The meat screamed from the scorching heat; spattering hot droplets of juice all over the stovetop. As it continued to cook on the one side, Tyler opened the beer and took a hard swig before pouring the rest of the bottle into the frying pan for added flavor as well as added thrill of defying his stepfather.

After flipping the steaks, he then went about cracking all of a nearly full carton of eggs into another frying pan and proceeded to make a sunny-side-up mess which he quickly dumped onto a plate along with the not-quite-done steaks. When he was happy that breakfast had been made, he grabbed a fork and proudly marched his food to the table and began to eat.

It wasn't until the steak was completely eaten and nearly all the eggs had been consumed that Kyle first stepped into the kitchen and walked past Tyler who glared hatefully at his entrance. Kyle continued his ignorant march to the fridge, throwing it open and studying its contents.

Tyler watched, waiting for the bastard to notice the missing steak and beer. Then, as if by some unheard cue, Kyle suddenly turned and narrowed his eyes at him and then looked back in the fridge, pausing to confirm his suspicions before slamming the door hard enough to shake the refrigerator and knock over most of its contents.

"Arrogant little fuck!" Kyle growled as he stomped towards Tyler, whose fists were tightly balled under the table and shaking in anticipation, "I should…"

Watching his living nightmare storm in his direction, he stopped listening to his threats and began to think of the beating from the night before. Then he thought of all the beatings he'd endured.

Then he thought of Kelly.

He wanted so badly to make him pay…

And then it began.

Tyler cried out from the intense pain that grew inside of him. He looked down at his arm and recoiled at the sight of it stretching, the bones inside it crunching loudly. There was a tightness that grew in his stomach and he wrapped his human arm around his gut and keeled over.

Kyle watched, stunned for a moment before glaring. A hard, solid force pushed against the agonized, misshapen teen then, forcing him against the wall and knocking several framed photos and a clock to the floor. Tyler, pinned by the unseen force against the wall, pried his eyes open and stared in disbelief at Kyle, who glared at him as he approached and shook his head. The gesture was accompanied by a throbbing ache in Tyler's head that forced his eyes shut again; his body thrown once again into painful spasms. When it was all over he opened his eyes only to see that his deadly, inhuman claw was once again a weak human hand.

As Kyle reached the wall he slammed his hand down and pinned Tyler, the invisible force lifting as he did.

"I see you've gone through some changes, son," Kyle said, sounding both angered and entertained. He sighed and shook his head, "This is probably—at least partially—my fault. If I'd have dug deep enough into this shithole"—he poked Tyler's forehead hard enough to make him flinch— "I'm sure I would have found out that you were…" he smiled wickedly, "… different. But honestly: you disgust me, so I never went *too* deep.

"So…" he shook his head, looking back at his breakfast plate, "you finally feel the change come over you—find yourself a way to get back at me for all the shit I've put you through—and you eat my steak?" he laughed in Tyler's face, "I mean—"

Tyler lunged forward and snarled—a sound like cinderblocks in a cement mixer—and Kyle grinned as his stepson's face collided with an invisible barrier. He recoiled, shaking his aching head, dazed and confused. He reached up slowly to touch his aching face but was slammed again and again against the wall as Kyle smiled and crossed his arms across his chest.

How was he doing this?

"Now you listen to me, you repulsive pile of dog shit!" Kyle spat before looking off into the distance for a moment, "I have bigger things to worry about than a prepubescent therion deciding to embrace his inner self; though I *do* appreciate the effort." He grinned and patted Tyler's head, flattening a ruffled portion of hair, "I haven't tasted determination this strong for quite some time." His playful features turned hard again and an agonizing wave filled Tyler's head, causing him to groan in pain, "I'll give you a choice, and I'm being *very* fucking generous in doing so!" Again he focused and again Tyler cried out, "I could kill you right here and now and then march my ass up those stairs and do the same to that worthless cunt you care about so dearly."

Stepping back several paces, Kyle chuckled at his own threat. Tyler, no longer pinned against the wall, lunged at his stepfather again, only to recoil at the sudden, screaming pain in his head.

"Now then," Kyle went on, "either you can use your newfound strength to fight for me when the time comes— and believe me when I say the time *is* coming—or I can end yours and Kelly's wretched existence right now!" The force that had kept Tyler standing drifted away and his body crashed down to the floor. Kyle calmly approached, his boots sounding as he did until he was standing directly over him, "So what will it be, son?"

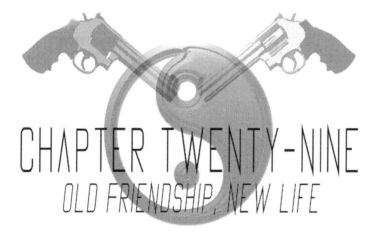

CHAPTER TWENTY-NINE
OLD FRIENDSHIP, NEW LIFE

IT WAS AN AWKWARD FEELING FOR

Xander when he realized he had nothing to wear. He was
relieved, however, that it was not so much a matter of vanity
as it was that he had nothing that didn't smell of dried blood
and BO from training.

Stan, who was reading a book on the couch with Trepis
sleeping nearby, suggested that he check Marcus' room.
Though his vampire trainer had assured the two of them he
was alright, was still clearly shaken and had left for "the

comforts of home", telling Xander before he left that his training was complete. In his haste to get out of the house and back to his apartment he had, however, neglected to bring most of his things. While Xander thought it a bit bizarre—and not to mention rude—to go rummaging around through someone else's belongings, he opted for being an impolite creeper rather than a filthy, reeking angel.

In the closet he found a pair of jeans and a black tee that had the faded, unreadable remains of what he could only assume was an old rock band on the front. He put them on and dug further, not seeing any reason to stop when he'd gone that far, to see what else his trainer had left behind. At the far end he came across a red leather jacket and ran his fingers across the worn material. Though most likely a bold fire-engine red when new, it had since lost some of its luster and was the color of dried blood—a color that Xander had become very familiar with over the past month. Out of curiosity, he pulled it from the closet and slipped it on, finding it somewhat loose but not at all uncomfortable.

Though it was nice and he had every intention of "borrowing" it, he felt that perhaps it would be overkill for the occasion at hand and hung it back up in the closet. He made a mental note to retrieve it later and walked to the bathroom to brush his fangs.

The night air was cool and refreshing as Xander jumped into overdrive and headed towards Estella's old house, hoping she hadn't moved since his last visit. It took only several seconds to travel the fifteen-or-so miles to her house, which was several seconds that he could have done without;

the anxiety to finally come face-to-face with his old friend and apologize for all of his wrongdoings had been eating away at his insides since he'd first heard that she'd been asking about him.

When, at last, he stood in front of the house, he was reassured by the slightly peeled letters on the mailbox that still read "EDASH". As he approached the entrance, he suddenly realized that he didn't want to knock and go through the discomfort of dealing with her parents and, instead, decided to make his entrance through the attic window—what he hoped was still Estella's bedroom.

Backing away to get a better view of his intended entrance he noticed that not only were the lights already on in her room but that the window was open as well. For a moment he entertained the notion that his old friend had been keeping her bedroom cool, but the nagging fact that it was early winter and too cold for comfort refused to let him hold on to that belief for very long. Left with no other truth other than the obvious, he took in a deep breath and tried to calm his racing heart.

It was an easy jump to the roof, though landing on the sharply angled roof proved a bit awkward. He teetered, the sharp slope threatening to drop him back over the edge, before he finally found his footing and began walking towards the window. Taking his time, hoping to elude—if no one but himself—of any views of him being clumsy, he dared his first peek into the room when the voice emerged:

"Come in, Xander. It's safe."

He paused as he was not only welcomed inside, but assured of the absence of any third parties. Slowly, he ducked his head and poked it inside. Estella sat on her bed at the other side of the room, which housed a combination of posters and several bookshelves crammed with an ample collection. His eyes quickly scanned a few of the titles, not surprised to find that many of them were somehow magical in nature.

He had not been completely shocked when Stan warned him that she had become a witch in the time they had spent apart, but, seeing her research material, he couldn't help but realize just how well versed she had become. Finally, his wandering eyes paused, having taken in every detail of the room around him and leaving him with no other option than to finally make eye contact.

"Just on time," her voice was soft and timid, as though she was afraid of startling a wild animal, "And you don't have to worry about Mom and Dad... they went to bed a few hours ago."

Xander took in a sharp inhale and nodded and looked up at her and her bright-orange aura shifted and she cringed and he frowned; she expected him to yell at her. Instead, he pulled a nearby office chair to himself and sat down, leaning forward and exhaling.

"I'm sorry," she said. "I'll get out of your head now. And I'm sorry about before."

Xander looked at her, "Before?"

She nodded and blushed as she realized that he didn't know what she was referring to, "About entering your mind... more than once." She smiled faintly and shrugged her left shoulder. "I guess you never picked up on the spells when I was casting them," she said with a twinge of pride.

Xander smiled at her. She had always been so sweet and innocent and he was glad to see that time hadn't tarnished that quality.

"It's... good to see you again. I will admit, though, I was

surprised to hear that you'd been asking about me," he finally said.

Estella smiled when she heard that and nodded, then suddenly grew still and laced her fingers together in her lap as if she'd done something wrong. "You... you've been gone for a while now," she looked down sadly, "The principal told me you'd moved away after the fire, but he got angry when I asked him where you'd gone." She smiled, "He always gets angry when someone catches him in a lie. It took forever to finally get Stan to tell me anything."

He looked up at her again, taking in for the first time how much she had changed. Her hair was still raven-black, though she had let it grow out and her eyes still shone with the same bright blue. As he looked more deeply, he couldn't help but notice that her pale face was still somewhat young-looking, though time appeared to have hardened some in the course of her life and giving the appearance of a marble statue. He was surprised that someone so beautiful would be so shy.

"Why *did* you ask about me?" he interrupted his own thoughts.

She blushed again, "I... never stopped caring about you, Xander. One day you just sort of cut away from the world and we fell apart. I didn't like it, but there wasn't much I could seem to do. Every time I—"

"I'm sorry," Xander frowned looking down, seeing where the conversation was leading. He didn't want to be reminded of his atrocities towards someone who had been such a good friend over the years.

A far better friend than he'd ever been.

She sat quietly and nodded, smiling slightly, "Can I ask what happened? Why you disappeared and what's happened to your…" she looked down.

Xander knew what she was thinking and raised a hand to his face, "My eye?" He nodded. She *was* owed an explanation, "I suppose I should start from the beginning."

After nearly two hours Xander finished telling Estella the story of what had happened. She sat on her bed for most of the time, leaning more and more forward in astonishment until she had finally asked him to pause so she could sit on the floor. Shortly after, he moved down from the chair as well feeling it rude to stay seated while she had sacrificed the mattress for his story. When it was over, her face shone with a combination of emotions, her tears flowing down flushed cheeks.

"I'm so sorry," she finally offered after a long, silent pause.

Xander blushed and looked away, "Don't be. You haven't done anything but be a better human being than I thought could exist." He looked at her and felt his own tears betray him as they burned down his cheek. He quickly wiped them away with the back of his hand, looking away from Estella's prying eyes in embarrassment.

She followed suit, beginning to wipe her own tears and dampening her face in the process. After several silent seconds, she smiled at him again, "So you're really a vampire?"

Xander nodded, "Two different kinds in one, actually."

She giggled and Xander noticed that her cheeks had brightened and she seemed less shy and he couldn't help but broaden his own smile.

"I've missed my best friend for so long," she confessed. Her eyes went wide as she remembered something and she sprung up, going to a nightstand by her bed and opening the top drawer. After retrieving whatever it was, she returned, holding a ring between her thumb and pointer finger. The stainless steel shone around the edge and Xander smiled at the present as he accepted it and examined the sequence of linear markings that traveled around the band.

"Stan said you'd gotten three already and that if I wanted to get you something it should be another ring," she explained, "Any style I wanted as long as it was a size eight."

Xander smirked as he looked back at his present. He didn't want to imagine how Stan would know his index finger size. He bit his lip, ignoring the pain as his fang pierced it, and took the ring and slid it on next to the others on his left hand.

"Oh! You're bleeding!" Estella exclaimed, seeing the trickle travel down his chin.

Xander sucked his lip and frowned, "Oh, I'm fine. Don't worry about it."

She didn't listen and grabbed a tissue and began patting at the tiny wound. Xander started to protest but something held him back. And then he realized it: for the first time since his grandmother had died he felt what it was like to be cared for. When at last the wound was cleaned, Estella marveled. The wound, during the process of cleaning, had healed and she mewed happily as she examined it. After a moment it occurred to both of them how close she was to his lips and they blushed and pulled away.

It was nearly dawn when Xander finally stood up and told his friend that it was time for him to leave.

The look on Estella's face showed all of the gloom one would expect from the end of such a wonderful situation, but there was no denying two facts: first—the sun was about to rise, and second—too much had to be done to prepare for Kyle to spend time towards something besides training.

"You need to make me a promise," Estella called out as he approached the window.

He turned back. After studying her face for a moment he nodded, "I'll do what I can," he offered.

Estella blushed and several bolts of orange shot out from her aura as she looked down to hide a tear that had wandered from her left eye and traced a path along the side of her thin nose, "I need you to promise me that you won't die," she blushed and looked up at him, "or, at least, not again." She walked towards him then and grabbed his left hand and ran her thumb over the stainless steel ring she had given him. She had laughed earlier, pointing out how cheap her gift looked next to all the others, and smiled when he'd assured her that it was no less valuable to him, "You have to promise me that I will get to see this"—she sniffled—"on your finger again after all this is over." Her tears began to flow more steadily.

Xander frowned. He had known death was a possibility the moment he heard of what Kyle was and the sort of power he would be going against. The truth of the matter was that he had not intended to live through it; not if it meant bringing Kyle down with him in the process. Looking into Estella's face, he almost resented her for making him have to aim higher. He sighed heavily and looked down.

How could he possibly explain to her what he was going

against?

Sighing, he slowly raised his left hand. He looked back into her eyes, drawn by the hypnotic gaze and a driving desire for the only answer that would make things alright. His hand touched her cheek and she started back as a rush of warmth—not unlike an electric shock—rushed into her skin.

And she saw.

She saw his mother and how she used to be.

She saw Kyle.

Saw the whirlwind of horrors and pain and the Hell of Xander's past.

When at last he removed his hand she collapsed forward with a heavy sob, pushing herself so far into Xander's chest he felt she might break through and seal herself within him. In a way, he realized, she already had.

As children, whenever they'd passed a dead animal on the road she was prone to fits of tears. She had always sworn against violence and gotten angry with Xander when he had had one of his malicious thoughts. She didn't have a violent bone in her body. All that set aside, though he knew she would never admit it, he knew that she agreed with his mission.

After a moment, she looked up at him with a saddened nod before another heaving sob was let out and she again buried herself into his chest. He was reluctant to hold her, afraid of what it meant to let himself care for somebody again, but finally he allowed his arms to wrap around her. He brought his right hand to her shoulder and began to draw in the sadness; surprising himself as instinct told him how. He felt her sorrow melt into his skin like wax and his insides cringed—the sensation was awful. Nonetheless, he continued to pull it all away until, at last, she sighed calmly and yawned.

He looked at her, pulling away and sitting on the window sill, and smiled. "I promise," he whispered, nodding. "I'll come back when it's all over."

She smiled at that and stepped to her desk, tearing out a piece of paper from an open notebook and scribbling on it before handing it to him. Giving it a glance, he recognized the seven digits of a phone number and looked up to see his renewed friend's orange aura bubble around her. Feeling his cheeks tighten with his growing smile, he stuffed the paper into his pocket, not needing to ask what it was for.

Finally turning away, Xander turned and climbed out the window and dropped down to the ground and started towards Stan's at a human pace.

CHAPTER THIRTY
TRAINING WITH STAN

XANDER HAD BARELY MADE IT HOME

before the sun rose, and the first touches of its rays made him want to kick a puppy. He recalled Range telling him that the first hour of exposure created unsettling paranoia and rage, and he forced himself to ignore the sensation, passing it off. Not wanting to tempt the sun's effects any further he took the rest of the trip back to Stan's in overdrive.

Stan had already left for work by the time he'd arrived, leaving behind a present under an old blanket with a note pinned on top. Xander set aside the letter in favor of the surprise and found himself, after flinging the blanket aside, staring at a white and brown rabbit in a wire cage. It hopped about its confines nervously when the cover was removed but calmed soon after and went back to gnawing a piece of lettuce. He frowned at the meal that Stan had left and shrugged, figuring that leaving a hobo on the kitchen counter would have been difficult.

He fed, being sure to end the animal's life painlessly and carefully disposed of the body in a garbage bag. When he was finished cleaning up he unfolded the note and began reading:

Xander,
I knew you would probably be hungry when you got home and found you a snack in the backyard after you left.
Stan
P.S.- hope you had a good time.

Stan was waiting in the living room—standing patiently beside the fireplace—when Xander woke up. He explained that the time had come to learn how to control his aura.

"I was wondering…" Xander started, a burning question nagging at him.

"Hmm?" Stan cocked his head, curious.

Xander held up his left hand, wiggling his fingers slightly

to call attention to his new jewelry, "I need to know what these are for."

Stan nodded and sat down, producing a cigarette for Xander, who gladly accepted it and lit it. He leaned back and breathed in before starting, "I know you never got to meet your father, much less see him and your mother together, but he loved her more than words can ever express... and more than telepathy can justify."

Xander frowned, looking away when he heard mention of his mother.

Stan went on, "The Odin Clan had been trying to take in smaller guilds and families that wanted the protection and honor that came with the territory. Other clans were against their motion to protect these 'lower' groups and turned to destroying them before the Clan could move to protect them."

Xander frowned, "Why would they be against it?"

Stan shrugged, "You have to realize, Xander, you were brought in by one of the best. Your father and Depok put a great deal of effort into creating a clan that housed *both* aurics and sangsuigas; something that is—for some—still frowned upon in our world. He—your father, I mean—had gotten the ring that you now wear on your pinky for your mother, but he was called to protect a sangsuiga house before he could give it to her. He left it and his own family band—which you're now wearing on your ring finger—with Depok in case he did not return," he shook his head and frowned, "It had become a habit of the two to pass over anything they wanted to keep safe in the event of the unimaginable.

"When you were born, Depok attempted to hand-deliver the rings, but your mother, as Depok told me, had tearfully turned him away saying that his lifestyle would not be yours."

Xander shivered despite the warm fire and he tightened his throat, desperately fighting the knot that was forming. He looked at the ring that Stan had just identified as his family crest and he let the light catch the engraved markings, which flashed like a lightning strike.

Stan could see the struggle to stay strong and smiled warmly, "The ring on your middle finger is the Odin Clan's band. Every time a new member joined or was turned within their walls they were presented with it. It is the act that completes the ceremony. I found it in Depok's study the night I found you."

Xander nodded and finally coughed a dry cry out, turning red in anger at having shown weakness. Never before had he illustrated his own frail humanity than the past few weeks, when he'd been taken from the human world.

"Why did you want me to have these?" Xander asked through a dry and chapped throat.

Stan's smile remained, "You need to be in the right mind to accept the training I have in store for you. Typically, like with Marcus, the act involves repetitive action and strengthening, but for this I needed you to have something you could look at and feel to bring the knowledge you already have in you to the surface. The next few weeks will not be about training you so much as it will be about *awakening* you. Once the natural warrior inside of you comes to surface, you'll find the rest comes naturally.

"Besides," Stan groaned as he rose from his seat, "it's nice to have a way to remember those who mean the most to you."

The rest of the week was dedicated to showing Xander how to control his aura; guiding it like a straw to absorb energy until he could reach inside the neighboring house and feed from their dog. Xander's curiosity had compelled him to reach further into the house, "seeing" the family's teenage boy discover his father's porno collection and the husband strike his wife in the other room for coming home late and drunk. He was captivated by the wave of energies that swirled about the household, but quickly recoiled, not wanting to be a part of it anymore. Stan had laughed at this, explaining that he had discovered his "mind's eye".

When he had mastered control of his aura for feeding, Stan taught him to use it as an invisible limb. Though he quickly learned how to pick up a pack of cigarettes, the idea of lifting himself off the ground or cushioning the blow of an attack seemed impossible. After several days, however, he was surprised to find himself deflecting tennis balls as they were hurled at him. Soon after he was practicing performing multiple tasks with his aura, catching several thrown objects at once while relying on his eyes to block a startlingly rapid set of punches from Stan. This particular exercise took several weeks of hard practice before he and Stan felt he had perfected it.

It was on the eighteenth night that the two got down to what Stan had called "the awakening".

They took their positions on the floor—Stan staring up at the shadows on the ceiling cast from the candles that lay about the room and waiting while Xander leaned against a wall in an Indian-style fashion. A strong, hallucinogenic tea had been consumed and Xander was struggling to keep his mind focused while staying on the same energy plane as Stan, who sat cross-legged across from him and kept track of his pupil's progress with his auric probes. Xander was unnerved about taking drugs while sitting in a candle-lit room with a teacher who used the term "probe", but stifled his laughter that threatened to throw him off and placed the blame on the tea.

When Stan was centered on Xander's auric field, he instructed him to look at the family band and remember anything he could about his father.

"But I never met—"

"Shh! Just concentrate," Stan instructed, his unblinking eyes open still focused on the ceiling.

Xander stared at his family crest and looked back at his time with Mind-Trepis. The being had been a constant voice in his mind, always talking to him when he needed a companion.

A father... of sorts.

Though he did not recall shutting his eyes, Xander was suddenly aware of being in complete darkness, and a man with thick brown hair and the beginnings of a beard stood in front of him with a smile.

"Hey, son," the figure said as it took a seat beside him.

Hearing that, Xander knew that for the first time he was being identified correctly and he smiled sadly, "Hey, Dad."

The man was tall, several inches greater than Xander, and he glowed with a brilliant blue-green; his entire form shaped by auric energy. He smiled and Xander felt his eyes burn through the resulting glare, like headlights in his vision, and his eyes watered.

"Come a long way, I see," Joseph said warmly.

Xander nodded and sobbed openly, feeling that he was finally with company that would not call him "weak" for it, "But I've failed so many times along the way!"

Joseph shook his head, "I've watched you, Xander. I've seen the events that shaped your life. You've survived darker horrors than many I could have lived through. I always knew you were stronger than you believed you were." He smiled over at him, "Why do you think I never took control to stop you during your ritual?"

Xander smiled and looked away, wiping his eyes, "Guess I thought you just wanted to let me play it out on my own."

"And I did. Every single time. Trust me, Xander. Watching my son stick a gun barrel in his mouth on a nightly basis and *not* doing something about it took a great deal of faith on my part."

Xander cried harder when he heard 'my son', "What if I'm too weak to move on with what needs to be done? What if I let you and Mom down?"

His father's ghost shook his head and patted his shoulder. "You've come this far and you've tried this hard already. If you were to drop this very minute I don't think either of us could accuse you of not trying. But you don't have it in you to quit that easily," he smiled and Xander felt the confidence rush through his mind as warmth emanated from his left ring finger, "do you?"

Xander clenched his eyes shut and looked down, the one question he feared most to ask seemed to flow from his mouth without his permitting it, "But am I strong enough? Do I have what it takes to be a warrior?"

There was silence, and Xander was afraid to look up and see disappointment in the ghost's eyes. At last the voice spoke up: "Xander, I am almost frightened to tell you that you most certainly have what it takes to succeed. No father truly wants to see their little man run off into a fight, let alone do so in a world like the one you've come to be a part of. But you are a Stryker, and you are my son. And that, Xander, means that you will succeed."

His eyes were closed as the final words entered his ears and he bit his lip hard and let the blood run down his chin and flood his mouth from the other side. Swallowing hard, he looked up, "Dad…"

But when he opened his eyes, the figure was gone, and he was sitting back in Stan's living room. His old friend looked at him through tear stained eyes, clearly having been moved by some memory of his old friend as he'd helped push Joseph Stryker's consciousness into his mind.

As he breathed in deeply, chasing his sobs away, he felt the warmth grow and pulsate within him. He felt his mind expand and soak in white light and suddenly he felt whole. When he looked up again, Stan nodded.

"You've awakened."

For several days after Xander's conversation with what Stan had referred to as an "auric reflection" the two practiced.

Xander was amazed at how much his skills had increased since the experience, utilizing skills he somehow knew he had but had never before learned to control or even known existed. He and Stan were both amazed when, while sparring in the house, Xander had released a wave of energy that had left half of the dividing wall between his living room and the garage in rubble.

The night finally arrived when Xander awoke—the month of training over—and found Stan getting dressed, instructing him to do the same.

"What's going on?" Xander yawned, stretching.

Stan smiled, "It's time to visit The Gamer!"

CHAPTER THIRTY-ONE
THE GAMER

UPON FURTHER INQUIRY AS TO

exactly *where* they were going, Xander finally got an answer.

"The Gamer is a friend who handles weaponry as well as giving tips on situations that call for a strategic mind."

"Is that why you call him 'The Gamer'?" Xander asked.

Stan frowned as he steered through the city, "I'm afraid not."

As it turned out, The Gamer was short and fat with a tuft of wiry hair the color of greased copper. His "headquarters"—as he'd referred to it upon their arrival— was a local videogame and roleplay gaming shop that advertised itself as being the best in the region; a bold statement coming from the *only* in the region. The store was empty, housing only shelves of merchandise as well as walls that were decorated in "Final Fantasy" and "Halo" posters.

The portly man was sitting behind the counter with a Penthouse open to a centerfold beside the register. He briefly scanned the porn before referring back to a copy of Game Informer. Stan pulled him from his task, nodding and showing a great deal more patience than he deserved as he explained that he wanted to confirm a rumor he'd heard that May of 2008's body-type had been used as a reference for a character in some upcoming project. He proudly declared that it wasn't before turning his full attention to them.

"And this must be the big-deal that had me working in the shop almost every night for the past month and a half," he said condescendingly to Xander as he rolled from the seat behind the counter and waddled to stand beside the two. "I must say, you're shorter than I would have thought."

Xander forced a smile and wondered when they would get around to the point of the visit. He was already growing tired of the stale smell of old hot pockets and cheap cologne covering up the man's flatulence.

The Gamer lingered on him a moment longer before finally turning away heading towards the back of the store. They stepped through an entrance that separated from the rest of the store from a doorway that read "Authorized Personnel Only".

Past this was a small kitchen which Xander saw was in need of at least several hours of hard manual labor before it even looked somewhat prepared to cook a sterile—let alone decent—meal. The Gamer turned away from the mess, not seeming to notice the mess or the disgusted looks it was receiving, and started down a flight of stairs.

Xander stayed quiet and kept pace behind Stan as they made their way into the basement, which had been gutted to serve as both a bedroom and a workshop, where a variety of guns and other weapons hung on the walls in a decorative manner. The "studio", which consisted mostly of a messy computer desk and a large table, took up the far side of the basement. The table housed a combination of bits and parts of guns as well as several different sized blades that gleamed under an over-head work light. Next to this, several clips of ammunition and some stray bullets rested in a small plastic bin beside several partially disassembled handguns.

"Now, about your toys," The Gamer wheezed in delight, "Marcus told me a simple cleaning and a few dozen custom rounds would do the trick just fine. But then he drops this case in my lap containing the most spectacular set I'd ever seen and I said 'what the shit!' and decided to do a full overhaul." He tugged Xander's shirt collar and laughed like a choking infant, "'You oh-ficially been pimped!'"

Xander frowned, suddenly beginning to wonder why a routine cleaning and a few "custom rounds" should take a month and a half. Realizing that he wasn't going to like what this man had done, he narrowed his eyes, "What exactly have you done to 'pimp me'?" he asked.

Misinterpreting his tone as a sign of impatience, The Gamer began heaving excitedly and hurried to pull two cases down from a shelf that hung over the table. One of the cases—the larger of the two—Xander recognized as his own. The other, though smaller and newer-looking, was similar in design. The Gamer snorted again, his excitement boiling over and his reddish-brown aura bubbling with the same ferocity, and set it down just out of Xander's reach, "I very rarely get a project that leads to this kind of inspiration. I mean, before this I simply dabbled in the custom jobs"—he smirked, his face beaming with pride—"but now I'd like to consider myself an *artiste.*"

Xander, seeing no way to get the fat man to hurry things along, looked at Stan, who had obviously been in this position before. He shrugged and gave him a hopeless look. The Gamer, they realized as they turned back to him, hadn't paused in his ramblings:

"... and I thought to myself: 'self, you can do that!'," he grinned broadly, exposing teeth that were laced with what Xander hoped were pepperoni fragments, "*And* put a little Gamer spin on it."

Stan sighed again, loud enough to get the man's attention. "We *do* need to wrap this up before sunrise," he pointed out.

The Gamer frowned but nodded and glanced at Xander with a sneer, "Vampires:"—he muttered as he turned back to the cases—"so needy."

Grabbing the larger box and setting it in front of his guests, he carefully undid the polished clasps and opened it. To Xander's relief, the twins, aside from looking a lot cleaner, were unchanged.

"While faced with Marcus' request for ammo," The Gamer began again, "I thought that simple rounds weren't nearly fun enough and basic hollow points were just too damn boring for *the* son of Joseph Stryker. So I go through my stash and begin to brainstorm." He reached for another box that was waiting under the work station and opened it next to the revolvers and pulled out two different bullets, "This one,"—he motioned to the first with a sausage-link finger—"follows along the same principles of a hollow point, but halfway through the shell I laced it with some personal Gamer magic that will increase the stopping power ten times over!"

Xander did a double-take at the mention of magic; what could a nerdy videogame merchant know of the arts?

"Now this one"—The Gamer gently lifted up the second—"is an explosive round that I added some concussive spells to."

Stan nodded, impressed.

Xander forced another smile, turning his attentions back to the revolvers and running a finger across Yang's shiny barrel, "So are we ready to go then?" he asked.

The Gamer looked at Xander with something that was both a glare and a pout, "Wait!" he said, scrambling to get his bulk to twist in order to retrieve the second case. Xander sighed, seeing no apparent end to the discomfort of the visit and leaned against the work table, folding his arms across his chest. The Gamer's excited snorts and wheezing laughs started up again, "I've saved the best for last!"

Xander frowned and glared towards Stan, "The best?"

Stan shrugged.

The Gamer let out another excited snort and unlatched the clasps on the smaller case and flipped it open, revealing a similar lining as the original, except instead of hugging a set of twin revolvers, there was a twin pair of pistols that followed the same white-and-black design.

Xander stared at the weapons, astounded.

The Gamer beamed, "I went with the same general design as Marcus' Berretta, but I guarantee you won't find anything like these on the streets.

"Now, I'm not sure how the original set was made, but there *is* magical residue on them, which is what inspired me to form, mold, and color the alloy through molecular manipulation." He wheezed and smiled at Stan and then at Xander, looking for praise. When none was issued, he went on, "That alone took four weeks!"

Xander, though he refused to show it any further than he already had, *was* impressed, but something deep inside of him felt enraged by the sight. "I don't want them," he said in a low tone.

The Gamer's wheezing laughter cut short and he turned to look at him, "W-what?"

Feeling that their business was over, Xander grabbed the original set and closed the case, thumbing the latches shut. Certain they were secure before tucking this under his arm, he grabbed the extra, magical ammunition and turned to head for the stairs.

Stan frowned, "Xander, I don't think he meant to—"

The Gamer snorted, "Not even a 'thank-you'?"

Xander stopped halfway up the stairs and shot the fat man a glare, "A 'thank you'?" he turned and took a step down. "Alright. Thanks for fixing what wasn't broken in the first place and putting your own personal greasy spin on an already perfect pair," he held up the original case. The heat of his anger was already wrapping around his spine as his fangs extended from his gums and he had to fight the urge to use them then and there.

Where was this outburst coming from?

Was he really that enraged by the new guns?

When he felt that he had his rage and impulses under control, he sneered and began up the stairs again, "Keep your knockoffs!" he spat behind him, "The originals and I have business to take care of!" As he stomped the rest of the way up the stairs, he could hear Stan and The Gamer exchange their farewells before the echo of feet started up behind him.

CHAPTER THIRTY-TWO
HARD GOODBYES

IT WAS THE NIGHT BEFORE HE WAS
supposed to go on his self-assigned mission and Xander was
practicing his aim.

He knew he didn't need to; since his father's abilities had
awakened within him he had been able to, as Stan put it,
"Take a fly off a fencepost from a hundred yards away". And
it wasn't a lie, his skills *had* grown exponentially since the
awakening ceremony, and he found himself capable of things
he never before thought possible.

Stan had gone off somewhere for a few hours, leaving
Tiger-Trepis to lie down on the back porch as Xander shot

301

again and again at a series of targets set up at the end of the backyard. He had gotten off about three shots before Stan stopped him and enshrouded the backyard in a silencing spell, asking that he not bring the cops around such a nice neighborhood. Putting a few more rounds into the center of the targets he'd set up against the trees that lined the backyard, he finally put the revolvers down and sat with a sigh next to the tiger and rubbed its head.

"You think I got what it takes, buddy?"

The animal looked up at him and bobbed his head. Xander wasn't sure if it was the motion of an overly exhausted big cat or of an overly intelligent one.

He hoped for the latter.

"Yea, that's what they're all telling me."

He sighed again, seeing no reason to rest when the moment of truth was so close to becoming the present. The tiger watched without much enthusiasm as he pushed himself off the porch with his aura, reclining in midair for a moment as Sophie had so many times before her death. Still hovering in midair, he pushed off, performing a flip before catching himself again and slowly lowering his feet to the grass.

"A thing of beauty!"

Xander jumped; startled. He'd never heard Stan come back.

He turned and nodded slowly to his friend, "I learned from the best."

Stan shook his head, showing a wide smile as he looked up at the clear night sky. "It was like watching your father practice," he said as he waved his hand, removing the spell, and turned back; his smile beginning to fade, "I have to tell you something."

Xander bit his lip and sat back down on the porch,

"What is it?"

Stan moved to sit on a deck chair and sighed as he lowered himself into it, "I won't be here when you get back."

Xander frowned, "What? But why?"

Stan looked down and several seconds passed in silence, "The Devil's paid his dues, I suppose."

"What the hell is that supposed to mean?" Xander asked.

"It means there's little more I can do for you here and now. You've become what you were meant to be and I need to gracefully exit the picture."

Xander glared, "And where will you go?"

"Not sure," Stan said with a shrug. If he'd picked up on Xander's rage, he wasn't acknowledging it.

"You're not sure? Then why are you leaving?" Xander yelled, rocketing to his feet.

Stan shrugged again, his calmness remaining, "That, Xander, will come up when we meet again."

"And how do you know we'll meet again?" he growled, starting to storm back-and-forth on the porch, "Since when are you so damn sure of the future?"

Stan continued to ignore the hostility and smiled. "It's just the way it is. Besides, you have things to do. When you get back you need to pay Estella a visit. You *did* promise, after all," he chided.

Xander turned his back to his old friend, "You've been in my head again?"

Stan chuckled and nodded, "It is such a *fascinating* place to visit."

Xander scoffed, feeling it was his last defense against the river of tears that threatened to break through.

"It's time for you to go now," Stan said, patting him on the shoulder.

Shaking his head, Xander turned back to face his friend, "C'mon, Stan! Give me another day. We can practice—y'know, spar some more! I'm not golden yet."

Stan lifted himself from the chair, locking his eyes on Xander's, and suddenly the young vampire was looking at his father once again.

"Son," the specter whispered, "you're beyond golden. And, moreover, you're a Stryker! Now stop stalling and go get that son of a bitch!"

The image wavered and faded then and suddenly Stan was standing before him again.

Xander's jaw trembled and he turned away to hide it and nodded. He knew Stan had nothing to do with the vision—his own mind was pushing him forward. He sighed sadly to himself, "Go get me a ride, Stan. I need to prepare."

There was no answer, and when he turned around he realized that his friend was already gone.

While Stan was out, Xander went into the guest room that had been Marcus'. He was eager to get the red leather jacket on. Though he wasn't sure why Marcus hadn't come back for his things yet; what he *did* know was that the coat was too damn sweet to let rot in Stan's closet.

He pulled the jacket on over his black turtleneck, once again marveling at the fit and admiring his reflection in the full-length mirror beside the closet. A grin tugged at the corner of his lip as he remembered Marcus' "Crimson Shadow" taunts. With this in mind, he ran his palms against the leather of his new jacket and went to work making sure Yin and Yang were loaded.

Stan showed up around midnight with the car that would take Xander to Maine: a blood-red Firebird with a pair of black racing stripes!

Though Xander wasn't sure of the year, he was quite aware that it was expensive and shuddered at the thought of how it had been obtained.

Stan smiled at him from behind the wheel as he watched his awe-filled approach, "I figured the Crimson Shadow needed a sweet ride to begin his legacy in!"

Xander shook his head, faking a scowl, "I'm really beginning to *hate* that nickname!"

Stan shrugged as he climbed out of the still-running car and laughed, "That just means it will stick with you even longer!"

Xander rolled his eyes, "Great…"

Stan smiled and nodded, "Oh, and I put a tarp in the trunk for you to keep from tanning when you stop it to rest."

Xander nodded his thanks and the two embraced. Despite still feeling bitter, he wished his friend well with his new life of travel—wherever it might take him. Stan thanked him, smiling briefly before his gaze moved downward and Xander frowned as he watched this, hoping he was merely choked up about their parting…

But he knew better.

"There's something you should know," Stan confessed.

Xander sighed, wishing he'd been wrong, but gave a nod for Stan to continue.

"Kyle knows that you're coming."

Xander scowled and tensed but gave a slow nod, "I

figured the motherfucker would pick up on my intentions."

Stan forced a smiled, but the gesture soon melted away into a calculated stare, "Listen: aurics often rely on distance to fight, and I doubt this Kyle is going to be any different. He's going to throw anything he can at you to keep you from getting too close."

"Like what?" Xander asked, knowing he wasn't going to like the answer.

Stan leaned gently against the car and looked up at the sky, "More than likely, he'll use humans."

Xander stood for a moment, considering his words. As the reality of what it meant settled in, he pinched the bridge of his nose, "Fuck!"

Stan nodded, dragging his gaze from the stars and locking them on him, "What are you prepared to do?"

Xander thought about the question, tapping his thigh with the case containing his guns. For a long moment he was afraid to say his answer out loud, scared of what it meant, but, finally, he cleared his throat and responded: "Anything." He nodded, fighting through the wave of guilt, "I'll do *anything* to get to him!"

Stan smiled, satisfied with the answer.

Xander's guts tied into a knot and he shook the bangs from his vision, "But…"

"But you don't want to kill all those innocent people," Stan finished for him.

Xander nodded.

Stan smirked, "How ironic that you'd find your humanity after *losing* it."

"It's not on purpose, I can tell you that much," Xander laughed.

"No," Stan said, grinning back, "I suppose it wouldn't

be."

A long silence followed and the two looked back up at the sky, each pondering what was to come.

"I can only hope that your sympathies don't get you killed," Stan finally said.

Xander bit his lip and nodded, not looking back down from the sky, "Me too."

"In this situation, however, you may be in luck." Xander looked up curiously as Stan's eyes lit up with realization, "An auric very often will need to empty out a mind in order to control it completely. If this is what Kyle has planned than those people are going to die anyway!"

"So they're dead one way or the other?" Xander sneered at the idea of someone being controlled by Kyle, "I'd be putting them out of their misery!"

"That's one way of looking at it," Stan said with a nod.

Xander shook his head, "It's the *only* way of looking at it in this case!"

With directions programmed into the GPS Stan had included with the car and everything he'd need packed up Xander hopped into the Firebird and gunned the engine, throwing it into gear and driving off.

A Doors album—left in the player—was blaring "Riders on the Storm" from the stereo as the knowledge that he was about to fulfill his life's mission drove him towards Maine and the completion of his life's mission.

CHAPTER THIRTY-THREE
A NIGHTMARE'S NIGHTMARE

HE WAS A MASTER OF TORMENT AND

a self-proclaimed artist of misery. He had shaped and been the source of so many horrid nightmares that simply thinking of all the dreamers and their screams made his mind ache with gluttonous pride.

But that night, his were the most horrible nightmares in the house:

No matter what he threw at it, it kept coming at him.

He tried several times to manifest weapons, knowing full well that in his dreams such things were possible, but they turned to scorpions and snakes in his hands.

He yelled out, but there were no ears to hear him; there was only the one gleaming red eye and a mouth that gaped like an ivory gate, swinging open to reveal hungry, gleaming fangs.

Laughter!

Insane, tormenting laughter all around him!

And he was too weak to fight it. There was nobody to feed from! No torment to make him strong enough to face the approaching threat! For the first time, he tasted his own fear.

Then, suddenly: a mind!

An aura!

A precious source to drain!

He dove into it, looking for sustenance to give him strength, but all he got was fire.

The burning scorched his brain, shooting down his spine and seizing his entire body. It boiled his skin and melted his insides and he felt himself fall into an empty, dark place with nothing but himself and his newfound torment...

And the gleaming red eye.

He woke up with a gasp and quickly scanned the room with both his eyes and his aura for any possible threat that might have gotten in. When nothing presented itself, he relaxed, looking down at his wife—his prey—and giving her rear a hard pinch.

He smiled at the pained whimper that escaped her lips as her dormant aura shifted and he greedily took in her pain. The meal was tarnished by the memories of the nightmare, however. He knew what was on its way to get him. Knew from the moment it had awakened.

He refused to let himself worry, however. He had seen the effect of his powers on the minds of those he had tormented in the past, and he was sure that this would give him the edge he needed.

He remembered the approaching threat as the boy that the other vampires had wanted dead.

Later on, after the horrendous failure and the resulting execution of his crew as a penalty, he'd found out that the boy was the son of an auric prodigy!

In retrospect, the boy's ties to their kind made sense, explaining how the twerp had been able to conceal himself that night.

He shook his head and peeked out the window at the calm winter scenery and imagined what it would be like when he finally arrived. He reached out to try and pinpoint it, but as soon as he felt a pattern and tried to lock on it snapped at him and chased him away.

"Bastard!"

The kid had skill.

A frown plagued his face for the first time in a long while and he turned away from the window and walked down the hall, reaching ahead with his aura and unlocking the latch to the therion's door so that it was accessible by the time he reached it. His stepson snored loudly, a leg hanging from the bed and an arm bent at an awkward angle over his face.

He'd lied when he'd told him that he'd let his mother live. After all, it was his right to do what he wanted with his wife! As for the boy…

Well, he made a decent puppet.

WAKE UP! Kyle roared in his head.

Tyler shot up with a growl; his lips pulled back and his human teeth exposed. When he saw his stepfather standing over him, however, he stopped in mid-growl and drew back.

"W-what is it?" he asked, his voice a blended tone of hatred and fear.

"It's coming!" Kyle answered as he shut the door behind

him, "It'll be arriving soon, and when it does it intends to destroy me." He watched as the boy grinned at the thought and glared down at him, "And if it succeeds I will bring you and Kelly down with me!" he grinned as he reached out and consumed a wave of resulting grief.

He probed momentarily, letting out a small chuckle as he tweaked his stepson's thoughts just enough to serve his purpose and a satisfied smile swept over his face as he finished his work and the young therion's eyes shone with the hungry gleam of a ravenous animal. Stepping back, he watched as the boy's body shook with the beginning of the transformation.

He was pleased to have such a weak-minded stepson.

He would be the first line of defense.

CHAPTER THIRTY-FOUR
"NO MORE PAIN"

XANDER WAS CAMPED OUT ABOUT AN
hour or so away from his target. Though he'd had it in him to make it the whole way, he knew that what he needed—like it or not—was rest. In the course of the night he'd already traveled several hundred miles, the speedometer stopping at one-twenty after he'd grown tired of the engine's limits and taken the car off the road.

Literally!

It might've have been a strange sight to see a car flying an inch off the ground doing more than three-hundred miles-per-hour, but after Xander swept the surrounding drivers' minds they had no recollection of ever having seen a Firebird that night.

Every time a cop had decided to flash their lights at him, Xander simply reached behind him with his aura and tweaked their minds until they were convinced that they were chasing nothing but a phantom. Then he would chuckle as the flashing lights shut off and their car slowed and took its place again at the side of the road.

The GPS predicted that the trip would take him nearly an entire day's worth of driving to get to Maine, but he had turned a twenty-two hour trip into an eight hour one.

About an hour before sunrise he lowered the Firebird onto the side of the road, being sure to park deep onto the shoulder and in the back-roads to avoid some nosy passer-by from poking around during the day and potentially turning him into a skin cancer victim. He hunted for the rest of the night, feeding from whatever he caught and using his aura to consume from whatever he didn't. Though the panic and fear "tasted" horrible, it *was* energy and it was what he needed.

As the sun began to peak over the trees and shine off the layer of snow, he pulled the tarp from the trunk and draped it over the car before sitting behind the wheel, reclining the seat, and forcing himself to sleep.

Xander was awake and on the road again before the sun had completely set; leaving as soon as he felt that it was safe to do so. Though the sunlight was still a risk, he was willing to deal with the anger and irritability that came with less-than an hour's exposure.

If nothing else it would certainly drive him that much faster.

Flooring the accelerator, he ignored the strained whine from the car's engine and let loose the full potential that lay under the hood. When the sun was finally down and no longer a drain on his energy, he once again wrapped the car in his aura and lifted it off the ground to hasten the trip.

He was three miles out, overlooking nothing but nighttime and trees, when he hit the animal.

The car shook as it collided with the hood and a sharp yelp and a pained whimper followed. Xander rolled his eyes; he'd hit a damn dog and dented the hood of the car!

So much for the integrity of The Crimson Shadow's ride!

Still listening to the creature carry on behind the car, he reached into the case and drew out Yang. Then, still cursing, he pulled himself from the driver's seat, slamming the door behind him. As he rounded the car he began to search for the dog he'd hit, keeping the white revolver ready in case he had to protect himself from whatever fight the injured creature might still have in it. He figured it was better to simply shoot it, since it was a miracle that it had lived through the impact of a floating car doing over two-hundred. He stopped in his tracks...

Not even a miracle could save a dog from that sort of collision!

His mind's eye alerted him of the danger a split second before the first attack caught him in the back and he hit the ground. Face buried in the snow, he gave thanks that he was still clutching the revolver. Before he had a chance to turn around and face his attacker, however, there was a pair of strong hands pressing on the back of his head. They pushed, forcing his face further into the frozen mound and held him there—suffocating him. Desperation filled his mind as his lungs screamed for oxygen and his aura flailed about.

He had to relax! His auric abilities were useless if he was reaching out in blind panic.

Unless...

Concentrating on the snow beneath him, he imagined a cup of cold water that he needed to boil; he imagined a cigarette that needed to be lit. He imagined anything and everything hot and burning and pushed more and more of the growing energy into the mound that was robbing him of breath and didn't stop until his face touched the cold, wet grass below and he got a breath of earth-laced air.

Denied the ability to drown him in the snow, the hands that still gripped the back of his head began to pound his face into the turf over and over. Xander screamed in rage and expanded his aura into a protective orb that forced his attacker off of him and he quickly jumped to his feet.

There was an inhuman growl as Xander turned to face his attacker and recoiled when he saw the therion. The thing's forehead was large and flat, caving the eyes in and making them look narrowed and fierce. The jaw was stretched and jutted out in a quivering maw that was filled with fierce teeth. Staring at it, he realized that it looked like a strange cross between a monkey and a starved wild-cat. It roared at him and Xander, desperate for energy, reached out and siphoned the rage from its earth-colored aura.

As the moon emerged from behind a patch of passing clouds and bathed the therion in light, he noticed the shredded remains of a button-up shirt that billowed in a passing breeze and what had once been a decent pair of jeans that were barely intact.

Xander glared as the therion hunched down, preparing

to pounce, and aimed Yang at its head. After playing around with The Gamers' rounds the day before he couldn't remember what he had in the ivory revolver's chambers, though he was certain that whatever it was would have no problem taking the beast's head off. The creature roared again at the sight of the weapon and swiped a long arm at it; its hooked claws whistling through the air. It bared its teeth at him when it came up short and he felt compelled to do the same and drew back his lips and, extending his fangs at it, hissed like a basket of shaken cobras.

The therion dropped to all fours and took a long, loping step forward and Xander regained his composure in time to pull the trigger and fire a round that hit a mound of snow in the distance and blew up, sending cold rain down on him and only him.

But where was the—

Clawed hands at his neck answered the question too early and in all the wrong ways and he felt himself hurled towards—and then into—the surrounding woods. Not wanting to see how a vampire's body would hold up against crashing head-first into an oak, Xander reached out and stopped himself with his aura before hurling himself back at the menace like a slingshot.

The therion tilted its head in confusion as he rocketed back in its direction and, at the last moment, it dodged the attack and grabbed Xander by the jacket, spinning him around and slamming him into the side of the Firebird. An immense pain shot through his body and he cried out in agony and gripped Yang tighter, preparing for another shot.

The therion circled like a wolf coming down on injured prey and Xander scowled at the creature as he pulled himself from the twisted metal of the Firebird and aimed at it before he squeezed the trigger three times.

The monster side-stepped at the last minute, dodging the first two shots and they exploded harmlessly in the forest a ways back. The third shot tore into the beast's forearm, tearing the limb off at the elbow. There was a bright flash of light then and the rest of the creature's arm singed away to its shoulder like a cigarette turning to ash.

The Gamers' magic. Xander thought to himself, pleased with the results.

The therion howled in agony as it stared in shock at the wound; its jaw hanging open and panting in pain. Though the rest of it was still monstrous and menacing, its eyes suddenly looked hurt and scared. Xander, seeing the human expression on the monster's face, slowly lowered his gun to his side.

The therion whimpered again, clutching at its stump of a shoulder and turned its all-too-human eyes towards Xander, moving its jaws but only producing pained barks.

Xander frowned and stepped forward, allowing his aura to reach out and wrap around the creature's head as he entered its mind. Inside, he came face to face with a teenage boy; brown hair that was unkempt yet stylish waved about from non-existing winds and the same terrified eyes looked at him with desperation as his lips moved wordlessly.

Xander frowned and focused harder on digging deeper into the therion's mind.

STOP-OP HIM-IM! It was the same voice—the same request—but shouted from what sounded like a dozen mouths at once. It was the only thought in the creature's head!

Xander turned back towards the boy and tightened his hold on the mind, being careful not to rupture the entire system and leave him brain-damaged. The boy, realizing what was happening, stepped forward and looked at Xander.

Please! The boy pleaded again, *You have to stop him!*

Xander blinked and when his eyes opened again he was back in the snow-capped woods with the one-armed therion—its breaths coming in ragged—in front of him. Its hot breath condensed in the air and made foul-smelling clouds and though Xander was free of the therion-boy's mind, he could still hear his plea. As he listened he could hear Kyle's voice as it jack-hammered inside the poor boy's mind.

He was overwhelmed by the realization that this was his old stepfather's most recent victim; his newest stepchild. Entering the mind again, he began searching his memories, seeing Kyle's manipulative entrance into his life and various degrading and humiliating acts against the boy—Tyler.

It was the exact same torture that he had experienced so many years ago.

Please! Tyler's voice continued to beg, *There's nothing I can do to stop him; to help her...* Xander frowned as he saw who Tyler meant and shuddered at the "sight". The bastard hadn't changed one bit! In the back of Tyler's head, Xander could sense Kyle's auric manipulations, "hearing" the command that he'd been given and was continuing to fight: the command to kill him, no matter what the cost, *Please... there will be no peace for any of us until he's dead!*

"Peace..." Xander looked down at Yang, lingering on his thoughts. Finally, he stepped forward and pressed the barrel to the creature's forehead.

The therion looked at him with sad eyes and breathed heavily, *No more pain?*

Xander shook his head. "No more pain," he recited as he pulled the trigger.

The blast echoed through the night, and the fluttering of

birds taking flight sounded in the distance. There was a moment of silence and then, suddenly, the thunder of an approaching army; coming at him from the woods. He turned away from Tyler—facing towards the new threat—as the magic from the bullet consumed his body and sent embers flying into the night sky.

CHAPTER THIRTY-FIVE
FODDER IN THE FOG

AS THE SOUND OF HIS ENEMY'S ARMY

drew closer, Xander hurried to the battered Firebird, fetching the spare ammo and beginning the process of reloading Yang with explosive rounds.

When he'd finished with the white revolver, he set it on the car's roof and grabbed Yin, repeating the process, this time with the magical hollow points. With both of the twins fully loaded, he grabbed the rest of the enchanted rounds and stuffed them into an old backpack. Finally, positive that he was ready, he thumbed back the hammers on both the guns and turned to face the onslaught.

The distance grew luminescent then as a mass number of auras—all shining a dull, bloody-grey—came at him. Xander scowled, the shared shade giving away what he had already guessed: they were all slaves of Kyle's mind control.

Just as Stan had predicted!

As he contemplated his next move he was startled by the roars of engines and lifted both revolvers abruptly, aiming into the forest and waiting for a target to present itself. Though his vampire eyes were sharp and the darkness meant little, something seemed to be clouding the army's approach.

Suddenly the clamor stopped, leaving the roars of several engines. Before Xander could figure out what had happened three snowmobiles came charging over the snow bank on the edge of the road and flew at him. Diving to avoid being struck, he caught himself with his aura before crashing to the road as the machines and their riders landed and sprayed sparks across the concrete.

Still suspended in midair, he twisted to face the slave-rider that had landed closest to him and fired a round from Yang. The rider swerved out of its path and the bullet exploded in the street, leaving a small, fiery crater.

Xander growled and touched down to the street before jumping into the air and landing on the roof of the Firebird, putting himself out of the vehicles' range. Crouched on the dented metal surface, he glared down at the mind-slaves as they all skidded to a stop and stared up at him with dull, mindless eyes.

A winter gust picked up, taking a hold of the stilled combatants and tugging at the hoods of the riders' parkas and kicking Xander's hair into a frenzy about his head. Momentarily blinded by his shifting bangs, he hurried to clear his vision with his forearm and was shocked to see that the three had taken the opportunity to draw their own weapons: hunting rifles.

Before he had a chance to raise his revolvers in retaliation the first shot was fired, piercing through his left shoulder and throwing him off the roof of the car and knocking Yin and Yang from his grip.

"SHIT!" he landed onto the road, clutching the wound and hissing in rage.

The riders dismounted their snowmobiles and circled the car. Snarling at them, he rolled to his feet, cringing slightly at the pain in his shoulder. Though he was sure being shot hurt a lot more for a human, the sensation was still an extremely painful one and he cursed again for being injured so early in the fight. Ignoring the burning sting, he crouched down in anticipation of the three as they charged at him. The leading attacker—a tall, balding man—turned his rifle in his grip and swung the gun at him like a club, catching Xander in the chest.

Doing his best to ignore the pain, he snarled, baring his fangs at the men despite their emotionless faces and grabbing the next swing of the rifle in his right hand, releasing his grip on his still-bleeding shoulder in the process. As the mind-slave struggled to regain his weapon, one of the other riders came around and repeated his comrade's attack: swinging the rifle in a wide arc and connecting with the young vampire's wound. A fiery inferno of agony wracked him and he dropped to his knees, cursing and sucking in frozen air in an attempt to numb the pain. As he did this, he became aware of the three rifles as they were cocked and leveled at his head.

Despite the threat of being shot, he couldn't avert his attention from the weapons' owners; especially their drumming heartbeats and the smell of the blood as it grew more and more pungent in their veins.

Forgetting the roaring pain in his shoulder he cried out in fury, a brief static crackling in the air as his aura shot from his chest and became a protective orb that surrounded him and forced the rifles from his attackers' hands, twisting and bending the barrels until they were nothing more than balls of metal.

The thirst was unbelievable! For the first time since his awakening he felt the uncontrollable drive to feed and he rose to his feet and glared at the mind-slaves.

Kyle thought he was buying himself a chance by putting humans—potential *energy*—in his path? He thought they would slow down or even *stop* him?

He was merely providing him with a meal!

Without their weapons the three drones were left with no other option but to charge forward empty-handed. Xander grinned, welcoming the advance, and drove his foot down with all his vampiric strength on the closest attacker's kneecap, his nostrils flaring as the force drove bone through flesh and filled the air with the scent of blood. The man gave a pained grunt and collapsed, unable to go on any further. Uncaring, the other two jumped over the injured obstruction that was their fallen comrade.

The man to Xander's left was cast aside easily with a swift backhand that drove him face-first into the street, further saturating the air with the sweet aroma. Down to the last of the riders, Xander turned to the third man as he pulled a serrated hunting knife from a sheath at his belt and swung his arm around, plunging the weapon into Xander's left side. Overcome by thirst, Xander ignored the pain and hissed again.

The man frowned—though his eyes remained lifeless—
and began to twist the submerged blade in an attempt to get
the upper hand. Before much progress could be made,
however, Xander lunged forward, grabbing the mind-slave's
head and ripping it from his shoulders. The resulting eruption
from the neck-stump covered the surroundings in blood and
Xander, overwhelmed by the scent, shot forward at the two
survivors.

Broken-kneecap was unaware of the attack until after the
fangs had torn into his neck, and as Xander fed, he sensed
the other as he pulled himself up. This one stumbled towards
him, reaching for the knife that was still embedded in his side.
Sensing the mind-slave's motives but not wanting to turn
away from his meal, Xander lashed out with his aura and
ensnared him, digging through his mind for any sort of
psychic energy but finding nothing of substance. Not wanting
to let the blood go to waste, he held him in his auric binds as
he finished his first course.

With his thirst subsided and his foggy mind cleared,
Xander turned back and fetched his guns. Lifting his left arm,
he cringed at the remaining pain from the still-healing
gunshot wound in his shoulder. The knife-wound was
completely healed but his shoulder still gaped. The bleeding,
thankfully, had stopped as the healing process took its effect,
but the wound still remained, serving as a reminder that he
was no longer at his peak fighting condition. He frowned at
this realization, silently willing his body to heal faster as he
gingerly rubbed the wound and moved forward.

He wasn't about to be swayed.

The eerie silence continued as he went into his backpack and refilled the empty chambers of his guns. He frowned as he finished up, realizing that Kyle was playing games with him. Shaking his head, he turned towards the thick haze that waited ahead of him—no doubt one of the bastard's mind-tricks—and extended his aura into the depths. He reached as far as he could, finding that his mind's eye was limited as well.

For nearly ten minutes he trudged forward towards the auric mass; the army seeming to be close but never showing with each advancing step. Unsure as to why Kyle was tormenting him with the suspense of holding his drones at bay, Xander was at least glad for the opportunity to heal further. Just as this thought was done forming in his mind the sound of the army picked up again.

Xander rolled his eyes. "Figures!" he growled.

As he looked ahead, a line of ghostly faces emerged from the haze. Wasting no time on the spectacle, he fired an explosive round into the group, watching as the night lit up with The Gamer's magic and the faces disappeared into the inferno, leaving behind sizzling embers and red-stained snow. With the lingering powder and mist dying down the auric haze that had haunted him began to recede and Xander found himself staring at the massive army.

The people, all void of any sort of expression, stood shoulder-to-shoulder, each armed with whatever weapon or potentially dangerous tool had been at hand. Many wielded a firearm of some sort while others carried axes and other farming equipment and one, he noticed, armed with nothing more than a steak knife.

All at once, like a single being, they charged.

Xander lifted both guns, firing a round from each into the approaching crowd. The explosive round went off—

filling the woods once again with its mystical light—and incinerated nearly a dozen mind-slaves in the process while the hollow point caught an advancing man in the chest and sent him rocketing back with bone-crushing force into the mind-slaves behind him, shattering their bones and leaving them unable to move.

Though many were taken down by the two rounds alone, others quickly stormed forward in their place, climbing over the dead and wounded in an attempt to reach their target. Xander, holding his focus, mentally recited applicable lessons from his training as he braced himself.

"'Fluid, never rigid'," he fired another round, "'Trust your instincts'!"

Two men wearing leather hooked around and came at him from either side—one wielding a tire-iron while the other swung a length of chain over his head—as a pimple-faced teen charged at him from the front with a fallen branch brandished like a spear. Xander rolled his eyes at the sight, raising his arm to get off a shot only to be caught off guard as the drone to his right brought the chain down onto his hand. Though nothing was broken, the force was enough to knock Yang from his grip and he cursed as the length of metal came around again and connected with his forehead. Swooning from the impact, he dropped to a knee as a wave of dizziness overcame him. He heard the jingle of the chain and sensed another attack coming and quickly rolled forward, deciding to take his chances with the kid and his branch instead. The rattle of the links coupled with a wet crack and he scanned the scene behind him with his mind's eye, "seeing" that his dodge had been effective and the chain had just crushed the other man's skull. His scanning mind picked up on branch-boy then as he swung downward for a head-shot and Xander caught it with an auric tendril, standing quickly and turning to the chain-wielder as he tried for another swing. Xander frowned, listening to the commotion from the rest of Kyle's drones, and jumped into overdrive.

All at once the blur of the swinging chain slowed to a stop as his vision changed to accommodate his heightened speed and reflexes. The roar of the mind-slaves' attack dulled to a near-silent hum. Knowing he didn't have much time before exhaustion would set in he lunged, throwing his fist forward and punching into the chain-man's chest. The force of the attack coupled with his advanced speed drove his hand through his attacker's torso until his arm burst out of the other side, grazing his spine as it exited. Startled by the effect he yanked his hand away, sneering in disgust at the viscera-coated forearm that emerged. Wasting no time he turned away from the man—already dead but not yet aware of it—to face the boy and the rest of the time-frozen mind-slave army.

The scene lurched momentarily as he started to drop out of overdrive; the drones beginning to move forward in slow-motion. Xander shot forward and bent to retrieve his fallen revolver and pulled the trigger, watching as the round crept from the barrel before he leaped into the air. Once off the ground and completely out of overdrive, he looked down and watched as the explosive round took its toll on the closest of the mind-slaves.

The force of his superhuman jump began to waver and gravity took hold of him then, pulling him back down to Earth. As the ground—and mind-slaves eager to kill him—grew closer with his descent, he fired a round at the base of a large nearby tree; the hollow-point struck the trunk, sending wood fragments spraying like shrapnel into the crowd and they scattered as the tree shuddered and started to topple.

Grabbing the closest branch, Xander steadied himself and began to work his way towards the top, leaping from branch to branch. As the tree became ever more horizontal with its collapse, what had been a steady ascent turned into a full-out sprint up its surface. Moments before crashing to the ground he threw himself off, landing and rolling to his feet several yards away. Behind him, the impact of the fallen tree shook the ground and sent clumps of snow raining down from neighboring trees' branches.

Xander, breathing hard from the exertion, turned and watched as the mind-slaves that had survived stumbled about in confusion before they suddenly went rigid. Xander frowned, watching as the drones were psychically fed new commands from Kyle and they turned all at once to face him.

"You can't expect them to hold me off forever," he shouted towards the crowd.

Kyle's response came in the form of a lone red-haired woman who stepped forward from the crowd and raised her arm at him. For a moment it appeared she was simply pointing until he noticed the small pistol in her hand.

The first shot grazed his cheek as he dove from its path, scurrying to put himself on the other side of the fallen tree as a line of shots traced his path. At that moment, every gun-toting drone marched to the front of the line and followed the redhead's example and a barrage of gunfire erupted; bullets filling the air and pelting Xander's wooden shield and the surrounding forest with their deadly spray.

"YOU BASTARD!" Xander screamed into the depths of the woods, "I *WILL* GET YOU!"

Not if you don't get up. Kyle taunted in his mind as the gunfire became more rapid and narrowed in on his location. A spray of woodchips rained into his face; like it or not, Kyle was right: he wouldn't make it any further if he stayed there and allowed himself to get shot up.

Reaching out with his aura and seeking out the closest of the shooters, he yanked the gun from their grip and snared the drone, pulling them behind the tree. All at once the gunfire stopped and the sound of snow crunching underfoot grew nearer. Xander growled and turned to face his captive, finding the redhead who'd started the bullet-storm squirming in his auric binds. As he looked at her, he once again became aware of the blood pulsing under her skin as the exhaustion tugging at his system became more demanding. Overcome with the sudden need to feed he yanked the woman's head to one side and moved to feed only to have his head snapped back before he could get his fangs in. He growled, struggling, as one of the drones clutched his hair and yanked him away again, keeping him from feeding.

Turning his head towards the drone, he hissed at the man and swiped at his throat. There was a sharp ripping noise as flesh was torn and blood began to gush from the obstructing drone's neck. Despite the injury and the loss of blood, however, his grip remained tight—Kyle's hold not wavering in the slightest. Xander narrowed his eyes, looking past the puppet and cursing Kyle's name.

The redhead—still held in his aura—struggled to get free and more mind-slaves climbed over and around the tree, taking their hold on him and keeping him from his meal. Xander hissed again and snapped his jaws at whatever flesh got close enough but was unable to score a bite as more and more hands took to holding him back. Before he could focus his aura to push the mob away a heavy set drone stepped into sight and leveled a sawed-off shotgun at him and fired it into his stomach.

Crying out, Xander shut his eyes and clenched his teeth as the pain coursed through his guts like a wildfire. Trying to focus his mind, he took several labored breaths, cringing as each inhale tore at his abdomen. Finally, he threw his aura out in a furious, whipping whirlwind that tore the drones from him and pitched them about the forest; scattering them. The shotgun mind-slave sneered, a familiar gleam entering his otherwise empty eyes.

"Having fun yet, son?" Kyle spoke through his puppet as he cocked the shotgun with an abrupt pump of a massive arm.

Xander narrowed his eyes, pushing the pain aside, and leapt like a wildcat, grabbing the barrel of the gun and pushing it away as it went off.

"I'm not your goddam son, you motherfucking bastard!" Xander spat in the drone's face, his eyes looking past the puppet.

The gleaming eyes remained focused and unwavering as the man gave a sadistic grin and issued out a bellow of laughter. Xander sneered and pushed forward, knocking the bulky body to the ground and pinning it as be began to drink from it. Part of him was disgusted at the source of his meal, but as the first coppery mouthful was swallowed he cast aside the thought and fed as fast as he could, already feeling his injuries start to heal. Even as he tore into the drone's neck, the laughter continued, though labored and lodged with blood.

"I'll... take that... as... a 'yes'," the mind-slave choked out as Xander dug his fangs deeper and deeper to try and silence the laughter.

He could sense others approaching from behind and wrapped himself and his meal in his aura as the first of them arrived. Though he expected an attack to be made, the drones instead lined up patiently just on the other side and watched; the same sadistic grin and evil eye pasted on each of their faces.

"Aren't you a clever boy?"

"Like father, like son."

Xander turned his head, glaring through his auric shield at the twisted ventriloquist act, "Shut the hell up!" he snarled.

Suddenly all of the mind-slaves let out a roar of laughter. Xander, returning to his meal, split his aura into segmented parts to grab and toss away the cackling annoyances. Once free of the mind-controlled pests, he fed freely, relishing in the sensation of the warm liquid rolling down his chin and smearing his face. The blood rejuvenated him as it coursed through his system and the snow below him was stained with the excess as his body rejected the buckshot from his stomach. As his body stitched itself back together, the aching exhaustion in his muscles subsided with each gulp, too.

He pulled away from the spurting wound before he'd had his fill—not wanting to completely sate his thirst before coming face to face with Kyle—and stared down at the still-twitching drone. He watched this for several seconds before crouching down and snapping the man's neck.

With the task completed he returned to the tree where he'd dropped his guns, finding only Yin. He frowned, lifting the lone revolver and looking around for any sign of its twin.

"Shit!" he muttered, dropping his shoulders and sighing heavily—a cloudy plume birthing from his lips and wafting off with the breeze.

"Quite the toy," a feminine voice cooed from behind a neighboring tree. As Xander turned the redhead strolled forward, still torn and battered from his auric attack, with

Yang hoisted against her right shoulder, "But don't you think it's a bit too dangerous for a little faggot like you?" her lips curled into a disturbingly attractive copy of Kyle's grin.

"Dangerous? Isn't that the point?" Xander muttered through clenched teeth. He wasn't worried about the redhead hearing his words; he knew that Kyle would have no problem receiving the message.

There was no witty retort. The drone simply grinned wider and leveled the stolen weapon with two shaky hands and pulled the trigger.

Xander was in overdrive before the hammer had a chance to drop, stepping quickly out of range and dropping out again. The round rocketed from the barrel—the force of the recoil throwing the woman's body backwards—and into the woods, exploding soon after with a chorus of falling trees and snapping branches. The young vampire was quick to snatch his weapon back from the woman as she struggled to get to her feet and aimed both barrels at her as she stood.

"Are you really going to make me kill all these people?" he growled, looking deep into the drone's eyes.

The woman grinned wider. "I don't see any reason not to," Kyle answered through her.

Xander scowled and shook his head, "You fucking coward!"

The woman laughed mockingly and stepped aside, holding her arms out as an invitation for him to advance, "Oh the mouth on you! I'll tell you what: I'll spare you the burden of killing this one. How does that sound?"

Xander narrowed his eyes and held his guns at his side, shaking his head as he walked past, "What does it matter? They're all dead already anyway."

"Too true," the woman's voice answered, "All too true."

A soft chuckle served as a twisted end to the conversation and, as Xander moved past, he felt the woman's aura surge as the control on her mind was lifted. Like a bulb in a power surge it grew brighter and then it dimmed and disappeared. Soon after the soft sound of the body hitting the snow could be heard.

"You fucking coward," he repeated.

The snowy hike deeper into the woods lasted five minutes before he saw Kyle's final line of defense standing several yards in front of his house. Like the rest of those he had enslaved, they looked like they had been pulled off the streets in the midst of living their lives.

Watching them stand there, unmoving and unresponsive without the auric vampire's command, Xander couldn't help but imagine Kyle as the sadistic piper leading an entourage of citizens down the street like hypnotized rats. Several more silent seconds passed before Kyle's command was given and the last of his slaves moved to attack.

Xander sighed, watching as the drones stumbled through the snow as they closed in, and pulled his backpack from his shoulders. Despite the oncoming threat, he was slow and careful in extracting one of the original rounds that had sat in Yang's chamber for so many years without his knowing and pocketing it in the battered jacket. When he was sure the bullet was secure, he emptied the chambers of both guns, saving one explosive round from Yang, and filled the bag with the rest.

The closest of the attackers raised a hatchet over his head as he drew nearer and Xander stepped forward, hurling the bag and its cargo of magical rounds at the onslaught. The man with the hatchet swung at the pack, hooking one of the straps on the blade and causing him to stumble back from the drag. He stopped and looked at the hefty weight that had snared on his weapon and began tugging at it in an effort to pull it free as Xander stepped forward and fired the one remaining round into the drone's torso. As the resulting explosion spread through the mind-slave's body, it set off the rest of the magic rounds in the bag, activating the dormant spells and creating a concussive and explosive reaction that consumed the clearing and all those within it.

Xander stood and watched as the combined spells took their toll on the army, and when the blast had finally died down he stepped around the resulting crater. The smell of blood was everywhere—though the explosion had left nothing large enough to feed from—and he forced himself to stay focused as he approached the house. He was happy to see, as the last of the dust settled, that the magic had taken out a portion of the nearby wall as well, giving him a clear entrance into the garage.

Come on in, son. Kyle's voice sounded in his head as he stepped through the makeshift entrance, *The little lady and I are waiting.*

Xander growled, throwing his fist into an already beat-up pickup truck that was parked inside, "I'm not your son!" he shook with rage and anticipation as the invitation repeated itself again and again in his mind and he sprinted through the door and up the stairs, "I'M NOT YOUR GODDAM SON!"

CHAPTER THIRTY-SIX
DEADLY REUNION

SHE WAS MORE DEAD THAN ALIVE;
kept breathing by the monster behind her as he fed off her
pain and misery. Her naked body shook under its own
weight, barely able to hold itself up, let alone hide its shame.
Xander stopped in his tracks at the top of the steps, stunned
and appalled by the sight. He recognized the woman from the
therion-boy's visions as she shivered in fear and
embarrassment; her dwindling aura shining dull grey and
lifeless like a wisp of smoke.

Kyle flashed his wicked grin from behind the slowly
dying woman and gave her a quick once-over before turning

to face Xander. "Quite the catch, huh son?" he began to laugh and clapped his hand down on her shoulder causing her to wince and stumble, "Quite the *fucking* catch!" His laugh deepened as he shoved her forward.

Xander caught the woman and stared into her sad, pained eyes as she mouthed her misery. He saw that she knew that he was responsible for the boy—her son's—death, but didn't bother to dig deeper to see if she knew *why* he'd done it. Not sure what sort of comfort he could offer the woman he instead entered her mind and cut the life painlessly from her body, refusing to allow another person to suffer any further at the hands of Kyle.

He was appalled with himself. Watching the woman's body slump to the floor, he knew that it had not been an act of heroism, but rather one of selfishness that he openly accepted as such. He couldn't allow her to live; couldn't allow anybody to serve as a reminder to Xander what he had gone through.

He looked up at the monster from his nightmares and scowled as he was greeted by the same terrible grin and the same cocky, sadistic brown eyes that looked at him like he could do *anything* and never have to face justice for it. The bastard looked just like he did the last night Xander had seen him: his light-brown hair was combed and neat and he wore a sports coat and freshly pressed khakis and Xander's body shook as a growl crawled up from deep inside his chest.

The son-of-a-bitch had tidied up for the moment!

All the collected rage from over the years grew and he tensed, letting his aura coil around him—a burning, electric-red serpent—and pulse like a second heart. The heat from the growing energy made his skin twitch anxiously and his nostrils flared as he took a deep breath to cool down his insides.

"What is this?" Kyle clutched his chest in a mocking gesture, "Is this the greeting I get after all these years? Not even a hug?"

Xander shuddered in fury and narrowed his eyes. Barely having to concentrate, his aura shot out, streaking across the room like a horizontal lightning bolt that forked again and again until it reached like a seven-fingered hand at the auric vampire. As his aura enclosed around its target a sickly yellow-green orb appeared around him, blocking the attack and sending the auric divisions off their path, three bolts crashing into the ceiling while the other four drove into the adjacent walls—three to the left and one to the right. The ceiling and wall crumbled, leaving behind clouds of drywall dust and cracked beams and dented piping.

"Not the hug I was hoping for, but what should I expect from an ungrateful fucking brat like you?" Kyle grinned wider.

Xander roared at the cocky monster's tone and lunged forward, dropping both of his empty revolvers behind him to free his hands. Kyle grinned at the advancement, side-stepping to the left and wrapping him in his aura, using it as a sling to rocket him into the dividing wall between the living room and the kitchen. The wall shattered under the force, raining down plaster and plywood as Xander flew through to the other side. Shaking from the impact, the refrigerator wavered unsteadily before collapsing to the kitchen floor and nearly crushing him.

Groaning and shaking the stars from his head and the dust from his hair, Xander looked up as Kyle marched towards him with the same confidence he'd had all those years ago when he was a child—those same damn boots crunching down on the scattered debris. The sight cleared the weariness from his mind and he snarled, reaching out with his aura again and ensnaring the fallen fridge.

Kyle stopped in mid-stride, raising a questioning brow as the appliance rose from the floor—encased in the semi-transparent neon red aura—and shot at him. The power cord ripped from the socket, briefly spitting sparks into the air and singeing the wall around it as Kyle dropped down and deflected the projectile with his own aura and sending it sailing over his head.

Seeing the attack miss, Xander pulled his weapon back around for a second pass; wielding the fridge as a massive hammer and dropping it straight down towards his old stepfather. Kyle watched this and sneered as he grabbed it and stopped the attack with his own aura and wrestled to pull it away. Refusing to relinquish his hold, Xander focused on getting control again, only to suddenly have an auric bolt from Kyle smash into him like a boulder and throw him deeper into the kitchen.

Various metallic and ceramic implements rattled inside their cupboards and drawers as the corner of the counter bit into the meat of Xander's shoulder with a sharp impact. A sudden flash of yellow-green drew his attention away from the searing pain and he quickly jumped into overdrive, dodging the refrigerator as it crashed down. Dropping out of overdrive to preserve energy he watched as the counter and the shelves above it fell victim to the attack that had been meant for him and looked around him at the rubble that the kitchen had become.

Picking up on the sound of Kyle's boots stomping closer he decided to try and turn the fight in his favor. Jumping back into overdrive he shot at the auric vampire and pulled back his fist, fully prepared to punch through the son-of-a-bitch just as he had done to the man back in the forest. As his attack was put into action, however, Kyle suddenly vanished from sight in front of him and the full force of the intended punch dragged him and sent him tumbling. Once off his feet, all control was gone and time came back into play as he rolled across the living room floor and crashed into the dead body of Tyler's mother and through the banister, falling halfway down the stairs in a twisted heap of limbs and lumber.

The miracle of his body's ability to withstand damage was fully realized when he determined that nothing had been broken—though that didn't stop the entire ordeal from hurting like hell—and he cursed as he pulled himself away from the naked corpse.

"Nice trick, huh?" Kyle called down from the living room. "It's not easy to hold an image in someone's head for very long, though. But I guess that means little when you're moving that fast." He laughed again, "All I needed was a fraction of a second!"

Xander frowned at the calm tone as well as the realization that he'd fallen for an auric mirage. Kyle had seen him coming; anticipated the attack before he'd even thrown it into motion. Deciding to keep things easy, he grabbed a length of broken banister and ran back up the stairs.

Kyle stood poised, once again seeing his intentions, and Xander growled that he was being so easily read and quickly put up an auric shield.

Kyle grinned at this, "Catching on, eh?"

Xander didn't answer.

He refused to stop for even a second and give the monster from his past the satisfaction of even the briefest moment of conversation. The rage that had remained constant and the added humiliation of not keeping his guard up from the beginning made his face redden until he was sure it matched his blood-stained eye. It wasn't a surprise that the bastard had been able to read and manipulate him without touching him with his aura; he *had* practiced the same thing with Stan, after all. But he'd been sloppy in not considering that it could be used *against* him. He scowled as he tightened his grip on his makeshift stake. There was no point in even trying to read Kyle. The auric vampire had been shielding his mind from the beginning.

As Kyle opened his mouth for another comment Xander started his attack. His vision shimmered as the auric vampire attempted to manipulate his mind again and he solidified his shield, blocking out the interference and swinging his weapon. Its length whistled through the air as Kyle jumped back and out of its range and, as Xander worked to stabilize himself and bring around the bludgeon for a second try, drove his right foot into his left leg and swung a tight fist into the side of his head. Startled and thrown off balance, Xander toppled, catching himself at the last minute with his aura only to have that knocked out from under him by Kyle's own.

"See?" Kyle smirked as he stood over him, "You're not the only one who can throw a punch!" Enraged by his mocking, Xander bared his fangs and lunged forward, ready to tear Kyle's head off. The auric vampire floated away, his green aura shooting out and wrapping around Xander's throat as he did, "And don't think you're the only one who can tear heads off either!" he boasted.

Caught in midair by the tightening auric grip, Xander gurgled as his breath was squeezed out. Just as Kyle had insinuated, as the hold tightened it threatened to pull his head from his shoulders and he fought to escape.

Kyle grinned at this, watching his old stepson struggle in his bonds, "But where's the fun in killing you so quickly?" he mused as he cracked his aura like a whip, smashing Xander into the shattered remains of the ceiling and flinging him across the room.

Landing at a bad angle, he cried out as something inside his body finally snapped.

So much for the indestructible sang body! Xander thought as a violent cough seized him and blood splattered from his mouth. The sight held his attention and for the first time in months he regretted the taste.

"Like losing your lunch, I suppose," Kyle cackled as he stepped casually toward him.

Xander heaved as another bout of blood erupted from his mouth and he pushed himself up, cringing as whatever was broken shifted inside his chest. The thirst came at him full force once again, and as his pupils dilated and his eyes narrowed on the only food source in the house he felt his body begin to numb the pain in his torso so that it wouldn't hold him back. Then, like a beaten and cornered wildcat, he lunged.

Kyle scowled at the sudden attack, shooting his aura out again and again in an attempt to take down the threat. Xander, however, was too driven.

Driven to maim!

Driven to feed!

Driven to destroy the life of the one who'd destroyed his!

The auric bolts missed narrowly as he advanced, the flat-screen television behind him bursting followed moments later by the couch as it was torn in half. With each and every one of Kyle's attacks Xander was no longer where he'd been. Like the beast he felt like, he circled his prey; hissing and snarling as Kyle grew angrier and more volatile.

"Stand still and let me kill you, brat!" he demanded through clenched teeth.

Xander complied then, stopping suddenly in front of him and grabbing his shoulders.

"Got you!" he snarled.

Kyle smiled at this, "Indeed you do."

Caught off guard by his prey's calmness, Xander paused; enough time for Kyle to completely wrap him up in an auric bind from below. Hissing and roaring in rage, Xander struggled in vain as he felt himself pulled away from his victory; watching as the snide, cocky face of his nightmares grew further away.

The slow push that distanced him further from Kyle shuddered and became a sudden whirlwind that smashed him into every available surface again and again. The chaotic flurry battering and dizzying him, going on for what felt like the remainder of the night. He cried out with each impact, feeling more pieces of himself break and rupture as more and more blood was lost through the multitude of fresh gashes. When, at last, the attack ended, he landed back inside the kitchen amongst even more rubble.

Xander groaned and looked up, watching as Kyle rounded the broken wall and entered the kitchen through the door, "If I'd known you were something valuable to the rest of the mythos community I might have simply handed you over." He grinned and Xander tried to stand, only to have the yellow-green aura shoot out at him and throw him against the wall all over again, "Some say your dad was a big deal, but I heard that he was just some radical, mind-feeding hippie." He lifted Xander, smashing him against the ceiling before throwing him onto the floor, leaving a bloody mess streaked across the hardwood floor, "I hate hippies, son, I really do."

Xander heaved, coughing up more blood, "I'm... not—"

"'—your son'? Yea yea! Heard it all before! You weren't the first and you weren't the last and neither was that ugly little shit-of-a-mutt you left smeared all over the road by your stolen car!" He shook his head, "And as many times as I hear it, I can't help but think that you *are* my son: a product of what I gave to you! Look at you! You wouldn't be the freak-show you are now if weren't for me!" He shook his head again, "You fucking kids. You think you're something special; something *original*. You think that pain can't come to you because Mommy and Daddy swear they won't let it!" He licked his lips, "But Daddy's dead and Mommy's dead and I *can* hurt you and it tastes de-fucking-licious!"

Xander groaned, still struggling to stand, "Don't you fucking talk about my—"

"What? Your mom?" Kyle smirked and shook his head, "Your mom was a dish! Something about that woman put a spice on *any* emotion that came out!"

"SHUT UP!" Xander roared and lunged at Kyle, ignoring his broken bones and lacerations. The auric bonds holding him back dropped suddenly and he lurched, stumbling forward as Kyle drove a fist into his face, doing more damage to his already broken nose and causing him to recoil back against the wall where he felt Kyle's aura trap him once again.

"Wow! A fighter to the end, huh? Just like your mother! Like the time I took her anti-depressants to get those negative juices basting her up good! Oh she went nuts that night! Said she'd call the cops on me and everything! Made a shit-load of noise." He shook his head disapprovingly, "But I've got ways of shutting up my food real fast." He moved his hand up until he was pointing to Xander's temple, "Many, many ways."

Kyle stepped back and narrowed his eyes and suddenly there was an explosion in Xander's head; an intense agony that seemed to drill its way out from the inside-out.

The pain was too much!

He screamed and saw, through his twisted vision, as Kyle smiled at him and soaked up his torment; bringing it into himself.

Feeding off of it!

Xander cringed, reaching for some bit of control in his mind to take on the monster, but his aura was immobilized by the pain and his body held tight in the sadistic auric's grip.

"My only regret," Kyle mused as he continued to drain Xander, "is that the bitch isn't alive and here so I could do it all over again."

There was nothing left in Xander to fight back with; not a thing he could do but feel his mind begin to shut down—piece-by-piece. His eyes lazily rose to see Kyle's grinning face through the growing haze of his approaching death. Though Kyle's mouth continued to move, Xander heard nothing except the dull hum of his mind being drained. He closed his eyes again and his muscles slacked as he began to feel tired and, as his head dropped in defeat, he felt the familiar warmth of the skin-heated metal under his chin and forced his eyes to open, filling his vision with his mother's pendant. Seeing the charm, Xander couldn't help but remember the sight of it as it fell from her beaten and ravaged neck.

There was the familiar surge of heat as his rage swelled within him and a sharp yank as Kyle ripped it from him just as fast. Again his anger and hate inflated his aura and again it was shrunk back down. With each new burst, however, something lingered in Xander and, though he was not strong enough to get free from Kyle's auric grip, he felt a portion of his life-force return to him. His tortured muscles flexed and he struggled against Kyle's force to reach up with his left hand until it clutched the pendant that had brought him back. Grabbing the pendant the rings that lined his fingers rattled with his quaking body against it.

And suddenly he was free.

Surprised, Xander stretched, finding all his limbs free of pain and capable of movement. This newfound freedom came with an even greater shock: he was no longer in Kyle's house!

He had no idea *where* he was!

It was foggy, first and foremost, and in the distance he could see the flashes of lightning and hear the rumbles of an approaching storm. Though he was bewildered, he did not feel lost. Rather, he felt oddly at peace.

The sound of soft footsteps drew his gaze away from the mist-filled distance and the raging storm that filled it and focused on a shadowed figure as it approached, hidden in the fog. Believing the environment and the figure to be a manifestation of Kyle, he tensed and watched as it emerged from the thick gray and into the small clearing he stood within. At first, he was sure it was some sort of trick, but as the familiar face of his father smiled at him he felt calmed and stepped forward to join him.

"Dad?" he croaked, his voice as choked in this world as it was in Kyle's home under his suffocating hold.

The ghost nodded and smiled, "Thought you might want some support."

"Not sure what good it'll do at this point…" Xander frowned and scanned their surroundings once again, "Where are we?"

The image of Joseph looked around as well and shrugged, "You're in that sadistic asshole's house, giving him the last of your essence."

Xander let out a heavy sigh and sat down on the ground. "He's too strong," he confessed, watching the swirling mist that served as this world's sky, "Any power I build up he takes away just as fast!"

The ghost mirrored Xander's stares into the distance, but remained standing. "You're confusing your emotions with power," he responded.

Xander looked up at the specter, "So what should I do?"

His father's image continued to stare off into the distance. When he was sure he would get no reply, he looked down at his feet.

Why do we like tigers? Xander's head shot up to find a source but his grandmother's voice sounded from all directions. He turned, eager to question his father's ghost but found himself alone. As the echo died down, he felt himself growing weaker and weaker.

His eyes opened suddenly, revealing the interior of the house and the bastard; still grinning and still feeding off of the last of his energy.

"My, my. Aren't we the bottomless pit of hatred and despair?" Kyle taunted, *The kids at school must have loved you.*

Xander cringed as he heard Kyle's voice ringing inside of his head. His left hand, despite his strange "trip", remained tightly wrapped around the pendant, its corners beginning to tear into his palm and sending drops of blood onto the floor.

Grace and intelligence. His grandmother's voice sounded in the back of his mind again.

Kyle furrowed his brow, "What do you have going on in there?" he growled in frustration, the pain in his head growing more intense.

Xander glared at the source of all his pain; the cuts in his hand deepening as his grip tightened around the pendant. Feeling the jewelry bite into him, a massive surge of scorching rage began to grow within him once again, and he cringed at the burning that was consuming him and fought to push it away, not wanting to feed Kyle any further.

Power... Grace... Intelligence... his grandmother's words repeated over and over in his mind.

Kyle snarled in frustration and took a step towards him, his boots landing hard on the floor, "I asked you a question, son!"

Xander saw his chance then and shot forward with his right hand, grabbing Kyle's face and digging into the soft flesh. He knew he had precious little time before the auric vampire would squirm free and quickly went about taking back the stolen energy through his hand. With every passing second he felt stronger, and his aura sprang angrily from his chest, pushing against Kyle's restraints until they buckled and shattered from the pressure. Finally free, Xander pulled him forward, holding him tighter in his energy-draining grip.

"I'm not your goddam son!" he growled, his fangs extending further than ever before and causing his gums to ache.

The blood that seeped from Kyle's face smelled too good to hold back any longer and he kicked off the wall, forcing both of them to the floor. Crouched over his old stepfather, Xander saw fear in his eyes and he shot forward with his aura, embracing the quivering energy mass and beginning to feed from it.

The ironic justice of feeding from Kyle's misery didn't distract him from the thirst and he quickly brought his fangs down on him, holding his struggling head to one side as he began to drink. Kyle thrashed and squirmed as Xander fed from both his fear of being conquered as well as his spilled blood. As he did, he felt his strength return and his body begin to heal and his grip tightened with his returning strength.

Finally, when he felt he'd had enough, he rose to his feet.

Kyle groaned, his weakened aura uselessly darting back-and-forth for energy that Xander refused to give. As he looked into the hate-filled glare of his old stepfather, he reached out with an auric tendril and brought Yang to his hand.

Seeing what was coming, Kyle sneered. "So what happens after you kill me?" his voice strained and croaked around his torn throat, "I've looked into your head, and you and I both know that you've got nothing more to live for!" He laughed and spat out a mouthful of blood, "You've got no clan. No family. NOTHING!" He grinned, glaring up at him, "So... you going to go back to trying to kill yourself?"

Xander frowned and fought the rage that Kyle wanted so desperately to well within him, knowing that if he let the auric vampire into his head he'd feed once more and grow stronger. Finally getting control of his emotions, he reached into his coat pocket and pulled out the bullet he had been saving and slipped it into the chamber, giving the barrel a spin and slapping it shut like he had so many times with Yin. As the raging inferno inside him shrunk down and disappeared, Xander pressed the barrel of the ivory revolver to Kyle's head and smiled, confident that this time the hammer would find the right chamber.

"If there's *anything* you've taught me"—he spoke slowly and deliberately—"it's that there is *always* one more thing to live for."

With that, he pulled the trigger and put an end to his nightmares.

CHAPTER THIRTY-SEVEN
SOMETHING TO LIVE FOR

XANDER SIGHED AS HE CLIMBED FROM the driver's seat of Kyle's beat-up truck. Scowling back at the vehicle, he cursed the fate that the Firebird had come to meet. It really had been such a sweet ride...

Rocking back on the heels of the stolen boots, he smiled; though they were a bit big on him they were comfortable and would serve as a reminder of his first real victory as a vampire and the conquest against the monster who had ruined his life. Kyle had clearly cared a great deal for the expensive footwear by keeping them in good condition for so many years. Their new owner, however, had every intention of wearing them until they came apart at the seams.

The truck idled noisily behind him, the rumbling beast causing the tall metal gates in front of him to rattle against the chains that held them shut. Despite looking like hell, the truck had survived the trip, though the tires had spent little time on the road, and when the sun had risen after the first night of travel the truck's wide bed, along with a black mesh cover, had served as a decent enough place to sleep.

Waking up the next night, Xander had taken a moment to find a payphone and give Estella a call. Keeping the discussion brief, he'd assured his friend that everything was alright and that he'd see her later that night. She had mewed happily at the news, promising to stay up and leave the light on for him.

He'd frowned as he hung up, feeling a twinge of guilt. Though he'd promised her that he'd see her as soon as he could he did have several places that he had to visit first.

And this was only his first stop.

He stood a bit longer at the gate, staring past the metal bars at the pale stones beyond it that shone under the moon's rays. It had been a long time since he'd last visited, and, despite everything he'd done and gone through, he found himself hesitant to move forward.

Kyle's injustice against him years ago had left Xander feeling weak and useless—a feeling that he'd revisited each time he'd walked past the gates. He'd hated that feeling and years ago had decided never to visit there again in an attempt to avoid it. For a long time he'd gotten away with it, exchanging a deep well of sadness for a deeper one of rage. Lately, however, he found that the despair was overflowing and refusing to be ignored.

He sighed and the exhale stuttered in his throat as he took the pendant of his mother's necklace once again into his left hand. Finally, unable to find any more reasons not to, he took a step forward and jumped over the cemetery gate.

His pace past the multitude of tombstones was slow-but-steady as he weaved through them, allowing himself to read the names and dates off of some. As he walked, he absentmindedly tightened his grip on the pendant as he drew nearer. Almost too soon, he found himself standing at the stone he sought and a long, bitter silence carried on for several minutes before he finally found the right words:

"I got him for you, Mom," he whispered, kneeling down beside her grave. He shook his head, feeling the first tear roll from his blood-stained eye, "I got him for *us*," he corrected himself.

The tears began to roll heavily down his cheeks as he dug a small hole and buried the necklace he'd worn for so long with her. He didn't have the patience or the heart to go six feet, so half-a-foot would have to suffice. When he was done he gave the pendant one last look before covering it with earth.

It was a beautiful piece of jewelry, and though he hated to part with it was no longer his.

It was never his to begin with.

And now that the human-Xander was dead it was only fitting that it be put in the ground for both of them.

Patting down the soil, he had one final flash of the event that had taken her and stood up. He wiped away the growing tears and allowed himself to gaze upon the grave in silence for a while longer before looking up at the clear night sky.

"I know you didn't want this for me," he spoke softly to the heavens, "But I don't think there was any other way for me…" he stopped and sighed, "It really is better this way.

"Besides…" his tone turned positive, "… I know Dad's proud of me." He stared for several minutes, waiting for some sign of acceptance, though he knew it wouldn't come. Finally, he just smiled weakly and nodded at the silence.

"I love you, Mom."

He stayed a bit longer, wordlessly pondering and letting out the occasional sob before turning and heading back to the truck. The night was drawing on, Estella was waiting, and he still had one more tomb to visit.

The truck sputtered and whined and Xander begged the heap to hold on a moment longer as he took it down the familiar winding path and up a hill. His destination was already visible in the distance but the truck didn't have the life left in it to make it the rest of the way and sputtered to a sudden stop. Having showed no kindness to Kyle's old ride, Xander wasn't surprised that it had died, but nonetheless pounded on the dash before climbing out.

There was no point in trying to carry it the rest of the way with his aura.

"Piece of shit!" he huffed, slamming the door with all of his vampiric strength and watching passively as it fell off the hinges and clattered to the road.

He retrieved his guns then and took the rest of the trip on foot; walking at a human pace. He let his thoughts distract him until the tall stone wall that surrounded the Odin mansion loomed above him. As he approached, he slowed to a stop, frowning at the front gate.

It had clearly been forced open…

Frowning at the obvious intrusion, he drew Yin and Yang from their case and pressed himself against the wall, reaching out with his aura and scanning what lay beyond.

After a moment of scanning the interior he caught "sight" of the intruder and chuckled, smiling at what he "saw". Relaxing his guns, he set them back in the case and snuck through the open gate.

The intruders stood motionless, staring at the remains of the once proud mansion; completely unaware of Xander's approach as he crept closer, masking the sounds of his steps and heartbeat with a simple tweak of the intruder's mind. When he was finally close enough, he pulled his aura away.

"Didn't see your car parked out front," he said, raising his voice to get the desired effect.

The trick worked, and both vampire and beast jumped in surprise.

Xander laughed as the sound of their heartbeats picked up and the two turned towards him.

Marcus took a deep, calming breath as Trepis excitedly pounced forward to greet Xander. "Yea," his voice was cold, though the beginnings of a grin gave his true emotions away, "I like to park in back." He shook his head, "Attracts less attention that way."

Xander nodded, petting the tiger and giving the animal's side a few soft pats.

"So... you're not dead," Marcus smiled, "I guess that says something."

Xander smirked, "It's more than I can say for the other guy."

"Messed him up *that* bad?" Marcus lifted an eyebrow.

"Put a bullet in his head and then blew up his house," Xander beamed.

"You blew up his house?"

Xander nodded, scratching behind Trepis' ears. "Tore a gas line and left my Zippo to do the rest," he grinned and laughed. "Almost didn't make it out in time."

Marcus stared for a moment and then joined in the laughter.

As their cackles died down they sighed, regaining a serious composure and turning their gazes back towards the building they had both come to visit.

Marcus didn't turn away as he wetted his lips, "So do you feel any better?"

Xander paused before he shrugged his left shoulder, "I feel better that I got to kill that sadistic son-of-a-bitch. But..." he sighed, trailing off and looking down.

Marcus nodded, "The old cliché: it didn't bring her back."

Xander looked over at him. He'd never gone into very much detail concerning what had happened to him and his mother, but he was sure Stan had filled his mentor in. He turned away, fighting back the tears that he thought he'd left back at the cemetery, "I didn't expect it to."

Marcus nodded, shifting his eyes slightly as he took in the remains of what had been his life. After a moment he let out a deep sigh, "But you *wanted* it to."

Xander scowled, shifting Kyle's boots in the ashy dirt.

After a long, uncomfortable silence Marcus clucked his tongue, this time turning to look at him, "Well it looks like he gave you quite a workout."

Xander frowned and nodded, happy that the subject had been changed. Despite this, a new wave of regret washed over him, "He used a lot of human mind-slaves against me," he confessed.

Marcus nodded, a slight frown creasing his features. "Typical cowardly auric trick," he said; his voice a slight growl. They stood a while longer before the burning question blossomed: "Did you feed from any of them?"

Xander, reluctant to answer, finally nodded. "A few."

"Dammit," Marcus groaned, shaking his head. "Not the smoothest way to enter our world, buddy." He scratched his head, moving his hand back until it rested on the back of his neck, "But I'm sure if this guy was as bad as you say I can get you a pardon from The Council; maybe even pass the whole thing off as a job that got a little fucked up along the way."

Xander nodded. Part of him was regretful. After thinking it over, however, he agreed that it *had* been necessary. He sighed as he came to this conclusion and stuffed his hands into the pockets of the jacket.

Marcus noticed and shook his head, "Y'know, I *liked* that coat."

"Sorry," Xander's voice was snotty and insincere. "I should've called a 'time out' and hung it up."

Marcus narrowed his eyes at the tone as he continued to explore the destroyed garment before looking at Xander's chest. "Where's your jewelry?"

Xander touched a hand to his chest where the pendant had once rested, "Yea. I... I gave it back to my mom."

Marcus studied him a moment and then smirked, "Everyone's got some ritual after the change." He smiled and looked down as the tiger licked at Xander's hand.

Xander smiled as well, looking at the tiger for a moment before looking back up at the building. "How'd you know I'd come here?"

"You think I'm here for you?" Marcus scoffed and shook his head. "The beast and I have been visiting the old stomping grounds the past few nights ever since Stan dropped the big lug off at my place." He rolled his eyes, "It was like a fucking magic show the way he made fuzz-nuts suddenly appear in my living room." He shook his head and laughed, "Scared the shit out of him, too! Literally!" he growled, looking back down at Trepis, "All over my floor, no less!"

Xander laughed at that. He thought about what Stan had said to him before he'd left for Maine and he shook his head, "So he's really gone then?"

Marcus frowned and nodded. "I'm afraid so," he sighed and laughed, "Guess this means I'd better watch my ass better from now on."

"What happened back there?" Xander bit his lip for a moment, :I mean, Stan stopped those attackers and saved us; so why'd you take off? Did you know those mythos or something?"

Marcus sighed and looked down. "I don't want to go into details, kid," he said, his voice low and even, "But I will say that that woman had every right to attack me. She would've had every right to kill me. She was trying to avenge the live of someone very special that I killed."

Xander looked over at him. "You mean special to her?"

Marcus nodded, but his shifting aura gave away that there was something more that he wasn't telling.

Xander didn't push the subject any further. He wasn't asking Xander to relive his pain, and he felt it only fair to offer the same courtesy. Letting out a heavy sigh, he returned his attention to what remained of the great Odin headquarters. Marcus' gaze followed, and the two shared a long, peaceful silence.

"You going to be alright?" Marcus asked in a low voice.

Xander nodded, unable to look away, "I suppose."

"You need a place to stay?"

He looked at Marcus, "Yea. I do…" he smiled. "But I

have to go see a friend first."

Marcus looked him over, taking in every filthy, tattered inch, "Hope they're a *real* good friend or else you won't make it past the door!" He chuckled and shook his head at his own joke, "Take your time. I'll have a bag of blood and a pack of cigs waiting."

Xander nodded, smiling, "Thanks, Marcus."

Turning to leave, he heard his mentor's voice and looked back to see him talking at the hollowed building, his left hand lazily rubbing the tiger's head. He frowned at the sight, wondering if he should say something encouraging to his mentor but unable to think of what he could possibly offer. Eventually, he turned away from the grieving vampire and stepped out through the gate.

He sighed as he walked around the wall to face the limited lights of the town at the base of the hill. A short distance away Marcus' car was parked, the hood cold from a while of misuse, and he wondered how long his mentor had been there. He sighed, looking back towards town and focused his energy. A wind-rustled bush a short distance away slowed to a near-stop as his muscles went into high-gear and his eyes refocused on the new time-stream and he shot off in overdrive.

As the nearly time-frozen world passed him by, Xander questioned where he'd take his life. Though he'd proven—if to nobody but himself—that he had what it took, he wondered what it was he was supposed to do next. It was a frightening realization that he would now live for hundreds of years, maybe a thousand, and a shiver threatened his concentration and he stuttered momentarily out of overdrive.

As the gloomy views of his existence and the foreboding speculations towards his future threatened to plunge him into an all-too-familiar state of mind and his thoughts shifted towards the contents of the case in his hands he noticed the attic light in the distance. Sure it was safe to do so he dropped out of overdrive, taking the rest of the distance at a human pace.

The rest of the lights in the house were long since out and a restless shadow scurried across the ceiling of Estella's room, giving her away. Xander couldn't help but smile and he quickly cast away the depressed and scared thoughts as he jumped onto the roof and made his way towards the window.

Knowing that his friend was waiting was all that he needed to live for at that moment.

THE DEVIL YOU KNOW

Nathan Squiers (The Literary Dark Emperor and the author formally known as "Prince") is a resident of Upstate New York. Living with his loving fiancé/fellow author, Megan J. Parker, and three incredibly demanding and out-of-control demon-cats, Nathan lives day-by-day on a steady diet of potentially lethal doses of caffeine and bacon. When not immersed in his writing, he often escapes reality through movie marathons, comics & anime, and gnarly tunes. While out-and-about, The Literary Dark Emperor can be found in the chair of a piercing studio/tattoo parlor, at the movies, or simply loving life with friends & loved ones.

Learn more about Nathan's work and join The Legion at
www.nathansquiers.com
~~~

OTHER TITLES BY NATHAN SQUIERS:
A HOWL AT THE MOON
*S(a)TAN
*FORBIDDEN PAINTS ON A WICKED CANVAS
**THE FIGHTER

*A prequel to the Crimson Shadow series
**A prequel to Scarlet Night (by Megan J. Parker)—coming soon from Tiger Dynasty Publishing

Read on for a thrilling excerpt from
Nathan Squiers' award-winning paranormal-thriller,

A DEATH METAL NOVEL

CURTAIN CALL

Now available from Tiger Dynasty Publishing.

PREVIEW

"ALRIGHT, EVERYBODY," THE

announcer's voice paused and allowed a squeal of feedback to pass, "GIVE IT UP FOR THE BLOODTONES!"

The audience's roar overwhelmed the booming voice's dying echo as a pair of fog machines began to pour a thick mist across the stage. With the ghostly wisps crawling across the stage floor, a series of backlights came to life and the five silhouettes of the band's members came into view. The cheers grew louder in response.

A soft percussive buildup began, mingling with the audience's cries and soon surpassing them. The sharp crash of a cymbal shrieked and a spotlight beam shot down a split-second before an explosive impact on the bass-drum, giving the audience their first look at William Jones—perched behind his custom drum set—as he raised his tattooed arms over his head before bringing them down to begin the song. Though he had done his best to reign in his messy brown hair several renegade strands pulled free from the elastic and fell in front of his green eyes. Ignoring the minor inconvenience, he pinched the ring at the left corner of his lip between his teeth and drove on.

A deep series of heavy thrums and growling twangs joined in then and resounded across the arena. At that moment two more spotlights shone down and illuminated Derek Sumner—stooped over his brick-red 5-string Squier Jaguar bass—and the band's rhythm guitarist, Brian Rains. As

Derek's nimble fingers galloped across the strings his bowed head and gold-dyed hair bobbed methodically to the beat; his black, sweat-glazed skin shimmering like obsidian under the intense light. On the opposite side of the stage, Brian worked the strings of his Warlock guitar; its blood-red body the exact shade of his swaying Mohawk.

Rampaging on, the bass-drum thundered again and another spotlight brought David, their lead guitarist, into view; his long, black hair partially covering a pair of gray-blue eyes that stared out at the audience with animal ferocity as his fingers stalked across the neck of his sandy-brown Fender Stratocaster.

As the intro's buildup climaxed Brian leapt into the air and Derek swung his bass out like a medieval warrior; a growling feminine voice calling out to the audience:

"LET ME HEAR YOU FUCKING SCREAM!"

The energy in the arena reached climactic heights and the audience's shrieks doubled in effort as the final spotlight turned on. There, on the edge of the stage, Rebecca Gespon came into view, perched and gazing out over the crowd. Though she was the smallest member of the band, what Bekka lacked in stature she more than made up for with enthusiasm; an enthusiasm that often had her band-mates struggling to keep up. Her bright blue eyes shimmered, fed by the roar of the crowd. Tossing her bright purple hair to the side, she brought the microphone to her black-painted lips and let loose a howl that trumped the combined cheers of the audience.

That sound—that raw, exuberant energy—was her entire purpose of being.

As the tempo shifted, Bekka stood and wetted her lips; bringing the microphone to her mouth:

"SLITHER AND SHAKE!
WITHER AND QUAKE!
NOTHING TO LEAVE,
EVERYTHING TO TAKE!"

Will slammed down on the cymbals and started an aggressive assault on the toms. His feet came down again and again on the pedals as he set the pace.

"COIL AND STRIKE!
TOIL AND STRIFE!
EVERYTHING'S THE SAME,
WHEN SCORED WITH A KNIFE!"

With Derek pumping out a strong bassline, David jumped in with another riff; his fingers a blur on the neck of his guitar as Brian leaned in towards his own microphone, letting out a deep growl that overlapped with Bekka's voice.

"WITH THEIR VENOM WE TAKE CHANCES!
WITH THEIR FLESH WE SEEK ROMANCES!
WE DARE NOT HONOR SECOND GLANCES,
AS THEY ENGAGE IN SERPENT DANCES!"

The two guitarists moved together towards Brian's microphone as Derek slapped a chord sharply with the side of his thumb before leaning towards his own microphone; all three syncing their voices to join with Bekka's.

"FEAR!
(SLITHER AND SHAKE)

REVERE!
(COIL AND STRIKE)"

As they finished, Brian took a step back and David returned to his mark. Bekka, looking over her shoulder as she rocked the microphone stand on its base with the beat, locked eyes with Brian and grinned. They were all harmonized; both in body and in mind.

Their performance was going perfectly!

"THEY MOVE AS ONE!
TOGETHER AS ONE!
NEVER FORGETTING:
THEY'RE FOREVER AS ONE!"

As Brian advanced on his microphone Bekka withdrew from hers and let her body succumb to the music— her tiny body thrashing with the beat—as her band-mate's growling voice returned:

"SO FAR FROM THE FANG,
BUT FOREVER TOO CLOSE!
BLESSED BE,
THE OROBOROS!"

Bekka continued moving to the music as she returned to her microphone; her and Brian's voices once again synchronizing:

"WITH THEIR VENOM WE TAKE CHANCES!
WITH THEIR FLESH WE SEEK ROMANCES!
WE DARE NOT GIVE THEM SECOND GLANCES,

AS THEY ENGAGE IN SERPENT DANCES!"

The crowd shrieked and hollered and thrashed before them; their combined mass taking on a serpentine shape that complimented the song's lyrics all-too-well. Soaking in their cheers, Bekka approached the edge of the stage and turned, smiling at her still-performing band-mates and spreading her arms a moment before allowing her body to fall from the stage. Somewhere in the distance the faint shout of an angered security guard could be heard, but it was too late.

The raised hands of the crowd caught and supported her, and as she allowed her body to be taken out into the sea of music-lovers she stared up at the arena's rooftop and took in the kaleidoscope of lights.

That was when she first spotted them.

At first she mistook them for plastic bags—possibly some trash that had fallen victim to a sporadic air current. However, focusing on them, she could see from the way they darted between the rafters that there was some sort of consciousness driving them. While there were already too many to count she was shocked to see that more were coming; emerging through a dark, shifting tear that faded rapidly behind them. As the rift vanished, the beings' colors—vibrant shades of blues, reds, and greens—became brighter. The beautiful display was short lived, however, and before Bekka could react they converged above her and began their descent.

Also available from Nathan Squiers & Tiger Dynasty Publishing:

CRIMSON SHADOW: SINS OF THE FATHER

No sins go unforgiven…

Xander's had it rough…

… and while the trials and tribulations of the young vampire's life have left him with a fiery rage, things are finally beginning to come together. Armed with his trusty revolvers, Yin and Yang, and a thirst for death and destruction, there is *nothing* that his expertise and fury can't stand against!

Except the spell-binding Estella.

****

Estella *finally* has her best friend back…

… and, despite her many years of training in the art of magic, it wasn't until recently that she discovered just how deep the paranormal world goes. But no matter how overwhelming the revelations might be, she's found reassurance and comfort in the depths…

… of Xander's supernatural embrace.

****

With their relationship's intensity growing, a new threat emerges from the depths of the Stryker family's past; one with a personal vendetta and visceral goals. Even with the help of some unlikely new allies, will the paranormal pair (and their blossoming relationship) be able survive the infernal rage?

CRIMSON SHADOW: FORBIDDEN DANCE

Xander Stryker has lost it all...

Now, living in the forest with a pack of therions, he sees little purpose in moving forward. With his legacy nearly forgotten, Xander spends his nights writing letters in a hope to cure a guilty conscience while searching for Estella.
However, when a ragtag group of mythos appears on his turf begging for his help in stopping a new enemy, Xander is thrown into making a decision that could end it all.
A choice that could change his life forever...

***

Estella Edash swore to never forgive Xander...

Now, surviving the elements has never been rougher for the new vampire and the need to feed has never been more destructive to her. With no hope and even less comfort, she spends each night hoping it will be her last.
However, when she finds herself confronted by her warring emotions, can she find the strength to not only forgive but to fight for the one thing that brings hope.
A choice that could change her life forever...

***

With the enemy and the binds of love growing stronger, can the unlikely crew find a way to survive the destruction at hand?

Or has the Crimson Shadow's legacy finally reached its end?

Made in the USA
Charleston, SC
02 July 2014